Fata Morgana

OTHER WORK BY THIS AUTHOR:

UNDERTOW (Novel)

# Fata Morgana

A Novel by

# Lynn Stegner

BASKERVILLE
PUBLISHERS, INC.
DALLAS • NEW YORK • DUBLIN

BASKERVILLE Publishers, Inc.
7616 LBJ Freeway, Suite 220, Dallas, TX 75251-1008

**Library of Congress Cataloging-in Publication Data**

Stegner, Lynn.
    Fata morgana :   a novel  /  by Lynn Stegner.
        p.    cm.
    ISBN No. 1-880909-29-4 : $22.00 ($30.00 Can.)
    I. Title.
PS3569.T33938F3  1995
813'.54--dc20                                             95-1261
                                                             CIP


Manufactured in the United States of America
First Printing, 1995

For Allen Wheelis

**FATA MORGANA,** *fä´tä môr-gä´nä:* The strange phenomenon known as the fata morgana is the rarest and most beautiful of mirages. This complex bending of light rays produces startling illusions where the images often bear no resemblance to the objects that have given rise to them. Like any mirage, a fata morgana can be photographed.

# 1

Her name was Dixie Darling and in 1981 she was living in the Los Angeles basin at the California Institution for Women-Frontera. I don't know what her name is today; it's been five years and it seems at some point she changed it. Dixie Darling was a stupid or a splendid name, but in either case a name hard to take seriously. It followed her about too, that name, witnessing, perhaps encouraging her to do things she might not have otherwise done. But that's just another chicken-and-egg theory, the first of many I turned inside out as I drove down to Los Angeles for what I thought would be an appropriately timed, redemptive visit. She was due to be released in three months. It was May, and the poppies were in bloom.

During the first eight years of her nine-year term I did not contact her in any way. Whenever thoughts of Dixie wandered in on me, I heard windows and doors slamming shut throughout my human house. But by the August of her eighth year, an August not unlike that last August of our time together in terms of heat and brush fires, I began writing her with a kind of creeping urgency. My first three letters went unanswered: the authorities were keeping them from her, I decided, though what threat they could find in my cleanly typed, impeccably benign chatter I couldn't imagine. In fact she was getting the letters, and as an attorney I knew this. Still, for the sake of peace or oblivion, I chose to suspect otherwise. Then hopeless fact and hopeful suspicion secured a patch of common ground in the backyard of my mind, and there, cohabiting, they seemed to cancel each other out: I felt nothing.

A few months passed, and by a crude intersection of trivia which occurred during my husband's and my anniversary junket to San Francisco—Irish coffees at the Buena Vista, the scented, cardboard pine tree hanging from the rearview mirror of the cab, and at the corner of Post and Powell, a pair of red suede pumps—I was reminded again of Dixie and of her impending freedom. I wrote a fourth letter by hand—in my work, an anomaly—large, jagged script careening down the page, and I signed off in caps, reverting to my maiden name to remind her as if she needed reminding, to let her know that SUSAN M. THATCHER might be hurt. Henry regarded this token of marital rejection with a bemused snort; to him, it was simply another quirk in a wholly unaccountable relationship. I shrugged—he was not the first to have wondered at my old association with Dixie Darling—and walked the letter out to the corner box.

I was working at the time on a relatively dramatic case. Corporate law does not often concern itself with the flux of human emotions, but this case involved a landscaping business and what is known as a "close" corporation, which is essentially a partnership. Corporations used to be the preferred form, because at that time it was virtually impossible to "pierce the corporate veil," an expression I found particularly appealing for its virginal connotations. One was always more inclined to protect what had yet to be lost than to salvage the already debauched.

Close corporations could not be pierced but they could be roughed up. One of the three shareholders, an innocent-appearing young man who liked to talk, was threatening to file for involuntary dissolution of the company in order to extract his initial investment. The other two stockholders were "doing me wrong," he claimed. Since I was the attorney representing the corporation, an entity in and of itself, I was bound to it alone and could not betray my sympathies. I enjoyed almost no real contact with any of my clients; by that I mean to say that during meetings I was obliged to remain emotionally blank. When drawing up a contract, I represented the Law; and when engaged to tend to the needs, financial interests, and legal health of a corporation, I was friend to no smiling, breathing thing, and yet this thing lived—as a mass of numbers, pages in a file, as the collective ambition of its holders. To this alone I allowed myself subjective response. It was a cold sort of romance but it seems I had always been well insulated.

On several occasions the young man came to my office, rocking in on mismatched legs—differently-abled, or challenged, as they instruct us to say now—and I was again reminded of that August of 1972, because I had been dating a fellow with damaged feet, and Dixie disapproved. She was intolerant of things not festive, not dressed up, turning away from our mortal uncertainty, from any signs, the least intimation of ruin, and courting danger as if to deny (or seduce) the ever-pending upshot.

I had the sense that the landscaping matter would come to a ragged end, and though I tried to summon the appropriate concern for the welfare of the corporation, the young man had spoiled it for me somehow. He seemed to think I had let him down, he became abusive in language and gesture, and when he left for good—removed by one of my partners—I found my thoughts were again ushered back to Dixie, as if that was where they should properly reside. With Dixie, for a time.

I left immediately. I told my secretary that I was not feeling up to par—and indeed I was rather hot and queasy—and went straight home where I found, layered among the usual bills and correspondence, a card postmarked "CIW-Frontera."

*Sue —Dixie here—Saturday is visitors day —Bring change for the machines.*

Above her signature were three illegible letters: she had always signed off in this manner, but I couldn't for the life of me recall what words the letters embodied. Card in hand, I stood in the vestibule of our home, absolutely halted, because two things were apparent: that she did not want to see me, but that she would—as a charity to *me*. It was astonishing.

Henry emerged from his darkroom, squinting. His sleeves were rolled up and he was wiping his hands on a soiled towel. Unable to speak, I held the card out for him to read, pointing to the mystery letters, and when he glanced at it, he said simply, "FYI."

"What?"

"'For your information.'"

I glared at him. These were not the words from the past; still, I couldn't rearrange them in a way that would trigger memory.

"She's sent you a memo from the slammer," he said, and essayed a wry chuckle.

It did in fact resemble a memorandum, the terms of the proposed transaction crisply outlined—date, money, names of the parties. Was this—so cold—characteristic of all her letters from the Institution, to other people, or was it reserved for me alone? Again I looked at the card,

4

but I lost its sense in the visual impression of plump letters leaning ever slightly backwards, like reluctant school children, the words seeming to take up too much space for all the little they said. And yet they said more than I could stand. Dixie, it seemed to me then, had blazed for no one, an entire life spent giving off light that was somehow warped and deflected and never returned. By some variant of gravitation her life had caved in, and she was a black hole into which I was again being drawn.

"You're going," Henry said in that definitive tone of his that always betrayed his misgivings. "Tomorrow, I suppose."

"Yes." The word came slowly, as though I had begun to try to say it years ago—yes, *yes*—approaching from behind and receding into the future, like the taillights of a ride I kept missing.

"It's an eight-hour drive," Henry remarked.

I nodded.

"This card," he held it out, as if it might be contagious, "it sounds as if you hardly know each other."

"We don't," I said, slumping down on the edge of the window seat. "Or I didn't. Isn't that odd? I knew her for . . . well, we went to school, we lived together, but it's hard to remember somehow. Just spaces in my life that never seemed to count. *She* never seemed to count."

"Obviously she does. You're going all the way to L.A."

"I guess. I guess I am."

"I don't get it."

"I don't either," I said. "Maybe it's just that Dixie was always there, almost cryptically, when something was ending for me. When I was at junctures, here came Dixie, bopping in as if it was the best news ever. That my life was a mess. And somehow I was there too, accidentally, well, maybe not so accidentally, when she was at junctures."

5

The bottom edge of the sun was just passing behind the roof of the Victorian across the street, a copper penny slipping into a child's bank. There was something heavy and tired about the light it sent through our window and against my skin, a weight, not a warmth any longer. "Maybe we can begin to know each other," I said.

"What kind of relationship can you possibly have now?"

"I don't want one now," I said, surprising myself. "The one I missed . . ." I couldn't seem to complete a thought: there were too many strands, all tangling, all resisting a coherent weave. "She can't be the same, can she?"

"No," Henry said.

He stood behind me, his hand squeezing the back of my neck, and together we looked out the window at the clean, urban street where an imaginary Dixie Darling had just pulled to the curb, and was brushing her hair and tipping her mascara and gathering up her usual flotsam before presenting herself to a distant and faintly amused, faintly perturbed world.

"Call me before you leave L.A. so I don't worry," he said finally. Henry is a nice man, a gentle man, with a smooth and somehow too-familiar face, the kind you can't easily picture when it's absent. He is a chronic smiler, and the smile, small and uniform, as if in expectation of something that will not really surprise him—like the one I saw reflected in the window—is sometimes inappropriate. But no one seems to mind, least of all me. It is simply how he wears his face. Generally his attitude, his position, is one of non-intervention, and as a nature photographer it is an attitude that serves him well. He married me, he said, because I was without illusion, and I married him, I suppose, because that didn't bother him.

"Do you want me to come with you?" he said. He was kneading the sides of my neck with his easy hands.

Abruptly I dropped my head out of reach, and he added quickly, "Not for the visit, just come along to help with the driving."

"I want to be alone for all of it. I don't know why."

"Okay," he said, kissing the top of my head as if in blessing, as if I was about to go on pilgrimage to the ruins of some once-great façade to climb about·the rubble, and to re-imagine the fabulous myth of Dixie Darling.

The warm day's evening had drawn the fog in off the Monterey Bay, long arms of it reaching up from the surf rocks and over the cliffs, through the pretty little villages of Pacific Grove and Carmel and the real town of Monterey where we lived, then continuing up the hills along the neighborhood streets, past the refurbished Victorians and the wee, mock villas, the beach bungalows, the ranch-styles, the recent, antediluvian manors of Pebble Beach and, following the rivers, the fog steals halfway up into the Salinas and Carmel Valleys where it usually plays itself out against the land's interior heat. The visitor seldom learns to appreciate the climatic irony of this region—that fog *means* heat, heat in the vast inland, dry hotness compelling cool wetness, and that neither can resist, and both are fascinated by, its obverse. Like Dixie, like me.

The absence of fog means change, moody clouds, a dissipating high pressure off the coast, lower temperatures, wind, perhaps even a wayward storm. It doesn't take long, an hour at the most, for the fog to fill up the hollows, seal all cracks, the backyards and byways of civilization erased by a cool gray even hand. Metaphorically, I suppose, it is a little like death on a daily basis. Or at the very least like an external tranquilizer. I like fog, the way it mutes and equalizes perception, obliterating any deceptive plays of light and fancy, and leaving flat patches of reality that can disappear with the next flick of wind.

Everything *is* what it appears to be, though not all of everything can be seen, and even when it is seen, it is not seen for long. One must make do with tatters and scraps, the seams all in the mind; one must watch the vanishing point for the brief moment it waxes, then watch again with humility and desperation as it wanes away. When the fog is just coming in, when, walking along the street, I feel it push damply past, smelling of kelp and salt and fish, then in the next block lag, almost crouching behind the heat, when I feel the cold and the hot and the cold again, that thin moment of turning, I experience a rush of anticipation, a sense that I must hurry to settle my business and take my place before the evening show begins. Of course it is the same show every night.

I didn't look at Dixie's card again; I suppose I couldn't bear to. Its very nakedness seemed to accuse me, as if I had denied her the basic charities . . . clothes, shoes, a crust of bread. No. I put the card in my purse and left the house. Having crossed Birch and Main, the fog had piled up at the foot of our street which ascended sharply from downtown Monterey. Cutting over one block, I started down the three to the corner, hurrying. I had forgotten to change from my dress shoes, and I began counting the coupled reports of heel and toe until I had far exceeded what it occurred to me was the probable radius of Dixie's current world. It was a sad strange thought. And not even halfway to the bank, not even beyond the aura of home territory. And I supposed that was the worst of her punishments—to suffer the insensibility of the familiar. Dixie thrived on the unknown, on the quixotic moment.

It was Friday afternoon, late, and there was a line out the door of our small local bank; ordinarily I would have postponed my business, but I took my place and waited. Several businessmen filled in behind me. One of them said, "Fog's coming in," and another replied, "Right on time."

*No, it's late*, I thought. It was late that summer too, that last August with Dixie. Everything was late then. Too late.

The walk and the closeness of the other waiters left me uncomfortably hot. A woman in front was wearing perfume which the heat seemed to tempt up from her skin and unleash back toward me. I wondered if Dixie wore perfume in prison.

Just as the last of us were moving into the bank itself, a draft of fog came quietly enveloping, and swirled up under the eaves a moment or two before it shoved in behind us with chilling insistence. It was a moment lifted from the current of moments: the heat, the perfume, the femaleness in front of me, and behind, the men, the cool, gray breath of fog, and the moment was neither mine nor Dixie's but the thin, lifted place between, as sheer as a veil, where we seemed to have known each other. It was how I thought of Dixie, and perhaps still do—in the context of that moment. Dixie caught between, exquisitely alive, but feeling the end, like fog at her back.

The teller smiled patiently at me, her eyes straying over my shoulder as if to tally those still waiting behind. She was young, about twenty, and I wondered if this was her first serious job. Her fingernails were flawlessly painted.

"I'd like a roll each of quarters, dimes, and nickels, please," I said, sliding a fifty dollar bill across to her.

As she filled out the cash receipt she said, "Laundry day?" There was a laundromat next to the bank; it was likely she had a lot of requests for change. Perhaps after work she washed her own clothes there with a girlfriend, a roommate, the way Dixie and I used to.

"It's for the machines," I said absently.

The teller nodded. She thought she knew what I meant; I had no idea what I meant, what machines, why. Communication. I smiled gratefully at her; she smiled back with a lovely and foolish self-assurance in her knowledge of laundromats and life, and of me in them with my handful of coins. Two smiles: thus we made a connection, never mind that it was founded on illusion and error.

Dixie had said to bring change for the machines, so that was what I would do. I would leave at eight the next morning in order to arrive by 4:00. I would bring (if they would allow it) her favorite meal: chorizo and a pineapple milk shake. I would be there with her because I had not been with her before, back when it could have mattered to her—and to me perhaps. Because if one saw what one really saw, not what one knew to see, getting thrown in prison, the whole thing, was a kind of counter-triumph for Dixie. And I don't say that because I didn't care about the man who was the cause, the last and strangely least distinguishable man; I didn't really know any of them. And Dixie couldn't have either. How could she, how could she have known *all* of them? I would go to Dixie because I had the sense that I was one of the conditions—shadowy and oblique, yet treacherously present, a negative image—that she had had to triumph over. If the camera recorded us, it was Dixie it saw, Dixie awash in light. Dixie who was really there.

# 2

High above the coast, much higher than usual, the fog had a metallic obstinacy about it, and I knew the small pale orb just bobbing up over the eastern hills would have trouble burning through. For Henry it would be a good Saturday—flat light was photographically ideal—and when he stepped out of the house, carrying my overnight bag, he flexed his habitual smile.

At the city limits my thoughts snapped directly to Dixie, and there relaxed, freed of the present. Alone I could wander over the past. And perhaps by the time I reached the L.A. basin I would know what there was to say, I would have a *position*. With Dixie it was always best to have one's position firmly settled in advance, she could so easily and cheerfully trip things up.

We were fourteen when we first met. My family had sent me to a boarding school on the Peninsula south of San Francisco, where we lived. My father was in education at the state level; he said that Reagan was ruining everything, and until father and others like him could reconstruct The System, his children would attend private institutions. Mother said he was a traitor to the cause, but she was a purist in everything.

So, Sunday nights my older brother caught a bus to

the Jesuit school north of the city, and I boarded the SP Commuter train with my suitcase and my pillow—I had an attachment to a feather pillow—and rode it south to the Menlo Park depot, the train making half a dozen stops along the way, disgorging weekend tourists from San Francisco and collecting students who attended the four private schools scattered throughout the city's bedroom communities. Upon boarding, we mustered according to uniform, forming noisy camps of gray corduroy, brown gabardine, black watch plaid. When traveling via public transportation to and from our respective keepers we were required to wear our uniforms, and it was generally assumed that this rule had been collectively established so that aged, near-sighted conductors could readily identify and report miscreants to the appropriate school. St. Agatha's uniform consisted of a blue plaid skirt, white blouse, navy blazer with the school's emblem—a burning torch—sewn into the breast pocket, white knee socks, and white oxfords which, after Sunday's arrival, swiftly reverted to the scuffed gray status of anarchy.

Those of us who took the train considered ourselves a breed apart. Like the businessmen, we carried worn monthly tickets with their punch holes of experience, we moved through the cars on legs accustomed to the sway of travel, and we had learned to evaluate fellow passengers with the courteously oblique peeks of veterans, not only expecting, but granting others the same opportunity to observe us. We never stared. We were commuters. We were *unchaperoned*.

At the South San Francisco depot Kelly, my best friend, joined me, flopping down on the opposite seat with her usual chaos of books and bags.

"Got any polish?" she asked.

I rolled my eyes. Last week she'd forgotten her blazer. "You're senile," I said, fishing the polish from my bag.

"It's the drugs," she said in an overly loud voice. The ladies across the aisle cast furtive scowls at us.

"Smack," I said, with casual confidence.

Kelly mumbled incomprehensibly, letting the word "weed" erupt now and then from the gibberish; finally she passed me a brown bag containing what I knew were red licorice whips. She always traveled with red licorice whips. Across the aisle the women leaned inward, apparently to discuss us young addicts and the imagined contents of the paper bag.

"The horror," I whispered. And Kelly whispered back, "The horror." We'd been reading *Heart of Darkness* for English, and "the horror, the horror" was our latest and almost exclusive commentary on life. Its applications seemed boundless.

Of course we'd never tried drugs, not even liquor, nothing except her aunt's Riesling, which she kept hidden in the vegetable crisper, a safe place, she'd reasoned. (Kelly's parents were in Greece for the year, and her aunt had been left in dubious charge.) But we had the drug patois down: it was 1968 and if one wasn't old enough to indulge, it was critical that one at least sounded as if one did.

I watched her with the bottle of polish, pressing the sponge tip against her shoe, spreading the watery white drips around. She even soaked the laces, and ran the sponge along the rubber edge of the soles, and when she moved her feet, there were two white outlines, like warped halos, on the floor.

"What a mess," I said.

Shrugging, she admired her work. "White is what she ordered." "She" was Sister Huerta, also known as Sister Weirdo, who was in charge of the junior dorm and who insisted that oxfords within her purview be polished white before lights out Sunday.

The train slid heavily to a stop at the Belmont Station, and several more of St. Agatha's finest joined us, candy and drinks and bags of chips comprising an alarming share of the accoutrements. I was sitting as usual (since I was first to board) next to the window and opposite Kelly. One thing I liked about the SP Commuter was that they really kept the windows clean, and there was a silent rule among all of us that you didn't mung them up with candy, or lean your face against them the way children or grubby people might. They were big, sleek parallelograms trimmed with black rubber, and the glass was thick, faintly rose-tinted, so that even on the brightest day you could see every little detail in the backyards of the houses along the tracks. The rails had been laid along an elevated mound of gravel which ran the length of the Peninsula like a backbone, the creosote in which the ties had been soaked warming as the day advanced and scenting the air, the packed gravel kept free of debris. Thus our path was always clean and straight. To this day the smell of creosote brings vaguely to mind things sanctified. And sometimes passing a telephone pole, I stop to sniff its bitter hide, as disinfected and preserved as we were in those early days, and perhaps some of us still are.

The SP Commuter eased away from the Belmont depot. Just beyond its swept lots in the depression along the tracks the shabby houses began, unlit and huddled down as if for bad weather. Broken cars and toys, overflowing garbage cans, scabrous lawns, windows blinded with aluminum foil, and the ridiculous, hopeless fences that kept out nothing, not even my sight. A woman wearing pink shorts scurried into her kitchen as the SP Commuter, like a silver ship, like a dream, sailed by. Further away on the other side of the town center where the middle class lived the occasional cool dot of a swimming pool or the green of a playing field soothed the eye. But up the slopes of the distant hills where the big houses sat under old, live oak trees, nothing was visible. I knew them—we all did. It was The Other that was exotic, and safe behind our tinted windows we enjoyed what we told ourselves were serious wonderings about poverty and women who scurry. Even our white oxfords, wherever they had rested, left halos. And our ignorance was a form of snobbery, perhaps the worst form.

The train accelerated, moving sleekly along toward the next station, and the shabby neighborhoods, the factories, the trucking companies and masonry yards became a murky wash of browns and grays. I turned away from the window. The girls from St. Agatha's were conferring over a science book; in it was a picture of an African man with elephantiasis.

"That really is horrible," Kelly said.

Someone giggled nervously.

"It says here it's caused by a worm."

"We don't have those kinds of worms," I said.

Already at fourteen in my St. Agatha's uniform I felt myself immune—to nematodes, to public schools, to the tattered ends of fortune. Not lucky. No. We were all matter-of-factly immune.

This struck me with a chill as I drove east up the Salinas Valley toward Highway 101. There were Mexican pickers in the strawberry fields that morning, and as an experiment I tried to imagine myself with them, bending over all day in the low green flats, the air damp, the world defined, while the cars on the highway went by, went some place exciting. But I couldn't. Then as always, they were a bright litter of color in the green space, another of the picturesque scenes that characterized the Monterey Bay area. I could not imagine myself as anyone else, I was purely me and that is a frightful state. To be one's own antibody.

Dixie would have stopped the car. She would have gone out and chatted in her frothy way, and maybe she'd have bought a carton of strawberries to eat—unwashed—in the car as we drove along. She would have left some kind of impression, not negative, that much I know. And the pickers, the fields, the newness of the hour would have infected her. Dixie was not immune. She seemed to know how to live, how to risk. Still, I sometimes thought there was a quality of the unreal about her living; that she was spending the days of her life like so many brightly colored Monopoly dollars, and that when the game was called she would find herself profoundly and gravely at a loss.

The SP Commuter sounded an advance warning, and the train pulled into the San Carlos Station. A group of Priory boys boarded, ambling through the car like young deities, over-sure and disrespectful. I had a crush on one of them, and I imagined him noticing me as he passed . . . *I am alone . . . he approaches, hesitates, tries to speak. No Jason, I say in a velvet voice, and he nods once slowly, his gaze still focused on me but relaxing now because he understands. We sit side by side. There is nothing we have to say to each other. It is all Fate. We're in a foreign country, riding the Orient Express, and it doesn't matter where we stop, it's all ours, the whole world. We're together. It's love.*

"Want some licorice?" Kelly's girl voice punctured my reverie, and I said, "No," curtly.

I watched the Priory boys settle across the aisle and one seat ahead of the scowling women. Kelly paid them no attention. She was small and plucky, with curly red hair, and a not-too-naughty reputation for making trouble. She had always been one of the more popular girls in our class. We had a fort in the loft above the stables. And one day a few years back we'd run away, leaving a co-authored note of long desperation for the nuns. I knew I loved her dearly. But in the last year her powers had diminished, and I was spending time with the taller, prettier girls, the ones Kelly and I had always referred to as the "wimp-ettes."

Prettiness, especially in an all-girls' school, never pulled much weight. It was personality all the way. When we were old enough to attend the dances that year, I remember being surprised by the girls chosen from out of the fringe. Don't the boys know? I thought, can't they *tell*, can't they *see*? Naturally seeing was all they could do. And when Jason, who was older, asked *me* to dance, I was genuinely embarrassed. It struck me as wrong that he should bypass the girls to whom I looked, and who watched me with obvious disgust as I followed him out. I didn't blame them, I shared their opinion—this was no legitimate measure of stature, this was a fluke, an error in judgement. Some part of me, however, began to see as the boys did. Occasionally after dinner I would ditch Kelly to hang out with the chosen ones in the phone alcove next to the Portry, to place group calls to boys we'd met. Traitor though I was, I couldn't help it. I was growing, and Kelly seemed like someone seen through the wrong end of the binoculars—smaller and less important, her once-endearing details too remote to matter. It was a confusing time for me.

On the SP Commuter Friday and Sunday nights, however, I reverted—with some relief—to Kelly's girlish ways, eating candy, finding amusements in other passengers, and speaking in our peculiar abbreviations.

Leaning forward, she whispered, "It's arrived."

"What?"

She gestured across the aisle, but the conductor was passing through, punching tickets along the way, and I couldn't see.

"What's arrived?" I said.

"What is a who," she said, winking. "Didn't you see the name? Sister Weirdo put it up Friday."

I shook my head. There was only one empty alcove in our dorm, recently vacated by a girl from Mexico City whose family had run out of money. That sort of boom-and-bust thing was always happening with the Mexican girls. It had something to do with the "dangers of a class society," we were told. And like some sad admonition to mourn the departed and give thanks for those of us still living behind St. Agatha's faithful gates, the girl's name had remained above the blue curtains. The empty alcove was next to mine, and because naturally Sister Huerta never checked it, it had lately served as a night meeting place. I was sorry it would soon be occupied.

The conductor punched our tickets and moved on. I saw then for the first time Dixie. Her hair was one of the undistinguished shades of brown. She had a puckish face, blue eyes, and suddenly a great smile, a smile that transformed the otherwise plain features. The nose lifted up slightly like a pixie's, the cheeks became pinked rounds, and the lights in her eyes went on and seemed to be so bright that she had to squint to suppress their dazzling effect. The squint was truly beguiling. Still, you wouldn't say she was pretty; but she *was* somehow pretty. Perhaps—and I have often since wondered about this—the answer lay in the question itself, in the uncertainty; perhaps she conjured up the sense of its possibility, of prettiness, and the viewer himself completed the picture. With Dixie imagination was essential.

She was sitting, to my utter consternation, next to Jason among the Priory boys; the smile was for them. She was wearing an obviously brand new St. Agatha's uniform, everything in model order—except the shoes. Red suede pumps.

Kelly and I eyeballed each other, and in perfect unison breathed the only and in this case intensely appropriate epithet that came to mind: "The horror, the horror."

About this time the train stopped, not at a station but in the middle of nowhere. It was a typically graceful stopping so we didn't think much of it. The passengers waited quietly, one or two trying to look through the thick tinted glass toward the engine. But we were the last car and it was impossible to see anything that far in front. I didn't bother trying. Eventually some men—not businessmen, but men in work clothes—got up and wandered forward, the sliding air door hissing with each defection. I remember thinking how funny it was that the women stayed put, even the ones who were traveling alone and who would have no reason to present an unconcerned front. I remember it because Dixie didn't; she got up, dragging a monstrous white suitcase plastered with travel stickers, and it seemed to follow the red pumps like a big ugly dog through the air door and forward to the heart of the matter.

The rest of us stayed, having every confidence in the SP Commuter. There had never been a problem before. If there was one now, it had to be of no consequence, not worth thinking about. The SP Commuter, to which we gave full allegiance, would deliver us safely to our customary destination. And anyway, curiosity simply wasn't cool.

It was immensely quiet. I could hear someone behind us unwrap a piece of gum and snap it between his teeth. Inhabitants of the shabby houses that backed on the tracks hopped their own fences and started up toward the engine, and even through the extra-thick glass I heard the rapid crunch of their shoes on the packed gravel. A white dog darted by; someone hollered, "Grab him." It was then I wondered if something serious had happened. The white dog. Why would anyone care about a stray dog, or where it went?

"Guess what her name is," Kelly said in the hushed voice she reserved for exchanges during Mass.

"Tell me."

"Dixie Darling."

"What kind of name is that?"

"Her mother must've been sick."

"But I mean, is Dixie Darling legal? Can you have a name like that?" I said.

Kelly shrugged, but Meredith, the girl next to her who was a year younger than us and who lived in our dorm said, "There's a go-go dancer in the City, her name is Serena Darling."

"That's a show name," Kelly said.

"Sister Huerta told me she's from Florida. Maybe they have names like that there."

I looked out the window and said vaguely, "Florida's a tacky state."

The debate then shifted to the red suede pumps, but they were so enormous a *faux pas*, so far outside our gates of comprehension that the talk was confined to single syllable emissions that were—to anyone listening— etymological orphans. At that point this new girl, this *element* occupying space somewhere on the SP Commuter struck me similarly—without origin and lacking development. Something truly new.

There were a lot more people standing on the gravel embankment now, I noticed, just standing there looking at the train, and at us as if we had done something wrong. The white dog was tugging at its collar; the man holding it finally gave a hard kick, and the dog crumpled down, rubbing its muzzle against the man's leg. I didn't like the kick and I didn't like being watched, so I made a point of staring at the man, but he regarded me with a thin smile, and I could tell he was feeling sorry for all of us sitting in the stalled train, and I felt even stranger.

Ten minutes passed. Kelly consumed the last of the licorice whips, its red tail wagging from between her lips. And I returned to my fantasies of Jason on the Orient Express.

Finally the conductor in his blue uniform suit walked by, making a pushing gesture with his hands, and the people strung out beside the train stepped back so that they were all lined up next to each other like spectators at a parade. A discussion followed but no one seemed particularly animated: they all looked sick and rundown, and as if talking was a required effort. An old woman was crying. Then slowly, tentatively the SP Commuter began to move. There was a throng of people about the place where the engine must have come to rest, several policemen among them. Otherwise, nothing apparently out of order. We were back on our way. The train gathered speed, and with the increasing distance I felt myself relax proportionately, relax enough to glance back a last time in order to satisfy what had become safe, idle curiosity. Abruptly my breath went jagged. Because I thought I saw on the packed gravel, pushed over on its side, Dixie Darling's ugly white suitcase. And for half a second it seemed as if the policemen and the poor people were all gathered around *it*; that the train had stopped to eject *it*; and where, I thought wildly, where was *she*, this impostor in a St. Agatha's uniform?

Yet I knew she was no impostor. It was the shoes. It was those damn crazy shoes that told me there was something credible, something indisputable about Dixie Darling.

At the Redwood City station the SP Commuter paused briefly, presumably trying to make up the lost time. As far as I knew it was the first occasion on which it had been late. In the eyes of the new passengers was concern tinged with irritation, but none of us had any explanation to offer them, and we kept our faces averted.

Finally in Menlo Park, the girls from St. Agatha's rose and went forward through the hissing doors. It was late afternoon, and as I stepped down off the train and saw the familiar station house, a small, mission-style structure soaked and saffroned in the nostalgia of day's end, I felt suddenly happy, gratefully happy, as if my world had been returned to me, unharmed. Behind the station in the lot the school van was parked, and Sister MacDonald, her hands tucked inside her great black cuffs, stood patiently beside the driver's door. The smell of creosote and diesel fuel rose warmly up from under the train. Behind me were the Priory boys, and I lagged back from my friends in order to appear older and different. At St. Agatha's dinner would be ready, the long walnut tables set. And afterward we would disperse to our dorms, to the cozy hubbub of girls unpacking, talking about their weekends, and displaying whatever acquisitions the days away had borne. By the time I reached the van I had very nearly forgotten the SP Commuter's unseemly delay.

Dixie was apparently one of the earliest to disembark, for she was already seated in the rear of the van with three kids from the lower dorm.

"She had great hair," Dixie was saying as I climbed in.

"Who's she talking about?" I whispered to Kelly.

"The lady that was hit."

"What?" A singular image flashed in my mind: the woman in the pink shorts who had scurried into her house. And for the space of a held breath it seemed Dixie's woman was my woman. But it could not be.

"A natural blond," Dixie went on.

"Did you see her face? Was it gory?"

"It was gone." She said this with unblinking wonder. A general gasp followed.

"There was just this great hair all over the place. And her arms were twisted together like a rope."

"What about her body, was it mushed?"

"I couldn't see," Dixie answered. "The conductor grabbed me."

Kelly leaned over the seat. "Do they think it was suicide?"

Dixie replied simply, "She was alone."

"Maybe she fell," one of the girls offered.

"She watched it come down the tracks," Dixie said in a trance-like voice. "Getting bigger and bigger and bigger, and the engineer told the policeman that he blew the horn but she wouldn't move. Not until the last second and then she stepped onto the tracks."

"Wow," someone said.

"Maybe she was deaf."

"She could still see, stupid."

"Maybe she was an MR."

"A what?"

"A mental retard."

"We didn't even feel it," Kelly said, and she glanced at the side of my face to include me, but getting no response she turned back to the others. "That's the creepy part. We were just talking and laughing and we didn't even know it. There wasn't even a bump."

I had settled with Kelly and Meredith in the second seat, but would not turn around. The whole thing made me mad. The flawless history, the impeccable tradition of the SP Commuter and the quiet achievement of Sunday afternoons of my life had been violated today for the first time. Dixie was at the center of it—Dixie Darling in her red pumps sitting next to Jason. And then *leaving* him, leaving our car to go and look at this lady who didn't have anything to do with us. And here she was with the details. She had brought the lady to us, among us. The awfulness of it all. They were watching her the way the grubby people outside had watched us. It seemed to diminish us. Me.

"There wasn't even a little bump," Kelly repeated.

"I felt it," said Dixie.

No one knew what to say to this, it was so clearly a lie. The engine of the SP Commuter weighed seventy *tons*, and practically nothing it might hit could be detected. Nothing.

I turned around then and even as I said it, maybe before I started to say it, I could see the thing behind her in the cargo area and I knew I was wrong. But I wanted to cut her, so I said: "You left your big ugly suitcase there."

Dixie never even flinched. Without missing a beat she seemed to accept, overlook, and forgive my nastiness. She said with convincing cheer, "You got it wrong, kiddo. That was her. They threw a sheet over her and the blood made spots all over it. Here's my trusty suitcase, right here," and she reached back to pat the monster. "It used to be my mom's. It's been everywhere."

I stared significantly at Kelly and offered up a sour "the horror." But she wouldn't echo my sentiments, and I must admit I felt pretty crumby then. The girls from St. Agatha's seemed to have excused Dixie her shoes and her suitcase and her snappy manner and her *kiddo*, excused all apparently because of a lady who had nothing to do with us. Except that we were on the train that killed her.

"She had great hair," Dixie repeated, as if this fact was somehow and still irreconcilable with suicide. "Like yours," she said to me. Which was odd. Because I have black hair, black as clean nothing.

24

# 3

About ten miles inland amid the foothills I reached the edge of the fog, and for a short while traveled beneath the thin fraying of light and haze. It would be a hot day but for now an open window sufficed. From the weeds and dried grasses warming under the morning sun the dampness excited an aroma that was neither a mutation nor a memory of spring, but rather an intensifying. It had a sharp, vulgar quality. The land humped and softly rolled, and wherever the fingers of fog caressed a curve or slid down a crease there remained after the fog had perished a brief localized humidity, like sweat drying on skin.

I was thinking about Dixie, and all her men, and then the last one. But that was getting ahead of myself, those most obvious and—ironically—mundane memories. There would be only one way to think about all of that.

Turning south onto Highway 101, following the Salinas River toward its source, I kept wanting to head east—that was where she seemed to be in my mind, east to beginnings—but I knew I had to make first the long run down to Paso Robles, then over into the dry heart of the state, and then down again into the desertic basin of southern California, down to Dixie.

The low land bordering the Salinas River was still
green, with cottonwoods and poplars parading along its
banks and a thinning, drying margin of fertility beyond.
White sandbars had begun to emerge from the river, and
it seemed that summer, though not officially here, was
already insinuating itself on the scene. Here and there
rounding a slow bend or dropping over smooth rocks the
water flashed on and off as it slid behind a hillock or a
thicket or under the path of the highway. Dixie too flashed
on and off; and I wondered if the visit today would provide the first circumstances for a good straight look at
her. Something about her had always defied flat light of
the sort Henry prefers. Dixie was a flicker and a shade
and nothing in between. Nothing. She appeared that winter of my fourteenth year and disappeared that June; reappeared at seventeen, vanished at eighteen. And
everything about her mimicked this pattern. When she
smiled it was a thing felt from the inside pushing out,
like a need; but whose need? Whose?

A trick of light, perhaps, that smile. Then a sudden
shadow, like a blow, and she was gone.

The river with its double strand of trees swung west,
shimmered a last blue-green moment, then vanished.
Without it the area around me was brightly exposed and
seemed far too blunt. A solitary oil rig—the first of many
to come—dropped its head up and down like a tired peasant working the fields. For awhile I listened to the wheels
whining along the old, cracked roadbed, and thought of
nothing except how hot the day would likely get. There
was very little traffic except for passing trucks, each of
which left a stain of exhaust against the sky and a foul
odor that clung to the path of the road. The inland sky, I
noticed, had already acquired the wan, bleached-out look
of summer.

I began to think that the visit was a mistake. I began to

crave the coast, the fog, Henry's easy presence and the life we shared, so agreeably tamed. This excursion was merely a spasm of insanity, and if I waited a moment, a mile or two, the muscles would relax, the spasm would pass, and I would be myself again—Susan Thatcher, attorney at law. Tall, willowy Susan, with straight hair, very black and long, and, owing to a dose of Castilian ancestry on mother's side, good skin, the kind that seldom requires amendments.

I gave the rearview mirror a perfunctory glance. *Susan*, I said matter-of-factly, and having no particular reaction, I adjusted the mirror to present a closer examination.

Father might have chosen for me an alternative nose. The one he provided—the most obvious of his genetic contributions—while having good English lines, has rather more scope than is desirable for a woman. But I am satisfied with it. It lends a certain credibility to an otherwise and perhaps immoderately perfect face. People relax—I have seen them physically soften, even offer a friendly smile—when they discover my nose. And since I prefer clients and associates, and anyone with whom I come in contact to be relaxed around me, my nose is, *in its effect*, perfect.

Dixie once suggested I have it fixed.

Again I looked in the mirror, this time trying to see myself the way she first might in the visiting room at CIW-Frontera. And I saw something—in the set of my mouth, or was it around the eyes? "Well, here you are, predictably," they seemed to say—that left me feeling vaguely ashamed. I don't know why. The whole thing—what happened, what led to it—struck me as so *in order*. Which for Dixie would be a kind of death.

And how might another see us? With half-closed eyes I pictured my visitor enter: there are crude chairs scattered about on a linoleum floor, barred windows, heartless overhead lights, and a dark blue smear against the far wall that is a row of guards looking on in a bored way. Somewhere in the midst my visitor sees my black hair neatly subdued with a band and Dixie's dyed blond curls—that's all. Hair. Even our hair is predictable, black-and-white as it were, real and unreal.

I decided to turn back at the next town, the very next. As it happened, though, the next town was Soledad whose existence depends almost exclusively on the presence of the correctional institution at its north edge. A men's prison. Chain-link fences capped with rolls of barbed wire, towers and aerials, low, gray, flat-roofed buildings checkered with tiny windows. But no inmates. Gradually the highway ascended, and I thought surely I would glimpse prisoners shuffling about in the yards, but in that whole walled expanse nothing moved except close by, atop the largest building two limp flags who offered up a desultory twitch, and in the distance dirty undulations of heat. It left me feeling entirely alone, and oddly too like a prisoner. But of what? Of the memory of those years?

I pulled off the highway into Soledad and found a gas station. It was a town of keepers and servers, and perhaps because I knew this I imagined a shabby, almost embarrassed silence hanging about. Of course it was only 9:00 on a Saturday morning; no reason to expect activity.

It was necessary to get out of my car in order to attract the station attendant. He was a tall, muscular black man with a broken front tooth which his upper lip never quite sheathed.

I asked him to fill it.

He jammed the nozzle in, spilling gas down the side of the car as he tried to engage the automatic catch. The car was a late-model, metallic gold BMW, and I supposed his carelessness was the result of some minor misplacement of jealousy. But when he commented about the "run of dog days," I decided it was the heat which caused his sloppy manner. I did not correct him on his use of the expression "dog days."

"Have they closed the prison?" I asked casually.

He was bent over the nozzle, hand-pumping the fuel, so he had to roll his head sideways and back to look at me. "Less they done it at six this mornin," he said.

I must have frowned.

"Thas when I get off. I'm a night guard." He rolled his head back. "Jes helpin a buddy out here. His ole lady's havin a baby."

"I didn't see any sign of activity as I passed," I offered, by way of explanation.

Returning the nozzle, he clicked off the pump. "Only took four gallons." There was a certain dull irritation in his tone.

"Really?" Truthfully, I hadn't even looked at the gauge: I had pulled in, I think, because I had wanted to make sure that there was another human being nearby. Also, I was still toying with the notion of turning back.

He ran my credit card through the machine, then, placing the card vertically on a writing pad, he walked around to the rear of the BMW to copy down the license plate number. "There's three lock-downs between you and me and Soledad, three more in the cell blocks," he said, still writing. "Thas six ways to hell you won't see in and the boys can't see out." He gave me what I believe was intended to be the disregardful glare of someone in the know. "But they do. In they heads, they lookin out an they gettin out. Specially the tykes."

"Tykes?"

"New boys."

"Ah."

"I got this," and he tapped his front tooth, "from a guy wasn't two days ole. He don't be lookin out no more. He is being there now. He was born agin the day they stripped him neked and give him prison blues. And they's all kina ugly inside to learn him how to git ole fast."

He handed me the pad, and as I signed it, I could feel him study me. It took him rather less time to size me up than I might have wished, because when I returned the pad he yawned and seemed to have already lost interest. I wondered if this was one of the skills he had acquired as a guard—the ability to swiftly classify inmates, determine the degree of threat, security risk, etc. However valuable, it was nevertheless disconcerting: one does not like to imagine oneself as easily pegged. So I said, "I'm on my way now to see a woman in CIW-Frontera," in order to make myself more interesting to him, to provide more contours as it were.

A groggy stare.

"The prison," I added, and waited for him to ask what crime she had committed: it was the usual question.

Instead, he glanced at the car and said, "You the lawyer?"

"No."

"We git a lot of lawyers. They all appealin, they all innocent."

"I'm not a lawyer."

"You say."

"Just a friend." It was not a lie. Technically, yes, perhaps, but the truth was I wasn't going as a lawyer; I was going as an old friend. The rest was out of the picture and seemed not to count, not even to exist. And I remember at that moment, standing in the gas station with the black man on an empty Saturday morning what a funny thing it was, because it was just the sort of quirky reasoning in which Dixie often engaged, and just the sort of chance encounter from which she seemed to flower. "She's been there awhile," I said. "I'm sure she's adjusted."

He ran his tongue thoughtfully along the broken edge of his tooth. "It's all long, day or life, there ain't no short of it. Cause it's a piss-poor way to be."

There was a pause then while we both, I think, appreciated the weight of his remark. The elastic nature of Time had been explored by many, including Bertrand Russell from a more philosophical position, and of course Einstein in his work on Relativity. Now, a night guard from Soledad.

"I haven't seen her for years." He tipped his head to indicate he was listening, but his gaze had landed somewhere behind me as if he was scanning my past. "Do the inmates you work with, do they *want* visitors?" I was thinking of the card Dixie had sent me, its coldness.

"Whal . . ." A long moment while he bunched up his chin and squinted. "They's some that do big ways, and other'n go sour jes thinkin on it."

"Yes, yes, I imagine so."

"But you don't know bout yo friend," he said, raising his eyebrows. There was a look of kindness—not pity—in his face.

"I can't tell. She didn't say much. I guess I'm a little scared." It was a feeling, and incredibly I had said it aloud. So that he could hear it, so that *I* could hear it. In that order.

The night guard laughed gently. "Lady Ma'am, ain't we all."

I glanced up to smile at him, and I seemed to see in an instant who he was; that is, he seemed to let me see him. He was very physical, the bulky contours of his torso showing in bas-relief through his T-shirt . . . yes, very physical—it was probably why they hired him—but there was a reluctance about it, and I think he wanted me to

31

see that, the reluctance . . . as if it was something we shared.

The white cement of the gas station had become a blinding field of glare, and behind him the sun kept rising, but for the moment he was a cool, dark eclipse of a man, a place to rest my eyes, and—*crazy, crazy*—I would have liked exceedingly well to stay there in his tired honest physical world.

The inappropriateness of the desire alarmed me: I moved to the car.

As an afterthought, or perhaps too because I had somehow earned it, he washed the windshield, the undersides of his arms stretching across my intimate vision. I noticed, I *thought*, how beautifully ripe his lips were: the thought was for me a kind of intruder, yet not unwelcome.

Standing back to let me go, he said, "Yo friend, she got some piece of luck today."

It was such a nice thing to say. *Nice.* I actually reached out and waved, as if he was an old friend I was reluctantly leaving, and several times I said thank you, even when clearly he could not have heard me, I said it anyway, because it seemed to be for me too. It was just what Dixie would have done, I realized; she was always so excessive, so infected with sudden feeling. It led me to wonder if I was infected with her, and how far the infection would go, how much of my being she would consume.

When I gained the highway it was to continue south toward Dixie. Though I hadn't the faintest idea what it would entail, I was determined to be for her, maybe for the first time, some piece of luck.

It didn't take Dixie long to transform the chaste simplicity of the alcoves provided by St. Agatha's—bed, dresser, closet, chair, white walls, blue curtains—into a preposterous mix of boudoir and beer hall. There were frilly decorator pillows scattered about, Victorian dolls, a stuffed poodle, and a stuffed black cat with glittering green lashes; sachets in the drawers; a vase of red silk roses; and a hideous gold jewelry/music box that played a stepped-up, tinkly version of "Strangers in the Night." On the walls, in obliterating quantity, were poster-sized photographs of a model—*one* model only—a long blond silky woman with wounded eyes like Ingrid Bergman's, a delicate face that looked as breakable as glass, and lips that were restrained though somehow sexy too. As was the fashion, her hair was pulled back and up in a tasteful French roll, like Grace Kelly's. She was posed with a variety of products—convertible car, refrigerator, hair spray, cigarettes. In one of the largest photos, wearing a red swim suit and a red plaid cap rakishly cocked back off her yellow hair, she was shown with a chain saw, her fingers brushing the ominous bar itself, as if her very femininity had tamed it. The model was Dixie's mother.

And as if this shrine wasn't enough, Dixie cut and pasted the magazine reproductions to the inside covers of her textbooks, so that every time she opened them, she and anyone sitting nearby met her mother's sad, luminous gaze. You could tell that Dixie didn't see much of her, that it was a novelty. The rest of us never paid much attention to our mothers. We were at that age. Of course Dixie hadn't inherited her mother's natural looks, in fact she was almost awkward, but she did—or could, it was always hard to say which—possess that certain air of femininity that was gaining importance in the world of the junior dorm.

Her father was a policeman originally from the east, Boston or Ithaca—some place cold. Because I learned (in the ways that girls do, through the side doors and cracked windows of communication) that they moved to Florida for the weather, though her mother as a model continued to travel a great deal. She was raised in Alabama—hence the name she gave her daughter. Now and then, and obviously for show, Dixie would say things like, "I *might could* do that," or "I *might will, might won't.*" A curious affectation. Probably it was just a way of feeling close to her mother. She was infatuated with her, and in some respects so were we all at age fourteen—or at least with anyone as purely helplessly female as Dixie's mother seemed to be.

Their names were Bill and Kate Slade, but the fine print beneath each photograph said Cheryl Darling. Personally, I didn't see much difference between Kate and Cheryl, except that maybe the former was more wholesome sounding, and models were supposed to have names that rang at night, kind of soft and easy and lingering on. There was no question, however, that Slade would not have done; still, it was odd that Dixie used her mother's professional name, Darling, as her surname. After all, she was just a girl. And it was odd that her parents sent her to a school in California, on the other side of the continent. There were plenty of good schools in the east; in fact, St. Agatha's maintained a sister school in Brooklyn Heights. What it meant, though, was that Dixie *lived* at St. Agatha's, never going home on the weekends as most of us did, to return with new clothes, or jewels, or adventures. Oh, packages came infrequently, some gaudy nicknack, more photos of mom languishing over a box of muffin mix, and within a week of her arrival, apparently after a distressed call from Mother Superior, a proper pair of white oxfords. But I in my distant way felt sorry for Dixie, even while Dixie seemed oblivious to her misfortunes and to the disaster of protocol that she was.

I say "in a distant way" because Dixie was always kept from the inner sanctum for several obvious reasons (which

I have already described), and for some not so obvious reasons. Girls schools are essentially a company of cliques. For instance, I belonged to a group of relatively studious girls, two of whom were also very popular and who "crossed over" to the popular girls' clique. Their presence elevated our clique further so that we were among the top two. But, either Dixie refused to recognize the existence of this order, or she might have decided that she comprised her own clique. Whatever the case, she hovered at satellite distance, usually cheerful and scrappy, a kind of one-girl improvisation.

The dorms at St. Agatha's were distinguished by theme and year in school. There was the Mexican dorm, Polynesian, Early American, and so on, with colors and decorations appropriate to each. Ours—seventh and eighth grades—was the Dutch dorm. Alcove curtains were alternately red and blue, the bedspreads a windmill pattern, the walls and furniture chalk white. The first thing Dixie did, the very first was to take her name tag from its frame above the curtains and to paint in neon colors flowers and butterflies and the like around Sister Huerta's excellent India ink italics. At St. Agatha's we used fountain pens and wrote everything in italics—it was the way. Even in the midnight dusk, the wild pinks and oranges and lime greens marking Dixie's alcove were visible, and one could not help but note the similarities between her place and a micro version of a red-light district.

Thus from the start Dixie Darling insisted upon her own solitary ethos, while apparently having no particular opinion about our carefully groomed homogeneity, or any inclination to adopt the St. Agatha's way.

In February Sister Olinger returned.

It was a school night, about 8:30. Dixie had put a 45 on the turntable which was kept just to the left of the entrance to the dorm. It was playing "Sugar, Sugar," by

The Archies. The older girls in the Polynesian and Mexican dorms, and the seniors in their rooms for two, they listened to Led Zeppelin and Creedence Clearwater Revival and the Moody Blues, and while we knew that one day when we got to be their age we would somehow *like* their music, we were happy with—if a little embarrassed by—The Archies. In the common area between the opposing ranks of alcoves girls were dancing. Dixie was sitting on the floor next to the record player shaving her legs with a Lady Remington electric. There was only the one outlet in the dorm, and she was the only one of us juniors whose parents permitted shaved legs. Probably they simply didn't care.

I usually heard Sister Olinger before I saw her. She had a distinctively heavy *heel*-toe cadence, and from one end to the other of the long oaken hallway I could easily detect the ascending and descending scales of her progress. The other nuns typically were quiet, almost recessive; this was likely an extension of their vows of humility. But Sister Olinger did not seem to mind people knowing who and where she was. And she was always laughing, a free, reckless sort of laugh that seemed to precede and trail behind her like a length of ethereal silk. It made her seem larger than life, because she arrived first as a sound and as an image inspired by the sound, then, full of anticipation, we watched her person arrive. When she departed, she *kept* departing . . . *heel*-toe, *heel*-toe, and the silken laugh fluttering back toward us. I suppose I was a little uneasy about her laugh, or confused . . . I don't know. It seemed to say "follow me," and at the same time, "hear where I am going merrily without you." It seemed to have a certain taunting aspect.

Before her mysterious departure Sister Olinger had been in charge of the Polynesian dorm. But I admit I had looked for or manufactured opportunities to be near her daily.

Dixie cranked up the volume on the record player, and for the sixth or seventh time we were dancing to "Sugar, Sugar." Outside it was raining, but the dorm was hot and bright, the air smelling of radiator heat, faintly burnt and metallic. We were all wearing our flannel nightgowns, sweating and shaking our hips to the untested rhythms of sexuality. I wasn't aware of Sister Olinger until the revelers began to drop out. By the time I saw her she was surrounded. I was not the only girl whom she had enchanted.

Dixie continued to shave her legs.

Having ceased to dance, I was hanging back by the entrance to my alcove, waiting, hoping she would come over and not force me to join the flock of common admirers, for there was nothing cheap or ordinary about my disposition toward Sister Olinger. I thought she knew that.

The record ended. Again Dixie lifted the stylus and swung the arm back, this time returning it to the "off" position. The high-pitched *buzz* of the Lady Remington became acutely noticeable to me, but Sister Olinger and my dorm mates maintained their bubbly exchange, and I maintained my miserably frustrated distance.

"Where have you been?" Sister Olinger was asked.

"Where do you think?" she said, almost coyly.

"Paris."

"On vacation."

"With your family," Meredith said. Then, "Where is your real family?"

Sister Olinger threw back her head, letting loose the fluttery laugh which brushed, like cool petals, against my still hot cheeks. "*You* are my family," she said. "You and the Community here at St. Agatha's."

"But where were you then?"

"In the Sierra, at our retreat house. I've been preparing to make my final vows. This summer I go to Rome, to the Pope," but when she said this she was wearing a stern frown and her voice was so serious it sounded angry, and the laugh just moments earlier seemed now like ancient history. It was then she noticed me, or decided to notice me—I don't know—and the smile she gave me was the one many of the nuns employed, a uniformly small neat placid smile, like a calling card.

I nodded. It was all I could do. My mouth was dry, and a rash of prickly heat had started at the nape of my neck and was radiating over the rest of my body. Had I hurt her by not joining the others? Was she angry? And why? Because I had been dancing, because I had told her I had wanted to be a nun and now upon her return she had caught me dancing? How serious, she might well have been asking, was my commitment to the order, to the Sisters of the Ascension of Christ?

I think I tried to look at her then, to let her know how sorry I was, how glad I was she had come back, to let her know the mess of feeling I was in. But it didn't work. Somehow I had walled off the mess so that neither one of us could see it. Numb, I watched her with the others.

Her round face was sunburned as if she'd spent a lot of time out of doors during her retreat in the mountains. She was wearing the shortened version of the black veil the younger sisters opted for, which permitted demure locks of hair to slip out from under the wimple. The locks upon Sister Olinger's forehead were maple brown and tightly curled. The color surprised me; I had expected something like red. Her eyes were not deep or contemplative or even vaguely melancholy like some of the other sisters'. They were hard blue lights, not eyes you wanted to gaze into, though I liked sometimes the electric shock feel of them. And she had breasts. Unambiguous ones. Beneath the flattening pleats of black linen *all* of the other nuns at St. Agatha's hid more or less successfully their womanly fact; at least it was not something of which you were consciously aware. But on Sister Olinger the black linen angled sharply out, then back, and because of the unfortunate design of the habits, the triangle dominated the whole of her chest to her waist producing a most unbecoming matronly impression. On one level it never occurred to me that in lay clothing she would be considered buxom; but probably on another level it did occur to me.

I was about to escape behind the curtains of my alcove when I heard her say, "You must be Dixie," and I paused only to see what Sister Olinger would make of our new recruit, Dixie Darling. "I've been hearing all about you," she added.

Dixie mouthed something inaudible, then oddly enough, she glanced over and winked at me, as if we two, by not joining the admiring throng, were together. I must say I was grateful, though I couldn't even tacitly agree with the sentiment.

"How are they?"

"What?" said Dixie, not bothering to look up.

"Your legs," Sister Olinger answered, and she bent down and brushed her fingertips along one of Dixie's legs.

No one seemed the least troubled by the gesture. "She gets to shave," one of the younger girls piped.

Dixie unplugged the Lady Remington, stood up, and casually started across the dorm toward me. "They're done," she chirped over her shoulder.

From Sister Olinger the reckless laugh flew again. "A pleasure to meet you," she said, her tone very sarcastic.

But Dixie must have missed it, because she replied in her usual airy way, "Likewise I'm sure." She then somehow enlisted me to join her in calling a boy from the pay phone down the hall which I had never before done with her, and never again during the rest of that term. Dixie's charities, I was to learn, were often so subtle that it was genuinely difficult to say whether they were accidents, she was simply and absolutely unaware, or *so* aware, so blithely aware that the seams never showed.

Nevertheless, I forsook boys. I forsook anything having to do with becoming a woman. I was going to be a nun. I would regain Sister Olinger's esteem by living in favor with Christ.

Dixie could worship her mother. I would worship God. And the rest of the girls in our dorm could content themselves with exploring the labyrinthine world of boys.


Every morning at 6:30 a.m. I rose and washed and put on a clean uniform, and atop my head like the pat of a benevolent hand—God's hand, I told myself—I set the small oval white lace veil, and alone I entered the chapel with the women in black, and offered myself up to Christ before breakfast. Sometimes from hunger I fainted. I suppose I hoped for that: it seemed to render my devotion more credible, more intense. Sometimes it was Sister Olinger who roused me, holding my head down between my knees, and in her eyes the penultimate reward of her loving concern. Naturally Christ was our ultimate reward.

On occasion I took to crying at night, or pretending to: suffering seemed a natural dimension of the calling. When the looked-for question came, I replied that there was nothing at all wrong, I was very happy here at St. Agatha's, and I provided as evidence my newly acquired and oft-practiced small neat placid smile. *My* calling card. Some of the other girls, Kelly included, began to mimic the smile. At Christ's recommendation I turned the other cheek, I smiled, but the smile felt like broken glass, and at night the tears became real. More and more of my time was spent alone contemplating Christ and His suffering.

Every other Friday night, from the moonlit palm court I could hear the rock 'n' roll beat of the dances I no longer attended, preferring the soft hymnal quiverings, like the heartbeats of a flock of birds, and the timorous giving of a higher sort of love.

On Wednesday afternoons I attended Benediction, kneeling as close to the altar as I could, intoxicated by the incense smoking and swirling, and by Father Moriarty in his satin vestments kneeling as we did, facing the altar, and the gleaming gold monstrance he lifted up like a small sun rising, and within it the greatest, the true Son, the Host; intoxicated by the deeply moving moaning chant of the Eucharist, and the accent of a single chime rung at intervals whose purpose it was, it seemed, to amaze all thought out of one's mind in order to leave it in its emptiness pure for the adoration of Christ Our Lord. While just beyond the chapel windows, my friends played like shadows—mere shadows I reminded myself—upon the still waters of eternal life.

Twice a week I confessed my sins—impure thoughts, jealousy, spiritual pride—standard fare for Father Moriarty, I imagined, although one day I recall he asked, and there was a note of kindly distress in his voice, perhaps even exasperation, if I had not *done* anything since my last confession.

Naturally I thought he was impugning my honesty. I replied, "No, Father. Besides what I have already told you, I have not hurt Our Lord since my last confession."

"What you have told me . . ." There was a pause while he formed his words. "What you have told me, these are things belonging to your inner world."

"Yes, Father."

"How old are you?"

"Fourteen."

"What do you do after school, for instance?"

41

"I pray. I contemplate Our Lord's sacrifice."

I hesitated then, and he said eagerly, "Yes, yes what is it, what else?"

"I play the piano," I confessed. "My parents pay for lessons, and I'm supposed to practice one hour each day. But I offer it up to The Lord. If it's good, I mean. If I play badly, I ask His forgiveness, and sometimes I . . ."

"What more?"

"I scrape the skin off the ends of my fingers with a bobby pin so that it hurts to play."

Through the iron grate I distinctly heard him sigh. "This again," he murmured.

"Music is an earthly pleasure," I hurried on. "So I thought, if I must do it, I ought to suffer to make myself more clean for Our Lord," I said cheerfully, proudly.

"You must not do this thing." His voice was tired, measured. "Several of the nuns . . ." but he did not finish his thought.

"But Father . . ."

"No more."

"Yes, Father."

"Who has taught you this?"

"No one. I thought it would bring me closer to God."

He was silent then, and I assumed he was devising my penance while I knelt in the soft murk of the cubicle, afraid of his displeasure, and confused by it too. He was a young priest, tall with dark hair and nice blue eyes, and I knew he smoked because I could smell it mingling with the just-ironed scent of his cassock. It was something I noticed at that moment, maybe because I didn't like feeling I had disappointed him, so I wondered about his smoking. It wasn't exactly a sin; still, you weren't supposed to indulge.

"Have you no special attachment, Susan?" he asked.

I was stunned. The confessional was supposed to be a

place and a time of anonymity, and despite the concern in his voice, I felt as if he had reached through the grate and slapped me.

"A boy perhaps?" he queried.

"No." A cold sweat troubled my palms. Why didn't he just give me my penance and let me go?

"Then a special friend, someone you share secrets with."

"I don't have any secrets," I answered. And in the interests of ending what was to me an increasingly uncomfortable exchange, I added, "I like especially Sister Olinger. She's helped me a lot, in my devotion." Of my plan to enter the order I told him nothing; I thought revealing it would smack of spiritual pride.

"Sister Olinger, yes, she is popular," he said vaguely.

"May I please have my penance, Father?"

"I want you to listen carefully to me. You are fourteen. You cannot give up things you have never had. The Lord did not mean for us to forsake our lives, but to live them in a way that demonstrates our love for Him *through* others and through living. He does not mean for us to manufacture suffering. You must stop this bobby pin business. Suffering is something that exists. We don't need to make more of it."

"Yes, Father."

"Your penance," he said, and he laughed a little, "is to play. Praise God by enjoying what He has given you, not rejecting it."

For one day, with a kind of dread I did as I was told. I played. Though anymore it wasn't clear to me what that meant. It seemed as phony and awkward as the standard penance of prayer likely was for most of the other girls. I then resumed my calling.

The campus of St. Agatha's comprised about a hundred acres of one of the most expensive—in terms of real estate—bedroom communities south of San Francisco. It was truly a world unto itself, having four separate schools ranging from grades kindergarten through high school, a rest home for the older nuns, a main building in which the six dormitories, infirmary, parlors, music rooms, two cafeterias—formal and informal—three indoor recreation rooms, countless enormous lavatories, and on the other side an entire cloistered community of nuns having presumably (for we never saw it) living quarters and dining rooms and such. The grounds included two sets of tennis courts, riding stables, a swimming pool, maintenance buildings and yards, a separate bakery, a "little" theater which was not little, hockey field, volley ball courts, and extensive gardens, in addition to the many paths that wound through wooded areas ending sometimes at shady grottoes of the Virgin Mary or fountains or a bench atop a sunlit knoll for the solitary contemplative walks the nuns took, their hands tucked inside their cuffs or clasped behind their backs, their heads slightly bowed, and their lips caressing words of silent endless devotion. There was even a cemetery reserved for the departed Sisters of the Ascension of Christ. It was here I spent my afternoons praying. Because someday, I was sure, carved into one of the tasteful white crosses would be the name *Sister Thatcher.*

I met Dixie there once. Or I saw her.

The cemetery was small, containing at that time no more than fifty crosses, and completely surrounded by redwood trees which had been pruned to a thick impenetrable hedge about eight foot high. It was arranged exactly like a church, with a center aisle or path from which the rows of crosses departed, and at the end a stone platform supporting a life-sized and surprisingly realistic crucifix. Someone had painted—probably Sister Martine—Christ's hair brown, His eyes and loincloth blue, and His wounds and sacred bleeding heart a deep red. It was upon His heart I usually fixed my gaze. From the back of the cemetery the heart was strikingly noticeable, even the small drips, red against the bloodless pallor of the unpainted marble.

I did not think myself clean enough to enter the cemetery; I sat at the back edge on a stone. Though if I was miserable about something real or imagined, if I was actually crying, I would sit at the foot of the cross, my suffering having cleansed me, temporarily at least. But not the day I saw Dixie.

I was on my stone, gazing at the heart when I noticed movement behind the crucifix. There were steps that descended from the back of the platform out through an opening in the hedge, and that was where Dixie was. With a boy, I realized. To me, where she was doing what she was doing was appalling.

I never moved. I thought to somehow counteract her behavior with mine: I prayed more intensely than ever.

*The body and blood of Christ our Redeemer who died for the sins of the world to set us free. Body and blood*, I repeated.

Every now and then I could hear them. And the funny thing was, Dixie sounded so *uninvolved*. At one point the boy said, "Come on, please Dixie." And she said, "Why, that's too much for TV." One of her favorite sayings, but it was her *everyday* voice she used, not the voice of a girl in the throes of what was then called "heavy petting." Her companion moaned on. It turned out to be John Cavanaugh, the brother of a St. Agatha's girl, and a nice enough fellow, nice enough looking, too, except for his complexion. It was a stopper. Apparently though it hadn't stopped Dixie.

I thought about how dirty it was back there. Bird droppings, redwood detritus, mud from the plowed fields beyond—and they were mauling each other in the dirt. They were sinning dirty.

*Jesus Christ*, I thought, but it wasn't clear whether I was thinking of Him, or of them, of His body and blood, or of theirs. Nothing was very clear after awhile. The halo of vision beyond the red heart went fuzzy and bright, like a slow explosion. It was one of the first, warm, spring days, and I began to feel woozy on my rock at the back of the cemetery. Somewhere behind me along one of the wooded paths I heard voices, girls heading for the stables, but I didn't move, and Dixie didn't stop. The slot in the hedge through which apparently they had first come lined up with the back of the crucifix, and the sun at that moment had dropped down into the slot so that they were perfectly silhouetted against the sun, the agonized body of Christ hanging before them, and His heart like a soft red light in the darkness of their sin. What I saw, heard, a shoulder or . . . a breast, then His and the cold limp flesh of His abdomen . . . a faint cry . . . exhalation. Exaltation. But whose? In what ecstasy of pain did He writhe? Did she? And what altar was this where dead virgins lay praying to sex and a bleeding heart?

I squeezed my eyes, I shook my head, I tried once more to focus on the heart, *body and blood*, but my gaze kept tracing the drops of red blood down His white skin, and I was thinking about Dixie's white skin, and wondering if there were now drops of blood on it, bright and sweet, wondering with a fascination I couldn't seem to restrain how far she had gone.

"Oh, not very," she chirped. I had confronted her that night after lights out. In the lavatory where I had followed her. "There's still lots more to try," she said, flashing me one of her exploding smiles.

"But Dixie, why there, why in the cemetery?"

"Same reason you were there. So no one could *see*.

Except you did see."

"We were not there for the same reason, not at all. I was praying."

"Oh, what's the difference."

"There's a huge difference, all difference."

"Look, I'm not a Catholic or anything like that, but the way it looks to me you're all trying to make this guy happy, right? Jesus. And there He is, He's half-naked and He's hanging there, and He's *suffering*, that's what they're always talking about, His suffering. Well," she said, and she tossed me a look of wicked delight, "John Cavanaugh was suffering, too."

I think I groaned.

"You should've come closer, Sue, you should've seen. He was so cute, quivering all over and pleading with me. Look," she said, tugging down the top of her nightie. On both sides of her neck just above the collar bones were hickeys. "Twins," she said proudly, and continued to put curlers in her hair.

Not knowing what to say I watched this proceeding for awhile from beside my sink. Mine was the first, next to the door, Dixie's was somewhere in the middle of the row, about six sinks away. Along another two walls were more sinks, all white enamel, all sporting a towel rack and a mirrored cabinet above. In the center of the room sat four bathtubs enclosed with metal half walls. From the high ceiling of the room itself light globes hung down, blindly intrusive, like eyes without pupils, and the bank of night windows along the fourth wall threw the empty gleam of the lavatory back at us. Despite the radiators beneath the windows, the room was always a cold cavernous place smelling of toothpaste and soap and towels that would never quite dry. Somewhere toward the far corner a faucet was trickling, but the sound in the hollow room seemed to rise up and circle relentlessly, like the pinched whine of a lone bird.

"It's a holy place," I murmured. "It's been sanctified, it's *clean.*"

"What? The cemetery?" With her front teeth she opened a bobby pin, then slid it onto one of the big pink rollers. She had borrowed the pins from me. "I think it's creepy, all those dead nuns. Anywho, it was John's idea. I said the stables. There's a big pile of hay in the back, and it's nice and dark."

"Do you love him?"

She laughed. "Why not? Sure. Does that make you feel better?"

"My feelings don't have anything to do with it."

"Are you sure, kiddo?"

"Yes, darn it, I'm sure. I'm talking about what you did."

"What you *think* I did," she said.

"Okay."

"Okay. So it bugs you I'm not in l. u. v. with a guy I was kissing. I like to kiss, okay? And he likes it." She shrugged. "Chateau no-problem." Leaning toward the mirror, she squeezed a blemish, ran a hand over the rest of her face and, apparently satisfied with the inspection, began putting away her assortment of hair articles. "How come you stayed for the show?"

"I told you, I was praying. I was there first. I go there every day." Suddenly, inexplicably she had me on the defensive. "I couldn't help it, you were right there, right behind the crucifix. It was really tacky, I mean it, Dixie, to do it there."

Pausing, she said, "You go every day?" In the silence the cry of the leaky faucet seemed to intensify.

"Yes."

"What do you think, Sue?" Softening her voice, she looked right at me with her luminous blue eyes, and it was funny when she said my name how it went right inside me, the way people like your parents who love you say your name at night when you go to bed. "That might could be a little weird, huh?"

"You don't understand."

For several long seconds she gazed at me, into me, then pulling one corner of her mouth, she headed for the door and in passing said, "This whole place is a little weird."

I wasn't ready to sleep. My stomach was in knots, my hands were cold. I turned on the faucet and held them under a column of increasingly hotter water, every now and then adjusting the cold until I had completely pinched it off. Several times I used the soap. Then I washed my face, in and behind my ears, back of the neck. Again that night, I brushed and flossed my teeth. Still, I didn't feel *right*. I kept hearing Dixie, I kept thinking about John Cavanaugh quivering, I kept seeing his mouth on her neck, and the leaking red heart, and Christ's loincloth, and suddenly I was wondering—God help me—wondering with appalling blasphemy what He looked like underneath.

A bath, I thought. But no, the noise would attract Sister Huerta.

The faucet in the distant corner leaked on, its cry incessant and still circling round and round like a trapped bird, and it seemed if I could just stop *it*, if I could find it and keep it from leaking water, or blood, or . . . From sink to sink I went, shutting each faucet tightly off, though I knew it was behind the tubs in the distant corner, I wanted to keep them all from leaking, all hearts, and when I finally reached it, His sacred heart and the blood trickling out, I think I was crying. Because I knew it would not shut off, not ever. It was broken.

# 4

The next morning I missed Mass. Though I had not slept well and had risen earlier than usual, I was too late to enter the chapel: Father Moriarty was already consecrating the bread and wine, in moments the nuns would be filing forward, and it would have been untoward of me to enter then without having earned my communion with the son of God.

What happened was I had gone to the showers, and perhaps I had taken a longer one than usual. The room was chilly and smelled of mildew, and the infinite amount of hot water St. Agatha's provided burned in a gratifying way. Also, after yesterday's events and a night of thrashing about I felt particularly grimy. So I took a long shower, and performed the remainder of my ablutions with perhaps a tad more exactitude than was my custom. I then went next door to use the toilet, following which I thought it best to shower again. When I was finally dressed and ready to leave the changing area, I paused to regard the door with its metal handle, undoubtedly a germy object. And after all the precautions I had taken that morning to be clean and ready to receive Christ, ready too for whatever the day would bring, for Dixie at the breakfast table, for my studies, and for my afternoon prayers in the cemetery, after all I had done to set off on the right foot, to have a good, ordinary, orderly day with no mishaps, I wasn't about to be undone by a door handle. I think I even congratulated myself on spotting the hazard; most people would have overlooked it.

Still, there was only the one way to open the door. Pulling the handle, I kicked the door block over and propped it ajar, then I scrubbed again and rushed downstairs, the skin on the back of my hands red and stinging. But, as I said, I was too late.

It was the first time, certainly not the last, that I understood what it was to be *at a loss*, for when I peered within I found that I had no feelings, or perhaps too many—there didn't seem to be a distinction—and not one would stand still long enough to be named. It was too early for breakfast, too late to return to the dorm and pretend to be just rising, dewy-eyed and innocent, as my dorm mates were at that moment. All the nuns were in Mass; all the workers already working in the kitchens, the bakery, the bathrooms and classrooms of the schools, preparing our felicitous way. A telephone rang, but Miss Hadleigh, our portress, had not yet arrived to take up her post in the cubicle reserved at the right of the foyer. Probably the front door was still locked, the Dobermans still loose. And outside, despite yesterday's balmy flirtation with spring, it was raining, a weary sort of rain, the sky brightening slowly and with apparent effort, as if neither rain nor sun would win this day.

Having set off on the right foot, I was ready, but for what, for whom?

The telephone kept ringing. A form of companionship at least, sound—someone else was alone and calling—and for awhile I considered answering, but the longer it went on the less I wanted to; it came to sound belligerently needy, and I was ashamed—in an abstract way, of course—for whoever it was who was calling. When it finally did stop, the silence that was there all along behind the ringing, a dry, insipid silence, seemed to waft up like disturbed dust as I passed through it.

I thought I had better remove my veil. I went to the end of the corridor, to the lavatory by the side door, and washed my hands, holding the door open with my foot throughout, and at the end rinsing off the faucet handles before touching them to shut them off. I then felt clean enough to remove the veil; which I did, folding it neatly and tucking it into my blazer pocket.

The main corridor at St. Agatha's was hung with fraying tapestries of hunting scenes and such, and a collection of brooding oils, many religious but many strangely heretical—wild-eyed horses with swelling, erotic hindquarters, noble women whose breasts were so milky, so untouchable they seemed to tempt the worst, Caravaggio's reclining Bacchus, very unctuous and obviously gay. Oh, there were lots depicting the baby Jesus, gray-faced and wrinkled, and looking more often than one wished like a little old man who was really angry with the world. I walked the length of the corridor, feeling alternately the gaze of beast and baby, and once when I passed between opposing oils, feeling the place where they intersected, the mighty and the almighty, and it was funny how thoroughly disorienting it was, being in that place. Being human, that is. Then I turned and went back halfway. I had been having dreams of this nature, dreams in which characters turn inside out—a grotesquely fat boy with tawny teeth and an oil slick for hair is sexy with me, good Sister Olinger kicks one of the girls from the lower dorm, Dixie in a black habit. Crazy dreams. It was probably why I wasn't sleeping well.

Between the tapestries and paintings chairs had been arranged at intervals along the walls, and though I had rarely seen them used, I occupied the one opposite the chapel door, a Victorian chair with a high straight back and solid rungs. Methodically I began to bite my nails. I didn't know what else to do. I had no place to go. In my mind it was impossible to reconcile tardiness with a whole history of order and precision. I really couldn't see how the day could go on without attending Mass. It would be all wrong, a real confusion. Though when eventually Sister Olinger emerged with the others, she raised her eyebrows and smiled as if she was pleased that I had missed Mass, that I had stumbled, as it were. It wasn't the least bit smug or disappointed, her smile. There was in fact a clear element of friendliness in it, not as if she had forgiven me, but as if *I* had forgiven *her*. This was even more disconcerting.

I washed my hands. It was the chair, I told myself, the old dusty chair, and it was only proper to wash one's hands before breakfast. But I think I knew even then that I was washing because of Sister Olinger and Dixie and God and those first vague stirrings of the flesh that had to be rejected out of hand but could not be rejected out of mind.

After a week or so, with some practice I devised a method of entering and exiting without my hands touching doors: if I was on the push side, I simply used my foot, and if on the other, I hooked my elbow inside the handle and wrenched it open just enough to twist by and slip out. For knobbed doors I relied upon companions, or if alone I waited for someone to come along, though sometimes I had to wait a good fifteen or twenty minutes, or as a last resort, fetch a friend or a nun on some pretext and tag along behind as she miraculously opened the door and passed through. Because the washing and waiting produced chronic lateness, I fell into disfavor with teachers, nuns, and friends alike. Father Moriarty even suggested I sleep in and not try to get to Mass on time, since I was increasingly unsuccessful. In this lay several ironies: true, I was not sleeping well, I was in fact awake and up earlier than I had ever been in the past, but I was so distressed at having been previously late, disappointing Our Lord, so ashamed that I really felt it was essential to wash all the more assiduously. Which, needless to say, further promoted the tardiness.

There were other complicating issues; there always are. My alcove, for instance. I liked it kept a certain way—this was nothing new. But I was so tired now I felt I couldn't trust myself to have done it right. Often and, toward the end, I admit every day, I returned to the dorm after breakfast when no one was there—they were all on their way to classes—to check that the bedspread was perfectly smooth, the closet curtains pulled so that nothing of my clothes showed, the little rug aligned with the edge of the bed, the dresser drawers all shut tight, the personal items atop the dresser—an earring tree, a photo of my family, a small statue of the Virgin Mary, a pair of scissors, and a white notepad on which I planned by the hour each day's activities—in their customary places. Pillowcases being a natural repository for a variety of nightly secretions, I changed it daily. I recall I had a nine-item checklist which I ran through twice, just to be sure. It also became necessary to forbid anyone from entering my alcove, though naturally I never said anything to this effect. If a girlfriend entered, I stood immediately and left, feigning interest in something beyond the limits of my area and, with perhaps excessive cheerfulness, luring her along; or, seeing her headed my direction, I rose and met her halfway. I was simply too tired to keep cleaning up after visitors. I kept the curtains to my alcove closed most of the time. Likewise, visits to other alcoves, despite the pleasantness of the camaraderie I was increasingly missing, did not finally justify elaborating the already elaborate schedule of washing in which I was engaged. Away from my own alcove, or dislodged from my habitual pattern, I felt utterly exposed and, as I said, at a loss. While this made isolation nearly a *fait accompli*, I nevertheless made a good show of normality, sitting at the foot of my bed gossiping across the dorm with Kelly or Meredith, or enlisting others to shower at the end of the day as if I had not already that morning, enlisting them so that I would not appear alone in my cleanliness. The younger girls were an easy mark; they were flattered to keep company with anyone older. And Jennifer who wasn't too bright; and Rita who was nice regardless. Hearing the other showers, the carefree chatter of girls, I felt almost okay, almost normal.

I timed everything. In part to curb the tardiness, but probably in the main because I couldn't seem to help it. It was simply an extension of the counting which gradually became irresistible. All things, all acts were subject to silent numeration—how many steps to the cafeteria from the chapel, how many bites in a bowl of oatmeal, how many tapestries on the third floor, the fourth, how many strokes in a lap of freestyle, of butterfly, how many Hail Marys or Our Fathers could be said in ten minutes if I concentrated on each word, if I didn't concentrate, how many boys had Dixie kissed and how many times would she say no before going all the way, and on and on and on. Once, I think, I even counted the number of times Sister Legare blinked in French class. But I really didn't mind. Counting kept me, if not focused on what I was counting, at least not at a loss, which was a most disturbing state.

I was profoundly tired, and functioning so much now on the frayed edge that I suppose others thought I was excitable, perhaps even nervous. I don't know. As much as was possible, without appearing odd, I kept to myself, my studies, my devotion. I even worked out a schedule for the eight lavatories in the main building and the three in the junior school which guaranteed secrecy. It was a good working schedule and after awhile I think I actually felt, if not comfortable, at least that I was not free-falling into the hole that had opened up at the center of my being.

I stopped going to confession. I couldn't tell Father Moriarty about the washing. So of course I could not take Communion. This was a terrible sadness for me. Oh, I went to Mass, slipping in late as usual, and, lost in my shame, I offered the Lord my filthy adoration, and hoped that he would not notice me in His house, contaminating it.

In late April Dixie found the book. I know it was Dixie because I was with her and the others that afternoon, making our weekly, off-campus excursion to the local town with Sister MacDonald; and I know it was April because the plum blossoms were blooming, but fading too, strung out along the main street like puffs of ashen pink smoke. I had come out of the five-and-dime with my purchase—stationery, I recall—to wait with the others on the sidewalk for the stragglers still shopping, and I remember wishing they would hurry because I was already anxious to get back to campus and wash, so it had to be late April, when my washing was *in medias res*.

The book was in a brown paper bag, lying in the gutter. It appeared as if someone had tossed it there suddenly, perhaps at a moment when discovery was imminent. Dixie slipped it in her tote and did not inspect it until we were back in the dorm. It was the first and probably worst form of pornography any of us would ever see. It took our imaginations and stretched them so far they snapped. Or at least mine did.

At fourteen, girls—and boys too, I presume—possess

a keen appetite for matters having even a whiff to do with sexuality. I admit, biologically speaking, it's natural. But this book was not natural, it was tainted food as it were, and over the course of a week, the simple natives of the junior dorm at St. Agatha's School for Girls made themselves sick consuming it.

There were scheduled reading groups. Though no one ever said, we all seemed to know exactly when and where—in the basement locker room after dinner, the dressing room of the Little Theater, the fourth floor maintenance closet, the seldom-used lavatory near the hockey field—all places without windows so that we could sit huddled and listen and not witness too closely, too intimately the mutating details of our expressions.

Even I attended. I couldn't seem to help it. The thing seemed impervious to thought or reason, especially to prayer, despite repeated applications, and I found myself—literally, as if I had been misplaced, or as if it were someone else who bore my name and face but who was decidedly not me—with the others in the fatal light, innocent, excited, and utterly in the clutch of a fascination so monstrous there was not room for anything else, not even shame. No discussions and, to my knowledge, no awkward experiments complete with smothered giggles and gasps followed the reading sessions. The things that went on—with men, with animals, with unthinkable objects—inside the book were so far outside our familiar borders, that if we felt anything—and we must have—it was not desire, but the sense of desire on the blade edge of violence. The sense too of something alien, yet not: at odd moments, listening to passages, all seemingly without plot, merely images with a kind of rough cadence, I felt as if I were trying to remember things I had not learned and perhaps never could learn, not in any intellectual way. Things felt vibrating in distant cells. The book, cloaked in brown paper, may have been found in the gutter, but the words seemed to escape from a fissure, wafting up like ashes on slow billows, and the fissure was within. I suppose it was something like a hell.

Often Dixie read. But others too. After awhile the identity of the voice was lost in the sound of flesh, and the color of flesh, and the smell of flesh, and the feel of our collective flesh quaking in the gloom . . . in the gloom, I remember thinking, of original sin. Still I listened and with the others imagined until that ability we call imagination, the elastic quality of the mind that enlarges upon a determined shape and either returns to its original size or remains stretched, lax, until it simply, abruptly snapped, as though it had gone rotten and could not tolerate the strain. Then the thing that was one piece, one mind, became two.

During the week of the book Sister Olinger disappeared. That was how I thought of it—as a disappearance. Of course it had nothing to do with the book. But in the end, in a funny way, it did. The backdrop against which my faith was projected had fallen away, and I was left exposed and alone, though in the spirit of my devotion I swiftly resolved the abandonment as a test. God was testing me. I was to go on now without my teacher, my example. I was to matriculate into the body of Christ, there to disappear likewise in the sublime chaos of His love.

I felt the book not as a contradiction, but merely as a presence that coincided with the deletion of another presence: Sister Olinger's. She was gone. It was here. There was no connection.

Dixie, our priestess, our Pythia, was the keeper of the book, and as such it was she who held the Delphian power, yet she was surprisingly free with it. Another girl might have been chary, dispensing its dubious charms for political favor. I even saw her in her nightgown one evening relaxing in the phone booth at the end of the dorm floor, her brown curls flattened against the glass, her face calm, her eyes twinkling as they often did, as she read from the book to one of the day students who could not attend the night session. I should say here that Dixie was not as affected by it as the rest of us were. There was a light, almost matter-of-fact yet studious quality in her voice; she might have been reading from an instruction manual. She seemed to take in the information in its totality, from its base assumption to the grimiest minutiae, and there was by all appearances plenty of room in Dixie for this book, this world and more. She was wide open.

After we had heard the book once through, Dixie got rid of it. One fresh morning, the grass and flower beds still dew laden, and on the air something shy, perhaps Magnolia, that seemed to vanish just at the moment it gained awareness. We were walking across campus to the junior school, past the kitchen service entrance when Dixie reached into her backpack—the book was with her at all times, you see, it could not be left in the dorm or any-where a nun might find it—and with an impressive lack of ceremony tossed it into the dumpster. Obviously not a premeditated act. Dixie was incapable of premeditation. She did not break stride, she did not even interrupt her-self . . . "If you got light skin like mine, you use blue shadow, that's what my mom says . . ." Then *flick*, out the book sailed. From the kitchen vents steam escaped, and even as I followed with my gaze the white columns rising heavenward, dissipating, I saw the book too rise a moment, then plunge down, like a lost soul, into the rub-bish.

"Blue eye shadow, that's the ticket."

No one tried to retrieve it though I think some of the girls wanted to. There was not any reason to save the thing, at least none that could be proffered without embarrassment, without evincing excessive prurient interest. And by that time the book had been partially cannibalized, whole passages, paragraphs here and there, even the occasional single word cut from its pages; indeed there wasn't much left but a collection of clumsy and (relatively) benign transitions between holes where the real sex had been. So with the meat scraps and vegetable cuttings and used serviettes the book stayed, appropriately rotting, until the truck came on Friday and hauled it from our lives.

My washing did not markedly change because of the book, though looking back it seems there was strong recommendation for an increase. Likely it did not for scheduling reasons: there was simply no time for anymore without risking discovery, even expulsion from St. Agatha's. I was a studious girl, as I said, and St. Agatha's had become my home, my world. Behind her gates I felt safe. But for Sister Olinger's disappearance—and the holes—the days filed neatly off. I won an honorable mention in the state science fair; my devotions proceeded apace, though now with labored effort, perhaps even a trace of *faux air*; Kelly finally had a boyfriend; and the SP Commuter made its runs without incident.

I suppose I ought to say something about the holes, since I was blamed for them, albeit erroneously. But they were so trivial they hardly seem worth mentioning. Gratuitous, baffling, a curiously random development, they began soon after the book. If they had had some significance, some detectable meaning, even metaphoric meaning, if there was evidence of order, if they intoned even the faintest note that could, or might could, as Dixie would have said, reverberate in the halls of my being I would have allowed the possibility that they were mine, my doing. However, there was none. The holes appeared in items having no obvious inherent connections, and no connection whatsoever to me over any other girl. In vestments, in the green curtains of the confessional, in my dorm mate's clothing, in books, in tapestries, in table cloths, in habits, even in a diaphragm belonging to one of the senior girls, though this last was not mentioned in the official report.

The senior accused me herself one night, after it had gone round that I was responsible. "You're a sicko," she said, in a graveled whisper.

I was very anxious; she seemed murderous. "I don't know what you're talking about."

"This, you crazy little bitch." And she held the thing less than an inch from my nose, a pale rubber moon with a meticulously cut peephole at its center through which, in fact, I could see her. She was very pretty. No doubt she needed the diaphragm, being that pretty.

"I'm sorry, but you're wrong," I said, backing away.

Dixie, who had a kind of weird talent for timing, drifted by at that moment, and perceived instantly the content of our exchange, since the holes, which had become a much-talked-about virus, were infecting everything. "What's up, Pam? Spring a leak?"

Pam made a disgusted sound and shoved the diaphragm back in her pocket. A nun passed us in the hall, and for ten seconds we stood communing in silence, though Dixie took the opportunity to pop a piece of gum in her mouth. She was never without resources. Then she said, "Maybe the last guy busted through," her voice wickedly soft.

The senior almost laughed, but in the end decided on the same marginally successful huff of disgust. "Just keep your mental friend away from my end of the hall." With that, she swished about and marched into the mysterious recesses of the senior world. Even the nuns avoided that end of the floor. Seniors were women (virtually) with rights to privacy that we had yet to earn.

As a free agent Dixie had friends, or associations—it was impossible to describe the nature of her relationships—among the seniors, her peers, lay teachers, and she was even known to consort with the grammar students, playing dodge ball with them out in the field, a lumbering goddess among the small quick bodies of the merely naive. So I was not surprised by her manner with the senior, and I was grateful—once again—for the inimitable way in which she had diffused the situation seemingly on my behalf. What did surprise me, though, was a gesture—her fingers brushing the back of my head—and these words which accompanied the gesture as we strolled back toward our dorm: "You wanna wash now? I'll go with you."

I must have nodded. It was clear she knew. What she thought about my washing I could not tell, but there was something effortless and touchingly casual in her tone, not as if what I was doing was acceptable; no, only that she, Dixie, had accepted it. That was all. Nothing more.

We went into the lavatory. Dazed, I turned on the faucets, held my hands under the water, fumbled for the soap, for the blind comforts. Next to me, at the next sink, Dixie leaned toward the mirror, pushed at her hair, examined her teeth. I kept washing, and for the first time I felt in the act the longing for *some degree of peace*. Then, peripherally, I saw her turn on a faucet, and I thought, *don't, oh don't do it, please Dixie, don't*. But she poked her index finger into the column of water, and with it combed her eyebrows. Afterwards when I had stopped crying, she rubbed some of her scented lotion into the backs of my hands, now so red and scaly that I had developed the habit of crossing my arms in order to hide them.

"You oughta use cream every time, kiddo."

"Yes," said I, with numb obedience.

Fata Morgana

My parents sent me to a psychiatrist. He was a short, gray-haired man with a penchant for cough drops which I noticed he sucked completely, resisting to the end the temptation to chew. I admired this, I recall. He had a warm, almost courtly smile, too, one presented as I arrived and the second as I rose to depart, a pair of parentheses that served to set off and shelter our interior dialogue. No further smiles corrupted the fifty minutes; this, too, I admired, even while I longed for more. His attitude seemed to be that we had a job to do in which the niceties of society had no play. I was bound by a strange and troubling freedom: the freedom to be frank.

"Tell me about your father," he said.

"Our Father, or my father?" I replied. And off we went.

I was directed to "steer toward emotionally charged subjects" in my free associations, which I must say wasn't easy. Naturally I wanted to cooperate, to be a good patient in much the same way I strove to be a good student, so I would willingly have traversed any ground I was instructed to. But there wasn't any that was "hot" as it were, none that I could detect.

In Dixie he seemed excessively interested, and it rather annoyed me: she was hardly worthy of opinion, let alone the time we spent circling round, like dogs, trying as he put it to feel comfortable with the idea of Dixie.

"She's just a girl," I said. "Not an idea."

"Yes," he said, as if I'd made a breakthrough. "A girl like you," he added.

"Not at all." I thought his a very stupid observation, since I had described at length Dixie's profligate habits. "I hardly know her, and I don't much *want* to know her."

"Yes," he said to himself, it seemed, but this time there was no note of triumph in his voice. He gazed at me with a sort of sadness, and as quickly erased it as if he'd been caught, presenting in its stead the second smile of the hour, which I understood concluded our session that week.

Nevertheless, on the way home in the taxi I tried to understand his meaning: Dixie and I were both girls, fourteen and, as he put it, beginning to mature as young women. She and I were also the only ones who were privy to my obsessive-compulsive behavior—besides the psychiatrist who had had the honor of naming it. In this regard I valued less Dixie's kindness than I would have another girl's, in the same way one values less the utterances of a fool than of someone with training. I wasn't even sure it was kindness. I wasn't sure of anything having to do with Dixie.

Turning right, the taxi shot down Balboa, then left and up toward the old big houses and the home of my family. The skies were clearing after a long Pacific storm, the pastel buildings of San Francisco clean and sharp and vulnerable in the new light. Blinking, I returned my gaze to the interior of the cab, for the light outside was painful.

I remember watching the back of the taxi driver's head, and thinking how really very personal the back of one's head is, and oddly how seldom one saw one's own. What had Dixie felt when she touched the back of my head? It occurred to me that she might have been repulsed—as I was by the greasy hair of the cab driver—but I knew she had not been. Just as I found the cab driver's hair, the rough unknowing intimacy of it, attractive.

And how were Dixie and I alike? I couldn't say. Perhaps I still can't. Perhaps though, I was trying to see in what essential ways the utterly unalike were alike.

Suffice it to say, St. Agatha's recovered from her rash of holes. I had nothing to do with them. Really.

Whenever Dixie happened to be around—which seemed more frequent—she opened doors for me, prattling on in her mindless way, or she waited for me as I washed, or while I bathed in the next tub she masturbated in hers. She had a method which employed the steady flow of warm water as the tub filled, a method she taught to some of the other girls. Sometimes all four of the tubs, bound by metal half walls, were occupied by girls learning the arts of physical pleasure. It might be even I tried it one night, but I was so sure that someone was watching, someone would peek over the metal wall, that I gave it up, announcing my defeat by mocking Dixie and her filthy ways. "You're a nympho," I believe I said, and loudly too. The outburst served to inhibit the other girls, at least as far as I knew, but Dixie smiled her Cheshire smile and said, "Aren't we all, Sue."

I should say that Dixie never joined me in my washing; which is to say, she never patronized my needs. She never joked, she never advised. In ways I cannot expressly recall, she simply acknowledged what I had to do, and went on. It was infuriating. It was disgusting, even while it moved me strangely, deeply, it was disgusting how she refused to judge the desperateness of my need to get clean, and my failure to do so. I felt like one of her weeds. She grew weeds, you see. There were pots of weeds on her dresser, on top of the closet, lined up on the floor, and in the spring when they flowered the place stank, the cloyingly sweet, pungent fume of a dirt lot at the wrong end of town.

It's possible I hated Dixie for knowing, or maybe it was for not denouncing me, as I would willingly have denounced her.

One day very near the end of the school year Sister Olinger returned for what was to be the last time I would see her.

Already the dorms were taking on the sad look of desertion, the incremental process of moving back into the homes of our families requiring several weekend trips before the close of school. The contents of my alcove had dwindled to one suitcase of clothing, a statuette of the Virgin Mary, and my pillow. Dixie had shipped most of her things east, including the poster prints of her mother, and her alcove for the first time exhibited the homogenized purity of St. Agatha's School for Girls. The weeds she set free in the hockey field, there to propagate until our clean white oxfords returned in the fall to pound them down. A few containers of perfume and unguents remained, the red suede pumps, her uniforms, wrinkled and more worn than mine looked though hers were much newer, the music box still playing its irrepressible *chanson*, "Strangers in the Night," and the ugly white suitcase which had reappeared from its long incarceration in St. Agatha's basement catacombs.

A June afternoon, I remember; the warm air swirled up, dusty with bugs and pollen and sensate promise, and the feel of summer like a slowing drug already affecting the campus. It had not been a good day for prayer. The swimming pool was near the cemetery, and while I sat on my customary rock I could hear the squeals, the occasional splash of a cannon ball, and shouted instructions from Sister Lawton whose voice, no matter the volume, seemed to travel great distances unimpaired. I had been hot. A swim seemed terribly agreeable. I had gone back to the dorm, possibly to change into my suit—I was still debating the probity of it—to yield to a bit of earthly pleasure. On the way back I had seen Dixie, off on one of the paths, riding her great horse. She was wearing hot pants—very popular at the time—lavender hot pants, and in the distance, through the shattered light of the oaks, her exposed skin was like milk spilling down the red flanks of the beast.

When Dixie first entered St. Agatha's she talked about her mother, her horse, and the gun her father had given her and taught her how to shoot. There was of course no opportunity to verify the latter. Evidence of her mother— her charms, her figure, her fame—was irrefutable. And one day in winter the horse arrived. A horse god, very tall, over 17 hands, sleek but not lean, and possessing an ineffable quality about the eyes, a kind of all-knowing peace. He was so superior a beast he could well afford to be humbled—and he knew it and so was not—by Dixie and me and some of the other girls who were invited to sit his back. A purebred Hunter, Dixie called him the improbable *Buck*. Or Bucky, if she was waxing lovingly about him. She was a magnificently natural equestrian. I and many of the other girls took riding lessons at the local polo club, but none had the grace and command— although it really was neither of these—none spoke the wordless language that was theirs. It was the one thing I could say I truly envied her for. Not having, but knowing that horse. Once only I rode him. I asked Dixie to take a picture, which I still have, of me in my horn-rimmed glasses, and black hair squared at the bangs, and my jodhpurs which we all—except Dixie—owned as a matter of course, looking as though I couldn't quite believe my good fortune, looking like a noisome bug upon the high flowing back of a god.

"Go ahead," she said. "Take him out."

A polo field is a very great thing, you know. A great space, a great green empty space which a horse, especially that horse, wants to fill up. The trouble was, unlike most horses, Dixie's Hunter *could* fill it up.

At my tentative bidding, he walked serenely through the whitewashed gate to the edge of the field. I turned to wave at Dixie. *Everything's under control*, the wave said, *I've got him*. Then the Hunter god exploded, bolting down the field, and the seconds crashed into each other until there wasn't anything left of time. No time to reach the end of the field where the dark trees shot up before my eyes, then back and across, while my heart crowded my throat, as if to escape this calamitous place, this body clinging to mane and pommel and flying, *flying*.

Dixie used an Australian saddle, much smaller than a western, slightly more substantial than an English, but I believe I thanked God a hundred times for the extra inches of leather, the wee rise in the pommel, the lip of cantle that kept me from shooting off his back. Because he had the bit between his teeth—probably he had had it all along, through the picture taking, the deceitfully placid approach to the field, my confident wave back—he had the bit and he was filling up that space with his thunderous being, and I was simply not there.

Eventually Dixie caught him. It seemed to take forever. Though detecting anger in Dixie was always a tricky matter, I think she was angry with me. "See ya later," she said. That was all. Then she led the horse, still quivering, into the riding ring, and put him through an hour's worth of paces—steady, calm, beautifully disciplined paces—to remind him, I suppose.

So I had seen Dixie and the splendid horse on my way back to the dorm. Passing the swimming pool, I heard the other girls. Along the path through the garden, sitting on a bench among the blooming flowers, I saw my old ally Kelly with her new boyfriend. And maybe by the time I got back to the empty dorm I was feeling sorry for myself. My bathing suit, I discovered, had already been packed home. Summer was coming, three months away from St. Agatha's sheltering halls, and maybe I was wondering what to make of my season of devotion and the solitude for which I had so readily volunteered. Maybe I was beginning to add up what I had turned down, to feel in the emptiness of the dorm and in the diminished contents of my alcove, the empty and diminished state of my being.

Thus I sat on my bed in the twilight of the unlighted dorm. Faintly through the windows behind the back of the alcove walls I heard the *clop clop, clop clop* of Buck coming round by the porte-cochère. And afternoon voices with their tingling quality of release now that competitions were over and St. Agatha's was on her final run into summer. A car pulling in. Upstairs where the senior classes met a janitor was waxing the hardwood floors. I knew that out on the Palm Court the graduation platform was mounting, the red and white bunting twined about the columnar trunks of the palms. Through the halls of St. Agatha's the sad contented giddy air of completion wafted, gently nudging us onward, out through her gates. But what had I gained? Completed? Of worship there was no end, not even death brought that to a close. I honestly could not say I had achieved anything. And I had no friend, no Sister Olinger, no Father Moriarty, certainly no similarly inclined peer who might tell me I was better than I had been before I gave myself to Christ. I had not even the hollow comforts my dorm mates enjoyed—a horse, a swim on a hot afternoon, a boy to admire flowers with.

I would not wash. I would not try anymore. I felt very tired. The blank white walls of my alcove stood about me, faceless and noncommittal. On the dresser my Virgin Mary offered her baked-on expression of serenity, the same no matter what I did, whether I was here or not. And I was not. It seemed there was nothing to say of my season of devotion. Of me. I had made of myself a very small, very meticulous hole.

Reaching for the statuette, I settled back on the bed and turned her idly about in my hands. She was chipped here and there, the ceramic showing through the blue of her veil, in one of her open hands, the tip of her nose, and rubbing my finger into the rough gouges, feeling her insides, it occurred to me that she was all veneer. A chunk of common ceramic. It was then, I believe, at that moment Dixie rushed into the dorm, calling my name.

"She's here," she shouted. "Sister Olinger." Her cheeks were flushed, her brown curls a tangle of excitement. She was excited for me. Dixie couldn't have cared less about Sister Olinger, but she knew, she had known all along, how much, how too terribly much Sister Olinger had meant to me.

And for the first time in a long time I leapt up and grabbed her, confused, alive, unchecked. "Dixie! Sister . . . where is she?"

"The Portry, the Portry." And together we charged out, sliding down the oaken bannister, racing each other through the long corridor lined with what struck me then as ridiculously somber oils and tapestries. Nearing the Portry, I skidded to a stop, letting Dixie go on, for I could hear Sister Olinger's voice, her laugh. I could feel a smile cracking my face. So I *was* to be validated. I tried to compose myself, gave up, gulped a breath, passed through the door. Stopped.

It was Sister Olinger. There were the electric blue eyes, the hair, the voice I knew, the magnetic enchantment filling up the small entry parlour. And it was not Sister Olinger. It was a woman wearing a lemon-yellow, doubleknit leisure suit, white wedge sandals, and swinging from her fingertips, a pair of sunglasses. The sunglasses, the way they swung, as if to entice, did me in. For me, the sunglasses settled the matter.

Miss Hadleigh, our good portress, called her Joanne.

I left. Saying nothing. Backing out. She had not deigned to notice me yet. Which was fine. Just fine.

I went back to the dorm and lay down on my bed. Dixie followed. I couldn't seem to hear what she was saying to me, but I remember being glad—no, not glad—I remember feeling that the force of the explosion inside me was somehow checked because she was there. I think she even lay down beside me for awhile, smelling of horse. At one point her voice pierced inward: she was talking about water-skiing in the Keys, and briefly I experienced a sort of crystalline other-reality—I was with Dixie, sending up white plumes across the aquamarine, feeling the prickle of cool spray on hot skin and the rushing movement through space, I was water-skiing with Dixie, laughing, and then I was not. In my ears the laugh rang on, though now there was something of the macabre about it. Then silence, a tinkling sort of silence, as of countless minute fragments settling in a void.

I was aware she was gone for awhile. When she had seen Joanne Olinger arrive, Dixie tied Buck to one of the columns of the porte-cochère. So she had to leave me to ride him back to the stables, to brush him down and feed him.

After dinner Dixie said, "Let's take a trip." I didn't care much what I did that night; I shrugged apathetically and went along with her to the senior end of the dorm floor, around the far corner into the laundry room where three girls, all seniors, were waiting. The meeting seemed planned. No one spoke. One of the girls produced two tabs of LSD. It was divided up, the older girls eating halves, while Dixie and I did quarters, I assume because we were younger. Of that night that was not night, not any form of category in time and space, I remember very little. Cartoon hallucinations. Someone (me?) playing Beethoven on the piano, scattered notes ricocheting off the walls of an empty classroom on the fourth floor. Reading an entire novel aloud to stave off surging images of chaos, the words not penetrating but vaporizing on the air. A mirror. Black holes where my eyes had been. Dixie in white, benign and spectral, appearing, disappearing. The bleary morning after, trying to hide my eyes from others, and from myself the colors I was still seeing, green and pink designs, when I stared too long, too far into the aftermath of disaster. I didn't bother to shower.

We were caught because one of the seniors "flipped out"—a sixties term used to describe those who couldn't hold their drugs—was found on the roof of the porte-cochère, readying for flight, and had to be taken to the nearest hospital where lab workers detected poison in the LSD we had consumed, a fine lacing of strychnine.

We were all separated. We were all sent away that same morning. If it hadn't happened so near the close of school—only two days hence—we would have been expelled. St. Agatha's sought to keep the whole matter under wraps, not for our protection but for the school's and its reputation. If any of the other parents found out . . . well, there may have been an investigation, a decline in enrollment. The three seniors were going anyway; they would miss graduation ceremonies, but that was small payment. Dixie's readmission to school next fall was seriously in question. "Susan Thatcher would be allowed to return because of her good and lengthy record at St. Agatha's," I overheard. A summer of penance was expected, however.

I went to the chapel to await my parents. I prayed to God that they wouldn't be too angry with me, that I wouldn't be grounded, etc. etc., and I realized with genuine elation that my relationship to God and the Church had reverted to the healthy, self-serving shallowness of most fourteen-year-old girls.

Sister Huerta summoned me. I passed through the Portry and out onto the granite steps of the porte-cochère where I saw that someone had brought and stacked my belongings. Above the live oaks and palms a June sun bobbed, the warm air soft about my body, and I felt as deliciously insubstantial as a piece of gauze in a breeze. There were two limousines, a Benz, my parents' car, and a taxi, presumably for Dixie, lined up awaiting the condemned. But I for one was not condemned. I was splendidly free.

I had not the opportunity to say good-bye to Dixie, and about this I felt vague regret, vague relief.

# 5

Down through Greenfield, King City, San Lucas, San Ardo, down below the hills, smooth and rounded as young muscles, down El Camino Real, the king's road—one day's walk between missions was the plan—become Highway 101, though now travelers prefer the Interstate through the Great Central Valley, a wide bleak fast streak north-south, making miles. But the old king's highway traces the Salinas, a minor river bisecting a lesser valley lying to the west of the Great Valley. No artery like the San Joaquin and Sacramento, the Salinas River in late spring is a pale blue vein twisting up, at times plunging beneath the trough that lies between the Gabilan and Santa Lucia Mountain ranges, a trough for which it cannot even take credit, for the valley was a sea inlet long since drained, reaching a hundred miles inland from Monterey Bay, and the bottoms are as rich and unroughened as a girl's first dream.

All its tributary creeks become at this season damp creases between hills, the year—1981—a dry one, the rains too early, too feeble, and the river itself not nearly enough river to quench the rolling flesh of the land, the river as if in shame hid underground, flowing through aquifers, coming up for a look here and there, ever dwindling between crusted borders of alkali, then diving again to escape.

Rounding a slow bend, the country flared open for a mile or two, and there in a great sunny scoop was blue, so blue that I could not fix my gaze but had to take it in obliquely, this fantastic rush of lupine. Higher up on the exposed shoulders and elbows and shins of the hills poppies blazed. Across fields lying idle the yellow mustard flourished. And in the working fields grew lettuce, artichokes, carrots, strawberries, Brussels sprouts, grape vines.

No, it was not the Great Valley, but a valley somehow more accessible and for that perhaps more important, a place one could know in the way that the smaller scene of one's youth was somehow more intense and more affective than the great impervious expanse of adulthood. Perhaps by then it was too late, all the cards had been played and it was merely a question of arrangement.

So it was as I drove south, and (oddly) up the Salinas, I felt at home in the lesser valley. A rising wind pushed from behind, tangling the spindly willows by the river, while making no apparent impression on the stolid live oaks which held the hills, like silent black sentries. It was not my home, this valley, but it reminded me of a home, just as some places would always be strange to me, the relationship forced. It was so in San Francisco where my family lived for years; not so in Berkeley throughout my higher education; strange—so very strange—in San Jose with Dixie, not in Monterey with Henry. At St. Agatha's, I suppose, I had felt most at home. There, past and future were laid out as neatly as the nap pads in the kindergarten room and the grave markers in the cemetery. Her routine provided each day with a comforting shape, and at any moment I could reach out and touch it and know where I was and where I should be, because there was never a difference. Her grounds were ample, not forbidding, conveying at once the quality of a home, the sense of a larger settlement. Finally, her air of righteous order and indubitable permanence gave me what I seemed to need most—a world apart.

Pulling off the highway in San Ardo, I bought some orange juice and a bag of peanuts from a gas station market, wishing I still smoked; left the stuff on the roof of the car and went back in for a pack of sugarless gum as consolation. It was a small, rudimentary market, a second thought to accommodate the traveler of the day who has goals, not time. Behind the smeared windows and the greasy counter the adolescent male was again drawn reluctantly away from a rerun of the Daytona 500 showing on an old black-and-white to ring up my purchase, again without noticing that a human being stood opposite him, offering a tentative smile. It was the best I could do, and indeed much more involvement than I was accustomed to allowing. Dixie, of course, would have insisted on involvement, asking charmingly stupid questions that drew the boy out, while drawing her in, toward his reality.

A tertiary and last act, prompted by nothing more than the vague impression of a pack in the young man's shirt pocket, and by a vague and desperate need to try to make some contact, and perhaps too by a vague desire to pay some small tribute to Dixie and our shared and youthfully foul habits, I asked for a pack of Lucky Strikes.

The young man looked pleasantly annoyed. Cigarettes: in this at least we were one. He tossed the pack and a book of matches on the counter, then returned to his vicarious race. And I to mine. Another small step in Dixie's direction.

As I was leaving, a truck driver filling his Thermos from a coffee machine adjacent to the door asked how I was "this prime morning."

"Reasonably well," I replied, still wearing my little smile.

His jeans were soiled, and there was a crusted ring of mud—or manure—just above the soles of his cowboy boots. Glancing outside, I saw that he was hauling cattle. "Reasonably well," he laughed. "Hah! I'm gonna keep that one. Hah." It was like the sound of a small pop gun firing, and he was still saying it—*reasonably well, hah*— as I left. I made a mental note not to say it with Dixie.

Shortly after, driving along the highway and remembering the three years following Dixie's departure from St. Agatha's, I mentally averred that I had got on reasonably well during that period: there was unavoidably no more accurate description.

Having proceeded with my life in sportsmanlike fashion, taking the wins and losses with not quite a sameness of attitude, yet with kindred dispositions, I felt the general consensus was that I would in the long run succeed.

At the beginning of my senior year Dixie reappeared.

Throughout the morning orientation meetings, the palm court luncheon with our parents, the endless filling out of forms and the somewhat furtive exchange of checks and receipts, (St. Agatha's was always tastefully embarrassed by commerce and other matters *of the world*), I kept my distance from Dixie, as if she were feral, and we trained creatures ought to be wary.

She had not so much changed as filled in between the lines of her erstwhile hyperbole. Taller, flashier, with broad, expressive hips and a smallish waist, legs a bit heavy but correctly curved, a moderately sized bust which apparently she sought to redeem with tight sweaters and dipping necklines and, at their twin summits, an unaccountable perkiness seldom subdued. Also, and thoroughly in character, she had dyed her hair blond. If she had been born with blond hair, I'm convinced she would not have kept it, for the color was not the issue: it was otherness that fascinated her, I suspect, the other person, a different way, unnatural color. In this respect she was the only true deviant I have ever known. The question was, from what norm, from whom did she deviate? Who was Dixie Darling?

Throughout most of the afternoon Dixie hovered near her mother, maintaining an orbit of no more than a yard's distance, and if one took account of appearances only, she was a pale moon by comparison. The posters had not done her mother justice, for she was especially fine to look at. There was a thin, blown-glass quality about her, and I almost felt just by staring at her—which I did, I confess, and others did too, many others—I could raise from her a single pure note, like a cry, that would eventually hurt the ear. Her hair was blond (natural, Dixie would remind us), and neatly subdued in a French roll. She was wearing a straw yellow suit of linen whose lines were so simple, so unobtrusive—no lapels, no pockets, no quirky cuffs, none of the usual riffraff touches fashion designers seem compelled to tack on at the last—that it almost seemed she was *of*, not *in* the suit, that it and she were one and the same. The blouse was eggshell white with a concealed-button placket and a jewel collar—once again so subtle, so *alarmingly* subtle, that it might all disappear in the next instant, and in a such a way that no one would notice.

If I say that her face was perfect, if I describe its parts, it yet does not fix the whole in my memory, and that day I found—as I have mentioned already—that I had to *keep* looking at her, as one might stare at an abstract painting in order to soak it in. Perhaps there was something of the *too ideal* about her: visually she slid through the eyes into the mind and out the back, lacking flaws and impurities, the jags of reality that catch in the memory. If I say that the chin was delicate, the nose small and straight, that even her nostrils were so perfectly petite that the effect was ornamental, almost symbolic, and that at one point I wondered how she breathed, except that all day long she kept her lips slightly parted, as if there was something she might say but didn't know how—if I say all this, I yet say nothing about her. It is all mental flailing. I can't see her, I can't feel her. Blown glass.

Dixie's eyes were more interesting, though, I must say. Oh, her mother's were pretty—blue and sort of extra-clean-looking, polished—but there was something vanquished about them, too, that the posters had disguised. Whereas Dixie's eyes, when she flashed them at me sometimes, could actually *change* how I felt, alter my mood. They were so full of life, *she* was so full of life, brimming with possibility. And one had the sense that wherever she was—which seemed to be an incidental proposition, pure happenstance—she was always and completely *there*, no part of her trailing elsewhere or casting about for more intriguing situations.

I know of but one thing Dixie's mother said that entire day, and though she was standing in line next to me— Dixie was behind her—and she said it to me, she seemed to be saying it for everyone; her contribution, so to speak.

"The palm trees, the palm trees are . . ." A pause then; it seemed she was teetering on the edge of a precipice, and when at length she spoke it was to fall into the word with relief all around. "Nice."

"Yes, they are," I said too eagerly, and quickly dropped my eyes.

*The palm trees are nice*—that was what she said, her voice every bit like thin glass splintering.

Her husband fetched her food. It was practically religious, the way he settled and arranged her as the group traveled from Portry to classroom to chapel, before he himself plunged into the proceedings, glancing back frequently to check that she was still there, still well appointed.

Dixie's father was large, Dixie's father was tall: he was both so successfully that neither category was eclipsed by the other. With his crew cut, frank blue eyes, and straight-shooting manner he was, while theoretically out of place in a convent, absolutely at home. He did most of the talking. He talked with all the nuns and half the girls, telling me that I was "prettier than Dixie said you were," and that "I hope my little *Chickadee* will pick up some of your study habits." I was then subjected to a pleasantly embarrassing bear hug, and in parting, a cuff, his great hand smelling of cigars and lavatory disinfectant.

Dixie maintained her post next to her mother. It was easy to see whom she was most like, and whom she most wanted to be like.

From the threshold of the Portry I watched them prepare to leave: they were the first that day to abdicate their parental office. Not, I know now, because he wanted to, but because, like the simple unobtrusive suit she wore, the suit that had begun to lose its shape at the end of a long day, she too was beginning to lose sense of her own shape. While he brought the car around, Dixie and her mother stood without speaking on the steps of the porte-cochère, listening to Mother Superior admire the roses, near bloom's end now, which were growing at the base of the columns. When he returned, Dixie's father shook Mother Superior's hand, and it was awfully cute, the way she shook it back in a lively, confident manner, her tine-like fingers barely navigating the broad continent of his palm. Words of a generic nature were exchanged. Then he hugged Dixie, glanced to Mother Superior, tousled Dixie's hair, and turned away—thus, the baton was passed. Mother Superior left, her customary beatific smile restored for the journey back to the palm court.

I then saw him lead Dixie's mother to the car—a turquoise Cadillac—and she simply stopped while he un-locked and opened the door for her, then he straightened, his big hand never moving from her shoulder, clasped in-congruously about its delicate curve. And there was a terrible little moment when all I could see was his hand, heavy and ursine, like a trained bear's, on her shoulder, and I felt as if something was going to happen, or could happen, that he was almost tempted to snap the glass only to have done with it, the tension of knowing that it could so easily happen to so fine and subtle a thing. *Just to get it over with.*

But when she had folded herself into the car, it was he who reached down and tucked in the hem of her skirt, then gently nudged shut the formidable door. Dixie kissed the glass next to her mother, who let her fingers flutter weakly, like a sick bird, in response. She did not even turn her head toward Dixie: the act seemed to be too much for her, everything seemed to be too much for her. At the end, I was again struck by her beauty, its vehe-mence and the fugitive reality of it.

Withdrawing, I sat down in one of the tapestried chairs of the Portry. For some reason I didn't want Dixie to know I had seen.

From her corner desk Miss Hadleigh raised her eye-brows at me, perhaps about to ask what I needed or where I ought to be, but the phone rang, and I was relieved of explanation. In a strange—I want to say *spiritual*—way, I felt queasy, as if I had been witness to some little drama, a parable enacted not for my or anyone else's sake, but only because it had to happen that way, it was and would happen that way, it would *be* that way. And nothing could change it. Dixie's relentless adoration. The big easy animalian presence of her father. Her glass mother.

I hoped I would never again see Dixie's mother, and when I left the Portry, it was to find my own parents, to hold my father's hand, to smell my mother's perfume, and to forget the little parable in the porte-cochère.

Dixie disappeared for about an hour. Perhaps she was crying. Many of the girls cried when their family left on the first day. It seemed the thing to do.

We were seniors now. Our territory encompassed the south end of the dorm floor from the TV room to the laundry room, and while Sister Flaherty maintained an office within our limits, she occupied it only during the day when we were in classes. At night and on weekends we were left to our own devices. There were 24 seniors who boarded, another 40 day students from the surrounding community. The ratio was about the same for the lower grades.

I believed—I still do—that God forgives, which is really quite a grand feat when one considers the odds. But He does not forget, or at least the Catholic Church does not forget. And the silence of those memories of sin is a far worse sort of pain than perpetual damning, because in the latter case one can, at the very least, enjoy the insulation of anger, but in the former one must perpetually acknowledge the forgiveness in the shared memory of past ill deeds, and wish, perhaps begin to erase those memories, and in so doing begin to erase oneself. Alexander Pope said, "to err is human, to forgive divine." However, if I were bold enough to rewrite Mr. Pope, I would say, to err is human, to forgive divinely inspired. But to *forget*, that is truly divine.

I remember as a young child when I attended a local day school, coming home with my week's folder of papers and projects, pausing along the way at some discreet locale to cull from the folder any work that had earned less than an A, and tossing the failures into the gutter. Not because I feared my parents, but because I resisted flaws. It was my nature. As far as I was concerned, a mistake was the exception that proved the rule.

When my father found out, he cried. He was that way, very susceptible. He said: "Success is generic." And to paraphrase him: there is, more often than not, a *right* way to do things, and we have all to learn that *right* way and once we do, we're all doing it and no one much notices. But there are many ways to fail, and no one wants to fail the way another fails, it is something to be avoided, that particular imitation; but we *do* fail, and the unique way we each fail, the pattern of our mistakes, tells us— and everyone else—who we are, perhaps where we've been, sometimes, unfortunately, where we're going. Failure is personal, my father told me, and it is that in you I have to love most. I have to, he repeated.

My mother, on the other hand, understood perfectly well why I had chucked the losers.

Well, when it came time to divvy up the ten private rooms to deserving seniors on that first day of school, I was found not deserving, despite an almost flawless record. That one mistake, that "trip" with Dixie three years before, the LSD caper, had not been forgotten. Needless to say, it was not mentioned either. It was simply there, behind me, a shadow of ruin that might, given the right circumstances, cast itself across my path and trip me up again. In effect, what that one mistake did was establish the permanence of possibility: I might do it—or something like it—again.

I was put in the senior dorm with Dixie and a dozen other lesser candidates. Oddly enough, though I had passed it a thousand times, I had never really taken it in, never *perceived* the senior dorm, perhaps because I took it for granted that I and it would have no commerce, ever. According to some perverse anti-reasoning, the senior dorm possessed not even the minimum of privacy. No three-walled alcoves with colorful curtains. No enchanting decorating theme—Polynesian, Mexican, Dutch, Early American. Instead, we were herded into a cavernous ward of 14 beds, seven on each side, and down the center of the room two ranks of seven pine dressers back-to-back, and a long open closet adjacent to the door which I realized—with some concern—we were expected to share. The beds were covered with worn cotton spreads which offered the only color—"poop brown," I heard Dixie mutter to no one in particular. The rest of the room was trying to be white.

It was hollow and cold in the dorm, and though all was swept and dust-free and sanitized for our arrival, an air of condemnation possessed our new quarters, and seemed somehow attached to the smell of moth balls and floor wax. Solemnly, we began to unpack. One of the overhead lights was out, and a few gray September clouds pressed against the windows, like a crowd of staring dullards. I felt conspicuous. The girl opposite me sat down on the edge of her bed, removed her sneakers, and began clipping her toenails, most of them falling to the floor, thankfully, though several times the clippers fired in unpredictable directions. I found a surprisingly large sickle nail, dirt still attached, lying upon my new, white, just-pressed uniform blouse which I had placed on my bed along with my other clothing. I brushed the toenail to the floor, kept unpacking.

Dixie had selected the bed next to mine. Mine was next to the window—a vain grasp at privacy. At least I could look to it and see no one. It was an hour until dinner. Pockets of conversations began to develop. I kept my back to the room, pretended to look for something, rearranged my belongings, picked idly at threads. Behind me, Dixie hummed. I heard pages flipping. A magazine. The bed creaked. I went out to the lavatory to install my toiletries and, returning, found that she had still not finished unpacking. In fact, she seemed uninterested in completing the task. Two of her dresser drawers hung open, some clothes had been stuffed in, but the bulk of her things remained in her satchel in a half-erupted state, and they had flowed partly into what I had already determined to be my territory.

At length, my belongings settled, the bed made up with linens from home, I straightened, preparing to survey the dorm. I really didn't know where to look . . . comfortably, that is; it seemed unseemly. But I did note that my good friend from last term, Eugenia, had not returned. She had learned English, and consequently her Ecuadorian family had summoned her back. I took up my chair— we were each given a cane chair—and placed it at an angle facing the window, selected a book from the several I had brought, and sat down. *My senior year*, I thought. *My glorious senior year at the top of the pecking order, the be-all-and-end-all of St. Agatha's.*

Dixie was still humming. Outside, the diminishing light cast a bruised and forbidding quality against the sky. At one point I stood and went to the window, raising it, but the menacing rattle of the fronds down below on the palm court and the blunt night air drove me back to my chair. A lump rose to my throat, it was like a wad of clay, I could hardly swallow.

"So you been here all this time?" Dixie said. Her voice was casual, as if we were taking up a conversation not years suspended but hours.

I realized I wanted to cry. I managed to say, "Yes."

"I've been in upstate New York. Holy Cross. You heard of it?"

"No."

"It was pretty cool. Coed, you know. That was pretty

85

cool. But the snow was a drag. Getting in an out of coats and boots and all that weather crap is a real dragola. Plus, I couldn't keep Bucky. Daddy sold him."

"I'm sorry," I said. Still, I had not looked up from my book. Still, I clung to the hope that the conversation would dwindle, that Dixie would please leave me alone.

"Whadda ya think of the dorm?" she said.

Then I looked at her, widened my eyes, as if to say, *what was there to think?*

"Yeah," she said, nodding. "It's the pits."

I made some sort of affirming sound.

"It's like we did something, you know? I don't get it. My mom'd have kittens if she saw it. She's footing the whole thing. She makes pots of dough. We're here now, you know. We moved to San Jose. My dad's an inspector for the P.D. there. We got a pool that looks like a bean."

"That's nice."

"It's a pretty cool place, our new house. I'm gonna be taking the train every week. How bout you? You still commuting?"

"I will be, yes."

"We can go to the station together."

I offered a cordial smile, and though I was not reading, turned a page of my book, as if to indicate that in spite of her I *would* progress, I would go on.

For a few minutes Dixie was silent, propped up on one elbow, canvassing the other girls who were likewise lolling about, talking of vacation or boys, things of that ilk. Several times, she called out: "Hey, Marg," or "Hey, Ginny, cool do," or something equally salutatory to the girls she remembered from her brief sojourn at St. Agatha's three years earlier. Finally, she turned to me and said, as if she'd been peripherally aware of me and my mood all along, "Hey, it's okay, Sue. I got a bunch of posters and stuff, we'll fix it up. It'll be A-okay." Then she gave me one of her exploding smiles—I had forgotten them, how sudden and complete they were, and strangely *not* to be remembered, like dreams or visions—only it was smaller with a faintly sexual quality. "I'm thinking graffiti," she said. "That'd doll up this place. Purple graffiti. They do it all the time in New York, it's like hunky-dunky there."

I had to laugh then, though it seemed my eyes were brimming, too.

"There you go," she said. "Graffiti."

I have yet to comprehend the message inherent in St. Agatha's contrast of rooming choices. As the eldest of the young, were we to understand that adulthood was a matter of irresolvable extremes, of privacy gone to sour isolation and unchecked eccentricities, or of longed-for company become oppressive society, the individual homogenized, lost? Or was it merely that we were not to be charmed into adulthood anymore; we were to accept it, the unvarnished reality, the white walls and shit-brown spreads and dirty toenails of life?

I never got used to the senior dorm. I missed the walls. It did improve, however. Fourteen adolescent girls can't help but introduce a certain homeyness to a single shared space. As expected, Dixie put up poster prints of her mother, along with some newer ones of horses, and an album cover of The Carpenters. She had corny taste in music. In clothes, too. Sometimes she wore outfits that looked like they belonged in an old Shelley Winters flick. And the way she talked now, it was stupid: all her old cute-isms combined with the slang of the day and some vaguely French constructions acquired from her years at French Catholic boarding schools, except that she got them wrong or mixed them up with slang that was ancient history, and she never actually said a real swear word which might have redeemed the rest. One of her favorite expressions was *tote la pits*, a hybrid of *tout* (translated

*all* in French), and *totally*, then *la* (article *the*), modifying
*pits*, something disagreeable, like prune pits or armpits.
It was quite a while before I got over flinching each time
she intoned that particular locution.

Autumn passed. It was unusually dry. Withered leaves
clung stiffly to the trees, everything of color was dust
muted and seemed to blur together, as if distinctions could
not be maintained in the heat. The fields went gray, the
sky a murky blue; summer had simply gone on, tired and
sallow, an old woman still trying. Nothing bloomed.
Nothing grew. Nothing seemed to happen. It was difficult—even for me—to get into the scholastic swing without a clear shift of season. We were instructed, because
of the heat, to wear our "summer" uniforms—loose, pastel dresses of cotton—and to leave our plaids and blazers
in the closet. We let our knee socks bunch down about
our ankles, hung our bathing suits over the ribs of silent
radiators, ate popsicles at *gouter*, and waited. I had looked
forward to my senior year, to the crescendo of my career
at St. Agatha's, and it seemed we were lingering over worn
passages, making no progress.

Out of lethargy I cultivated a temperate enthusiasm
for boys. As a senior it was almost prescriptive. And the
nuns were in collusion; they were trying to be "modern,"
to keep up with the times in order to appear attractive to
new families with new daughters and new money. Dances,
permissible dating, occasional parties were simply St.
Agatha's survival throes. Personally, it broke my heart to
see her driven so.

The weeks simmered by.

Only Coach Humphrey seemed pleased by the stay of
season. He kept us out on the volleyball courts till mid-
November, by which time we'd knocked out all our ri-
vals except Notre Dame, and they were next. Coach
Humphrey had a long torso and short legs with bunchy

muscles, and I often thought that his occupation was more than fortuitous, in terms of his dress, because it meant he could wear Bermuda shorts most of the time. On him, slacks were not becoming. But he had pleasant pup eyes, curly hair, and a hail-fellow-well-met attitude that did not seem the least bit political. He was proud of his red Mustang, and of the girls' volleyball team. At lunchtime, I noticed, the nuns seemed to enjoy watching him eat, which he did with great gusto.

I used to see Dixie in his office after school. Who knows what they talked about? She had such odd affiliations, after awhile no one paid much attention. "Humpy," as she called him (there was nothing to say about *that*, it was so preposterous), arranged with Mother Superior to give Dixie a ride to her afternoon job. Of course she had to walk back, but I guessed since he was going home at that time anyway, the ride over was naturally allowed. Other seniors had work experience too; it was considered part of our final training. I was a "candy stripe" volunteer in the pediatrics ward at the local hospital. Dixie worked in an ice cream parlour. There were jobs in the city library, the country club office, the downtown deli.

During the first week of December the senior boarders made a four-day Christmas retreat to a sister convent in the coastal mountains south of St. Agatha's. Indian summer still held, though its grip was beginning to loosen— we'd had some cooler days, no rain, now and then small bands of rangy clouds that scuttled furtively east toward the Sierra. But for the first time I was glad for the dry weather. Dixie brought along some kind of winter sun lotion that had orange dye in it and was guaranteed to provide a practically instant tan. I had met a young man from the Priory who drove a white MG convertible, and who had already let me try it out in the parking lot behind the junior building. There were clear possibilities and I wanted to look good. His father was a doctor. My mother would approve.

The convent, a collection of stone buildings established at the turn of the century, was now a glorified camp from which one could see to the southwest the bright white haze of the ocean, and it gave one, I must say, a grand feeling, the haze rising up off the illimitable blue, and the mountains tumbling down from one's feet toward it as if they had just that moment been disturbed, and were seeking their lost repose. Though the knoll had been cleared, a handful of live oaks had been reserved—gray, muscular, some branches so massive that they had grown down, crawling like Goliath snakes along the ground before twisting back up to rejoin their brethren. The presence of the oaks lent a certain invulnerable quality to the place, as if having been protected themselves decades ago, they would now protect the old convent, the little knoll of paradise, and its transient citizens. There were even a few apple trees, though by now the fruit was long gone.

Sister Flaherty allowed that we had three hours of free time before our first retreat discussion in the lounge.

It would be false of me to imply that I spent much time with Dixie: I did not. But she was "one of us" as it were, a senior boarder at St. Agatha's School for Girls, and especially when we were off campus, we tended not only to overlook each other's idiosyncrasies and shortfalls, but to meld in the same way that the young of any species tends to bond together when away from home territory.

After we dumped all our stuff in the bunk room, Dixie and I and four or five others snuck up to a secluded rooftop niche, stripped down to our underwear, slathered on the orange lotion and, as we listened to the others who took the suggested walk under the oaks, contemplating the vicissitudes of God and life, we waited for the sun to activate the dye. I could hear St. Agatha's bus, empty now, corkscrew back down the road, its brakes protesting, as Humpy took it home (he doubled as the bus driver), and the sound of the whining brakes growing more remote and feeble, like a dying beast, then finally the silence welling up, left me steeped in an exhilarating sense of isolation. We had no homework, nothing we *had* to do, no place we could or wanted to go. We were here at God's behest, we had been invited back to the garden, we females all. At that moment it seemed to me that we ought to have been here all along throughout this unnatural autumn, this season that wouldn't be; that we ought to have simply succumbed, that we ought not to have insisted it was time for school, time to move ahead, executing our prescribed achievements in the prescribed increments. We ought to have suspended ourselves, as the season had.

So it was I found myself practically naked next to Dixie on the flat tar roof of an old convent in the mountains. An airplane droned overhead, distant and unreal, part of another world into which it passed like a half-remembered dream, then we were again left alone with the sun. There was no wind, no movement except the heat which seemed to press down into me, tentatively at first, then with an intensity, a delicious insistence I was prepared to welcome. I wanted a tan, I wanted that young man in the white MG.

"Anyone like to hear some music?" one of the girls asked. She fiddled with a radio.

No one answered. Maybe some were asleep. We had been waked early, and it was a long drive. But I said, rather boldly, "I don't." And that was it. It gave me a dumb sense of power, and I was awfully glad to be there with my friends who, with their silence, seemed to agree. *No, no music, no reminders. We are suspended. We have drifted into abeyance.*

Presently Dixie murmured, "It's like sex"—so quietly, so sweetly almost, like a tiny bird sound in the background, the kind you don't hear unless you make a point, that I was sure no one had heard it, or sure I had imagined it. Because there was another silence, not of the first order, but a wide open, falling-into sort of silence. I thought no one would comment. Maybe I hoped.

But eventually a girl named Ingrid found the first handhold, the first word, and indolently, as if she could barely muster the energy to speak, she said, "What's like sex?" the words melting off her lips.

I opened my eyes. Small white rafts of panties and bras floated in a sea of pink flesh. Bordering the sea was a stone wall no more than a foot high streaked with lichen. Above the wall, only blue, a fierce December blue, except within the sun's territory, the blue weakened. As we did.

"The sun," Dixie said. "It's like it's doing it to me."

Turning my head, I tried to look at her now, but in the compact geography of the niche we were staggered. My head was even with her stomach, which I found myself examining, idly, while waiting for Dixie's next installment on the theme of sex. It was really very beautiful, her stomach, not sunken in, but smooth from her ribs down, then it rose the tiniest little bit just below her navel, like Marilyn Monroe's. The navel seemed to be winking. She had fair skin, and exposed as it was to the noonday sun, her tummy was already blushing. I felt the strangest urge to put my hand on it; it would be warm, and it seemed it might somehow tell me who she was, though I couldn't imagine why at that moment I wanted to know.

"You've never done it," said Ingrid. "You don't even have a boyfriend."

Dixie said nothing.

"Ingrid's got a boyfriend," Carol said. "He's a real

fox."

"We've been going together for eighteen months," Ingrid added proudly. "But I only see him on the weekend. He's up at St. Mary's."

Here Dixie said, "Quelle bummer," by way of commiseration, though I thought I detected a note of sarcasm.

There followed an open forum on the subject of "how far each of us had gone," the discussion moving from "tonguing in the ear" (Carol), through heavy petting, to Kelly's confession that her uncle had "copped a feel" between her legs one night when he was drunk and she was sleeping.

"That's appalling," I said, and enlisted the others to agree, or to at least talk so that Kelly would not regret her revelation. I even made up something about my cousin, just to keep her company, and in the end, when Kelly's turn was over, we had taken her under our wings, so to speak, like protective sisters. I remember feeling proud of us St. Agatha's girls, very close and very adult. We had, by sheer communal spirit, overcome the thing.

A voice said, "And what about you, Dixie." We all knew, of course, that she would have the most to say, and I'm convinced that we'd've just as soon not hear. But there was something compelling about that rooftop niche where we had assembled in the heat of the sun, unseen and seeing nothing but flesh and stone and sky. I closed my eyes. The smell of tar mingled with the vanilla and fruit scent of the lotion, and hung over me in that still, too closely mingled state, and I experienced a spark of panic which Dixie's cool voice seemed to put out.

"What about me, what?" she said.

"How far have you gone in entertaining the male of the species?"

"Well," she said. "Let's see. First base, second base, third base, and home run. *Tote la way.*"

After that, I was so disturbed I lost track of who was speaking.

"When?" somebody asked.

"Well, let me think . . . the last time was yesterday."

"*Yesterday*! Where?"

"In a car."

"Whose car?"

"Who is it?"

Sitting up to rub on more of the sun lotion, I said, "I hope you used some form of protection, Dixie." Even I noticed the tone of formality stiffening my voice: it always inspired Dixie to even worse degenerations of the English language, and this was no exception.

"Hell's bells, kiddo, that's boy work. They have these little rubber sockies they tug on that makes 'em shrivel right down." I couldn't see her, but I knew she was winking and twinkling, I knew it. I knew it. "That's when girl work gets going. You have to pick that little fella up and make him stand up proud."

"What? What is she talking about?"

"His *penis*," someone answered angrily. Suddenly everyone was edgy.

"Are you going to tell us who it was? Do we know him?"

"He's a real wolf," she said.

"Fox," I said coldly. "You mean fox."

She giggled. "Can't keep animals straight."

"Where does he go to school?"

"St. Agatha's," Dixie said, in an eerie, singsong voice.

I sat up, wearing my best bored expression, and scooted backwards to the stone wall, hung my head over its crest. I needed to see the ground, places where human beings walked upright. I was waiting for the name that I knew then, and when she said it, then re-said it the right way, and went back in her fashion to tell the whole story, the pot bubbling over by now, needing no encouragement, I gathered up my clothes and climbed back down the secret ladder that ended in our bunk room. Ingrid followed. For some reason she was crying.

Curious how popular Dixie became throughout the rest of our retreat. Even Ingrid recovered from her initial shock— I suspect she harbored some ultra romantic *Casablanca* illusions about making love someday with her "fox"—and I watched her with the others, dogging after Dixie who hardly seemed to notice her new rank, except that when she said things during the retreat discussions and no one challenged her as they usually did—she reveled in setting that sort of fire—she looked mildly disappointed. Naturally her fame was specious, a temporary accident of perception, and I may have anticipated—with some glee even—the hour when a meritorious achievement, a wind of substance brought down her tawdry house of cards. When someone else's house— perhaps mine—became the mansion on the hill.

On the third afternoon of our retreat one of the other seniors, Fiona, who had not attended the tanning session on the roof, asked me "What is the story with Dixie?" Fiona was one of the invisible girls. There was something wrong with her vision; in order to see, she had to look sideways which, even if you knew about her problem, was disconcerting, because it *felt* rude. I'm afraid it colored most of her relationships: like her vision, she was simply peripheral to the social scene at St. Agatha's. But she was awfully bright which connected us to a certain extent, and her parents knew mine, and I guess I liked her because she accepted her exclusion not with bitter resignation, but with the sort of wise forgiveness you see in handicapped people. Often she came to me for information on the more subterranean issues concerning St. Agatha's seniors, and there was nothing gossipy about her interest; she simply liked to be kept apprised of shifts in the environment.

"Oh," I said, as if it was nothing, nothing worthy of attention, "Apparently Dixie's been having sexual relations."

Fiona gave me her sideways gaze. "With whom?" she said. I was pleased to hear a kindred note of bored disgust. We might have been chatting about the antics of a child.

"Coach Humphrey."

Fiona simply nodded and returned to her book—Voltaire, I recall. What I can't recall is whether or not it was before or after our brief conversation I noticed a shadow cross diagonally through the lounge where we were seated. A shadow that was not a shadow but felt like one, because it was the black habit, as mobile and ever present as a shadow, belonging to Sister Flaherty.

When the bus came the next day, a woman of indecipherable age with short-cropped hair, no breasts, and a stainless steel whistle hanging around her neck, a woman named Miss Gunn, was driving.

Not to me, not to anyone else did Dixie ever mention Coach Humphrey. She was grounded until the Christmas holiday. She was not allowed to use the telephone. She lost her job at the ice cream parlour. For all intents and purposes, she looked brokenhearted. It was something I hadn't counted on. Love.

However, you can't have male instructors at an all-girls school sampling the goods. You simply can't. Also, it's against the law. Once again, St. Agatha's kept the whole thing quiet. They did not press charges—statutory rape it was, technically. They did not expel Dixie—though they wanted to, oh yes. Enrollment was down that year; Dixie was a senior—I suppose they figured in less than six months she would be gone.

As it turned out, though, we were both gone by February. I because of my father's susceptibility, simply put. Dixie because in January her mother committed suicide.

# 6

**M**y birthday is January 23rd. That is important.

Not to me, really. It's just a date, it could be any date on which one is forced to coddle oneself because one is that much closer to the end. It's like a name, which is to say it's like nothing. No inborn meaning. It is all layered on and just as easily peeled off. To me, a birth date is simply a convenient way to keep track of one's personal time on the planet. And perhaps, too, a reminder that to Time one cannot be impervious, even while to that end one may make successful forays in other quarters.

But for Dixie Darling it was important. My birthday. And specifically, my birthday that eighteenth year of my personal time on the planet.

She thought in connections, you see . . . or she lived in them, in the places between things; it's hard to say. The way she spoke, for example, mixing up old and new slang, and French and English constructions, vocabulary; the way she could look boyish, like an endearing punk, then suddenly be as showy and flirtatious as a peony. And, as I have already said, she had nonsensical affiliations—it didn't seem to matter whom she was with, only *that* she was *with* someone. I could go on. Suffice it to say, Dixie made a disorderly wash, a blur of life that drove me to distraction. While I found myself ever more focused on elements and distinctions, on orderly arrangements.

So it seems she made a pitiful connection involving my birthday that year. Pitiful and tragic and if I had only realized it sooner, if I had felt the eerie ambiance of that connection during our time together over the following year, maybe I would not have responded the way I did the night before I moved out. That awful awful night.

And if *that* hadn't happened, or if, by some shift on my part, some oblique sleight of hand, it had happened differently, then what happened when she made her last brutal connection and was finally distinct, unconnected to anyone, to anything, to life itself—maybe that would not have happened. Maybe I would not have had to go all the way down to the California Institution for Women-Frontera, in order to see her. My friend.


It started to rain in mid-December, and stayed soggy pretty much through the first week of January. Then we had a run of those winter days when the air is as hard and clear as leaded crystal, and the sky an unforgivable blue, and one feels one can do anything. It made my new status at St. Agatha's even more difficult.

Frequently I was left alone in the kitchen with the giant-sized pots and the trays of glasses my school mates shoved indifferently onto the stainless-steel ramp and on through the small opening between the cafeteria and the machine I ran. Through pity, then covert mocking (not quite covert enough), my friends had passed swiftly, I admit. Now they simply didn't see me: I had faded to background, into the shade of shadows. Even the cook and his helpers, since I had learned to run the machine adequately, left me alone in my dismal labor. I was engaged in what St. Agatha's euphemistically called "work study." I was the dishwasher. Father arranged it.

On Christmas Eve, because, he said, he didn't want to make a mockery of the season, father had delivered the news—to all of us as we sat about in our crushed velvets and cashmeres, sipping egg nog—that he had made an "unpropitious" investment in an "aggressive, smallish company," and that we would henceforth rely solely upon his income as a low-level appointment to the governor. That gave us nine months at a substantially reduced level of income, longer if the governor was re-elected and kept father on.

(It may have been this event that seeded my later desire to pursue corporate law; it seems likely.)

For five dazed minutes, no one said a word; then mother sobbed; then, remembering her "proud and austere" (I had heard these two adjectives all my life, they were like a family mantra) Castilian heritage, she wrapped up the rest of the canapes, actually extracting one from between my fingers, and put them in the freezer, presumably to be saved for a later day when we would be starving.

Father felt strongly that I should graduate with my class at St. Agatha's. Mother, who assumed an extremity of attitude toward the new situation, thought I should be yanked immediately, and for the last six months of my required education, sent to the local public high school where home economics was the acme of life training. One day during the holidays I saw her—her expression like a crazed pioneer's—actually walk in the rain the two miles to the grocery store (to save on gas), except that she wore a pair of lizard-skin pumps, ($425 at Saks), which were totally destroyed, along with her feet, by the time she reached home. She was trying so hard. She simply hadn't integrated the habits and trappings of her former existence with the new scheme of things.

I felt I should try too.

But I hated it. After years at St. Agatha's, I was relegated to the kitchen where I became part of the unseen machinery behind swinging doors and greasy windows, behind a smile tight with jealousy and embarrassment. And the fact that I was now engaged in a fiercely real version of "home economics" did not escape me.

The nuns were kindly in a practical-minded way. After all, they had taken vows of poverty; there was no shame in it. Their attitude helped a little, but not much, for I had long ago forsworn my callow decision to "be a nun."

I began to fantasize ways out. I had a plethora of credits; maybe I could graduate early, skip the platform-and-rose ceremony on the palm court, skip the whole damn meaningless thing. Because to me, now, St. Agatha's, her quiet corridors, her paradisiacal grounds, her protective gates, her good and righteous shining way meant nothing: reality had overflowed her bounds and swept me up, and while I yet remained with St. Agatha, I was awash in the very tangible concerns of survival.

In the evenings, sometimes until 8:00 or 9:00, I lingered alone, rolling the giant pots and bowls along the steel counters, searching for errant spots, the burned black scabs that lesser dishwashers had overlooked. I meant to make some small stake of honor in my diminished rank. The pots gleamed, the dishes squeaked. And in my steamy room behind the main cafeteria the hours scrabbled by. Thankfully, there were no windows, only caged vents behind which fans whirred continuously. It was easy not to think. It was easier not to see what I was missing. As it was, imagination did enough damage.

At the same time I snubbed all that had once meant everything to me. I took up smoking. I neglected—partly from fatigue—my studies. I enchanted (quite handily, I thought) a young man named Delano from the "wrong side of the tracks" (literally, for his family rented one of those shabby ranch-styles along the SP line, and I knew I had gazed at it and others a thousand times, safely wrapped in my idle curiosity as the train sped by). It was his job to deliver crates of dairy products to the milk-fed girls of St. Agatha's. Every morning his white refrigerated truck pulled up next to the kitchen entrance, and in he came without knocking, pushing his loaded dolly. Usually he grabbed a bran muffin or an orange on his way out, sometimes bacon if the cook wasn't looking. He was twenty, quiet and lanky, with high, sculpted cheek bones, very classic in a primitive way; he was black, too. That was half the attraction for me, doubtless for him too. Our reverse colors. Also, I liked his self-assured manner: it seemed based on so little, and yet there it was. One morning he glided into the dishwashing room, slapped my behind, and left, allowing me no time to respond: in its way the act displayed an accuracy of percipience with which I would not have credited him. I was not to be had by asking, or by any means that engaged thought processes. Even Dixie knew that.

With other young people on their own he rented a house in the next town, a much less desirable district in terms of real estate value, though the trees and sod, the flowers, shrubbery, even the creek which passed south through St. Agatha's, were identical. Only the people and the stuff of people were different. (That meager realization was the first of several cracks in my exceptionally small, hard social consciousness; of course I learned quickly that even the people were identical, of the same rags and bones, that it was to *stuff* we had all clung to tell us who we were.)

Once I visited Delano's room. There was a mess of things in it, multiples of things, and I had the feeling that they might be stolen. With a certain fascination I wondered if I too had been "lifted" as it were, a piece of white taffy from St. Agatha's candy shop. Indeed, I hoped so.

He led me into the twilight, between heaps of clothes, old milk crates containing records, sunglasses (dozens), packaged food, portable radios, flashlights, a half-eaten sack of dried peaches, to the center of the room where a mattress lay on the floor. At the corner of its coverlet, just visible, was a St. Agatha's laundry brand.

He said, "Let's get naked."

If he had phrased it differently, if he had couched his suggestion in the soft deceptions of language I would have developed qualms, a rash of qualms. He said what he meant, though, and said also all that it *would* mean to him, our being naked together, and I was moved by his honesty as I would not have been at another time in my life, reduced as I was to needs and impulses, and the express satisfaction of both.

I said, "Do you have a condom?"

From his delivery shirt pocket he produced one. (I was impressed by his preparedness.) His name was stitched into the pocket with red thread, *Delano*, in cursive.

I resisted the impulse to say his name.

He leaned into me, over me.

"You're a looker," he whispered. "You got a taste too."

"A taste?"

"Yeah. For wild."

We had sexual relations that afternoon; actually, I thought it was great stuff, if unruly. I think I may have even told him in the twilight, in the collapsed moment just after, just that I loved him. I think I had to at that moment. I think I just had to love him. Perhaps for me it was the last reduction. Love. I knew with a heart that seemed to be breaking up, like spring ice, I knew that I meant it, too. I can't imagine why.

Afterward he passed me the half-eaten sack of dried peaches, and when we'd finished them, we drove to St.

Agatha's, to the back gate where in I slipped, returning just in time for the disorderly queue of soiled dinner dishes advancing on my cell behind the cafeteria. Immediately, I loaded a rack of glasses, performing the job with rote accuracy and at a veritable clockwork pace, then continued on to a second. When I had several racks loaded, I flipped the red switch to awaken the machine which protested thunderingly, then settled into a steady, sullen rumble. For me, the noise had become a comfort, a form of insulation. I thought of the afternoon—I loaded a rack of cups—I let the details play slowly again and again until they became a mantra of images which now and again elicited a lovely physical *zing* from way down in where those secrets are best kept, and which inevitably give themselves away in a pinked effervescence about the cheeks, and dewily overloaded, all-consuming eyes. I loaded the first rack of plates. I wondered what he would do or say the next morning when he came with the milk. I thought that I might smile this time. I thought I would.

But, as he never called for me again, I concluded that I was not his cup of tea.

Dixie—bless her heart—came to visit me at night in the dishwashing room. Not every night, but often enough that I rushed to get the machine work done so that I could hear her. Then by the time she arrived I had only the pots to scrub, and the monster mixing bowls to wash out by hand in the tub sinks. She would fill me in, (as I used to fill in the invisible Fiona, I remember thinking), on the familiar, perhaps not so cherished life I was missing at St. Agatha's.

She never knew how her tryst with Coach Humphrey was discovered, and although on several occasions I was near confession, I did not tell her of my accidental breach. I suppose I didn't think she would think it was accidental. And I needed her now as I had not before, her presence, even while I was convinced that it did not matter to Dixie one whit whom she was with at any moment.

Now of course I know—too well—that it did matter, that everything mattered intensely to Dixie. Until it didn't matter at all. Maybe the two are inseparable—real caring, real as blood and bones and as fine as the light in her eyes . . . and the unbearableness of it.

Mother had secured a weekend job at the public library near our home, sorting and stocking returned books. In terms of employment, it was the best she could do. She'd had no work experience, she was a reader, she'd organized fund raisers to build the children's room at the library, presided at its dedication. I suppose when she came in asking, they felt obliged.

Father got through the weeks in satisfactory order, but on the weekends spent most of his time either in his cups or in his bed recovering. He told us his malaria was acting up. Mother told us the same thing; I think she believed it. (He'd been employed briefly by the Agency for International Development in Columbia.) But since mother was working and I was left to clean and care for the house, it was I who found the empty bottles of scotch—off-labels now—so I knew his malaria had been cheaply purchased, and was liquid, not airborne. Poor father. He was terribly susceptible.

My brother was almost twenty at the time of our family misfortune, graduated from high school, and enjoying an intermission in his education, having informed our parents that before matriculating at MIT School of Engineering he needed time to "get real," and to that ambiguous end they had agreed. But it was all moot now. He got a job at an auto body shop on California Street. I had never seen him happier.

So when Dixie asked me to spend the weekend of my

birthday at her house, my parents, even my brother James, encouraged me to accept.

"Try to enjoy yourself, honey. Try to be carefree," father said, looking careworn.

"We'll have a nice dinner the next weekend," said mother. "To celebrate." I wondered if then she would bring out from the freezer the Christmas canapes, if we would ever again "dine" as we had before father's unpropitious investment. Lately, we fed. In the kitchen, in silence. And there was nothing of the old grace about it. The food was dished directly from the pots onto plates, the napkins were paper, the condiments stood huddled in the center of the table dressed in their original containers, as we seemed to be. Mother cooked (badly). Father drank. And James and I refueled. It had come to that.

"Hey kid," James said, squeezing the back of my neck. "You're going to be legal."

That was what I thought about on the train the following Friday afternoon with Dixie as we headed south to San Jose, to her house. Being legal, being eighteen. What did it mean, and what did it mean I could do, and what would doing it mean to others? How would I stack up as an adult?

My parents could not now afford to send me to a private college, or, if I went to a state-funded institution, to support me away from home. In June, when I graduated from St. Agatha's, I decided I did not want to live at home, not to reject my parents as most eighteen-year-olds feel compelled to do, but so as not to participate in what mother called *noble labor*. It was neither the nobility nor the toil that bothered me; it was the communal factor.

Someone once said, someone who made the finest of distinctions, that *deprivation is worse than privation*—to be deprived of something one possessed for a time, or never to have had it at all. Living with my parents, watching their lives erode, like sandstone banks, as a rougher sort of reality flooded in, and the way they flinched when they saw my hands made raw by the dishwashing (perhaps it reminded them of my earlier hands, chapped and chastened during the obsessive-compulsive campaign); living at St. Agatha's, catching glimpses of my friends through my little window as they slid their dirty dishes up the ramp into my cell, their eyes blinded to me now, hearing the bustle of mealtimes, happy, flagrantly happy it seemed, I decided it would be best to be alone. It would be just fine. I would not feel I had been deprived. I would feel—and others would think, more importantly—that my life had always been thus.

The only one with whom I was not ashamed to be was Dixie. Everything, everybody was always all right with Dixie. She was wide open.

Dixie's father met us at the San Jose train station, wearing a brown suit and a pair of cordovan wing tips in need of polish. He'd obviously just come from the police department, because a photo ID with his name—Inspector Slade—was still clipped to his shirt pocket, and I found myself looking at it as if it was a sign all travelers were well advised to heed. "Bill," he said, removing the ID. He took our bags. "Everyone calls me Bill, even the street scum. Big Bill." He laughed heartily, stopped. It was eerie how abruptly he could shut it off, mirth.

"Where's my mom?" Dixie said. I thought it queer, her use of the possessive.

"She's resting. She hasn't been sleeping so good this week."

"Why?"

Shrugging, he frowned at Dixie, as if the question was unnecessary.

I had the sense that she knew why, but was trying to make him say it. I had the sense that Dixie had com-

106

pletely forgotten I was there, and it wasn't until we reached the car and a seating arrangement was required that she remembered there was a third party.

The car was brown too, with county plates and a police radio, generic vinyl bench seats, a notepad suction-cupped to the dash. It occurred to me that probably hundreds of different people had ridden in it—criminals, informants, battered wives. On the front seat floor were the remains of a take-out lunch, and the whole car smelled of tired onions. There was something sticky on the armrest, and I had to scoot over close to Dixie who was hanging out the window, letting the wind brush her hair.

Suddenly I wished I had gone home to my fallen family. At least they were aware of the possibilities.

Heading east, we reached the foothills and started climbing past fenced developments of new, stucco homes, then acres of barren hills, another development where the houses seemed a little bigger, more balding gray land, then finally higher up the live oaks began, and we wandered through an enclave of big homes, still obviously new but looking more established because of the trees and expensive landscaping. The car stopped before an iron gate guarded by two, grinning, midget, black lackeys, all done up in painted jodhpurs and jackets, their lips as red as waxed apples. Bill reached under the seat for a remote control, pressed the button, and the gate swung open. The drive was cobbled and circular, with a statue at its center of a nude woman holding an urn upon her shoulder from which water dribbled into a pool below. It was a crude cement replica; I had seen dozens like it in corner lots behind a phalanx of paintings on velvet. The house itself was a monstrous, imitation Spanish villa.

Dixie was watching me.

"It's cool," said I. I meant to sound sincere, I really tried to.

She smiled then, not one of her bright expansive smiles, but a small, wrapped up present of a smile which said, *I know and it's okay, I'm just glad you're here, none of this really matters.* The other funny thing about that smile was how it made me feel, as if she was taking care of me, as if I had lost something, an arm or a leg, and she knew and was helping me get used to it, my limping, scrabbling life. Perhaps Dixie was to be my artificial limb, perhaps for awhile most things would be forgiven, even chronic snobbism, but there would surely come a time, I predicted, when all smiles would cease.

Dixie's father carried our bags into the foyer, and told us he had to get back to work, that he'd see us at dinnertime. Hermia, their housekeeper, appeared.

"The pool's been heated," she said. "And I've laid out a snack in the kitchen." It wasn't clear whom she was addressing.

Introductions were made. I said, "How do you do?" She nodded my direction, but there was no verbal response.

As Dixie and I started for the kitchen I saw her father and Hermia by the front door, having a discussion, something about a coat. Bill Slade shook his head while he clipped his photo ID to his shirt pocket, then he left. Hermia was still standing in the doorway when, five minutes later, we passed back through the foyer.

There was something profoundly common about Hermia. I saw her several times over the years, and each encounter failed to complicate my first impression of her. We all have seen her face, her shapeless shape, in grocery stores, laundromats, in post office lines, at the theater, occupying space the way a stone does, as if it will be there dependably each time you come, and will never break, and never change. Someone to whom one becomes unwittingly accustomed, and yet with whom one is never quite comfortable. Everything about her was tangible and outward, from her broad, peasant feet to her flat gaze. One had the sense that even her emotions—if she had any—were not inwrought, but acquired conditions, the way a stone warms in the sun and cools at night. One knew always what to expect from Hermia. Even so, she was a disconcerting presence.

I never knew how old she was: she might have been thirty, she might have been in her fifties. It didn't seem applicable.

Dixie and I spent the remainder of the afternoon in the swimming pool, seldom emerging into the blunt January air. But it was sunny, and the water was a delicious 85 degrees, and we dallied about her bean-shaped pool, exploring our futures. Dixie wanted to be a hairdresser. Someday she would have her own shop and call it *Dixie's Darling Dos*. It was almost clever.

With an excitement that surprised me, I told her that I was thinking of law school—also a surprise to me. We even talked about getting an apartment together while I waited out the application procedures, and she put in her 1600 hours of required practice at Harold's College of Beauty in downtown San Jose. Her education would take ten months, while mine would last seven to eight years: Dixie found this hilarious. She was laughing so hard she kept going under, and I was engaged in performing a mock rescue—arm under chin, side stroke to the edge—when her mother came out onto the patio.

She was wrapped in a white wool coat, but there was a foot or so of peach satin hanging below it, billowing and snapping against her bare legs. On her brow was the sweetest of frowns, like a child when it is seeing something for the first time.

"My baby," she said, and smiled gently.

"Did we wake you, mom? I hope we didn't . . . did we

wake you?"

"I don't know," she said, then added an enigmatic, "Maybe."

Dixie gestured at me. "Do you remember Sue?"

"Sue? It's Sue, is it?"

"Hello Mrs. Slade."

"Darling," she said, and smiled gently again.

I thought it was awfully nice of her until Dixie turned to me to say, "My mom's name is Cheryl Darling. Just say 'Cheryl.'" To this day I still believe, I want to believe, she was using a form of endearment, not correcting me.

But, ever obedient, I said, "Cheryl," as if practicing.

And Dixie's mother said, "Sue." It seemed we were engaged in a kind of elementary game of call-and-response, and so far we had only managed to get through names.

"I'm glad you came."

"Dixie's a good friend," I said, realizing the sentiment for the first time. "And your place is real nice."

Cheryl Darling looked around, a glint of alarm in her eyes, as if she too had arrived here for the first time. "Is it?"

"Oh, yes. It's terrific."

We studied each other, and the embarrassment, if there had been any, seemed to thin away. Dixie watched; she was right to, for some intangible thing had passed between us, and I had neither the words nor the desire for words to describe it. It scared me a little.

Hunkering down into the pool, I let the water warm my shoulders as I waited for the deeper meaning of the exchange to be revealed.

A parody of confusion mixed up the fine and delicately balanced features of Cheryl Darling's face. "Where's daddy?" she said.

"He'll be back," Dixie piped, a little too eagerly, I

thought. "For dinner. Will you come down and eat with us tonight? Did you get enough rest?"

"I'm going," she answered. Her arms were crossed over her breasts, her hands began to caress the lapels of the coat, while about her slender legs the peach satin flowed indifferently. She looked cold, very cold. "I may as well," she added, her voice dissipating like the drifting mist of her gaze.

"That's great, mom. Hermia's cooking eggplant. My mom loves eggplant," Dixie said to me. "She's a vegetarian."

I wonder if Dixie has learned to make distinctions now, to hear the difference between "coming" and "going" as I did that day, because it was clear to me that Cheryl Darling was not coming down to join us for dinner. She was going somewhere. She had her coat on, and she was already gazing off, into her future, and unknowingly into our future too.

Dixie climbed out of the pool and toweled off behind her mother. I stayed in the water, head just above the surface, the rest of me wavering in the blue depths, like a long pale fish about to be caught. I was acutely aware of Cheryl Darling, aware of the steady movement of her hands as if they meant to comfort—or forgive—the white coat. I watched my own hands in the water, and wondered what or who they would comfort someday, if they would know how.

Suddenly, Cheryl's face brightened—"Happy birthday," she said—really brightened, as if she was seeing the whole of something, a trajectory of birthdays ending with mine.

I gave her a pleased smile, one to Dixie, too, for telling her that it was my eighteenth birthday, and said, "Thank you."

"Today you're a woman, today until you die, you're that. A woman. We have to hold on, don't we, don't you think, Sue, to the part that, to the part . . ." She couldn't seem to find the rest, settled on, "the real part, when we're pretty like you. It keeps sinking, doesn't it?" She stared into the water. "It's a birthday today," she added, frowning. There was something fiercely present about her now, as if she had gathered all of herself for this last, most trivial of meetings. As if she had brought it all to the surface, whatever there was of her to grasp—and there didn't seem to be much left within her reach. Her hands had fallen loosely to her sides, and a passing breeze slipped in her coat, leaving one edge of it flung open, and, like a stranger taking liberties, fingered the curves of her satin, peach-colored skin. Then the breeze dropped, and nothing moved, not her hands, not the satin, not even her polished blue eyes which held me in a sweet and shining glaze of sad benevolence. At that moment I saw her as perhaps Dixie and Bill Slade did, and surely as the thousands who had flipped through magazines and seen her without seeing her; as an American icon, ritualistic, yes, but representing nothing so morally complicated as religion, nothing so profound as philosophy, but merely as a canvas for the more important fall outfit, a prop for a brand of detergent, an attendant to the latest Ford coupe. Again, the icon spoke: "My daughter, Dixie, knows what it means. She has always known what it means. Do you?"

I glanced at Dixie who was looking at her mother with a kind of creeping horror.

"What it means . . . ?" I began.

"To be a woman," Dixie cried. "That's what she's asking you. Do you know what it means to be a woman. Because it's your birthday today. That's all she's asking, it's a perfectly *normal* thing to ask. Do you know what it means, or are you tote la deaf?" It was the first time I had heard something like anger in Dixie's voice. Or desperation, helpless desperation.

I shook my head *no*, but it felt more like a reflexive jerk away from a terrible danger, something tiny and contained and deadly and right here, because it seemed that we had slid through some undetected crack in the smooth scheme of things, and I didn't know where I was. I had no idea. Ideas were alien. I waited for Dixie's mother to tell me what it meant to be a woman, for I thought, of all women she would know, but no answer came, no saving sound, no distant siren or siren song, and at length I said, "I guess I'll find out."

"I ordered a cake," she said. The immediacy had departed her voice, and the drifty quality returned with the breeze. Shivering, she drew the white coat about her.

"That's awfully nice of you, *Cheryl*." The name felt improper, like the name of a newborn baby, pasted on and forced, without history, without associations. "That's so nice," I repeated.

She turned to go, but there seemed to be no decision inherent in the act: it was almost as though the breeze had simply turned her about, like a rudderless toy boat, the satin sails fluttering loose, the delicate limbs tensing and trembling for the journey.

I wanted to say something to her, something that would tie her down, something meaningful or real, something strong, but all I could think of was how beautiful she was, pure and simple, and that seemed to have no weight at all. None. So I couldn't say *that* to her, I knew I couldn't. It would've been the keenest insult. It would've driven her further from the shore.

Suddenly, almost shouting, she said, "Red," and swung about as if to accuse me of my thoughts.

*Red?* I mouthed.

"Don't you think, Dixie, with her dark coloring, don't you think red lipstick?"

I stared at the two of them, so essentially different; on

113

this, however, they agreed.

"That's the ticket."

I shrugged, I tried a smile, I was in their hands. I was strangely, totally, fatally in their spell.

Dinner transpired at a table that would have been well placed in one of those mock castles they have at amusement parks. Dark and thick-legged, and about as long as the room itself, it suited Bill Slade somehow, who occupied the northern shore of the oaken sea, like a tanker at port. Dixie and I shoved in along its sides, while the chair at its southernmost reach sat empty, though a place had been faithfully laid.

Under the table at Bill's end was a button which, when he stepped on it, rang in the kitchen. But it seemed to fluster him: he would call for Hermia, and just about when she pushed through the door, he would remember the button, press it, then glance up apologetically. The calling and the ringing conveyed a sense of impatience, but Hermia seemed aware that it was not so. Finally, in frustration, he asked Hermia to please sit down and eat with us, gesturing toward the unoccupied seat at the distant end of the table.

Dixie sent her father a dark look.

Chatting with Hermia about household matters, he slid the casserole dish of eggplant parmigiana down the length of the table, like a mug of beer at a bar, and when Hermia caught it with not so much as a flick of notice, he let out one of his unique, TNT blasts of mirth which never failed to straighten my spine a little. He seemed so much more at ease with the housekeeper.

It was Dixie who brought out the cake, an angel food with lemon frosting and eighteen candles. Peering over the host of jiggling flames, I saw she was as usual smiling, but in an oblique way, as if there was someone standing behind me. I made a wish for Dixie, whatever she wanted.

Presently, Hermia stated—she seemed capable only of statements, her voice as toneless as stone—"Tomorrow is my day off. I have errands. There are some prepared meals in the freezer."

Bill Slade nodded thoughtfully. "Good, good," he said, then, clearing his throat, he added, "Listen, I've got to take a guy up to the city for booking, I could give you a ride into town, save you the bus fare."

"That'd be fine," said Hermia, and she cleaved off a large bite of cake.

Dixie pushed away from the table, and I rose to follow.

"I'm gonna watch some TV," she said. It was clear she wanted to be alone.

"I'd like to thank your mother for the cake."

"Yeah?" In her eyes a faint twinkle, but not effortless this time. Artificial light.

"If it wouldn't disturb her too much."

"Naw, go ahead. She'd like it. She likes you. Second floor, down at the end of the hall. She's got her own rooms."

To this I said nothing; I thought it best. But as I started away, she explained, "My dad keeps weird hours. Like tomorrow, he's gotta take this probably totally rot-*tone* . . ." she pronounced it as if it were French ". . . guy to San Francisco 'cause he's probably done things there too, he's probably a druggie who offed someone and . . . anyway, my dad sleeps in a guest room. We have tons of guest rooms," she muttered, straying off toward the TV room.

So I went upstairs to thank Dixie's mother for the cake. Though the door to her suite was ajar and a light was on, I knocked loudly to give her an opportunity to prepare herself. No answer. I then nudged the door, leaned in, and called out softly, *Cheryl.* Waited.

The outer sitting room was as tasteful as any I had seen, and unlike any other room in the house—simple, chaste, neither inviting nor forbidding, a beautiful room. On the white Berber carpets and arranged not for conversation but for solitary enjoyment were a fainting couch and a stuffed chair with an ottoman, all upholstered in the same sky-blue fabric. In front of the hearth stood a low table, birch or some other sort of pale wood, and on it a white alabaster swan dish and a stack of coasters. There were no books, no mirror. Several reproductions adorned the white walls, light impressionistic types, pleasant colors, scenes without import. Moments of prettiness.

A dark opening led through to the bedroom itself.

I took three steps into the sitting room, toward the opening. The illumination, I discovered, was all firelight. Behind the glass doors shapely flames bowed and swayed, and I found myself briefly hypnotized, for there was something too tame about it, a postcard image of the perfect fire; I wondered idly if I opened the doors and poked in my finger whether or not I would feel anything at all. Then, above the mantle, I saw it—a mask. An appallingly gaudy mask, Indonesian, I guessed, with wild eyes and a crooked, obscene mouth, red tear drops on one of its cheeks, a fantastic headdress from which horns sprouted. Anywhere else the mask would have been interesting, even amusing. But here, in this room, there was something direful about it.

I left, glancing back over my shoulder. Through the dark opening the firelight had slipped, and for an instant it drew across an ankle, down along a silken arch, then feathered off toes into the surrounding dark. I was sure I saw her foot stir, as if in response to the light. I was sure.

But they said no. They said I couldn't have.

The next morning I awoke early. Dixie was still asleep. I knew she liked to linger when she could. And anyway, even if she was awake, there would be her ablutions to contend with, which occupied the better part of an hour if you didn't count her hair. Her hair was an entirely separate matter which *evolved* along an apparently nomadic course, though the evolution itself was fixed: wash, blow-dry, curl, apply setting mousse, wait twenty minutes, remove curlers, brush, followed by a sequence of violent head-flipping designed, she once informed me, to fluff the curls like Farrah Fawcett's. Throughout this process Dixie, still in her bathrobe, ranged from room to room, her make-up without the soft corona of curls seeming too graphic, almost militant.

So I let her sleep. And when I heard the electric gate, and glanced out the window at the west end of the hall in time to see the gate close in ghostly fashion on the already departed, it was *I* who ranged from room to room. There were, indeed, too many guest quarters, an eerie row of welcoming arms, all empty. Heading downstairs into the kitchen, I made a pot of coffee—a taste I had lately and with some effort achieved—and took a cup out to the patio where I lit up a cigarette, testing the fresh waters of adulthood. Another beautiful January day. The pool sweep hummed softly as it toiled the perimeters of its little world, steamy and chlorinous, *fire burn and caldron bubble* . . . trouble, I thought. Very shortly, I stubbed out the cigarette, went inside, and dropped the butt into the kitchen garbage, first rinsing it under the faucet to be sure. The candles from my birthday cake lay on the counter; several times I arranged them, a square, a triangle, a star was too difficult. Now and then the coffee machine sighed or gurgled or clicked, its small, mechanical, almost human sounds seeming only to amplify the profound somnolence of the house. Pocketing one of the candles as a memento, I suppose, I then tried finishing my coffee at the oaken table in the dining room, but I kept staring at its southern end where a place had been laid, like the two along its sides for Dixie and for me. The window behind had become a sheet of bright light, the chair before it was rendered darkly obscure. Increasingly restless, I wandered into the TV room, took one look at the inanimate screen, and found myself rushing up the stairs.

To wake Dixie? I wondered. No, for I passed her room, I passed it like someone who knew all along and had been engaged in a ruse of delays. I moved swiftly to the white and sky-blue rooms at the end of the hall.

To thank her for the cake.

As before, I knocked, but this time I did not wait before pushing open the door and entering. And this time when I called her name, it was not softly, but with the bold assertion of morning on my side. When no answer came—and I seemed to know it wouldn't—I strode through the opening that was not dark anymore, but drenched with sunlight from the window on the far wall, I strode through to find her.

I seemed to know she would be dead. Her skin had grayed and pulled back against her teeth, conveying a skeletal appearance. Her lips, too, were gray. She was dressed as I had last seen her, in the satin nightgown and the white wool coat, and lying on top of the spread. Caged within her hand was a small white diary, the name "Kate" in gold embossed letters on its cover. I removed the diary to read her last entry, but there was no last entry; there were no entries at all. Every page was blank. There was just the name "Kate" on its cover. Her real name. That's all.

I returned the diary, hearing in my mind a whispered, *I'm sorry*, as if there had been something to read, an intimate view of a total stranger.

The room was neat and clean. She had even replaced the cap on the sleeping pill bottle. Over on the dresser, I noticed, a tiny package meticulously wrapped with flowered paper, a tag that read *for Sue*. I picked it up and made a tight fist around it, as tight as I could, in the same way that one might, in great pain, bite down on a piece of wood. My other hand felt strangely ashamed and dove into the pocket of my robe where it found the birthday candle from the cake she had ordered. It was half its original length, the wick black and curled and, rubbing it, it left a black smudge of ash on my too pinkly alive fingertips. I lay the birthday candle on the table beside the bed: it was hers, you see, it was really her birthday. Then I sat down in a blue chair facing her.

*Now you are real*, I thought. *You have taken hold of our common flaw. Mortality. You have embraced your very own death, and made it personal, made it happen.* There was something to be said, after all, for not waiting and wondering.

Thankfully, her eyes were closed, and though her skin was cinerous, her lips, too, ashen and collapsed, (the lips really bothered me); though her hand about the unfilled book seemed like the hand of a statue, the book ironically the prop now to display the hand, or perhaps the artist's skill; though she was still beautiful in death, it was an ordinary beauty now, a negotiable beauty. I could look at her, study her, without faltering. Whatever there had been about her that was extraordinary, whatever it was that had left the viewer with the sense of something unworldly, had vanished.

Perhaps she had groped about for the "real part," as she had called it, everything else having slipped away, and in the end, in the darkness, it was death her fingers brushed across, death that was finally real and tangible and touchable. It may very well have been her only flaw, if one didn't take into account the probability that she hadn't the least idea how to live. Dear lady, dear icon.

The tiny package in my fist announced itself. Inside was a tube of red lipstick; it was not new, it had been used—by her, I hoped. Rising, I leaned toward the vanity mirror and carefully applied the red lipstick. At the moment it seemed the highest tribute I might pay her. I then resumed my post in the blue chair to await Dixie and her wandering evolution. I would let her awaken naturally, I would meet her at the door, I would try, *god help me*, to prepare her.

Again I felt the tube in my hand and squeezed hard. It was not my pain I clamped down on, it was Dixie's.

*Look away, Dixie,* I thought, *look away, look away, look away . . .*

# 7

Considering Cheryl Darling's occupation, the people she had met, the places she had been, all the products she had enhanced and served, considering the wide distribution of her image alone, there were not many people at her funeral. Maybe fifty, not counting the attendants from the funeral home in their dark suits, shiny from too many pressings and too many hours in church pews and stretch limousines.

Having endured a strange service at a local Baptist church—strange to me, a Catholic—for Dixie's mother had been born into that southern arm of the Protestant Church, we then convoyed to a graveside ceremony at a vast cemetery in south San Jose, just around the corner from a dog food factory which we passed on our way there. The early morning stench from the factory was almost unbearable; it became in my mind confused with the imagined smell of the dead, and impelled me to stand as close to Sister Flaherty, who had come down to represent St. Agatha's, that I might catch now and then the dry, chaste scent of her linen habit. I overheard the funeral director, in fact, apologize to Bill Slade for the "unfortunate air," was how he put it. Glancing nervously up into the sky, squinting, Dixie's father frowned, as if he could not detect what was wrong with the air, then he turned to the immutable Hermia for explanation. When none came, he simply smiled politely at the director, and took his seat in the row of chairs alongside the open grave.

Dixie refused to sit. Alone, she stood at the foot of the grave. She'd also, apparently, declined to wear the customary black, choosing instead a pale pink suit of her mother's which was a little too small for her and conveyed, I'm afraid, a vaguely cheap quality, as did the oversized dinner ring of gold and alexandrite, also belonging to her mother. Her hair, however, was perfect in Dixie's terms, the height of the evolutionary process, a Farrah Fawcett replica. Her make-up, too, perfectly executed, though from my point of view it failed to encourage her own features—perhaps it was not meant to—and rather drew in a precise and obliterating manner a picture upon an utterly erased surface. The picture was not of Dixie but of The Daughter—two distinct entities, I realized.

Next to Bill Slade sat Cheryl's sister, who had always been called "Sister," as if she were some generic version of her older sibling and indeed, while she shared a good many of the icon's physical features, they simply did not add up to the same total quality: her appearance was pleasant, but prosaic. According to Dixie, Sister suffered imaginary rapes followed by imaginary miscarriages; no one knew why. It seemed a shrugging matter. The fellow sitting next to her was her husband, Milt, who ran a boat rental outfit in Galveston and who was "too nice," Dixie once told me. When I asked her why, she said, "Because he believes her."

Beside Milt sat Cheryl Darling's career manager, a small, nervous fellow, Lucas Sharp, whom Dixie always referred to as Lucas Not-so. Not so sharp, because somehow, incredible to Dixie, he had been unable to get her mother into the movies, or at the very least into TV commercials. She had remained a glossy still life, never achieving even the simulated life of film. I thought I understood why Lucas Sharp had not been successful, but naturally I never communicated this to Dixie. Perhaps I ought to have.

Behind Lucas Sharp a chorus of three beautiful women darkly, elegantly dressed—Cheryl Darling's peers, I assumed, and from the way Sharp kept turning to check on them, clients of his. They were younger than Cheryl—she had been thirty-five, Dixie told me, approaching the shadowing edge of a model's career. Some of the photographers had already begun using a soft lens and softer lighting, but probably to Dixie's mother it was merely a temporary and technical forgiveness. She had had too many birthdays, she could not be a model forever. She would have to settle for being the real thing and that, it seemed, had long ago unraveled to this scene this January morning.

The rest of the gathered appeared to be associates of Bill Slade's, law enforcement types with their wives who looked, I must say, almost relieved to be paying respects not to one of their own—a likelihood they no doubt feared—but to a woman who had chosen to pre-pay the last debt, a woman none of them had ever actually met.

Thankfully, the ceremony was brief, for the breeze had flagged and the stenchy fumes from the dog food factory had seeped in among us, like a tule fog. I tried breathing through my mouth, but once I'd started I found I could not return to full breathing capacity, for it was nearly impossible to re-acclimate to the "unfortunate air."

Sister Flaherty and I were standing on the other side of the grave, opposite the seats reserved for close family, so I had a good view of both Bill Slade and Dixie. And what struck me throughout was how utterly diametric they were, their expressions, their little, new-fledged feats of survival. Bill Slade's face was a symphony of ticks, each one a single and different emotion *staccato*, as though he were trying them all out, all notes, to assure himself of their existence. And of his, perhaps. He would stare into the hole, then peer up sharply to the white casket suspended over it, to the crown of flowers, then his gaze seemed to ricochet not from face to face, but from the smallest movement to the next and then on to another— someone scratching his nose, a turning head, a handkerchief withdrawn, even the most minor shift in weight from one foot to another, every moving, every ordinary emblem of life living seemed both to fascinate and comfort him. Then back to the open grave and up and around we went again. Mostly he seemed dazed, but there was about this state an element of relief, as if he had survived some strange and lovely ordeal and could now settle back into the mediocrity that appeared to be his natural wont. It was over. One might even venture to say that if selections of that sort were possible in the seamless, schemeless flow of things, if he could have halted for an instant his west-running brook and cried, "*this*, not that way," he would have chosen differently.

And Dixie's face . . . it was not that there was *no* expression, it was that it was somehow *invisible*. I knew, I *knew* that in that conspicuous absence all the world was present and falling in as if into a great maw. She had got herself up in her mother's things to ward off Dixie, what Dixie might feel; she had put on a mask, shadow and blush, mascara like rays of dark light escaping her eyes. She had put on the armour of faithfulness. Several times by subtle gesture or glance I tried to offer sympathy, but the mask didn't flinch, and wavering in the stars of her eyes was the feeling of not-feeling, the distant thinning light of illusion. I wondered how long she could sustain it. I wondered when the maw clamped shut on her sorrow if there would be anything left of the world for Dixie to care about. There had been something obscenely religious about Dixie's devotion to her mother.

Suddenly spent, I took my study away from her to the quiet white casket, the dark and waiting space below. The minister's voice buzzed on; I found it annoying for its utter neutrality. I had overheard him mention to the funeral director that he had "two to bury and two to marry" that day, and when the director asked how he, the minister, could tell the difference, he dropped his head to hide his amusement. I supposed it was the sort of shoptalk that made it all tolerable, but for Dixie's sake I was put off.

Bill Slade coughed to conceal his tears, while Sister, having no such concerns, unleashed her sentiments. She was a messy weeper.

One of the beautiful chorus whispered to the middle one, the third bent in to receive the gossip, then they resumed their three-headed pose, sad-but-true. The Fates.

Dixie remained as oblivious as her mother.

*Extreme infatuation*, I thought, *maybe only that*. And Dixie, lacking what all infatuations require, what defines them—time, not much time, but enough to ground down the infatuation, to wear it away to something approaching a normal relationship, a realistic appraisal—Dixie, lacking that simple, most ordinary of opportunities, would be condemned to the infatuation. Now with the icon dead it would probably get worse, I thought. No "real part" to trip it up. No wrinkles, no extra pounds, no cranky moods, no arguments about boys and cars and late night parties, no chance to hate, no time to forgive. Just this haunting, heedless infatuation.

The minister closed his book, and the four attendants moved in, each one grasping an end of the double sling on which the casket hung. There was a basket of single, long-stemmed yellow roses next to Bill Slade which was passed around, and each in his turn tossed a rose on the slowly descending casket. When it had finally reached bottom—it seemed to take forever—the minister whispered last instructions to Dixie's father, and he pawed up a handful of dirt and let it shatter on the lovely spill of flowers.

I looked at Dixie. A moment, a flash like the flash one sees on a pitchy night, a flash of the eyes' creation, pure and complete, the night snapped inside out, and I saw in her face a bolt of absolute pain. *Gone*, the mask restored. In her pink silk pumps she was moving, she was walking up the mound of dirt to the edge of the grave. To throw herself in, it was clear. Someone grabbed an arm. And another. There was a struggle. Her head flung back. Blond hair, the evolution undone.

*Dixie, Dixie.*

Sister Flaherty took hold of my hand and squeezed. I shook my head, I sent Dixie, I *kept* sending her a fiercely silent plea, and when at last she seemed to recognize me— or someone near me, behind me—her body went lax, and they led her away. It was the first of only two times I would ever see her cry, and I must say she did it, she *cried* with an essential and most lovely grace; there was a purity to it, a rightness, as if it had come from the very first and simplest order of things. For Dixie spirit and flesh were one.

Nevertheless, it was too much for Bill Slade. Collapsing in a chair, he studied the palms of his hands: it seemed unsafe to look anywhere else.

Sister, having been upstaged, was talking petulantly with hubby, Milt.

Sharp was herding the three Fates toward his car, and when he had them headed the right direction, he started back to the graveside, peered round at the slumping hulk of Bill Slade, changed his mind, and hurried after the models. Probably he had wanted to discuss the estate. All of Cheryl Darling's income was filtered through him. Somewhat too eagerly, everyone else dispersed.

It was Hermia, I noted, who stood the customary exchange with the minister, who slipped him the white envelope containing the "tip"; Hermia who spoke for the family. After which, the minister glanced at his watch, flagged the funeral director and together, the two of them left, presumably to bundle off another to the kingdom.

That was January 30th, a Friday. Sister Flaherty and I caught the SP Commuter back up the Peninsula, she detraining for St. Agatha's, and I continuing on to San Francisco and the home of my family. I could not help remembering the first time I had met Dixie that day on the train, and the woman who had thrown herself in front as we sped along. A stranger. Perhaps this last too, another kind of stranger.

My family were solicitous if mildly uncomfortable around me. Father kept calling me Susan, not Sue or Susy as he usually did, as if I was somehow older, had grown into the last letters the way James had grown his last two inches in one year. Later when father poured himself a drink, he asked if I too would care for one, a "*soupçon*" he suggested, and I accepted, though I felt a little guilty because of his problem. The scotch was very nice, not exciting as I had always anticipated, rather like a warm hand soothing back the hair from one's brow.

Mother, on the other hand, reverted to terms of endearment I had not heard since even I considered myself a child. "Honey-Q" (as in Susy-Q) was one of her favorites, and out it came that weekend as she tried to shrink me back to a protectable size. James avoided me mostly, though in a valiant moment following dinner when we were left to clean up the kitchen, he did offer up a blow-by-blow account of a job he was doing, "banging out a Classic," a Ferrari, at the body shop on California Street. The sound of his own words, the comforting minimalism of slang he settled into when our parents weren't around, seemed to ease things some. I asked him what color the car would be when it was finished.

"Red," he said, as if I ought to have known.

And remembering, my voice seemed to whither away in the back of my throat to dust.

No one, not even father who was the likeliest candidate, asked for any details. I think they all thought the whole thing was too bizarre, and silently I agreed with them. But I was stuck with it, with the knowledge and possession of the details. Details can do you in. When the whole of a thing has receded, when the names have slipped and the faces blurred, when what happened even, sequence and configuration, becomes an equation with missing factors, a few details or perhaps only one will remain, like a fish hook snagged in the memory, as small and keen and sometimes just as painful as it was the day it caught. For me the details would be a tube of red lipstick; the look on Dixie's face, as if she was imploding, when she saw her mother on the bed with the empty diary; and the mockery of the sunlight pouring in, *pouring* like a bright and weightless fall and the two of us drenched in it by the window when the dark men came to take her away to the darkest of places. And after, sneaking past Dixie's closed door and down to the guest bathroom to wash my hands, as if Death were contagious.

My sense of Dixie's sense of her mother's death seemed not to be the usual experience of loss, of an untenanted position, an empty seat beside her. Rather, it seemed that something had appeared, a disturbing and drafty opening in the person of Dixie, a kind of psychological leak into which, it seemed (like the boy and the dike), she would have to thrust more and more of herself in order to keep the despair from flooding in.

No, my parents never asked me for the details, though I think I wished they had: telling might have helped me get rid of the memory, or master it, perhaps even embrace it.


At eight o'clock I went up to my room. It was good to be alone. I stretched out on my bed and faced the abandoned dolls, their stiff arms forever reaching out. At that moment the painted wonder of their expressions struck me in a vague way as ghastly. On the shelves stood books I had long ago read, and near the door a bag of too-small clothes mother had culled in order to sell them at a consignment shop to help make ends meet. The flowered bedspread, I realized with a weird sort of surprise, I hated. It was funny, but I couldn't even say when I had started to hate it. But I knew I had and that it wasn't until that night that I found something like the courage to admit it. The room, though large, was cluttered—photos of friends left behind, tired posters whose one-line sentiments seemed embarrassingly trite, a stack of record albums by musicians long since faded from the scene. A pillow I had embroidered—badly—for Girl Scouts. My old book bag. A pair of baby-blue ballet slippers pinned to the wall. All seemed to belong to someone else, someone who, like the musicians, had faded from the scene. I couldn't say who she had been, or why these things were still here in my room, or why she had done some things and not others. Or why, like the dolls, I was reaching stiffly out and not touching anyone.

Around 8:30 mother came in, tight-lipped, ominously

calm, and brandishing a tampon. "What is this?"

I made a dumb face. "A tampon."

"Why was it in your purse?"

"Why were *you* in my purse?" I said, glaring back.

"How long have you been using these?" Again, she waved the white cylinder at me. "Do you use these?"

"Once a month."

"These are for women, *married* women. Not girls who haven't any, who shouldn't have any experience . . ." desperately, she searched the carpet, ". . . putting things there." In all, mother was a purist.

The hateful bedspread peered up from between my outstretched legs. Mother and I had chosen it together, I recall, but I think I understood then that there was a chance that I had *never felt* attracted to the bedspread, I had *thought* it attractive for her sake, or because it didn't matter . . . I don't know. I had thought too much. Maybe there had never been sufficient reason to feel anything. Or maybe because I could not impose any rational order on feelings, I made a habit of sidestepping them, the impossible mess of them. Genetically speaking, father's susceptibility was of some concern to me.

I looked at mother, her immaculate Castilian skin, her big eyes, her beautiful beauty. And suddenly I was furious that she couldn't see that father was drinking himself to death, or that James was wasting his life as a grease monkey, or that I couldn't stand to see her trotting down to the low-rent quarters with my used clothes to make a few bucks. I just couldn't stand it. I said, "Maybe I have a little experience."

"What have you done? What have you done, Susan Thatcher?"

"Not enough," I heard myself yell. Then, in a whisper, "Not enough, mom," as she fled the room. "Oh, mom."

At 9:00 the phone rang. "Which do you like, gold or blue?" Dixie said.

"Gold or blue what?"

"Carpet."

"What are you talking about?"

"I found us a place. The Penthouse Apartments. It's got a pool and a laundry and they'll put in new carpet and the landlord's daughter says there's some cute guys renting on the fourth floor. We're on the fifth. The *top*, Sue. The *penthouse*."

"Dixie," I sighed, thinking of St. Agatha's, money, my parents—all of it. My life. "For one, I can't afford it."

"Don't sweat it. I'll float us for awhile, till we get jobs. I know a guy, he owns a restaurant."

"Dixie."

There was a silence on the end of the line, but not much of one. "I gotta get out of here, Sue." Her voice was level, but it rose immediately. "I gotta get out of this house. Daddy's practically back to normal, I mean it's sick, how *normal* he is. And *she* eats with us now, every time. Hermia. She sits where my mom sits like some big weird toad, and I swear she's deaf 'cause you have to yell everything at her and finally she'll croak something back that has totally nothing to do with what I want, she's so frigging cold and ugly and efficient. Sue, she sits where, where my mom used to be. The fat toad. He says the company's nice, he *says*. He says we need it, it's good for us."

"Maybe he's right."

"But it's all so frigging normal around here, it's like she wasn't ever here, they're making it so I can't even feel her in the house. The TV's on and the washing machine's going and he picks up the phone and, like, says hello the same way. *The same way*."

"I guess that's what you do," I said feebly. "I guess you just keep going."

"But it's different. Everything's different. *I'm* different."

Somehow I heard these words as if they were coming from inside me; I even worked my lips around them silently as Dixie rushed on about the apartment, how she had everything figured out, etc. Probably it had something to do with Dixie's mother, the shock of death, the recognition and all that. But after all, she was Dixie's mother. I had my own mother, my own problems, and they had been grinding away at me so that I, too, was beginning to change. Ready to change.

I suppose, too, I may have been a little upset with father. Oh, he was a fine fellow, and I knew he was terribly fond of me and I of him, but he had let us down, he had really let us down. He was *so* susceptible. And unlike James, I *did* want a career. And unlike mother, I was not going to be found unprepared for any ill turning of events. It was all so pathetic. It was all so different. *I* was different.

So I said, "Gold."

"Gold?" Then, triumphantly, "Gold. Far out."

# 8

Once again, arrangements were made, but this time it was I, not my parents, who effected them. Sunday night upon my return to St. Agatha's I presented my case to Mother Superior who sat behind her desk wearing her usual expression of melancholic love. Several times I recall having to fend off the urge to bury my face in her lap and weep for what I was asking, what I realized it would mean. Without question she was the best, a female incarnation of the Lord's disposition, and the only one to whom many of us, long after the practice had been abandoned, continued to curtsy. There were nuns who were stronger, or more worldly, or more pious, some with keener minds, perhaps one or two with greater poise, but Mother Superior was the heart of St. Agatha's. She felt for everyone. And I was awfully glad it was to the heart I appealed at the last, for it was the heart's response I most required.

She let me go. Sure, I had more than satisfied the requirements for a high school diploma. Naturally, the dishwashing was a trial. Granted, I was eighteen and could legally do as I wished, didn't really need her permission. But on none of these accounts did she give her blessing.

"St. Agatha's," I tried, "St. Agatha's has been . . ." But there was everything to say, and she knew it, and finally

I blurted out, "I can't bear to go."

Her head floated downward in a soft, compassionate nod, rose up, and then she gazed at me straight from the place in the heart where warm and cold keep even company but somehow do not cancel out each other. Because I felt both when she said, "Then you must go."

Looking back, it seems an awfully Zen thing for a Catholic to say. That was the way she was. I remember when I lost my confirmation medal out on the softball field (she was my confirmation sponsor), and we spent a good hour pawing into gopher holes, searching for it, she stood at length, dusted off her hands, and said, "The chain is enough." A week later in the dressing room at the swimming pool someone stole the chain, and despite her request for honesty, no one came forward. At which point she said to me, "*You* are enough."

I kind of laughed then, bitterly, for the chain was sterling and after all it was she who had given it to me on the day of my confirmation. "And when I'm lost," I said with a certain challenge in my voice, "What then?"

"God is enough." And she smiled her forgiveness.

I recall this because it was like something she said to Dixie's father after the arrangements had been made for *her* to leave St. Agatha's before her time. It was far more complicated, of course, liberating Dixie from the school of youth. Bill Slade came up and gave his best imitation histrionics—he was most profoundly not excitable.

From the hallway Dixie and I listened.

He told how traumatic things had been for Dixie (true), how important it was for her now to find her "own footing," was how he put it, "on *new* ground" he emphasized, that she was planning to go to college but needed the high school diploma (he did not say it was Harold's College of Beauty, he may not have known), how St. Agatha's would really not be enough for her since the recent large events of her life. Too limited, he added.

"I have my doubts, Mr. Slade, that any world as Dixie experiences it will be enough. In the *next* world she evinces no interest whatsoever. I have my doubts, Mr. Slade, I simply have my doubts about our dear Dixie altogether."

"Whad'ya mean?" he said, brought up short.

"She is out of bounds."

"Bounds?"

"She seems unconscious of them."

"*Out of bounds*," Dixie whispered to me. "*I like that.*"

We had to leave then; someone was coming. But I did hear Mother Superior say in a hopeless tone the word *feral*, and the irony of Dixie and her parents struck me as I followed her down the main corridor. A father committed to law enforcement; a mother not just restrained but utterly quashed by her beauty, the cultural expectations of it; and Dixie bound by nothing less than the law of nature, colliding at every turn with life.

I think it was Sister Flaherty who finally convinced Mother Superior, and I suspect the lingering shadow of "Humpy" had quite a lot to do with it.

Oh, they gave Dixie some equivalency tests, and she did surprisingly well, I must say, it made me stop and think. She did about as well as I would have done. It was unsettling. So I knew then that she wasn't stupid, she wasn't ignorant, she was simply indifferent to book learning. It was the sort of discovery that while having no effect on actual behavior, does alter one's slant somewhat, and I was viewing Dixie and the apartment as less a matter of expediency and more one of choice, perhaps even as a pleasant adventure with a quirky sort of equal. Mole and Ratty in the Wild Wood.

With clear conscience St. Agatha's conferred upon us our high school diplomas. Ten days later we matriculated at the Penthouse Apartments. As a house warming, Bill

Slade stocked the freezer with New York steaks—I had never seen such a wall of dark and waiting flesh—and the cupboards with enough peanut butter and jelly and crackers to adequately feed the local elementary school. Whatever would please Dixie, that seemed to be the prod and the policy. He kept calling her *Chickadee* as we hauled up boxes, and I rather suspect that he had transferred a leaky version of his devotion to Cheryl over to Dixie, because he also seemed relieved she was moving out of the house, that the distance would safely attenuate their relationship. He did not apparently want to go through again what he had with his wife. Anyway, things were heating up between him and Hermia—though that seems the wrong metaphor—things were *congealing*: Dixie said she was getting the "big chill." Personally, I doubted this. Hermia was a constant, not Dixie. Slade was somewhere in the middle.

My family's attitudes were predictable. Father "understood," father understood even when he didn't, bless his squishy soul.

Mother engaged her "proud and austere" Castilian heritage, starting slowly with a chat about the Importance of The Family in Today's Society, followed by a lecture concerning The Compass of Duty, and (the old hardtop barreling down the road now), a full sermon on The Threadbare Fabric of Morality; then, shifting into overdrive, she let go a string of tired quotations from Bartlett's (in which she delved on a nightly basis), including "adversity doth best discover virtue," something about tigers and degenerate daughters, and finally, veering out of control, a slam against "rats deserting a sinking ship." Father and James cleaned up the wreckage of poor mother. The rat departed in silence.

The Penthouse Apartments was a five-story, cinderblock, faded imitation of a faded and faulty dream, a Midwest housewife's guess at Hollywood glamor. There was no actual "penthouse," of course, and the apartments—ten to a floor—were old and small and crypt-like because of the concrete walls. Everything was white, lavatory white, even the cinderblock wore a thick veneer of high gloss paint; you could press your thumb nail into it and make bamboo letters, and indeed, someone named "Jake" had asserted himself repeatedly on the wall next to the toilet. Unfortunately, Dixie's furniture—the only furniture we had—was mostly white too, with gold doodads and curving legs, that faux-French style popular with the domesticated ladies of the sixties. There was only one bedroom, about which both of us tried to appear indifferent. Dixie's father donated a couple of twin beds from the unnumbered guest quarters at the house; the closet, two white dressers, and several orange crates accommodated the clothes; and with a seedy assemblage of leftovers culled from their garage we pieced out the living room. As requested, the new carpet was gold, and sculpted—an effect of varying heights that brought to mind a very bad haircut—and composed of some petroleum derivative that infected the air for the better part of a month, and led me to wonder several times in the pitchy hours before dawn if I had not awakened very near the La Brea Tar Pits.

The kitchen was a closet. The balcony was half a closet—you could jam in one chaise longue, but you had to mount its webbing directly from the living room, which inevitably collapsed either you or the chair or both. A white, ceramic lion lounged near the TV. A plastic crystal chandelier dangled down over the dining room table we didn't have. Someone (Jake?) had punched an apparently irreparable hole in the bathroom door. The ceiling over the entry cubicle had been covered with mirrored tiles sporting a gold (again) marbled design; two tiles were missing, revealing nasty scabs of old glue. The rest of the ceilings were the classic cottage-cheese-with-glitter often found in motel rooms let by the hour.

In all, our first apartment was a triumph of wincing bad taste.

Dixie adored it. She went about enthusiastically arranging and rearranging our motley collection of knickknacks and posters, photo albums (of which she was an avid producer), back issues of *Cosmopolitan*, potted ferns and wandering Jews which struggled through thick hammocks of macramé. When she had it all just right she placed on the small white table in the entry cubicle someone's unused, discarded, wedding guest register, and wrote on the inside page, "Sue and Dixie's pad," and underneath she drew a heart, and inside the heart a happy face. *God*, it was corny. And yet, *and yet* I remember thinking in some secret way that it was sort of *neat*, the idea and all, of our place and the register, that there would be a record of the friends who came to visit and, indirectly, of the things we had done. And some day in the waning future it might tell us who we had been at this moment in our passing through.

The steaks and the peanut butter and jelly lasted almost two weeks. Used to being fed at St. Agatha's and at our homes, it never occurred to either one of us to supplement these staples with other food items—they were there, they were *it*. We simply waited until they were gone, then one morning Dixie extracted from her jewelry box a roll of cash—as long as I knew Dixie, she always preferred the immediacy of cash—and together we went to the grocery store. Then we lived on spaghetti, iced coffee, Oreos, and a ten-pound sack of pulpy Golden Delicious apples. Eventually, of course, working our way through the immersion theory of consumption, we maintained a more balanced diet, or at least kept it on hand. Because Dixie tended to be a reflexive feeder, I took over the kitchen.

Most of my early days were spent at the coffee table, filling out college applications, scholarship and grant forms, and arranging for the forwarding of my transcripts and letters of recommendation to a dozen or so campuses around the country. I did register (late) for three classes at the local community college, just to keep my hand in the business of learning—Sociology 1A, taught by a midget who kept getting into arguments with a Vietnam vet in the group, "Swimmer-cize," an exercise class not wildly popular during the winter months, and Psych 1A in which we read such formidable texts as *I Never Promised You a Rose Garden*. Truly, I was desperate to get to a university.

Until noon Dixie slept. Because immediately and virtually every night, she went out to restaurants, bars, private parties, wherever the action was, she had a nose for it. Not bad action, not drugs or anything illegal—except for the one LSD junket at St. Agatha's, Dixie was, illogically, straight. No, she liked to dance, liked being around a lot of guys, and she liked to drink. Mixed drinks—piña colada, Irish coffee, margarita, that sort of folly (in De Voto terms). With extra make-up, and dressed to the nines, she easily passed for twenty-one.

"Come on, Sue. You gotta get some fun going."

It was an almost balmy March afternoon, and I had been studying all day at the coffee table, gazing perhaps too frequently out through the balcony doors at the velvet of new grass dressing up the west hills. "I have to study," I said automatically.

"It's been three weeks and you haven't partied once."

"This paper's due tomorrow."

"We're going to Pedro's. You can dance." Dixie knew I loved to dance, probably in the main because I had a knack for it. Often in the afternoons we practiced, crank-

ing up the volume on her stereo until the people below us
got home from work and yelled up at us from their balcony.

"You can't be a brain tote la time," she said. "You got
a body, don't ya? Gotta shake it to wake it."

I made a wry face, but nevertheless gave the air a few
tentative bumps with my hips just to please her.

"There you go," she said.

The books on the coffee table stared up at me. "I don't
know."

"Look," she said, lowering her voice. "I didn't want
to tell you this, 'cause I know you like things au naturel
'n all, but there's this guy, Earl, he's a total fox, and I told
him all about you."

"What?" I said. "What did you tell him?"

She was rolling her hair up in the ubiquitous pink curlers, getting ready for yet another night out, but she
dropped her hands, and gave me a simple, informative
look. "You're beautiful." It seemed she was not relaying
what she had told the fellow, but stating an otherwise
unrecognized (by me) fact.

Turning away, I walked over to the balcony. "What
does he do?" I said.

"Do?"

"His occupation."

"He's off-season, he said. Football or something." She
was working her hair again.

"Well, how did you meet him?"

"In our parking lot. I think he's got a cleaning service.
Cleans apartments when people move out."

"A cleaning service?"

"I don't know that he actually does it himself. He has
people, like, working for him. Yeah, that's probably how
it works. I didn't pay much attention."

Maybe I groaned—I don't know—or slumped, because

Dixie returned to the bathroom to continue the evolution of her hair. I think she was disgusted with me. I think I was too—probably for different reasons.

Ever since I had left The Known behind—St. Agatha's, my family, San Francisco—I had begun to focus exclusively on the future, on getting shut of the present. The present had really not been part of the plan. The present was at worst a correctable mistake, and at best one of those youthful choices one regards in later years with a whimsical smile and a shrug, the implication being that one has survived despite. The present was not to be enjoyed; it was to be got over, like a case of flu.

Dixie was disgusted, I think, because I was behaving like a snob, and I admit I was beginning to learn to feel pretty crumby about that part of me, thanks to Dixie. So I said loudly, cheerfully, "What time would we be going?"

From around the corner she appeared, one eye made up, the other big and blue and peering through a haze of disbelief.

"If we went," I added.

"7:00."

"But he's your date, isn't he? Earl."

"He's got a friend. You take Earl, I *want* you to take Earl. I'll take the crapshoot."

"I don't know, Dixie . . . deciding this sort of thing before he's even met me. What if . . ."

"Jeez, Sue," she interrupted. "All this humming and hawing for an eeny night out. I mean, he's a really nice guy. You don't have to hire him or anything. He'll buy you dinner and drinks, and ask you to dance, and at the end if he's *tray* lucky, you can let him kiss you."

The kiss was out of the question, dinner would be Dutch, and drinks, as far as I was concerned, were illegal. That was the plan. It was all in my head when, two hours later, the gentlemen knocked on our door.

"*Sue*," Dixie croaked, as she paused in the entry cubicle. "Lay off the brakes, will ya?"

I rolled my eyes but nevertheless tried to look casual.

There was always a lot that Dixie did not say. I still don't know if she simply did not notice, or if she chose not to predispose by making her own report in advance, or if she did notice but it wasn't important to her. In any case, what she did not tell me about Earl Buckner, my date that evening, was a lot. A lot of Earl, that is. When she opened the door I instinctively stepped back to make room for him.

A mountainous young man with black curls and beautiful teeth, a bright half moon of a smile that shone appreciatively on me, the little live thing in the path beneath him, he was not, as Dixie had said, a "total fox," but he was uniquely attractive. He reminded me of an Italian tenor. "Whatever you're selling, I'm buying," he boomed, coming toward me.

"I'm not selling anything." It was a little offensive, his opening line. A little flattering, too.

For the longest moment he said nothing; he simply left his black eyes resting on me, a candid, unhurried appraisal. Then he said, "Okay good, we're anted up. Now we can play."

No formal introductions were ever made. There was a Dixie-like immediacy to our foursome, and it gave me the strangest sensations, as though this was the first and last time we would all be together and we would make the absolute most of it, because in its not mattering at all, it seemed to matter intensely that the evening flow uninhibited through us, and we through the evening, that in all we be nakedly open and fixed securely in each passing moment.

"You have to sign the book," Dixie said, giving

Randall, her date, a long white pen.

Randall seemed deeply moved by the guest register; he actually straightened his tie before accepting the pen, then crouched monkishly over the book to inscribe his meticulous little name. Conventional good looks, preppy clothes, and terribly earnest manners, Randall was difficult to notice. Except to invoke Dixie's name, I don't think he said more than a half dozen things the entire evening, and one of those things was to ask her to marry him. He was serious too.

Then Earl Buckner took the pen in his great fist and shoved it across the page, leaving the tangled trail of his signature, and at the end he drew a tiny football with wings, his personal logo.

Thus our wedding register lost its clean white virginity, and after that the names came thick and fast.

Pedro's was on South 1st in the old part of town near the theaters which had in recent years degenerated to splatter and porno flicks. But the restaurant was so popular a landmark that it wouldn't give up its location and move like the rest of the businesses to the newer, sanitized parts of the city. A vast, windowless cellar below the streets, candle-lit, crowded, and so flooded with noise that it was hours before the residual sound drained completely from the ear canals, Pedro's was a world unto itself, and its denizens were swiftly naturalized.

Officially we never ate dinner. Earl kept ordering platters of nachos, and Dixie kept ordering pitchers of margarita, and Randall and I obeyed the laws of physics: if matter was on the table we consumed it, thus providing the energy for dance.

It was funny how Dixie changed around men. She became almost kittenish, yet I never had the sense that she had resigned her command. Leaning back in her chair, smoking—she had moved beyond the experimental stage

(where I still lingered) and was a regular smoker now—
she surveyed the scene and the company with a sort of
cute confidence, winking her response to observations of
which she approved, glancing around when she was
bored, dabbing her lips with a cocktail napkin and, after
dancing, fanning herself with one hand in a pleasantly
feminine but totally futile manner. Sometimes I wondered
if it had more to do with my being there than with the
men. Because once during a conversation between Earl
and me—he was a devotee of all things Japanese, and
since my experience of that culture was the most cursory,
I was interested in his knowledge—Dixie leaned over and
pinched my cheek, as if to say, "see, I knew you could do
it, I knew you could have fun, I'm proud of you." And
again I felt the feeling that no one hitherto, except my
parents, had stirred—that I was being taken care of. By,
of all people, Dixie Darling. I could not imagine anyone
less qualified, anyone whose guidance I less respected.
Yet I seemed to need it and, embarrassed by the pinch
but grateful for its motivation, I smiled a warm smile back
at her.

Earl was a good dancer, surprisingly nimble. At some
point I switched to soda and lime, just to keep up with
him; anyway, the margaritas were going to my head. Earl
was wearing a dark blazer, and I was wearing a dark dress
mother had given me: with its high collar, and alternat-
ing black and ruby flowered panels, ribboned cuffs and
full skirt, it had a rich Spanish flavor. In more ways than
one, Earl and I overshadowed the other dancers. Together,
we were big and smooth and we took up more than our
share of the dance floor.

Like a wind-up doll, Randall never altered his moves
with the music, keeping them tightly repetitive and as
close to Dixie as he dared. In the same way she resisted
order in her life, Dixie disobeyed form and rhythm in

dance. She was wearing a pink jersey dress with spaghetti straps that made her look abundant and bouncy, but not graceful. It didn't seem to bother her that she didn't dance well. Dixie was careless about achievements of any sort: if it didn't come easy, it didn't come at all. At one point she bumped into us, her perky, jersey breast flattening against my upper arm, then popping back like some toddler toy as she danced away. I don't think she even noticed.

Around midnight I was ready to leave. Everyone was getting more drunk, while I was getting sober, and that is the sort of imbalance that leaves one clinging to a raft of smugness on a sea of not-belonging.

Dixie went to the restroom to fluff her hair and fix her make-up, and this time I followed in order to suggest departure.

"So what do you think?" she said, as the door shut. Pushing her face toward the mirror, she brushed up her mascara.

"Of Earl?"

"Sure."

"He's nice. You were right. And he's interesting," I added, just to remind her that that mattered to me. I went in to use the toilet, and through the closed stall door I said, "What do you think of Randall?"

"He watches me breathe." I could hear her rattling through her cosmetic bag. "Pretty soon, *I'm* watching me breathe and then I'm not breathing so good. It's weird."

I joined her at the vanity. "Does he really watch you breathe?"

"Yeah."

"Why?"

She shrugged. "I know how to breathe." If anyone else had said this, I would have taken from it a metaphoric meaning, but with Dixie I was never sure.

"Well," I said, not knowing what to say, "He seems perfectly nice."

"Totally."

"That's good, isn't it?"

"Not totally."

Laughing, I dried my hands on the towel roll. "Don't you want to date someone nice?"

"You mean like Uncle Milt?"

"Well . . ."

She put down her lipstick and looked at me. "See, Randall's nice, like, really McCoy. I could be bad and I bet he'd be nice, and then I'm dying to be bad worse just to see how deluxe his niceness really is. The rest of the time I feel like his ma." Picking up the lipstick, she drew it across her mouth, then kissed the air with mock seductiveness. "I bet that's what he calls her, *ma*."

"Ma," I echoed.

"Anywho, sure, I want a guy who can be nice, I want a guy who can be it all, and the trouble with Randall is he *is* nice, he's stuck there. He could be pure mean, what's the difference? He's 100 percent stuck dead fast. You know what it's like?" she said.

"What?"

"It's like being with one of those one-way mirrors. He looks at me, and when I try to look at him, I see me, not Randall. Yeah, he's *tray* smooth," she said. "Cold and smooth and not *ici*. So," she said . . .

"He watches you breathe."

"There you go," she winked. "Breathing lessons."

The exchange in the restroom left me so stunned—I didn't know why—that I forgot to tell Dixie I was ready to go home. I watched Randall watch Dixie, then I watched Dixie, then I danced to forget the watching, and then at 1:45 a.m. when they called out "last round," I ordered a double shot of tequila, which I had never done before, and leaned my head against Earl Buckner's amazing shoulder, feeling the evening flow in and out of me like breath, and thinking that whatever it was that was required of me in this new world, it was not bravery. It was something, I suspected, Dixie knew.

Earl and Randall went to get the car which had been parked about five blocks away because of the theater and restaurant crowds; Dixie and I were supposed to wait at Pedro's, but she said *forget it* when the busboy flipped on the vacuum cleaner, and we started walking up South 1st Street at 2:30 in the morning which was just about the time the porno theater on the next block let out.

There must have been spring clouds high above, because there was no moon in sight. A light rain had recently drifted through, and the air was tingling with city seasonings, and the shiny pavement made wet paint of the blinking yellow street lights and of the white marquee far ahead. Maybe it was only that we were outside after the long spell in the crowded and smoky cellar; maybe it was the cleanness of the rain and the dirty street; or maybe it was just that the men were gone, and the loud music was gone so we could hear plainly our own voices, sharp like the air, and sharp in the air, like metal and glass; or maybe we were feeling the tequila solidarity of an evening out of time. But the moment after Pedro's was all contrast, the place where opposites touched and were somehow briefly the same. In it, we smarted with life, we were girls again, and if we skipped or sang or laughed, even if we cried, the acts were invincible, we were invincible; then it seemed we were one girl on any one of a thousand night streets. And when the dark shapes surrounded us, especially then we were one girl, one St. Agatha's girl wearing the armour of faithfulness.

They were one too.

One dark tide of shapes flowing around us, cold but deeply hot. I could smell Dixie, she was close, her perfume, too sweet. I could smell the men like seaweed tangling around us tighter. Then I could not tell the difference—perfumed seaweed, her skin and man skin, hands, hands, hands.

I said: *no*, sharp like metal in the air. Dixie laughed, a lost giddy childlike sound that reeled up with the *no* like the tail of kite, and suddenly we were wagging free, pulling further away, pulling Dixie away. Once I glanced back: the men had come apart and were scattering, black seeds sowing the black fields of the night.

I have often since thought of that near miss. Two things I have thought: how desperately innocent we were, as if it was our last chance, and yet strangely, how much more innocent the men were, freshly aroused from the porno theater, and streaming, almost magnetically, along a natural course our direction, happening upon us in their hunger, and naturally seizing its natural and likely satisfaction. Perhaps that is the greatest form of innocence—the assumption that desire will be swiftly answered. I have never thought of them or what they tried to do as evil; if anything, I have felt apologetic, as if I had refused to keep some ancient promise.

The other thing I have wondered about was our improbable escape, and I keep returning to the place Dixie and I were when we were surrounded, the place where opposites meet and live, maybe only fleetingly, but live with an invincible and thorough intensity. I said *no*/Dixie *laughed*. And the confluence of the two, refusal and acceptance, seemed to lift us up above the fray in the sheer and confused glory of our forces.

We told Earl and Randall about it when we got in the

car. Randall was driving. He was so horrified by the gang of men that his driving became increasingly reckless, and finally I had to chat him down with a lame monologue on the Ik of Africa (about whom I had just read for Sociology 1A), how the Ik tribe uses only one language tense, the present, and how it has shaped their entire culture, etc. etc., just to keep Randall focused on the road presently spilling under the front wheels of the car.

Apparently our adventure turned Earl on. I heard him in the back seat with Dixie, talking about football and the samurais of feudal Japan (of which he considered himself to be a modern equivalent), and by the time we got to the Penthouse parking lot, he had unzipped his pants with a kind of proud fury, and freed (for our benefits) what was a most impressive erection. His samurai sword.

Obviously, our dates were drunk.

"You oughta get that taken care of," Dixie giggled.

So was Dixie. Drunk.

On the way up in the elevator, Randall asked Dixie to marry him.

"What should I say, Sue?"

I peered around her at Randall. "Tell him you have promises to keep."

"Did you catch that? Promises."

Randall nodded. I think he had forgotten the question.

When we got home, Dixie gave Earl a "tour" of the apartment which meant, since everything else was immediately visible when one opened the door, a tour of the bedroom, and as far as I know, she took care of his samurai sword, too.

Helping himself to an end of the couch, Randall picked up one of Dixie's photo albums, and began methodically turning its pages. His hair, I noticed, was still as smooth as the fur of a short-haired dog, his tie was straight, his clothes still clean and wrinkle-free: as far as his habiliments were concerned, the evening had not yet transpired. Indeed, I thought, glancing at the tiny, one-way mirrors of his eyes, perhaps Randall had not yet transpired.

At the opposite end of the couch I sat waiting for the tour's conclusion. No longer was the evening flowing uninhibited; it had piled up outside my door and I wanted it to simply go away. No longer did I feel invincible.

Of time and of our respective dates, Randall seemed unaware. But I noted each of fifteen minutes come and go on the clock in the kitchen, the second hand making desolate circumnavigations and the minute hand jerking reluctantly forward.

Reaching the latter pages of the album, Randall tapped a photograph Dixie had recently taken of me. "Gee, you're beautiful," he said, somewhat surprised and glancing from the photo to me, and back, as if he was having trouble reconciling the two, image and reality.

"Gee, thanks," I said, emphasis on the "gee."

Then Earl came out, looking sheepish; not looking at me. And our dates departed.

That night I slept on the couch. I couldn't imagine why.

# 9

On Easter Sunday we started work as hostesses at Sambo's Pancake Paradise. Dixie indeed "knew a guy" at the restaurant but he was the manager, not the owner— a distinction to which she was oblivious—and he didn't call us until a month after we had submitted our applications and résumés (high school graduates, *c'est tout*), and not until that same Easter morning when he himself had received a call from his regular hostess with the probably false news that she was ill and (regrettably) could not perform her duties. I suspect the manager, A. L. Lemucchi, had telephoned a legion of other young women before resorting to us, because there was a clearly unctuous note of desperation in his voice when he asked if we could start immediately, after which he fairly hung up lest we reconsider our reckless assent.

Dixie was delighted: she had been knocking about for something to do. I was dubious, but needed the money.

We were told to wear nice dresses. Excited by the idea of bona fide employment, the first fat oyster of adultdom at last in our grasp, we interpreted the manager's directive to mean, for safety's sake, our best dresses. So at 7:45 a.m. we rustled finery into Dixie's turquoise VW bug (another gifty from Daddy Slade about which I was not a little bit jealous, confined as I was to a three-speed two-wheeler) and chain-smoked throughout the fifteen-minute drive, keeping the windows open to combat the smoke and the heat on to combat the inadequacies of our apparel. Giddy and dizzy, we emerged into the brightly deserted parking lot of Sambo's Pancake Paradise in time to witness a local panhandler urinating against the dumpster behind the restaurant. As he turned around, his sleepiness vanished on the gust of our visual wind. I can only imagine what we must have seemed to him. Angels of death. Fumes and figments wafting up from delirium tremens in the celestial light of Easter, while the stucco walls of pancake paradise rose behind him. (Stucco? . . . *twitches of vague misgiving* . . . )

Dixie was performing some last-minute head-flinging to excite her hair to the Farrah Fawcett ideal, which she had exceeded: it was beyond fluffy, it was explosive, a corona of sunny wanton curls. At this weird ritual the mendicant stared with a kind of puppy-like anxiety, his head cocked, his lips trembling over faded prayers, inappropriate pleas. I stood behind Dixie, a little scared maybe (for he was bad-looking), and self-conscious in my sleeveless blue and dangling silver and insensible heels towering stiffly up from the desolate pavement.

"Hi," chirped Dixie.

His gaze skittered across the parking lot.

From her purse—a satchel really—she removed a bottle of *eau de toilette* and impelled two toxic puffs to inundate her ear lobes, then she leaned forward, tugging at the front of her dress, and sent a veritable cloud blustering into her *décolletage*. "Want some?" she asked me.

"No, thanks."

"You?" Aiming the bottle at the panhandler, she smiled flirtatiously.

I think he meant to shake his head *no*—clearly he did—

moving it to one side, but there his nerve seemed to ossify, and he could not complete the negative swing back.

Dixie shrugged, dropped the bottle in her purse, and as we passed our solitary witness she handed him a wad of bills. "Happy Easter," she winked.

It seemed he might cry.

"I love doing that," she said to me as we strode toward the restaurant.

"What do you mean?"

"Blowing 'em away. He's gonna have a day, and he didn't even know it. A capital D *day*. From no pot to jackpot."

"You know what he'll spend it on," I said, trying to sound world-weary, or at least worldly.

"Thunder Chicken," she giggled.

She was referring to Thunderbird, a fortified wine with the highest allowable alcohol content (21 percent) and the lowest conceivable price tag. We had frequently seen the bird's green glass remains—often broken or crushed as though there had been some deadly skirmish—about the benches in the park downtown where we had lately made a habit of consuming cups of coffee and sweet rolls in order to watch the businessmen heading for their offices, and speculate which might make the most desirable mates.

"And maybe," she was saying, "a Bruce Lee movie, and a one-inch steak, and a bed with sheets. That's what I'd do."

"For Christ's sake, how much did you give him?"

She shrugged. "I don't know." A helpless smile enchanted her face, a smile that for some reason infuriated me, even while in a distant way I felt that just by association, I too shared in the random benevolence of her heart, and the panhandler might regard me with a similar amazed gratitude. On the other hand, he may have simply thought we were the worst sort of fools, despicable but necessary to his wretched survival.

A. L. Lemucchi, the manager and interim host of Sambo's Pancake Paradise, met us at the door. He was lean and moderately tall, with ashen skin and sad little eyes like souvenirs of some poignant event, and down one cheek there was a messy, creased scar. The attitude of the scar, as if he hadn't cared about the injury or its tidy repair, was faintly seductive. He was wearing a short-sleeved white shirt (gone gray), a brown tie, a pair of rust-brown slacks of an unnaturally stretchy fabric, and brown socks burrowing into brown shoes. I never saw him wear anything else.

"Are you . . . ?"

"Susan Thatcher," I said, extending my hand with confidence (though I was not possessed of it), "and this is Dixie Darling," I added as quietly as possible. It was never easy for me to say Dixie's full name, it was so preposterous.

A. L. Lemucchi smiled, and I realized that it was not the name that amused him—which he, of course, had already read on her application—but, quickly glancing around the restaurant at the checkerboard of orange vinyl booths and black vinyl booths (Sambo and the Tigers motif), at the no-nonsence formica, at the centrally located and exposed busing station with its teetering towers of dirty mugs and syrupy plates, its dribbling coffee makers and overfed garbage can, and at a waitress with impressive, no-nonsense calves who barreled past us wearing a white uniform and a wee, paper, Sultan's hat nesting in frowsy hair, taking it all in at one swoop, as it were, I realized that it was our attire, the swish and shine, the fluff and fume, the wild surrealism of our hereness in a paradise of a decidedly lower order.

It was Dixie who had delivered the applications a month before. I could have kicked her for not warning me. There is nothing more small-making that being massively overdressed. But, as I have already mentioned, there was always a lot that Dixie did not say or notice or care about—I honestly don't know which it was. For she was just as overdressed as I. And her hair, the sheer volume of it, a yellow riot screaming for attention, and inside it the blue lights of her eyes twinkled like the nuclei of a double supernova.

After his initial amusement, Manager Lemucchi seemed flattered: we were taking the jobs seriously, his look said, we conferred upon his restaurant the esteem and respect it deserved and that others hitherto had failed to appreciate, we would confer upon its patrons the same, we were young and fresh, we were on time, and we were still smiling at 1:00 when the third post-Easter Mass rush hit us with the ferocity of a tidal wave.

Whole families lined up from our makeshift podium through the glass doors into the vestibule of potted plastic plants and out into the glaring light of the parking lot where children played games between cars, and parents in their Easter pastels listened with mock attentiveness to the grand generation.

Dixie and I worked out a system. She kept the people in line happy, delivering tiger balloons to the younglings, menus to oldsters, and chatting in her soda-pop fashion with the ones who would likely pay for the privilege of Easter brunch at Sambo's Pancake Paradise. (I suspected that many of the guests had tried other, more elegant restaurants whose lines were even longer, and had had to make a hasty and relatively crude port at Sambo's.)

It was my job to determine which tables would soon be available, alert the busboys and, once they had cleared and re-set the tables, call out the name of the winning party and show them with masterful grace and fluidity to their table. Once I'd got the hang of it, the whole thing was awfully fun, I must say. I began to behave as if it was *my* restaurant, *my* party, as I ushered across the checker-board *my* guests and saw to their first needs—coffee—before signaling to the waitress to tend to their subsequent desires.

Some of the waitresses, as the day whirled on, became downright rude. "Cut with the hand signs, will ya? I know when I got a table, I got eyes." Her name was Pearl, though she was not.

"I was trying to help."

"Yeah, well, this ain't the Ritz," staring significantly at my dress, "and you ain't my mother."

Honestly I couldn't imagine her with a mother; it was like trying to imagine a suckling pit bull.

She shoved a sticky stack of plates at me, and I was obliged to leave my post for the kitchen to deliver them. At that point, the overwhelming crockery in the busing station seemed to have induced a kind of gridlock, and the station had simply been abandoned.

"Forget Pearl," another waitress whispered. Her name was Toni, and she was young and dismally unattractive—stocky, horse-faced, a stricken quality about the eyes. I wished she'd been pretty if only for the sake of her kind-ness. "Pearl's a lifer. Even Lemucchi don't mess with her. We let her have all the eighty-sixes, that's the only time she's happy. When she gets to eighty-six some poor sucker." We were standing behind the counter, but Toni was picking up an order while she talked, and the loaded plates had mounted up her left arm, the stacks of pan-cakes ascending too, like columns to a temple of the ed-ible, and then she scooped four balls of whipped butter onto each plate, dispersed some tired parsley—it didn't

156

seem to matter where the sprigs lit—filled two juice glasses, checked the tag and shoved it into her pocket, picked up the glasses, made a huffty-puffty face, and said, "I'd better shuffle and deal," and was gone before I could find out what form of sadism an "eighty-six" was.

In the kitchen I discovered that the plates had left egg and syrup deposits on my front. I must have been feeling a bit frazzled by then, because I think I almost cried: it was my best dress, my first job. My feet were killing me. And here came Mr. Lemucchi from the dishwashing station, in a hurry. (He was always in a hurry, even when it might have been nicer all around if he hadn't been in a hurry.)

"Problem?"

I pulled at the front of my dress.

He led me back to the employees' room, to a bottle of liquid spot remover.

"I can do it," I said, knowing how busy he was, knowing my nadiral place in the pecking order (even lower than busboys, I learned, who, if they were helpful, obsequious, eager to be terrorized by the fairer sex, at least received a percentage of the waitresses' tips).

"It's industrial stuff," Lemucchi said. "There's a knack to it, so you don't hurt the fabric."

"All right," I said, believing him.

And kneeling before me, dishwashing fumes rising up from his brown curls, and not looking at my face as he dabbed at the egg, he said, "The dress is very pretty." His wedding band, I noticed, was too tight. His hand, the huddled back of it, kept accidentally brushing the inward declension of my right breast.

For some reason I was having difficulty getting a clear shot at some air to breathe, though I did manage by snatches the minimum requirement and was able to sputter an appropriate response to my especially considerate first boss. "We weren't sure what you meant. You said to wear something nice."

He smiled and kept dabbing and kept accidentally brushing my breathless breast, and soon enough expunged Pearl's nastiness from my blue and fortuitously pretty dress. I'd seen him taking meals to tables, and ringing up checks, and even mopping up a flooded toilet: in reality, it seemed he had the all-around worst job in Paradise.

"There. Now you can use the hand dryer in the ladies' room and you'll be good as new."

"Dixie's alone."

He was trying to twist his wedding band, but it was still too tight. "I'll check on her."

In the ladies' room my dress and I recovered, though the former took considerably less time than the latter which could not simply be subjected to a hand dryer.

When I got back to the podium, Dixie was gone, Lemucchi was wiping off menus, and the line was half as long.

"Where is she?" I asked with some alarm.

He lifted his chin toward the parking lot, and it wasn't anger but amusement that revitalized his souvenir eyes.

I found her around the corner of the building, giving the panhandler a stern talking-to. He had come back, he had been working the line on Easter Sunday. It was probably why he was there waiting in the first place, to cash in on Christian benevolence when victims were most susceptible, the biblical words fresh.

"Ah, go fuck yourself, lady," I heard him say as he shuffled off.

Dixie turned, came toward me, her expression caged. "I don't get it," I said. "*You* gave him money."

"That was different. He didn't ask. He shouldn't be asking, that's all."

"He's a beggar, it's what he does. It's like a job." Why

was I defending him?

"Naw. Asking wrecks it. It's sposed to just *come.*" She stopped to adjust her dress, then she flicked her head haughtily and gave me what seemed an artificial (and so, for Dixie, totally out of character) look of nonchalance. "Anywho," she said, "I gave him enough."

"For what? A few days maybe? He was only planning ahead. Saving for the future. He's got one too, you know, a future."

"A future? No such beastie."

It struck me as sad, what she said, though I wasn't sure what she meant. I wondered if it had to do with her mother's death, or if it was only a symptom of the immediacy that sprang from Dixie with the suddenness of an idea that would not ever be examined. That infinitesimal event—of the beggar beyond the walls of paradise and Dixie's two, opposing responses—became in my mind one of those contradictions that from time to time afflict humankind, and in a queer sort of way end up describing it too. For Dixie it was just this sort of contradiction, though of a more weighty cast, that was to account for her, and, finally, to bring about her ruin. At times, Dixie seemed less a person than a philosophy, defiantly reigning, and very much alive, oh yes, there could be no doubting *that.* She was an anarchist, a solo revolution incarnate, a deviant, a tacit devotee of absolute naturalism, and simultaneously the greatest pretender I have ever known, an illusionist, a mirage on the mind's horizon. *Fata Morgana,* close your eyes and hope for the best.

We finished out the shift in good order, and by the time we were wiping off the last of the menus, Dixie was calling A. L. Lemucchi "Al" despite gentle corrections from himself: he finally gave up. (I never did learn what the "A. L." stood for, though, as it turned out, I of all people ought to have been privy to that.)

It was 3:30. I felt tired but exhilarated too. We had done it. Customers had thinned to a few regulars drinking bottomless cups of coffee at the counter, and a dozen or so stragglers in the booths against the windows. The overflow back room had been cleared, and now waitresses going off shift were seated at a big round top, counting up their tips in columns of silver, smoothing out the ones, the lucky fivers, and cashing in for the more meaningful compact bills. Gossiping, laughing, their wee sultan's hats nodding at silly angles, their treasures bountiful, the camaraderie of the scene was infectious, and to Dixie, irresistible. She made us a couple of iced coffees, and we sat down with them for awhile. Dixie had a way of simply including herself which could sometimes embarrass me, but the waitresses were so pleased with the money they'd made and with the hectic shift being over that it seemed okay.

While Dixie was inquiring about the "hunk" in the end booth—was he a regular, did he always wear those "tray sexy" sunglasses—I asked Toni how much she'd made.

One waitress stood up. Another made a roll of her bills and stuffed it into her uniform pocket. Toni said, as nicely as possible: "Get yourself another iced coffee, Sue. You look tired." Thus I learned the first rule of the Amazons in Sambo's Paradise. It seemed about the same as asking how far each of them had gone with the same man.

Naturally, Dixie would never have asked: she didn't care a dot about that sort of thing—money or comparisons, measures of success.

We gathered ourselves to leave. The manager said he'd try to work us into the regular hostess shifts.

"Mr. Lemucchi," I began.

"Al," he said, and actually laughed.

"Al. If you foresee any openings for waitresses, we'd

be very interested. I don't think we would disappoint you or the fine tradition of Sambo's Pancake Paradise."

He smiled.

I tried not to notice his scar.

"A breakfast shift would be best. You see, I'm putting myself through college," I added, in order to make our cause worthy. I already knew Dixie wanted to waitress, but I hoped she wouldn't say why: it was the uniform, "the white uniform with the darling little hats," was how she put it at some point that day. For me it was the money. Only the money.

"Sue's a brain," Dixie said. "She's got a future. It's all in her brain." She squeezed the back of my neck which annoyed me, since as far as she was concerned there was "no such beastie" as a future.

"I'll see what I can do," Lemucchi said, peering into my eyes and behind, it seemed, as if indeed to see this future I possessed back there in the recesses, waiting for me to simply step into it, like some tailor-made suit of the finest wool.

Then especially I was grateful for his scar: in its bold ugliness it seemed to forgive us our flaws, our pretensions, our dreams for unequivocal success. It seemed to ask us to fail, if only for the camaraderie of the human condition.

We smoked all the way back to the apartment. There were a lot of people out, walking dogs, working off Easter meals, easing back into normality—probably with relief. A sheet of pale thin clouds had drawn in from the west, the Easter blue was washed out, here and there the wind turned a page of newspaper or stirred a clot of old leaves. Smoke twisted from chimneys, while in the distance silvery new high rises and broad, squat, brick buildings worn with age seemed to wait expectantly for Monday to come rcund again. San Jose was just beginning to emerge from its ragtag chrysalis, and it was plain what it had been and what it might be. And I remember feeling a part of it, of the change coming and of the leaving behind, too, as we putt-putted along the holiday streets in Dixie's turquoise VW, the windows open to the cooling air, the cigarette searing, and best for that. And Dixie and I debating—without really caring who was right—about the ingredients in a piña colada which we were going to make—a whole pitcher—as soon as we got home.

Within the week we had waitress jobs. Dixie took the graveyard shift—she actually wanted it—and I had an early-morning schedule which left my afternoons free for classes and my evenings for homework. As employees of Sambo's, we were required to join the union which I took very seriously, regarding it as naturally coincident with my new working-class status in my new life. One day, in fact, I encountered a former St. Agatha's student emerging, arms laden with purchases, from *I. Magnin* in whose windows I had been gazing with wan nostalgia; after a cursory inspection of my grease-stained uniform, she asked, "Didn't you go to St. Agatha's?"

"St. Who?" I replied, inspecting *her*. "Who's got time for saints."

The uniforms were provided by Sambo's, but we were supposed to buy our own white shoes. I was hoping for the first time to make up my share of the rent, all of which Dixie hitherto had been paying with her inheritance, and maybe even pitch in on the food costs, so the thought of having to buy white shoes in order to work in order to make the money was practically devastating. I couldn't ask mother. She was still too mad at me, and anyway, her purist attitude was prohibitive: if I wanted to live on my own, I would have to make it on my own. And I wouldn't ask father, because I was (probably) still too mad at him; plus, he'd've shorted mother to help me and since I silently agreed with her about making it on my own, it would have been morally intolerable for me to accept his help. So, for the first several days, I rode my bike to Sambo's early enough to catch Dixie just going off shift and, feigning that I had forgotten my uniform shoes, I borrowed hers for my shift. But she was a half size smaller than I, and it wasn't long before a purplish stain spread beneath the nail of my left big toe which was jammed up tight against the end of the shoe. (My left foot was larger than my right.) Lemucchi kept asking me why I was limping and, in spite of the authenticity of my complaint (which I kept under wraps), I found his solicitous souvenir eyes a pleasant side benefit.

Not surprisingly, Dixie always made more in tips, *always*, even when it was slow. I can still see her those mornings when I arrived early and sat drinking coffee and eating my one-free-meal-per-shift at the counter, or when on occasion we picked up an extra shift and worked together, I can still remember her swinging from around the counter with her arms full and her hat perfect, an attitude of cheery anticipation as she traipsed off to deliver meals, as though they were gifts, long-fancied, from her to the world. She was utterly unflappable, thoroughly in her element as a waitress, and yet there were so many circumstances in which Dixie seemed a natural. And I can still remember me, fleeing behind the kitchen doors to sob between orders, because I hadn't gotten the juice to table 12 before the omelettes, or because the guy on 33 had stuck out his foot as I passed to get my attention and I had dropped a mug, or because I couldn't seem to get to the deuce by the back door and they were being so patient and I had sacrificed them to the crankier tables in my station and was feeling horribly guilty. In waitressing, perfection is not something to be achieved In Time With Effort. It is a willingness to give oneself over to a fundamentally reactive and timeless state. It requires a fluid percipience, an ability to sense the whole which is in flux while responding to distinct and express parts, all soluble, suspended in the mind. Being a good waitress has nothing to do with order, or even efficiency. In the world of one's station, it is the equivalent of a sort of omnipotence. I don't know how Dixie did it. I used to see her in the back room, having a quick cigarette, her eyes rolled up as she mentally reviewed the tables within her charge. "Happy, happy, happy, happy," she'd say. Or maybe, "Happy, happy, refill, happy, check, happy," and then she'd sit down and let the cigarette loll between her lips and, squinting through smoke and blue mascara, add up a ticket or two.

After Dixie's first four shifts she had already had dates with two men: a short fat older fellow with a lot of money and an eager face, too eager I thought, faintly false, and a Chicano youth who *never* spoke and with whom she had sex in the bed next to mine while I was napping. I was wearing a mask. It was in the afternoon. It was awkward, to put it blandly. I didn't want them to know I was awake, and yet I wanted to get up and leave. The sound of the scene was, well, it was just *too much*; I seemed not to hear it but to feel it *twinging and twanging* in the darkest inland of muscles. And though I did try not to peek, truly it was impossible not to catch a glimpse now and then, just under the right edge of my eye mask, of her loose lace bra, puckered berries seeing through, of his face imparadised between her milken silken legs, his black hair brushing the pink hillock of her belly. When they had finished and the Chicano had gone into the bathroom, Dixie appeared beside me, brought her lips to my ear and, in a post-sex voice, like a still-hot liquid in which my face was being poached, she said, "Peekaboo."

Why? *Why?* Was she taunting me? Was she including me? Was their secret ours? Was I *supposed* to feel, well, quickened, or tactfully immune? Or impressed? Amused? Shocked? Disgusted? *Rien?* I couldn't fathom her, I hadn't the least idea what she was about, and I didn't possess and it seemed would never possess the right tool that might pry open the treasure chest that held the Meaning of Dixie.

Of course I pretended to sleep on, poached face, twanging muscles, and all.

Of course she knew I was not sleeping.

After *my* first four shifts I had saved $13.75 in tips. We weren't to be paid salary until the end of our second week's work. My toenail having by now heaved up, suitable white shoes seemed a medical necessity: I had begun to horrify myself with visions of podiatry bills, collection agents badly in need of manners and a shave. About a mile from the apartment was a discount clothing store which I passed on my way to class, and on the afternoon of my fourth bout with employment, after soaking my foot in warm salt water to no avail—it was still throbbing—I gathered up my tips and limped into the store. Maybe I'd find something in the seconds bin.

But there was nothing in my size. I summoned a clerk to fetch some examples from the regular stock, even though I knew I couldn't afford to buy them. Maybe it was because I was already there in the store, or because I needed them so, or maybe it was simply a function of the old habit of having. Or maybe I was only pretending for the clerk's sake.

He seemed a dependable young man, his gait unhurried yet determined, as if he knew what to do though what there was to do was still relatively new to him, and his features had a fine, resilient quality, and he was wearing a handsome blue blazer—obviously not purchased from the store in which he worked—and I liked the feel of his hand curling round my instep as he slipped on each of the white shoes, and, too, the feel of the memory it reawakened, the memory of Dixie's quiet Chicano and his not-quiet hands as they curled round the inside of her prodigal thighs toward the plumpened little bounty they offered. His name tag said "Clark." We seemed to be the only two people in the store. Holding my foot with the greatest care, he sat before me, below me, and asked tenderly, "How do they feel?"

Standing, I ventured a few steps. They felt wonderful, they had been created for my feet alone, hugged them with just the right pressure, an equable warmth, stable, dependable, yet soft too, I thought, gazing at the young man. "The length is good . . . but I'm afraid they're a little snug."

A look of deep concern. Undaunted, he disappeared behind the curtain, reappeared, breathless, with three more boxes. And three more times we enacted our poignant playlet until at the end it seemed we had become a kind of *tableau vivant*: Clark the clerk, dazed and heartbroken, kneeling before me, open boxes strewn about, their perfectly lovely contents rejected, and I, the young woman, sitting above, anguished to the quick because I could not give to him and could not tell him why, it was all a selfish ruse, could never have given him what he wanted—a sale.

Some customers drifted in.

Clerk Clark rose, gave me a keen, beseeching look of apology, and then he wheeled off toward the mundane.

I limped into the clothing department, hating myself, hating my poverty, and sensing too a familiarity about it, like the deep reverberations of the bass felt before it is heard if it is heard at all; sensing another sort of poverty, a poverty of spirit, and wanting desperately to shut out the hollow feel of it and the low down rasping sound of it before it undid me altogether.

Deliberately, calmly, I watched myself select items—a pretty cotton skirt, some bras, a pair of gabardine slacks, two silk blouses—and actually take them into a dressing room. I spent a long time trying things on, looking at my body with other eyes, Clark's eyes, going out twice for more clothes, different sizes, as if I was really going to purchase something—a spring outfit perhaps, something that might please the boyfriend I didn't have. And would never have, it seemed. Then, beaming casually in Clerk Clark's direction, I watched as I returned every item to its original rack. Except a bra. One bra. I didn't even need a bra. The bra. A pretty pink lace bra. Sort of like Dixie's. Which apparently I had stuffed in my pants and with which I exited, not-hurrying-but-hurrying out to my bike.

The policeman kept disappearing with Clark who turned out to be some sort of para-manager, taking the entrustment very seriously, as ill luck would have it. I could hear them through the open office door. The policeman tried to persuade the para-manager not to press shoplifting charges. The policeman had been moved by my tears, my apology, my youth (I was technically an adult, which was bad), my distress over prospective scholarships that would be imperiled by my having a RECORD, and perhaps by my hand, my soft, susceptible female hand trembling on the professionally-ironed cuff of his profession.

"Please help me," I said, as they emerged.

"*Give the kid a break*," he said.

"It's my first time," I said.

"*It's her first time*," he said.

"*Store policy*," said the para-manager. "*Prosecute all*

*shoplifters."*
"I'll pay."
*"She'll pay for it."*
*"No dice."*
Tears and trembling.
*"Ah, come on. She's all broken up. Whadya want from her? She's just a kid, she's on a bike, fer Criminy's sake, she's on her own, so she slipped over the line once, so we all have. Cut her some slack."*
*"No way."*
"What does he want?"
*"Whadya want from her?"*
Then, only then, did Clerk Clark cast his eyes upon the diminished me, his mouth twisting into an angry grimace. *"All those shoes . . ."* he said hoarsely.
And I knew there would be no forgiveness.
I told Dixie everything. Dixie never asked me why— why I did it, why the bra, why anything. What would I have told her, anyway? *Perversity, Dixie, it was out and out perversity.* She would've said, *No such beastie,* or something to that flippant effect. Or, borrowing a psychiatric vernacularism, I might have tried this: *I was merely acting-out, Dixie, improperly registering a legitimate complaint about the state of my life by means of a totally gratuitous, meaningless and, most importantly, unconnected act so as to conceal from myself the real object of the complaint—against which I am powerless—as well as the pain it causes me.* Dixie: *Huh?* Or I might have simply resorted to: *I took the bra because I didn't have the money for a bra and though a pair of uniform shoes was what I needed, what I wanted was a bra like yours and a boyfriend like yours so that I could have sex like yours.* Probably this last would have been the only explanation both of us could have understood in any real sense of the word.

A pair of uniform white shoes in my size, along with the actual bra I had tried to steal, appeared that fateful and very evening, placed at the foot of my bed, an offering to the human-all-too-human corpse of the formerly flawless S. Thatcher. Even my sub-clinical obsessive-compulsive traits did not flare: I suppose my subconscious considered me a hopeless cause.

Three weeks later I had to appear in court. Dixie drove me over, and I asked her not to come in with me, partly because I wanted to spare her this particular public association with me—I was finding that I *really* did like Dixie, I really did—and partly because for some reason I thought the judge might be less sympathetic, or that I might appear less pitiful, less in need of his mercy, with Dixie Darling's ever cheerful dazzle, like a guardian consolation, seated beside me. I left her in the VW with the newest issue of *Vogue* and a pineapple milkshake, filing her nails.

With the drunk drivers and barroom brawlers and child neglecters and repeat recidivists and car thieves and the appallingly occasional lawyer, I sat waiting my turn wearing my best blue dress and trying not to look to the left or to the right along the long cold courtroom pew of my unholy new life. When, two hours later, my turn came, I instructed the noodles that were my legs to stretch upward and, clinging to the pew in front, tried to respond to the Judge's queries. But the eyes of everyone in the room combined to create a heat wave of atomic proportions, a 360-degree searing heat wave, and I was its nucleus melting down. Crying was something people did; I, I was boiling over, I was molten, I was the very beat and blood of unstoppable, unbearable shame, I was emoting in the purest sense of the verb, and without *any* fear of *any* successful subdual, without any presentiment that there would be an end to it. It was the first time I could palpably feel Eternity.

The Judge—strong voice, a lax fatherly face, small wen near his temple, touchingly hideous—kept peering down at my case report which was too brief to require such attention, then he would steal a hopeful glance at me, try to ask questions, each one diminishing in volume, and flee back to the report. Somewhere on the far side of the heat wave, on the far side of Eternity, laughter began.

Sighing dismally, the Judge surveyed the courtroom, crowded with real criminals, and handed off my case report to his assistant. "At any rate," he said, now not looking at me at all, "you seem very sorry for what you . . . for what happened," he snapped. "Ninety-dollar fine. Probation unnecessary." This said sharply, in form. Then, shaken, sickened, he muttered, "Get her out of here."

When we returned to the apartment Dixie made us a couple of Irish coffees—a new favorite—and I spent the rest of the afternoon with her, getting drunk and watching her soap operas (instead of studying), just to convey my gratitude for her support, even though in some back room of the brain where decisions of a quiet, vulgarly truthful (not necessarily factual) sort are made, I considered Dixie Darling liable. For what happened. For everything.

# 10

Since the crime, I noticed that Dixie in her quiet, cavalier fashion became more involved with me, maybe over-involved. She offered advice on my clothing and my hair, and persuaded me to wear make-up. Whenever I came home from work or class, she inquired about my activities, people I'd met, and such. She took me to lunch every sunny Saturday at an outdoor restaurant on the coast, with a live band and cool, foamy drinks, Skip's-on-the-Sand, it was called—very *au courant*—and while I resisted, she insisted, and I was glad for that. For each of us she bought a pair of straw flip-flops with velvet trim which were all the rage, and we wore them, along with identical tank tops and blue overalls to a rock concert at Kezar Stadium in San Francisco, and when we got home we had identical sunburns. I can recall standing with her before the bathroom mirror, the bibs of our overalls hanging upside down, tank tops and bras off, and comparing (with coy pride) the ruddled and synonymously meandering outlines of our dual dueling breasts. It was at such times I felt acutely the unmitigated femaleness between us, which I found to be a comforting sort of oppression.

One day our high school diplomas arrived, along with (in my case) achievement award certificates etc., and an official letter of congratulations from St. Agatha's announcing that I had graduated second in my class. I tossed all of them, still punishing myself for my shabby and inexplicable crime. But in my absence Dixie retrieved from the trash all the parchments of praise, and had them framed in one of those multi-picture mattes, then she hung the thing over the couch where no one could possibly miss it. It was strangely embarrassing. Our relationship, it seemed, had taken on some of the characteristics of a marriage.

"Well," I said (not knowing what to say), "It's like a little shrine." I had just come home from work.

"It's to perk you up." she said, and added, "when you need it," without looking at me. She was referring to my dark days, days when just the thought of having to speak was almost too much to bear, as though I feared it would have used up the last of a thing reserved for basic sustenance. While at the outset of our tandem journey it had been pleasant to think of the total control I would possess over my activities, my friends, the establishment of an equable routine, now it had begun to seem that there was no control, that I was being swept along, at times swept beneath the very crosscurrents of life. Dixie, too, I suppose, though by all outward appearances, the sweeping along, the currents, the chaos, didn't bother her; indeed, she seemed to delight in it, like an otter frolicking in waves.

I made appreciative noises before the shrine. Though I doubted these emblems of past glory would relieve the present void, I told Dixie it was a sweet thing to do—which it was—and I meant it.

"Anytime," she said with her airy, summery, blond hair cheer.

Still in her robe (for she had slept all morning after her graveyard shift), she was sprawled on the carpet, playing solitaire backgammon. In the heavy amber ashtray a new cigarette sent up a brief clean line, then it seemed to hesitate a half space before corkscrewing into the glittering cottage-cheese sky of our alleged penthouse. Her matchbook collection which she kept in a fish bowl on the floor of the entry cubicle was next to her, and I supposed she had been making additions to it. From the TV I recognized the familiar organ histrionics, the comely, clumsy *tragedians* of daytime operas stumbling into each other's lines, into each other's arms.

Suddenly I felt an uncommon sadness for Dixie.

She gestured toward the backgammon board. "You wanna play?"

"No, I'll never get it. I'm not good at games."

"You try," she said.

"Of course I try."

"No, I mean you shouldn't," she said, dragging on her cigarette. "You have to not think *at* it, you know, you have to be, like, sideways to it, pretend *for sure* that it's not there so that it's not there at all, and let it come curling around you and sneak in. Then," she opened her palms, "there it'll be."

I laughed, I laughed too loudly. "What is *it?*"

"Whatever," she said, a fay squint through smoke, a slanted smile. "Whatever you like."

"You should write some of this stuff down Dixie, your philosophy. It's definitely one of a kind."

"Write it down?" she said, incredulous, and staring in a glazed-over way at the end of her cigarette. "Break it into itty-bitty pieces so they could all eat me up in itty-bitty bites? That wouldn't be *tray sporteef.*"

Shaking my head, I went into the kitchen, poured a cup of coffee, found the bowl of whipped cream Dixie always kept on hand, plopped a white mound into my cup, and took a couple of deceptively searing sips.

Dixie was reaching into the pocket of her robe. "Got another notelet for you."

"From Toni?"

"There you go."

I didn't move.

"Come and get it," she said flirtatiously.

Nervous smile. "I don't think I want to." But I came toward her, feeling obscurely guilty.

"What're you *skeered* of?"

"Let me bum a cigarette."

She lit one, then handed it to me filter first, along with the note, and I kicked off my uniform shoes and sat down on the couch.

"Read it aloud." No smile now. Taut voice. Blue ice eyes.

> *Howdy Lady, How are you doing? I'm sorry I couldn't stay around for your shift this morning, but Dixie said really that you didn't want company.*

Here I paused to look at Dixie. She was moving the backgammon pieces about, silently, aimlessly. I went on.

> *I often wonder if I distort my image of "I want" with "I need." I want people to love me and want me and show it but then is it really that I want them to be that way or is it that "I need" this from people. This I guess is an insecurity but I have human needs to [sic] and this is perhaps my greatest. I think everybody is like this but only few are free to admit it truly. I feel independent to people themselves but I feel somewhat dependent on their emotional responses to me if that makes any sense. I know what I mean anyhow.*

*I want you to come to me and I need the emotional satisfaction you fulfill me with. You can't satisfy me all the time no-one [sic] does no-one ever will and I don't expect this from anyone it would be far-out but I think we are incapapble [sic] of achieving this. Not really incapapble as much as non-knowledgeable as how to achieve this. I sense in you so much warmth and sensiveness [sic] Lady I did the day you started at Sambo's when you came to me because Pearl's such a crusher. You are beautiful and if you would only put some of it out it would be far-out. I need for you again to come to me. I wish and pray for you so much happiness and love in the adventure of your life ahead of you and the curiousitys [sic] within you.*

*I switched with Holly so I'm on with you tomorrow and it would be totally so far-out if we could talk. You are really special Lady. Believe me. If you can't believe my words feel my feelings.*

It was signed, *Your buddy, Toni*

I could not believe much less understand her words, and as for the *feelings*, they practically made my skin crawl. I couldn't begin to address the syntax. A generous peppering of commas might have alleviated symptoms (while not even approaching the ailment itself), for there was also a breathless quality, as of a child making an otherwise simple appeal with a handful of newly acquired, experimental words which were lamentably so oblique to the real issue that the real issue remained clouded. It was all gibberish—mangled, homegrown philosophy, mawkish sentiments overdressed in misused, multisyllabic misspellings all for the dazzling of an audience which expressly was me. And the unprotected, the *unashamed* candor of the thing . . . god help me. All for naught. All gibberish. And yet, *and yet* I sensed some singular, un-named, (perhaps even familiar) potency ordering our fel-low worker's pouring forth, and I was (in my distant way) touched, though loath to admit it in company with Dixie. I had, in fact, saved all of Toni's previous notes. I really don't know why. Maybe for all those feelings, whatever they were, the purity of them.

My hand with the note had dropped.

Dixie said, "Far-out," her voice as toneless as stone.

"I don't get it."

"Which part didn't you get?"

"All parts," I said. "All of it, and all the notes before. What *is* this?" I said, shaking the pathetic thing.

"Look at it sideways."

"Shit," I said (swearing having become what I consid-ered to be one of the many intrinsic coefficients of my plebification), "say something straight for a change."

"Okeydokey," she said. Then rising (and suspending me), she began putting things away—the fish bowl with the matchbook collection, the backgammon set, the ash-tray which, courteously, she brought over to me—then she went into the kitchen, poured herself some more cof-fee along with a dollop of Irish whiskey (it was just 1:00), and a dollop of whipped cream, and leaned over the bar toward me. "Toni isn't."

"Isn't?"

"Straight."

Silence. Silence because I wanted to hear Dixie say it, I wanted to hear the details, the explanations in Dixie's inimitable, keynote, offbeat way; because I was ready to be flattered by it, annoyed by it, amused by it. I was ready to be aggrandized. In front of Dixie—somehow that was important.

So Dixie tried again. "Toni's in l.u.v. With you."

"No."

"Because you're so nice to her."

"I try to be," I murmured, "to everyone."

She drew in one corner of her mouth and tossed her head. "Yeah, you're nice to her 'cause she's got bruises for eyes, and she's dumb and u-gly and she's oh-so-grateful just to sniff around after you, telling herself that she's *helping*, and you let her think that she is, you shine her on 'cause she's no threat and she's there like a stray dog."

I stared at the carpet, throat painfully knotted, tears welling, subsiding. It was the first time Dixie had hurt me, and it was clear that she had meant to. "What does any of that have to do with love?" I said helplessly.

"Nothing."

"You said she loved me, that, that that's what these notes mean."

"Yeah, well, look at her. What kinda selection you think she's got? Zippo. And look at you, how you look, and you know what else she sees, she sees guys hitting on you all the time, *on the breakfast shift* when that's supposed to be the last thing in anyone's head, and Lemucchi letting you go without stockings 'cause you *don't like stockings . . .*" this last singsonged, "but your legs are *so* brown and *so* smooth no one can tell, not even the health department so he says hunky-fine. But the most main thing she sees, your buddy Toni, and this is the part that must've grooved like a neon sign from The Man who made the signs in the first place, this is the part where the sky busts open and Barbie, *you*, come riding down on one of those rays of hope, 'cause what she *sees, Susan,* is you *nixing* all these guys with their shadows throbbing around you. And she thinks, Do my eyes reveal me, 'cause what else can she think? Huh?"

"I don't know."

"What else can Toni, stubby ugly Toni think when all she probably ever wanted was one guy with a dingdong to ring her bell *once*, and she thinks it'll never happen. And there you are, telling all the dingdongs to peal off." Turning away from me, affecting a solemn archness, Dixie reached the pith and pitch of her argument. "She thinks you prefer women."

"Oh Dixie," I cried. "Dixie, but I don't."

She left a moment, came back with a box of tissue, pushing it toward me, then she sat down beside me on the couch. "Naw, you don't," she said, stroking my hair, but her voice seemed to pull away from me, like a train whistle receding into the belly of a black night.

I thought the conversation might be over, and for some murky reason I didn't want it to be over, so I said, "I'd like to meet a nice guy, somebody I could think of loving, but not waitressing, not just anywhere. Somebody I could really think of . . ."

"*Think* of love?" Shaking her head, she rose and went to the stereo, fiddled with the knobs, picked a book from the shelves below, fanned its pages, replaced it, came back toward me and, it seemed, changed her mind and took a seat in a chair sideways to the couch. Away from me. "*Think?*" she repeated. "It's something that's just there, you know, and when you dip your mug in, it comes up full, maybe if you're lucky spilling over. Or it comes up empty. Or maybe there's only a little swill in the bottom, maybe just the spit-end of something mostly used up but you want it anyway 'cause you're thirsty for that *particular* swill and you'll take what you can get of it. Or maybe, like I said, there's nothing there, not a drop. But whatever, you can't *think* it into your mug, it doesn't know how to think, it's way past *that*. It only knows how to be." She inhaled, dispatching four perfect smoke rings which we both watched with keen attention until the last dispersed. "Anywho," she said, "what's the sin in meeting a guy on the job?"

"I don't know, it seems so, so precarious. It seems that it would just have to be, by definition, impermanent. And I would want something permanent, something to count on, not like, like . . ."

"Like me."

"I didn't mean to imply. . ."

"Forget it. I *comprende* what you're saying."

"No, you don't," I said, scrambling. "I was going to say like my dad, that's what I meant."

"Naw, you were talking about the guys I meet at Sambo's, the ones I date."

Giving up, and still feeling stung, I said, "Yes, indiscriminately."

"All righty, yeah, indifferently."

Sighing, I dropped my eyes. What did it matter? Both words worked.

"You know what I think?" she said.

"Actually, Dixie, I *don't* know what you think, I never know what you think, because I'm too busy thinking myself, it's what I do, is think about . . . I don't know," I snapped, "whatever *you're* doing when you're not thinking, I think about that, among all the far more interesting things in the world to think about and worth thinking about, I think about the fact that you *don't* think." Quietly, I added, "And I do. Which is maybe why I don't." *Fragments of dementia*, I thought.

For the longest minute neither of us spoke. We might have been waiting for the *fragmentia* of my explosion to sift and settle out and collect in the shoals of the gold sea carpet surrounding us. We might have been waiting for the sun to blink and shine again. But we were not. We were not waiting for anything because it was all there, inside us, between us, around us, like a swift liquid flowing clear and carrying us toward some place neither of us had been before.

"Yeah, all that," she said, "all that thinking that stops doing. You're afraid you might like it, and then if you do you're afraid you can't hang on to it, and if you can't hang on to it, then it's no good. And then, and *then* you feel real dumb just for liking it in the first place. For letting yourself."

"Once again, Dixie," I said in a positively Arctic voice, (because she was right), "you've lost your referent, if you ever possessed one."

"You got it wrong, kiddo. I find stuff, I find stuff anywheres. And I haven't lost one itsy thing."

"Your virginity, let's not forget that, though it's been awhile since you had it, and understandably, you may have forgotten."

Silence and a Cheshire smile; the rest of her seemed to have vanished.

"How many guys *have* you fucked?" Erupted words, like pressurized steam from an undetected crack in my reality, and I heard alarms clanging inside the boney cavern of my head.

She made as if to tally a pleasant batch of data, her eyes gazing up to her left, agreeably cogitative, her breath coming slow and languorously, as if at that moment she reposed, smoldering, *déshabillé*, in the very arms of memory. Now giggling, now striking a pouty face, here wonder, mock ire, now dropping her lids to half-mast and lifting one shoulder as if to nuzzle seductively the numbered memory at which she had arrived, now a string of satisfied smiles broken by a childlike frown, satisfied smiles resuming—all in remembrance of things past. The tally apparently complete, she leveled a pair of blank eyes at me. (No, not *blank*, I rescind that word. They were deeply *admissive*, as if anything, anyone might enter and disappear in those violet-blue pools, even light, even the darkness, and never again to surface as its particular self, as its known self, but to mingle indiscriminately, to confound light with dark so that light was dark and dark was light, and all that had fallen in the pools and all that was to fall in the pools would be the same and one, and would be that only by entering, by confounding, by dispersing.) So it was those eyes, those beckoning pools into which I gazed, mesmerized, as she said, "Fifty? Give or take. Can you get next to fifty?" No embarrassment, maybe a dash of pride, the merest mist of a challenge—I didn't know, it was so hard to read her at that moment. In fact, it almost seemed she was waiting to see what *I* thought, in order as it were to *acquire* the proper, *de rigueur* disposition to this amazing statistic.

Carefully, like the victim of an accident, I stood and took myself to the balcony door, gazed down into the swimming pool with its pale lifeless bottom and its chlorinated solution of human detritus—lost Band-Aids, tiny drift nets of hair, exfoliated skin, peeled scabs, child urine—so utterly unlike the vital and mercurial blue pools of Dixie's eyes; gazed out over the checkered parking lot, and beyond to the west hills that were overqualified yet definitely not mountains. I could see cows grazing, but the distance between them and me was so great that they had turned into statues, and I supposed if they could think, if they could see, they would regard me as similarly static. With sudden urgency, I slid open the door to smell the outside, the cool, clean, simple, predictable, undemanding air that the cows were smelling and breathing and living, the air outside the twilight cave-in of our interior world. The accumulated smoke in the apartment began to swirl past me and out, and I experienced one of those strange instantaneous fantasies in which I was the young heroine caught between a burning apartment and a terrible leap of faith, except there was no one waiting below to catch me, just a tall anonymous man I couldn't possibly trust, so the only way out was back through the fire. Through Dixie. I don't know how I felt: panicked, in over my head, defeated. Then, as if I had popped unexpectedly out the end of something, I felt myself to be within—that is, *entirely present for*—a moment of being from which I knew with surprising lucidity I could not shrink. What I said was: "Let's assume that figure is accurate. Fifty. You've been in bed with fifty men. You've had sex with fifty men in a bed." I turned so she could see me. "I've had sex with fifty men in my head. Maybe there isn't much difference. One of us, though, seems a whit happier than the other."

Leaning back, eyes softly casting over, she pulled on her cigarette. "You know what your problem is, Sue, your problem is you don't have any respect for Fun. You think it has no future, and you're into the future big time."

Probably I nodded. I was feeling so charged internally that it had an odd numbing effect on outward awareness.

"It's not even on your list," she added.

"What do you mean?"

"Those lists you make every morning."

"Who in their right mind would put *fun* on a list of things that *have to be* done? It's not as if one needs to be reminded."

"You do."

"It's optional," I said, squirming.

"Not for me."

"No, never for you."

"And you think it's low class, too. Having fun. In fact-o, you think there's something low class about any feeling 'cause you can't pin it down and dissect it and dust off your hands and walk away. You can't put them out of your misery. You got 'em all caged up, your feelings, but then sometimes when you don't expect it because you don't see them, you don't see them on purpose, sometimes one'll escape, and by then, you know, it's real strong and sorta mad like crazy and it comes out all wrong and you get embarrassed, like your underwear's showing or something. So there they are, all jammed up inside and getting squirrelly on you . . . If you ask me . . . "

We looked at each other, *really looked.*

"I guess I'm asking, Dixie, I'm asking you."

Then, inexplicably, *she* got teary-eyed, and had to stand up, fumble for another cigarette, cough once or twice, not return to her chair, keep her back to me and her tangled blond curls, and keep away from me that smile that could have saved me, those eyes that could have spared me—as they always had.

"I don't know what I was going to say," she said.

"Please, Dixie."

Sigh. "What I was going to say, I guess, was that there's stuff that goes by us all the time, that goes through, stuff that goes on, that *goes*, you know, just goes and happens and it doesn't *mean* anything because it doesn't have to, because it's just going and that's all it's supposed to do. Is go. And if you try to make it mean something, if you try to pull it down and make it fit into your head, it stops. And I think, well, what I think is that deep down below there's a whole part of you that's not going, that's stopped. *Optional* stuff. Because you're so grooved on everything meaning so much and getting you some place that's permanent, like you said."

"Like death." It was the absent me speaking, absently, absently.

"I don't think about it."

"Probably you don't, but you behave as if you do, as if

it's always with you, the flip side of everything."

Still, she would not turn around. "You're like your mom, the way you say she is, chock-full of principles. And then you're like your dad, the way you say *he* is, loaded with feelings, and squishy so you can't count on him. So you got this hard stuff and this squishy stuff and the squishy stuff is what scares you because you can't say ever for sure what it's going to do, or even when, but don't you see, Sue, that's the best part, not knowing."

"Not dependable," I murmured, but I was thinking. I was thinking that, without the routine of a well-ordered, well-appointed life, a life I once possessed, all my usual methods of staving off emotion had begun to fail, had indeed failed. And out of the failure rose this absurd and impossible Phoenix—Dixie Darling.

"What I think you got," she was saying, "is, like, a wall, a big glass wall between the hard and the squishy, and there they are looking at each other and wishing, oh boy, I bet they're wishing, but there's no way they can ever kiss and make up."

"What would be the point?"

"So you can have some fun," she said, spinning around and smiling, *thank god*, smiling.

A sort of belching laugh—derisive, pathetic, defenseless—broke loose. "*Fun?* I don't even know what it is. I don't know how." Followed swiftly by rising panic on a rising voice. "I don't have *any idea*, Dixie, what in god's name fun is. I, I just don't know how to do it."

With charged intensity she gazed at me, the blue pools very dark now, dark and magnetic, and I could tell that she was debating what was for Dixie an unusually serious matter. "Are you," she tried, "are you, well, *anticlimaxic?*"

*Oh*, how I laughed then, with delight, with bitterness and bubbling tears. "If you mean am I capable of climax, of an orgasm, then yes. And if you mean anticlimactic, am I living my life in a place that is essentially beyond some great significant event, then I suppose the answer is yes, too."

"What great event? Tell me," she said eagerly, ready (as always) to be excited.

"Well, that's a good question, Dixie." I was still laughing and crying simultaneously, and it occurred to me (as a mere blip on a peripheral screen of observation) that this was just the sort of confluence of estranged emotions, estranged *anythings*, that Dixie thrived on. "I could say St. Agatha's, having to leave it, and daddy's loss, and all my great plans reduced to scrabbling and cursing the bread. But I think it's older, much older. I think at some point far back, maybe when I was just a kid, maybe when my uncle died who was, well, I mean, I guess I might've really loved him, anyway, maybe somewhere around then I was infected with a sense of the profound shabbiness of life, even the 'good life' which used to be mine. And what a shabby trick it is, too, Life. Because you can't count on it, it stops, and you don't know when."

She said, "Yeah," in the most casual manner, as if this was not only incredibly obvious, but also *no big deal*.

"So maybe I've spent a lot of time primping it up. Life, I mean. Trying to find or make meaning just to give the whole proposition some weight."

"It won't last longer than it's gonna."

"No, it won't. It doesn't." I went into the kitchen and poured my own, though more generous dollop of Irish whiskey, then came back, sipping and hacking as I walked. "So maybe that was why I was so into God for awhile back then, because He's supposed to last."

"I thought it was 'cause you were chicken to meet guys."

This last interruption I ignored. I had to, simply had

to. "And now it's the Law," I went on, "because the Law is supposed to last." Abruptly, I gulped down the rest of the whiskey, enjoying its burning path down my esophagus and the backwash of alcoholic fumes as it crashed into the walls of my stomach. "What you said, Dixie, what you said about my feelings, well, you were right. Because they seem to me just as flimsy and impermanent, just as uncertain as living, and maybe that's the whole point. Maybe that was your point. That I don't know how to live, that I'm afraid if I do, it'll end. It'll end just when I'm having fun, just to teach me a lesson."

Long pause. Dixie picking at her nail polish.

Finally I said, "It's a setup, Dixie, a grand sting."

"You mean like a joke?"

"Right. A joke. And the punch line is, you die. And there are lesser punch lines, too, along the way."

"I like jokes."

"Well, I don't like being made a fool of."

"But we're all in on it, the big joke, so it's not really a joke 'cause it's not a surprise. It's like a, like a story, a kid's story that you know the ending of but you still like to have it read to you every night before bed, 'cause every time you notice something different, and you look forward to different parts, till one day you don't want to hear it anymore because you know it by heart, all the different things that aren't different anymore, all the fantastic people in it you've pretended to become so you've been already. One day the story is yours, all of it yours, and then you just want to go to sleep."

So. So, I thought, she *did* think, in her inimitable, sideways way, Dixie thought.

"What about the great event?" Dixie queried. "The one that made you anticlimaxic?"

"Shit, I don't know. Maybe there was a string of little great events, like Sister Olinger, and every one made me less willing to put it out, to desire and lose and then have to find something else to desire only to lose it too."

"You mean change, is that what losing is?"

I think I stared at her. "Dixie," I said, disgusted with myself, "it may very well be that the Great Event that has rendered my life anticlimactic, the finest hour I have outlived, was birth."

"Birth?"

"My birth. Maybe after that, everything seemed ludicrous, and everything I have done, everything I am has been a wretched and very often miserable pursuit of serious, lasting meaning where there is no meaning and where nothing ever lasts."

"Dying is serious, it lasts forever."

"Yes."

"So why not have fun?" Rising, she went to her purse, rummaged about in it, and came back, brushing her hair. "You know what I heard the other day, I heard it from this guy in the Safeway, he had teeny weeny glasses and a yummy beard, and right in front of the cucumbers he started giving me this hoodoo Zen line. He said his asteroid body was feeling *my* asteroid body, can you believe that? In front of the cucumbers. Then he goes, do you know what tantric practice is? And I say no, is it like football, like a sport?"

"Dixie . . ."

"He didn't laugh and I was trying to make him laugh. His beard was real neat, Sue, like a black bush on fire. So anywhose, I pick up this cucumber and I'm standing there holding it and he keeps looking at the cucumber in my hand like it's a ding-a-ling, and then he says in this pinchy voice, like someone's squeezing his neck, that my asteroid is *merging* with his, and do I wanna practice tantrums with him, and I go, naw, I gotta work. Then he kinda gulps, like this someone still has his neck, and says

187

that some cat named Roshi says, 'When you're taking life too seriously, you're not taking it seriously enough.' And it made me think of you, isn't that weird?"

"Oh, Dixie," I said, helplessly charmed, and then I hugged her and kissed her on the cheek, and it was odd how flustered she became, how much effort she had to exert to keep herself light and frothy.

"I think he just wanted to dip his wicky," she said.

"There you go."

Later, when she was getting dressed, she leaned out of the bathroom in her pink bikini panties and said, "Hey, let's have a party."

"All right. *Very* all right," replied The New Me.

Naturally, I considered a decision made to be a decision that stayed. Language; awareness; thought processes arriving at reasonable conclusions; the brawn of mental resolve—these were more than enough to alter the very bone and sinew of one's personality. Action (and flesh) would follow.

Naturally, for Dixie, action was *it*, and the rest—if she considered the rest at all—would (if it must) tag along.

# 11

$F$riday morning we cleaned the apartment.

Friday afternoon we broiled poolside, Dixie listening to a motley assortment of music—*Karen Carpenter, Chicago, The Captain and Tennille, Fleetwood Mac, Elton John* singing the sad tale of Norma Jean (one of Dixie's favorites)—while I read my Psych 1A textbook, a chapter on conditioning, salivating dogs and bells, that sort of thing, and tried to keep the bottom edge of the pages from the rivulets of tropical oils coursing across my stomach. Somehow the prospect of the party corrupted my usually clear and undeviating lines of concentration, Norma Jean got tangled up with the salivating dogs, and I gave up (rather easily); took a nap instead.

Friday night we put on cotton dresses (floral and pastel puffs, midcalf innocence) and shoes with tamed heels, and scrubbed, guileless faces (which for Dixie, in spite of her apparently vast experience, was genuine, and which for me, in spite of my vast inexperience, was thoroughly fallacious), and went from door to door alerting those neighbors at the Penthouse Apartments who occupied our floor and the one below that we would be having a *soirée* Saturday evening, and if they would care to join us we would be most honored. A safety measure, suggested by

189

me, in case the *soirée* swarmed. It was better, I reasoned, to invite potential complainers; then even if they were annoyed, they would be mollified by having snubbed our invitation and thus more inclined to suffer in silence. Dixie thought it was a great idea, inviting "surprise people," and I think she honestly believed in both the authenticity of the invitation and in the verisimilitude of their responses—we were inviting them and they were all coming, as far as she was concerned.

By Saturday Dixie was positively airborne, and I was, well, I was not exactly grounded either. Not only had we been excused from work for two days, but Lemucchi, who was invited, was planning to attend our gala, and since he was the only figure of authority in our current incarnation, we considered the event sanctioned.

The liquor had to be purchased. For this second mission we wore knee-length skirts, button-down collars, blazers, sensible heels. Dixie spilled out all her make-up on the vanity, and we slathered on foundation (to appear as though we had wrinkles to hide) and powder, dabbed counterfeit shadows under our eyes, browned our lids and blackened our lashes, partook of none of the *faux* youthful blushes, and smeared our lips with a priggish peach. This done, we ran the hot water and hung our faces in the rising steam in order to *undo* just a *soupçon* our carefully forged faces: this, we believed, would make us look as if we had tried to look younger but had (somewhat) failed, and the failure itself would make us look older, would provide that futile quality, that tired, nononsense, brown obscurity which was our objective. All of this was my idea; Dixie would have waltzed in the liquor store and simply charmed the clerk out of daring to card her. But since we were buying so much, I really felt we had to go in like world-weary wives (another cocktail party, ho hum), with a list, and a stern eye, and cash (large, fresh-from-hubby bills).

In the car I told Dixie not to say anything, not to open her mouth once.

"How come?"

"And get rid of your gum."

"How come I can't talk?"

"Because you sound too young, too happy," I said.

"And you don't?"

"We're supposed to be old. We're shopping for yet another boring party, that's the idea. We have to sound old and, and staid."

"I think that's sad," Dixie said.

"What?"

"That you can do that, sound that way."

I thought it was too. Sad. And I'm convinced it was the sudden verity of this negative emotion that infused our liquor purchasing mission with the old, staid, futile lifeblood it required for success. The clerk, a middle-aged man eating a powdered donut, hardly looked up from the morning sports section long enough to ring up our rather substantial purchase, though when he did notice the total, he noticed us and, I think, might have considered carding us if not for the instant reply to the total—a pile of cash on his counter.

He offered to carry the two boxes out to our car.

"No thanks," said I with haste that verged on annoyance, and hoping he would think we were simply women's libbers, intent on doing for ourselves. But the real reason was that I was afraid the car—not an Olds or a Buick or a slick black Lincoln, but a turquoise VW bug with a scented pine tree dangling from its mirror and a fuzzy gearshift knob—might push our luck.

Of course I may have imagined all of this. It may have never occurred to him to card us. Or, if he thought we were underage, he may not have cared. Or, since Dixie

Lynn Stegner

had shopped at that liquor store in the past, and since I
distinctly saw the clerk sneak a wink at her, it occurred
to me—smugness evaporating to dismal desert—that he
might have been one of Dixie's 50. In which case our
success was owing not to my clever deceit, but solely to
Dixie's philosophy of fun and one of its more well-trod-
den paths of expression—sex.

And again, for the $n$th time since our conversation I
considered the very real possibility that Dixie was right,
that life lay *between*, in connections, which is to say in
feelings since they alone can pass across, that one's sense
of one's self was embedded in relationships; that to seek
a value and a meaning independent of others was to seek
isolation, and if achieved, to abandon life. Not a partial
death, but death by dissociation. Nothing, not meaning,
not value, not even power, could be realized except
through relationships. Oh, no doubt they could be
achieved independently, meaning and value, but not realized. Not *known*. Power, of course, was entirely depen-
dent upon extant relationships.

And even while I exhorted myself those days and especially that day of the party to reach out and "let it flow"
(to use an idiom of the time), I really couldn't help but
wonder how Dixie would feel, how in fact she did feel, if
and when she found herself alone, when there was no
one present to tell her who she was. Because if she felt
desirable around men, and if that in turn converted to
value—she felt valuable—what *would* happen when there
were no men around? Which may, I concluded, handily
explain the 50. (I spent a lot of time trying to explain
that 50.) It was also at this point that I began to wonder
about Dixie's mother, less about their relationship *per se*,
and more about its reverberations. I had never figured
out what Cheryl Darling meant that last afternoon of her
life when she talked about the "real part," about having

to "hang on to that"; really, I was far more interested in what Dixie thought was the "real part," and further, how *she* hung on to it. And I had to conclude—there was statistically no way around it—that whatever it was for Dixie, hanging on to it *had* to have *something* to do with those 50 undiscriminated men.

Still, I had long ago learned that handy explanations of Dixie never had much staying power; she usually neutralized them the minute I had writ them in some small, carefully selected, flat gray stone, picking it up (as it were) and skipping it across the dazzling, light-stippled and profoundly capricious waters of Dixie. There to disappear without the proverbial trace.

If the truth be known, I was far more interested in my deficiency of relationships, feelings, fun, etc. etc. than in her *embarras de richesses,* no matter what unhealthy, perhaps even sad, coloration with which I tried to tint her motives. I may have been jealous; or curious; or jealously curious. Or indirectly, comparatively trying to explain me. In any case, her plenitude was all relative to *me*. Indeed, the word itself—*relative*—I thought a fine first step in the right direction.

As everyone knows, the best part of most parties, the best part of most things, lies in the anticipation. If we dispensed with the thing itself—the event, the gift, the trip, the sex, whatever—if we simply constructed a ruse of successive events and strung them together, each promised jewel more glittering than the one before, and spent our time in happy self-deception, excitedly preparing for each, we should spare ourselves a great deal of expense and heartache and the inevitable belly flop of disappointment. It would be a world of infinites, of soaring swan-dives-of-the-mind, of provocative tales without tragic endings, imagined parties without the bother and mess, the indigestion and hangover, imagined romances without love's attenuation, imagined rises to success without fame's declination. With our minds alone we would crowd the impossible out of existence. Nothing would be finite because nothing would really *be*.

Looking back, I feel sure it would have been far better if that party had not been. I was bent on putting to a first test the new "wild-and-crazy" me, and I approached the task with blind determination, prepared to hack my way through teeming jungles of fun. And while Dixie was incapable of being *bent* on anything, that evening she was possessed of (or possessed by)—and for quite some time before and after that evening, I have to suppose—a secret, a vitally simple and thoroughly internal cryptogram that was ordering everything from the color of her hair to the color of our carpet, from her non-selection of men to her selection of a roommate, ordering, shaping, directing, and ultimately composing with the precision of music—notes, sequence, time and phrasing, *presto, crescendo, diminuendo*—her apparently haphazard life. All of which, if it was known, would have been fine. Really. But it *could not be known*, not by Dixie, not then, and not even later when it surfaced, this sad little secret gasping for its rightful air. Because even in its honesty, its *rightness*, it served not to authenticate Dixie, but to utterly nullify everything Dixie was about, and everything Dixie was about seemed to nullify it. It was an antibody, it was *anti*-Dixie. And yet *it* was Dixie. My Dixie, alas, dearest chimera.

So, in splendid anticipation, we absorbed hours trying on clothes. Dixie decided that each outfit with its particular mood should be recorded, and out came her ubiquitous camera along with props—book, wine glass, fountain pen, half a sandwich, shoes. Two of the photos I kept for their deeply touching incongruity: Dixie lying on the carpet, wearing one of my linen blouses, cigarette languishing in a *faux* crystal ashtray, cheeks as yet not rouged and too pale, hair as yet not curled, not fluffed, looking flat, the textbook open before her and clearly upside down (dear Dixie), and a pen poised over the page—something no one who reads would ever do. And there in the second photo am I, pretending to have just come through the door, "A happy homecoming," reads the caption. I am wearing Dixie's tube top—stretchy, strapless, and sexy—long hair sweeping back in gay abandon, and dangling from my fingers are a pair of wedge sandals. It seems I have just returned, barefoot, flushed and dreamy, from love's very nest.

We were both trying so hard to take each other seriously, though sometimes the effort seemed merely a function of the happenstance of our living together and of having no other politic selection.

In the end I wore a floor-length, emerald-green gown, with halter straps (thus permitting no bra) and an empire waist, a dress that had belonged to Dixie's mother. I didn't want to. It was overmuch. But Dixie insisted. She said, "You look *gorgee-oso*. You look like there's a *seething cauldron* of womanhood deep down below."

The *seething cauldron* bit I figured she'd picked up from her soaps. "I don't want to seethe," I said. "I want *them* to seethe."

"They won't seethe without you seething first."

"Okay. I'll make a concerted effort to seethe."

Her face, her eyes went dark, as if someone had literally turned out Dixie's lights. "Don't try," she said, almost sadly. "It's there. Just take the lid off."

"Yeah, right, and I'll try not to burn myself when I do." It was cocky and dismissive, but something in her look had made me uncomfortable.

Since I wore almost no make-up, and since she had taken primary interest in my fitting, I was ready long before Dixie. Camped at the breakfast bar, nibbling on chips, I watched idly as she went into her dressing routine. For someone so, so, well, whimsical, there was a coldly businesslike quality about her system, as if she was preparing to engage in some highly refined, technical activity requiring not only elaborate, but uniform preliminary measures each time. She seemed to be in the grip of something, I didn't know what to call it, the exigencies of femaleness perhaps, and yet I had the sense that it was her own hand gripping her and that to let go would have been equal to a terrible and imperfect fatality.

Emerging from the bathroom, she pulled her hair back in a taut roll, posed a moment, then shook it loose and posed again. "Stuffy or fluffy?" she chirped.

A choice? This was new. "Which do you feel like?"

"Oh, I don't know," she said, turning obliquely. "You decide. What you like."

"It's not my hair. It should be the way you like it."

She drifted closer to the bathroom, yet did not reenter, and I could tell this was not the breezy issue it ought to have been. A long minute passed. She mumbled something, "forget it," maybe, but whatever it was it had such a wretchedly lost quality that I cried, "Fluffy," with triumph, as if the question had been well-considered; fluffy to affirm the way she had always worn her hair. Because honestly I didn't care, but it seemed that that might disappoint her.

So it was fluffy. And the dress was gold, long, shiny, and form-fitting (worse than form-fitting, *skintight*), with useless spaghetti straps and a wide leopard print belt, a two-pound gaudy, gold-painted buckle, jewelry *partout*, dripping from lobes, girding ankles, plunging and pooling in her *décolletage*. Her make-up was Egyptian in its excess, the eyes more purple now than blue, like the ring she wore, the alexandrite that had belonged to her mother and which, depending upon the ambient light, changed its color from shades of blue to violet to a cool purple. Taken in parts, everything was savagely tasteless, tragi-comical, staggering out of all bounds. But *tout ensemble*—which was at the time the only successful method of negotiating Dixie—she was burning bright, she was phantasmagoria, she was the blood, sweat and tears of the male subconscious.

"Wow," I said. "You look like a figment of *everyone's* imagination, Dixie, they're all going to seethe, *I'm* seething. Come to me, love of my life," and I threw open my arms and put on a hopeful, desperately-in-love look.

The moment after seemed to splinter. And in the first of those splinters of time, I swear Dixie was not Dixie. It was as if a negative jolt had traveled through her being. I was sitting on one of the breakfast stools, and I remember spinning around because I thought something had happened behind me, some frightening thing that she alone had seen, a thing had fallen or broken or caught fire. She was so strange. When I turned back around, Dixie was gone.

At 7:00, a trickle of guests. 7:30, a steady stream. 8:00 and the door was flung open so that people could simply flow osmotically between our apartment and the hallway which by then had become a necessary appendage to the beast that was our party.

Toni came. I tried to be rude to her, but it only seemed to inspire her to further feats of neediness. Every now and then I became aware of her at the edge of things—that is the only accurate phraseology—her cow eyes locking on to me as if to draw me into their doleful vacuum. Finally I told her in mock confidence that I was going to screw somebody tonight, that I was "really in the mood for a Man."

"You don't have to, Sue," she said, her voice oozing

Lynn Stegner

*tendresse.* "You're so special, lady, and we don't have to do that. Feel my feelings, lady."

"Feel them yourself," I said.

A dozen or so of my classmates came, too, including a young man, an intellectual, whom I had briefly considered dating, mainly because he had boasted to me (and I believed him) that during a recent junket to Yosemite with "associates" (he always referred to his friends as "associates") he had remained in his tent reading Kierkegaard while the others enjoyed the temporal splendor of the valley, skiing, hiking and such. That night of the party, watching him with his sherry glass, and his poetically longish hair which he flipped off his brow with passionate airs, and his thin, leather volume of imported thoughts clutched effetely against his forearm, watching him engaged in that self-important, point-making, high-flown hand gesture of his as he conversed with an "associate," I decided he was simply a wimp. That he had stayed in his tent with Kierkegaard, inert and dreading, because the natural magnificence of the world outside would have squashed him like a bug. Maybe Kierkegaard as well. (Dixie was just behind me at the time, and I'm sure her proximity emboldened my thoughts to a certain reductive economy.)

There were also employees and customers we knew from Sambo's, girls from Harold's College of Beauty where Dixie had recently begun her studies, but mostly just a ragtag of people we'd met at the swimming pool, at Skip's-on-the-Sand, at the bakery where we bought our morning Danish—people we'd encountered and didn't really know. And of course there were Dixie's 50. Most of whom, it seemed, were well aware of their reiterative status with Dixie. But it was curious, it was more than curious, it was appalling in a way, how nonpartisan they were about this fact. They all seemed to be on the most cheerful terms with each other, as if not one of them was burdened with any overwhelming emotion relating to Dixie. It made me sort of mad, considering the lengths she went to to please them.

I drank too much. It was part of the plan. Dixie offered encouragement in the form of occasional pats on the butt and a chirping "That's the ticket, kiddo," every time I swam over to the bar for another blended bomb. At some point I peered at her through the noisy haze and shouted, "A ticket to where?"

"You name it, I'll frame it," she said, which still makes perfect sense to me: with Dixie, imagination was essential, representation was everything.

Someone in a purple velvet bathrobe and a pair of swimming fins, a man, I think (because of the cigar), had taken over the Osterizer, and with a lovely-to-watch masterful flair was commingling the liquefiable contents of our kitchenette. One batch, I noted, with only the faintest misgiving (I noted also), included two tomatoes, leftover coffee, Dixie's famous whipped cream, and half a bottle of rum, served on the rocks with a head of soda and a speared green grape. Received with gusto.

Men held the majority, though there were enough women to provide the necessary contrast, while reserving for most the pleasantness of choice—presuming choices would be made at some fateful hour. I had made mine practically at the outset. Stratford Standish. Or Standish Stratford. He seemed to answer to Strat, which left the order in question.

When first seen, he was standing before the framed awards and notices Dixie had seen fit to hang over the couch, his eyebrows lifting with appreciation, and at that moment I could have kissed Dixie on the mouth for her absurd little gesture of cheer. In his dark blue suit and white button-down collar, patterned burgundy tie (silk), slim Italian loafers, he was hands-down the best dressed, perhaps the only real man at the party—as far as I was concerned. Also, he was handsome, ridiculously handsome; I mean, I practically had to laugh. Ebony waves of hair, limpid gray eyes, a strong, pensive brow, nose as straight as a rule, not full yet ample lips which conveyed an impression of compactness, as if they might be otherwise, they might ripen to lush proportions if applied to the right surface. (Me, I hoped.) And he had a cleft in his chin, a wonderful, personal, trademark, this-is-who-I-am sort of cleft in his chin.

Next to him, like a secondhand car of which one is only nostalgically fond, idled Lemucchi, and when Stratford Standish turned and the two exchanged words, Lemucchi then peered (in his restaurant manager way, taking everything in) around the apartment, spotted me, and pointed.

I dropped my eyes.

Though not before I saw Standish Stratford offer an elegantly quiet nod, which sent a bolt through the crowd and straight into the heart of my heart where it sizzled and simmered of delights to come.

"I want him," I told Dixie.

"Him?"

"Him."

"He's so square looking."

"Dixie. I'm square."

"That's what I mean. You need a guy who'll sand off the edges."

Saying nothing, I gazed significantly at her.

"Okay," she sighed, "I'll get him for you."

"Wait a minute. I'll get him myself. I was only telling you that there was a man here, an actual man present whom I found attractive. I was just telling you . . ." Why was I telling her? For her approval? Congratulatory pride?

Or so that she would indeed help me "get him"?

Lemucchi drifted over. "You girls" (he always referred to us as "you girls" even when there was only one of us present, as if we were simply two sides of the same coin), "you girls *shuwer* have a party here." He waved a sloppy hand to include the entire apartment.

"Yeah, it's a doozer," said Dixie, and I watched, jealous, as she slipped away, leaving me with a seriously drunk boss.

I said, "Maybe you shouldn't drink anymore, Al."

He shook his head and rattled the ice in his glass. "Got to. Got a migraine. Sss medininal. See, look," he said, shoving his face toward mine. "The eyes."

I made an obligatory inspection of his eyes.

"Pinholes, ya see. That's how to tell, when my pupils become pinholes." Smiling helplessly, he raised his glass in salute, then chugged the rest. "Pain'sss gone now. All gone," he added in a childlike singsong, referring now to his drink.

"Well," I said, desperate to get away, for I could see Dixie now with Stratford Standish, talking, smiling in my direction, and I was afraid, I was worried that she would foul my chances, that if he knew I had a roommate like her, who talked and looked like her, he would dismiss "us girls." "Well," I tried again.

Lemucchi cocked his head, ready and willing for me to speak. And I knew I would have to, not because he was my employer, but because he had really been very kind to us, to me especially whom it seemed he might favor. I had never heard him yell at anyone, never seen him dally while others labored. Once he gave me a ride home from work in his souped-up, orange Honda (about the size of an overgrown basketball), the long, windy way that followed the edge of the hills, demonstrating for me how to take the curves fast without quite losing control, and in those desperate, curving moments he seemed to be invoking a freedom not successfully forgotten. He seemed almost happy. On the radio, a John Denver song, and he turned it up, said it reminded him of his youth. He couldn't have been more than thirty. Said he was married, his voice flat and lonesome; said he had two great kids, but he didn't see much of them because of the restaurant; said he used to ski, used to be "something" on the slopes, he said. Then in the Penthouse parking lot, with his souvenir eyes almost asking, he said goodbye to me. And I remember how sad, how resigned the little orange Honda sounded as it putt-putted away when only minutes before it was wide open and flying.

So, in spite of myself, I asked him what caused his migraine.

"Dishwasher." And he lurched into a tangled discourse about the dishwashing machine at Sambo's Pancake Paradise, how it had broken down that afternoon, how he had had to jerry-rig it until the repair man arrived, but all I could hear was Dixie's inimitable trilling coming in loop-the-loops through the crowd toward me, all I could smell were the kitchen fumes lingering in A. L. Lemucchi's always brown, always faintly damp attire, and all I could really see before me were his pinholes and his scar superimposed on the distant man of my immediate dreams who was standing much too close to Dixie Darling.

"I wonder, would you please excuse me?" I said.

"Ah, yeah," he said, genuinely moved, "the way you talk, you girls, you girls *shuwer* are a class act."

It was Dixie who introduced us, and while I tried to think of the perfect opening, I watched her recede, thinking "the beauty of motion on the edge of violence." I can't imagine why, or even where I had read it, but Dixie at a party was that—beautiful motion on the blade edge of violence.

"Your roommate's quite a gal," he said.

Gal. I liked that. "She is unique," said I.

"And it must be you are too," he said, gesturing toward the framed, not-to-be-forgotten glories, adding, "Two beauties, too."

I blushed and, so he would not think me conceited, hastened to say that it was Dixie who had had the awards mounted. "Are you a friend of . . . ?" I made as if to fumble for a name, because I knew Dixie didn't know him, and of course I didn't.

"Mauro."

Blank face.

"Guy down the hall who works on imports. I was just picking up my car, and as I'm leaving he tells me that everyone's invited here. The fact is, there was no way to avoid your party."

We both glanced in the direction of the open apartment door, the clot of people beyond.

"It is a big party," I said lamely. He was impossibly handsome.

"Your roommate says I'm a surprise. What did she mean?"

"Ah, you never know with her," I said, not wanting to explain.

"Well," he laughed, "and I was just picking up my car. Must be my lucky day."

Then there was a positively sodden pause, and it seemed perilous to simply leap across it, to say "Let's get out of here, *Strat*, let's go to the beach and take off our clothes and wade into the obsidian salt waters of Time, hand in hand, and then dance back up the sand and seethe together beneath the prickling stars, because my darling Strat we were meant for each other"; really, it seemed far too dangerous, that pause, and I thought it best to simply plod carefully through it. So I said: "What kind of

car do you have?" The question had some of the quali-
ties of a death knell.

"Lotus."

I nodded, excessively appreciative.

"Gave it to myself as kind of achievement award," and
again he fluttered his long, manly fingers toward my tri-
fling awards on the wall. "When I'd passed a certain figure at the firm."

"You're a lawyer?"

"Stockbroker."

"Ah." What figure he had passed I didn't ask but I
imagined it was large. A million, maybe two. The fact
that he didn't say I considered yet another mark in his
favor. He was modest. Discreet.

"Speaking of firms, I intend to pursue law," said I.
"This is just a, a way station. It's funny," I said, trying to
sound light and frothy (like Dixie) and self-possessed (like
me), "I've been acquainted with my roommate off and
on for some time, but we don't really know each other.
We're very different," I added, almost under my breath,
as if to reassure him. "I'll begin my studies this coming
fall. Probably specialize in corporate law."

A frown rippled faintly across the exquisite brow of
the man of my dreams. Did he doubt me or, or, did he *not*
doubt me? And which was worse?

"And your roommate, does she have plans?"

Here I was somewhat stumped. Because I was currently
associated with Dixie, I didn't want to diminish her, yet I
didn't want to aggrandize her either, because I was pur-
portedly intending to disassociate from her. So I said,
"Cosmetology," hoping the multisyllables would cancel
out the euphemism, and leave him indifferent to her.

All at once he threw back his head, he smiled, he
clapped his hands. "Perfect!"

If he had reached out and slapped me I would have

been less annoyed. Getting off the subject of Dixie, though, was proving troublesome, since I seemed to have value solely in relation to her, as if one of us should act as background for the other's foreground, and vice versa.

We were standing next to the bar, and Strat leaned over and poured himself additional Scotch with a splash of soda, sipped, then removed a pristine handkerchief from his pocket and dabbed at his (unfortunately) still compact, unripened lips.

Someone had turned up the music and now there was a nucleus of vibrating bodies expanding our direction.

"Do you like to dance?" I said.

He took a step closer to the bar, and for a second it seemed he might actually try to fold his beautifully attired self beneath it. "Well," he coughed.

So he didn't. But heedless, I plodded on, thinking that even if he didn't like to dance, it was important, it was critical, that he know that I *did* like to dance; that indeed I could "cut loose," "cut a rug," be "wild-and-crazy." "I guess I do. It's a hobby, I guess. It's something I do, well, I suppose rather well, and I suppose one ends up liking what one does rather well, don't you think?"

His expression was queer, almost relieved, as though he had mentally dismissed some noisome thing, a bug perhaps. And when he asked what my roommate liked to do with *her* spare time, the effort to please had gone out of his voice. Still, I wouldn't give up. I wouldn't tell him that men were Dixie's hobby, I wouldn't give him that satisfaction. "She rides," I said. "Horses. Obsessed with them. In fact," I went on, (and this was true), "she recently purchased a Thoroughbred even though," and here I made a smug face, "the man who sold it to her implied that the animal was unridable."

The cleft in the chin of Standish Stratford twitched. "Why?" he said.

Smirking, I replied, "It's a stallion. She spent two grand on a rank stallion."

"Of course." At the corners of his lips a whiff of a smile stirred. Then he added almost to himself, "I'm not surprised." Which I thought a very odd thing to say since he didn't know the tiniest little thing about my roommate, Dixie Darling.

"I'm waiting for the broken bones," said I, sighing affectionately, as if over an unruly child. "I'm waiting."

At which point Dixie appeared. On cue. Looking not the least bit broken in her shiny gold dress.

Standish Stratford pulled himself up regally, his smile radiating relief (though of an altogether different sort than that previously witnessed), his lips ripening on the spot, his limpid gray eyes all a-twinkle now in Dixie's sunny, sudden presence.

"How're you kids doing?" she said.

"Fine. Just dandy," and off I plowed through the madding crowd.


Still, as I said, I was bent on having fun. *Bent.* I was not going to fail this first test. I was going to meet someone. I was going to sleep with someone. And I told myself that it wasn't Dixie's fault about Standish Stratford, it wasn't her fault that the man of my dreams was whistling Dixie. Intellectually, I took myself by the shoulders and told myself it didn't matter, over and over, throughout the next two hours as I went about nuzzling up to strange men, making cruel gibes about Toni to people who knew her and to people who didn't know her, taking refuge in the always-receptive Lemucchi (an interim consolation) or in Kierkegaard by way of my classmate, Sir Cerebral, when there was no one else available, and slipping downstairs and out into the cool air in order to give myself time-out pep talks.

Dixie joined me during one of these time-outs.

Smoking cigarettes, we strolled to the edge of the parking lot where there was a cyclone fence and a ravine beyond, and then the west hills mounting in pitchy billows against a sky bereft of light. We leaned our backs against the cyclone fence, gazing up occasionally at the windows of our fifth-floor apartment where the shadows of our guests scribbled across sheets of light. Behind us from the ravine a dank, weedy tang strayed up and drifted by.

Our cigarettes were mostly gone; still, neither of us had spoken. Then Dixie heard something, or she said she did, something in the ravine, an animal cry. Maybe a kitten or puppy, I thought. And the next thing I knew she had clipped her cigarette purse to her belt, hitched up her gown, and was going over the fence, and then I was too, in keeping with the general tenor of the pep talks to go with the flow.

Scrambling first, she grabbed for my hand, and we angled our way down through the scrubby bushes and litter, the broken glass and broken-down trees, discarded tires, bits of sheet metal; down together like that, using each other for balance, muscles flexing, going slack, our shoulders touching, then two arm-lengths apart. It was entirely dark, but I could see a kind of negative image of parts of her, a place that was somehow less dark that was her hair, and a vertical shaft of less-dark that was the shiny gold gown of the party—the party that now seemed worlds away.

Maybe five minutes passed. We were nearing what must have been the bottom. She paused, squeezed my hand. There was a sound. And I whispered, "Yes." And we continued. At that moment I suppose it didn't matter to me that the sound was clearly not a kitten or a puppy; I don't know why it didn't matter. Maybe because we were going, and it was so dark and so late and I didn't care what it meant, I was holding a hand and not thinking and just *going* down through the dark behind Dixie.

When she stopped, it was as if it was simply time to stop. Because I remember feeling not the least bit alarmed in those two or three seconds before the first one spoke, I remember that there was nothing, absolutely nothing in the feel of Dixie's hand that would have let me know.

"I smell cunt," a voice said.

"Young cunt." A second voice, lower and rugged.

"Real cuntlets," and the first one laughed, high, attenuated squeaks. Our lost puppy, I realized.

Then Dixie did something truly astonishing: she dropped my hand and lit a cigarette as if we were to linger here in the belly of the beast, engaging in pleasant chitchat. In the brief flicker I saw a stubbled chin, glassy eyes, thatches of hair, army fatigue jackets. And they saw us.

"Dressed to kill, too," the rugged voice said.

I fumbled for Dixie's hand, found it, still warm and dry, still unperturbed. "If you'll excuse us," I said, pulling on her.

"Why?" he said.

I stopped. I had to. "We live right up there, at the top of the ravine. We're having a . . ." *don't say party*, I thought, "we have friends over this evening." I wanted to sound pleasant, calm, I didn't want to incite them, I didn't want them to know how frightened I was. I wanted to get out of it before we got into it. And I knew we could not outrun them. I knew that in a horrid and infuriating way we had to get their permission, we had to ask their leave. "Our friends will be looking for us."

This was met with several more of the attenuated squeaks. "And you left these friends all alone?" *Squeak squeak.*

"Yes," I said, without thinking, words rushing. "We

wanted to be alone. We were just taking a walk because we don't get to be alone very often, and there are a lot of friends up there and they don't understand that we like to be alone sometimes and we don't get to be very much. Alone. Do you understand? We don't get to be alone, and we just want to be together. The two of us, left alone."

Afterward there was such a strange silence that even I paused.

And then the second one said, "Oh," his tone suddenly soft and bewildered.

And we started back.

And they let us.

And that was it.

Except that it wasn't it for Dixie. I want to say that for her it was the start of something, though I know it wasn't, I know it started long before, even before her mother's death, which, granted, was the main tributary, perhaps at the time even larger than the river itself and bringing with it such a confusion of matter that it changed forever the color and texture of the main current. Of Dixie. And this last event, just a trickle feeding in, that was all. Not a start at all.

It was still pitchy out. I was leading us up, back, pulling hard.

Dixie said: "Did you hear what you said?"

"We had to get out of there, Dixie. That was serious trouble. I can't believe you didn't realize what kind of *serious* trouble we were in. You were practically suicidal. I mean, you were no help with your fucking cigarette, you were no fucking help at all."

"But did you hear . . . ?"

"I don't care. We got away."

"Yeah, but do you know *why*?"

"Just shut up, Dixie. Shut the fuck up."

We went back to the party. It seemed it would never end. Finally around 3:00 in the morning, the last guests sloshed out the door, except for Lemucchi who, either out of habit, or because he was the nice guy he seemed, or because he would do anything to delay going home, was bravely busing glassware.

Dixie was nowhere in sight.

I called Lemucchi a cab, then wandered down to the lobby to watch for it.

The moon was up now, up high and coldly bright and fixing its stark cyclopean eye upon me as if to say, "So, it's over, everyone's gone, you're alone, some fun."

Presently, from across the parking lot I heard the unmistakable musical trill of Dixie, though slower than usual and with a cool, confidently relaxed quality as if in the aftermath of some *fait accompli*. Which of her 50—the Chicano, the golf pro, the vegetable packer from Salinas, the insurance man, the cabinet maker, etc. etc. etc.—had she ended up with? I wondered idly.

Over the metallic sheen of car roofs I saw the two figures, thinking it odd that the car next to which they stood was so much shorter than the others around it. And just about the time I heard his voice, I realized it was his car, his sleek, low-down Lotus, not red as I had hoped, but blue, like Dixie's eyes. Into which I assumed he was gazing at that very moment. With the love that was to have been mine.

Then I stopped thinking. It was that simple and that complete.

I went back up to the apartment, shut the door, shut off the lights and, between pewter sheets of moonlight, found A. L. Lemucchi. I put my hand where it would immediately count, and we fumbled down to the carpet. Strong, much stronger than I expected, and quick in a determined, old-knowing, old-brain way, he actually picked me up and carried me with my legs wrapped around his waist, over by the balcony door, slammed my back against the wall and while he held me there, penetrated, thrusting with piston-like regularity. It was good and hard and entirely mindless. His eyes were all pupil now, black pools, his sweat tangy like the smell of the ravine, his eccentrically messy, mannish scar telling me all at once what he was about, what this was about.

Then the door opened and in came Dixie towing Standish Stratford.

Lemucchi was beyond stopping, beyond caring, beyond humanity.

I groaned.

He came.

They left.

Simultaneously.

And in the overexposed, black-and-white documentary moonlight of the apartment, my mind crawled back to its diminished throne.

Morning.

Nausea. Sore thighs.

Smell of coffee, like faraway skunk.

Drunk, I thought. I was.

A yellow blur—Dixie?—settling on the edge of my bed. "He was for you, kiddo," she was saying. "I was bringing him back for you." Stroking my hair . . . *painful, painful,* the touch of her hand so tender.

So it seemed that my sex with men, my two men, my two sexual experiences, were just like all of Dixie's— meaningless. *I* was just like Dixie, qualitatively; there was only the very minor quantitative factor that distinguished us. Well, I suppose they weren't altogether without meaning; palatable meaning, yes, but not without *any* meaning at all. Or maybe that too. No meaning nowhere.

# 12

There was an unworldly stillness about the heat that summer, as if all meaning had drained from the emblems of life, and left us like dazed survivors of a cataclysmic event, wondering if anything was really worth doing. But there wasn't any cataclysmic event, none of which we were aware, except for the dogged continuation of life, which, in the orderless order of things, struck me as a groaning, wrenching, slow-motion upheaval of sorts; life, that is, the effort of it. Maybe it was the heat; it seemed impossible to try in heat so incorruptible. It seemed impossible to get out of bed, ragged and sticky and smelling too familiarly of one's primitive beginnings, and drink tepid coffee for the sake of caffeine, and shower only to sweat anew, and speak only to imagine the disturbance of air between us, or to frighten it away with voice—this heat, this presence, this pervasive omen.

That was how it seemed to me: that something was going to happen that *had* to happen, because the heat could not be quenched—there was that quality about it. Something else would have to give.

Early mornings standing on the balcony looking west, I could see fog here and there peeking seductively over dips in the ridgeline of the mountains, or on the most promising days a thick white outline, and it seemed I could almost smell the transient humidity, the revived pungency of dried grasses and weeds, the piqued, medicinal scent of Eucalyptus, almost feel the summer camp comfort of redwood needles underfoot, the dusty shade and shapeless days and the occasional waft—cool and fetid—from some place low. But within an hour or so of dawn the fog, like Sisyphus, slid back down the western flank of the range, back toward the birth-conjuring ocean, and we were left facing the parched expanse of another day without relief. Another day of wondering.

The other thing about the heat that summer was that it was sentiently inclusive. Naturally, one felt it, pressing into one's body, lingering in creases and vales of skin and webbing through hair, cleaving like a weightless hand about one's neck. But I began to think I could hear it, a listless droning pitched high, and while reduced to parts, a minute or two, the sound was feeble, could even be ignored, received as a whole it seemed to eke itself out, forward, and back too, like the worm of Time, and the very monotony of it conferred upon the sound an eerie strength. From the parking lots, from the rooftops of houses and cars, from the metal railing of our balcony, hot tides ebbed, flowed, receded back into the sky which was as bleached and hardhearted as an alkali flat. Smell, it was a burning smell, like dried spices cooking in a dry pan, faintly East Indian, and mingling with one's own sweet-and-sour response, it kept relentless company. The taste recalled the distilled essence of an unlikely vegetation, a bad *eau de vie*. This heat was not healthy, grew more ominous as the days wavered on.

102. 105. A fiery leap to 114. Down to 108, holding, holding. Down again to the low 100s, there to idle for weeks. A teasing plunge to 92. Back up. Eventually I could call it within two degrees. Not Dixie. Functioning *tout*

*ensemble,* she worked with gross values: it was hot, it was cold, it was just right. She was impressionistic; I was pointillistic. But the effect was the same: it was formidably hot.

While I tended to reject the heat, to pay it the grudging regard it deserved—for example, persisting with my daily jog (on principle), though changing its accustomed time slot from afternoon to early morning—Dixie simply and completely evolved with it, into it. The heat was present, the heat was happening, Dixie was at all times in the here and now. She switched from Irish coffees to piña coladas, and spent more (though not exclusive) time with a cop she'd met at Sambo's, I think mainly because he had a motorcycle and they went for rides along the dappled roads of the west hills, avoiding the east hills which, except in the deepest creases or within walled enclaves of houses miming each other, were treeless, a cracked and grizzled hide angry with heat. Changing her dress, her habits, she accepted the weather, accommodated it, as if it was a not very likeable family member: she was always one to welcome with equanimity her own, and everyone was her own. But eventually it got to her, or something did.

Now, four or five afternoons a week she visited the horse. Owing to the heat, I assumed.

"Aren't you ever going to name him?" I asked her one June evening.

Having returned from her ride, she had showered and was sprawled on the couch, massaging perfumed cream along the insides of her legs which were sore and chafed. She refused to wear jodhpurs, or anything remotely appropriate—always a pair of shorts so she could feel his muscles, the rhythm of them, that sort of thing, she implied, but personally I didn't see that the more intimate contact made any significant difference in her skills as an equestrienne, which were exceptional.

"A name?" She seemed then to consider it, though I knew she wasn't. I began to think it had never occurred to her. "Naw," she said, her lassitude like a slow, tonal expression of the heat itself. "He doesn't need one."

"Why not?"

"Ah, he's crazy. He thinks he's all horses, like, he got elected or something. He'd give me that funny look he's got, like I oughta know better."

"He's a horse, Dixie."

"Kinda, yeah. Just horse, in a totally 100 percent full throttle kinda way." Dabbing more cream onto the palm of her hand, she made slow circles on the insides of her thighs where several small bruises reposed like jade pebbles in milk. "Yeah, that's him," she said, smiling, but there was a nervous shimmer about her blue eyes, as if a gust had come up suddenly from nowhere and roughed the surface.

I said, "I think he's dangerous."

"Yeah?"

"Well, isn't he?"

Head tipped speculatively, she squeezed one eye and fairly whispered, "He might could be."

"Well?"

"He isn't now."

"Well, what the hell is he now?"

"A blast," and she laughed, "a total blast of being, like I'm him, you know, and he's me, and then pretty soon *bang bang*, we're not either of us there."

"A transcendent experience," said I, musingly, and mostly to myself, too, because I figured she wouldn't know what I meant.

But she replied, "No, no, not that. We don't get *out* of it, we get *into* it, way into it where nothing is a thing anymore and I'm not me, a person, anymore and he's not a horse anymore, you know, like, it's just moving there, only there's no *it* and no *there* 'cause there isn't any room for the piddly stuff. Just big moving."

Honestly I didn't know what to say except, "Big moving, well," and then after another awkward pause, "Well, he does sound dangerous."

Looking disappointed (in a silent, "big" way, if she were describing it), she recapped the cream, jade bruises disappearing as she closed her sprawling, perfumed legs, then she got up and flipped on the TV and went into the kitchen where presently I heard the desultory popping of popcorn, sloshed liquid and rattling ice, and then the punishing explosions of the blender as it chomped through cubes and dispatched the first alcoholic installment on the evening's mood—which seemed to have flagged.

By June the letters from campuses began to arrive, and it wasn't long before I had a flattering fan of acceptances, some with scholastic scholarships, others with only work scholarships, just two offering both: University of California at Berkeley, and Michigan. Between these two I saved and savored the happy task of choice, and though never in front of Dixie did I discuss even idly the various pros and cons of divergent paths, I knew eventually an announcement would have to be made.

So one Sunday morning I paced about the apartment, lingered conspicuously before the sliding glass doors to make my usual a.m. pronouncement about the heat— "Christ, will it ever end?"—which had about as much consequence as a mantra, all form, all in the saying; then taking a deep breath, cinching the ties on my robe, and reeling about, I blurted, "I'll be moving out at the end of August."

She was frying up chorizo and scrambling eggs in another pan, the coffee machine gurgling steamily behind her. Her curls from the night before had separated and hung in limp, isolated corkscrews about her face; there were blue mascara shadows under her eyes; her lips were wan and recessive—in all, her appearance was about as plain and as authentic as I'd ever seen, and I confess to some discomfiture, having, like her men, grown accustomed to the ongoing fanfare of Dixie Darling. It made my news easier to report.

"You don't have to tell me that," she said, not looking over.

And of course I didn't have to tell her, I thought, studying her closed profile, the unoccupied face. She knew about all the applications, the hopes, she'd watched the two stacks on my dresser—the short, bad news stack, the taller one of promise and welcome, signifying departure.

"You might want to start thinking about another roommate, that's all."

"Yeah. Perf."

Well, what had she thought? *What?* That we would simply go on living together indefinitely at the Henhouse Apartments, and shuffling pancakes at Sambo's, and cashing in our tips like the days of our lives for a roll of soiled bills lavishly dropped at a bar with men we didn't know, their minds stubbed, their fingernails dirty? This was a way station—didn't she know that?—a wobbly, half-submerged stone in a trail of ever greater, ever more stable stones on my way across a mighty river. Dixie . . . Dixie was stuck in the current. And having, it seemed, less fun the more she twirled and twisted, now and then her movements, her expressions flashing like *memento mori*. As they seemed to that morning. I felt bad; hadn't even fully repaid her the rent she'd fronted those early months; hadn't realistically considered what would become of Dixie Darling. Hadn't deeply cared.

But then, why should I have *deeply* cared? We were

just roommates, we had been that in a way throughout our entire hopscotching relationship, just roomies. Disjunction was inherent in the very nature of that sort of fugitive connection. In fact, traditionally, disjunction betokened success of one brand or another; it meant one was moving on, had secured the coveted job, had saved enough money for a first house, had met the man/woman of one's dreams, had been accepted to a college of one's choice.

Though I knew, I suppose I had known since, well, since her mother's suicide, that there was an alien presence in our roomie, not-so-roomy relationship, something crowding standard rules of conduct and injecting normal expectations with a faint tremble of urgency, as though something far more important than the temporary economic convenience of shared quarters, more important than the pleasantness of ephemeral friendship, was at stake. It seemed to lurk behind the most trivial gestures so that they meant far too much, to have a weight that was not their own, borrowed and secret; which in turn served to push sensibilities out to the skin-edge, and cast a spell of acute exposure about our incidental encountering; and finally to arouse in me an ultra awareness of my own actions, of Dixie's, of this slow, Sunday morning exchange. For instance, I realized I was noticing, just there in the pale down above her lip, flecks of perspiration, like a band of dainty, dewy stars.

"Hey," she said, with suspect zest, "the book's full."

"What book?"

"The guest book. Thumper's the last." Thumper was her cop friend—big ears, no embarrassment, a cuddly disposition, and oh-so-grateful to have on his arm, even on a time-share basis, the twinkling spectacle of Dixie.

I picked up the made-over wedding register and fanned its pages, stopping now and then to read down the names, mostly men, mostly unknown to me, except at the door in a late-night blurring of borders, their faces nuzzling through Dixie's curls. Few had lingered with her in the current, but all, I suspected, had had some lovely moments paddling through.

"You take it," she said, "when you go."

"Well . . . they're mostly your friends. Wouldn't you like to save it?" I knew it meant something to her, records of any sort did. She was always taking pictures, "pics" she called them, or "happy snaps"; she was practically wasteful about it, recording the most inconsequential acts—Thumper watching TV, or me brushing out my hair, or Lemucchi ringing up a check at the cash register. And whenever we went out—an idle excursion to the market, a drive to the city for a concert, *anywhere*—she kept in a steno notebook a journal of things we'd seen, even street signs if they struck her fancy, anybody we happened to talk to or ask directions of, names of restaurants, food we ate, numbering each entry and circling the number, and tucking the notebook back in her purse until the urge to chronicle surfaced again. There was never any future examination of the data, no questions asked of past events: they were merely recorded as though she meant to subject the contents of her life to the rigor of science, yet she never troubled to impose any interpretive order, never drew conclusions, never pushed the entries beyond their manifest states. Just lists of flotsam and jetsam snagged in the current, coming loose and drifting down, but it was only that moment, that encountering interruption in the flow—so utterly brief—she sought to note while she herself drifted down and away. It seemed not to occur to her to climb above and see the whole, to ask where or why. Perhaps that was a blessing.

Flipping to the front page, I read in Dixie's backward-leaning script, "Sue and Dixie's pad," and underneath, the faded heart with its bravely smiling, interior face. The guest book meant nothing to me. Another list. To-ing-and-fro-ing of no consequence.

Dixie had not answered me. "I think you should keep it here," I tried again. "I mean, it's part of the place."

"I'm moving," she said.

"What? Why?"

A flippant shrug. "Closer to work."

"But it's only fifteen minutes now."

"She'll want her own room."

"Who?"

"Whoever. The new one. The roommate I'm supposed to get."

"It was just a suggestion, Dixie. Someone to help with the rent." A pang of guilt, since I hadn't helped as much as I should have with the rent; determined then and there to repay her before I left.

"Rent," she said, and jerked her head dismissively. She had never cared about money.

"Well, then, for the company. I've been meaning to tell you about a woman I met in my Psych class, she's been looking . . ."

A series of thin, merry notes tinkled forth, like shards of glass, and having, it seemed, very little to do with mirth, I was again aware of my awareness around Dixie, the mental poise she excited, as though in each other's presence we were both in some sort of danger and ought to stay alert. "You don't need to pimp roommates for me, Sue. I got oodles of friends."

"Sure, I know," I said, backpedaling, waving the guest register with mock appreciation, "you'll have no problem . . ."

"I got a friend . . ."

"Sure . . ."

"This lady, in facto, she comes into Harold's once a

month, I do her hair. She likes it like mine, you know, lots of volume." Here Dixie shook her uncharacteristically subdued hair. "She saw my do and said 'that's what I want.' She's going to be a historian, *artistic* historian. Goes to State, and works part-time at a bank. It's a good place to meet guys with money, she says, they all come in making deposits, and she can see what they got, she says." Dixie tossed off a simulated naughty glance.

I smiled wanly. "She sounds like a natural."

"Jewish," Dixie added. "That'd be a switcheroo."

"Would it?"

"You're Catholic."

"Was."

"Yeah, well, like, you believe in things. Certain things."

"I'm beginning to wonder if it matters what people believe in so long as they care about belief," I said.

"Ah, for peeties sake and sanity, let's not have one of your philosophy rags."

"No problem," I said, and slipped behind her to pour myself a cup of coffee, declining the whipped cream— one of Dixie's few gustatory contributions—just to spurn her.

"You hungry?"

"Fine." And she handed me my plate, the surprisingly orange grease from the chorizo staining the yellow eggs, and I remember feeling that the day, too, had been stained by our conversation. *Guys with money,* I thought, *and she didn't even care about money. Artistic historian . . . should have at least got that right.*

At the breakfast bar we sat side by side, not looking left or right at each other. Dixie smoked a cigarette before starting on her meal; it seemed she'd temporarily lost her usual a.m. appetite for heavy, greasy foods. Presently I said, "So, what's her name?"

"Who?"

"The art historian."

In her neat, feline way, which conveyed a remotely trained quality, she slid a forkful of chorizo between her lips and finished chewing. "I don't know," she said, with incurious eyes fixed on the blank wall of the refrigerator.

What was there to say? I felt terrible, reverted to my original sentiments—that I was abandoning her—thence to the original argument—why should I feel I was abandoning her? we were just roomies—thence to the conclusion that it was best I was getting out before things got even stickier. The trouble was—it seemed the trouble would always be—that I didn't know, couldn't fathom, *why* things were sticky. And at that moment it occurred to me that I didn't want to know. Which, of course, led me unerringly to one closed door: that I suspected something, something that was so intolerable, so outrageous that my mind refused to open the door and peer in, even while it recognized the ghostly existence of the door, and lingered with a painful and angry ambivalence on its threshold.

"I have a hard time with names, too," I said, making a lame and thoroughly transparent offering.

Rising, she carried her dishes around the bar and into the kitchen and, for the smaller half of a second, she looked at me wonderingly before wiping from her face, as from the plate in her hand, all residual content. "No you don't," she said, her voice as smooth and impenetrable as the closed door before which I shrank even further.

I took a night job, 5:00 - 9:00 p.m., telephone soliciting for the local newspaper. Classes were over for the summer, I was still working the breakfast shift at Sambo's Pancake Paradise, it was too hot in the afternoons to do more than exist at a minimum standard level, and besides wanting to pay back Dixie before I moved, I thought to save some spending money for sundries, like shampoo—I liked expensive shampoos—during my first semester of college. Plus, it was close enough to the Penthouse for biking: I wouldn't have to rely on Dixie's VW, I wouldn't have to incur further debt.

*The Herald* maintained perhaps a dozen of these operations throughout the county, and there was about them a shady, bustling quality that reminded me of card rooms and gambling clubs with conspicuously nondescript, darkened façades. It was an old bungalow-style house located just off the freeway in an area that in the late forties had been a thriving middle-class district with regular daddies, resident moms, and 3 percent mortgages that were actually paid off. Now there was nothing left but *The Herald's* bungalow, cheaply purchased through probate of an old woman who had dug in and finally died. The rest of the neighborhood had long been razed, soft industry moved softly and silently in, put up monolithic, two-story hulls with flat tops, and strips of ornamental lawns, like sad, inadequate Band-Aids on a losing land, and logogrammatic signs that, impressively, no one could decipher.

But no sign announced the bungalow's intentions, no light illumined the door, and the windows, because of the interior configuration of phone cubicles, were all blinded. There wasn't any parking lot; most of the employees were alcoholics or drug addicts whose licenses had been pulled, or simple bums, or (very occasionally) working students like me who couldn't afford a car. The sole occupant of the driveway was a dented yellow Cadillac from a later vintage, the year they demoted the shark fins to guppy rank, with Texas plates, bald tires, and a molting white vinyl roof.

Inside the bungalow, the majority of walls had been

knocked out, but underfoot a patchwork of faded, nicked linoleum and pine boards and carpet revealed, like pentimenti, the lost anatomy of a home. My cubicle was situated on the carpet, looped and powder pink, worn thin in places, in others where ancient furniture had spared it, still respectably clean and thickly resistant—and sometimes I found myself looking at the carpet as if with the old woman's eyes as she welcomed into her parlour relatives and friends, perhaps the local minister to discuss her daughter's wedding, or the sheriff with news of her husband's accident, gazing at the carpet with its touching pink pride, the simplicity and earned goodness it evoked, and I remember feeling a pang of sadness for what now possessed this home.

Everyone working for *The Herald* smoked. The light from the dangling bulbs settled through the sallow haze like a toxin, the smoke saturating clothes and hair, stinging eyes, desiccating throats.

Each work space consisted of a metal folding chair, a three-by-three square of desk on which awaited a black, rotary phone, a stack of blank order forms, a list of phone numbers arranged by streets, and several capless ballpoint pens, their crowns misshapen and incised by the anxious mandibles of fellow workers. The three walls which formed the cubicle itself were of acoustic board, multiples of perforated white squares whose thousands of holes provided a near-ideal canvas for doodling connect-the-dot masterpieces, like constellation diagrams, which became an eerie parallel record of true sentiment during the prescribed and ever-enthusiastic, mostly unrequited singsong of the sales pitch.

None of us used our real names; initially it wasn't clear to me why, but it seemed *de rigueur*, an unchallenged issue, and so I came up with *Dorothy Johnson* for its wholesome allure of the girl-next-door. I was the only female in the building. No one (except Paul, and one could never be clear about him) seemed to notice or care. Indeed, gender was entirely off the subject.

For every newspaper subscription we sold on the two-month "special" (two for the price of one), fifty cents (avowedly) would go to the HOPE foundation for crippled children—that was the bait. Altruism. They could cancel at any time (though the odds were they wouldn't). They would be helping disabled children (though neither they nor I would ever receive any written documentation to that effect). *The Herald* (it was implied) was experiencing a one-time-only spasm of generosity, and the fund raiser would likely soon end (though I discovered that HOPE was an old, rusty hook long employed by the newspaper and its motley crews of solicitors).

The alkies were good, their voices caressing with a soft, mannered quality that registered the irresistible charm and authority of an older world, and there was always (delicately, delicately) the impression of a larger purpose shadowing forth—need—but it was their need they were selling, that the listeners heard at the other end in their kitchens and living rooms of sobriety. Working odd hours, they disappeared with their checks, went directly to the liquor store down the street, thence to their rented hotel rooms where they sojourned in the lonely (and limited) recesses of a bottle, returning two or three days later, broke and inspired anew to romance the addressees on the day's list. If they came drunk, they were sent away. If they came smelling too foul, they were likewise sent away, and though standards were sympathetically low, the hygiene rule was seldom invoked. For even though it was absurdly short-lived, and even though it was compulsory, a question of economic lack, the alkies took pride in their fleeting sobriety, and usually arrived with their hair combed and their faces scrubbed, even shaved now and

225

then, and their cleanest dirty shirt scrupulously tucked in. It was more than touching; it was courage, stark and brief, and honor sweet as a child tying his own shoelaces. And more than once I felt my eyes tingling as I bent to my work.

They were good, the alkies, but not as good as I was. Talking on the telephone, not having to relate to an incarnate human being with all the confusion of eyes and bodies and moods, only words and a quality of voice, a youthful, stammering eagerness, designedly lax and ungrammatic, and an innocence born not of belief in the words themselves but of belief in *their* ability to believe, in the ultimate principle of belief, buoyed me along to the shores of success. I believed that they *would* want to help the crippled children, I believed in altruism. What did it matter if it was a trick, a lie, that stirred it? Altruism was alive and it was I who had labored and begat it. In my shabby little cubicle I was Dorothy and Oz and the good witch all.

A back bedroom functioned as the boss's office. And he was, in the old-fashioned, pecking order, yes-siring sense of the word, a boss: his clothes were nicer, his manner paternally authoritative, his directions short and never explained, never questioned, even his swearing seemed admirably *pro forma*. In the beginning, every time I made a sale, I brought the order to him, like a cat bringing its kill to the master. Later I learned restraint, waiting discreetly until the end of my shift. The boss was a tall, bony Texan with circle eyes and small, perfectly centered green pupils, like the seeds of some exotic white fruit that had been halved and which had fallen wondrously open. From the arch of his forehead to the nape of his neck comb stripes ran neatly, seeming as immutable as lines scored in gray slate. He had a good-humored, suspicious manner, as though there was something naughty about whatever it was you were doing, but he would say nothing, only wanted you to know that *he* knew what you were up to. It always left me feeling obscurely uneasy, because I couldn't think what it was I had done—some little thing I had said, or my very presence in the bungalow?—and if I couldn't know it, I couldn't right it.

Grif (for Griffin) kept his dog—a fat, white, short-haired mutt about the size of an overgrown casaba—with him at all times, and he and the dog, whose name was Boy, shared Hershey's bars on the hour, Grif breaking off two squares and dropping them between his shoes where Boy always lay—"my Boy," he would say—and the rest he dipped in his coffee before popping the slick card of chocolate into his ill-furnished mouth. Even when I had had a particularly remarkable night, was standing beside his desk with a gin hand of orders, he never offered me any chocolate, and I came to understand that he too was an alcoholic, not drinking for the nonce, and was as covetous and protective of the chocolate (for its sugar content) as doubtless he had been of his booze. Grif always had the radio on, turned down low, western swing and such, I think so he wouldn't have to hear from the front room the smooth drone of dishonesty which, even though he understood it, approved of it, seemed to offend him in some residual way as though at some time in his past, life had been otherwise.

It was Grif who telephoned the names on the order forms a day later to confirm the sale. I had a near 100 percent confirmation rate; most everyone else was down around 50 percent. No one was paid for non-confirmed orders. The others, the alkies and addicts, they sold for the most part on greed—two months for the price of one—and greed, swiftly perceiving greed, will repudiate in self-righteous disgust. But I sold on the wings of goodwill, HOPE for the children, hope too for the philanthropists, and seldom did they dispute their blink of generosity, quit what might be a rare light in the darkness of themselves, and rescind the gift to HOPE.

Because of my success, Grif, with his silent, wide open eyes, seemed to regard me as worse than the others; it seemed to amuse him, too, the incongruity of it. It didn't surprise him. Nothing surprised him. Nothing surprised anyone there.

And oh, how I loved my nights in *The Herald's* bungalow—the smoky bustle, the serious black rotary phones of the old school, the thin coffee and powdered creamer with its never-washed spoon, and all around me men voices, deep and soothing, a vibration that spoke of the presence of Otherness. Mostly, though, it was the stunning artfulness of the con in the service of undisguised, unflattering need that affected me strangely. At the time, poised between the wallows of deprivation and the high road—its gate now swung open—that would lead me out, this passage through *The Herald's* shabby underpinnings seemed the kind of revelation that often comes at the end of one's association with a place or a time, with a friend perhaps, just as one is parting. I was fully and fulfillingly aware of its naked meaningfulness, and felt not that I had been shamed but that I had been secretly honored. Life had stripped itself bare to addiction, money, lies, to blessed survival, and was dancing in the dinning gloom with me. We, the tattered ends of society gathered in the night, in the fumes of our own exhaust, to feed on the unseen and unseeing body of humanity, and yet the body accepted it, agreed to it—for HOPE! That was the miserable, crashing beauty of it. HOPE.

Dialing the phone an average of seventy times per night with a 60 percent contact rate, I typically made twelve sales, and was paid $4.50 for each. Within two weeks I had settled my debt with Dixie (about which she seemed vaguely disappointed), and was saving for a swelling list of college extras. If I sacrificed the multiples of expensive shampoo, the tastier clothes and sheets of single-stitch cotton, if I tightened the budget till it squeaked, an actual car of my own began to seem achievable. And more than anything, a car meant freedom. Thus, my obsession with the world of the bungalow intensified.

We rarely spoke to one another, I and my fellow solicitors. A no-nonsense nod at the beginning of the shift, a Styrofoam cup passed at the coffee machine, and at the end, when it became increasingly risky to call, when just a ringing phone in the faraway living rooms might spark anger and the failure of the pitch would be foregone, we stole glances, making private estimations of each other's success as we wended our separate ways to the boss's office, to Grif's amused, collusive eyes and Boy's semi-exalted place at his feet, to the whining love songs of the Texas Troubadours that persisted, like chants, in spite of the encroaching buzz of a far lowlier world. Indeed, there was something churchly about the place, each call a kind of obscene prayer, mostly unanswered, but enough need combined with enough reinforcement, and we kept believing in ill-begat belief, in money, in back seat, fag end, tooth and nail survival. And, in my case, in blind altruism.

But Dixie . . . how she detested that place, what we did, all of it. Even HOPE. Never before had I seen her so desperately—that really was the word for it—so *desperately* confounded by a thing. To her, we with our phony names and idiocratic pitches, and the little bungalow gutted into service, and the fleshless Grif at the head and the fat white Boy at his feet slavering chocolate, all of it embodied some kind of egregious organism, a boogey beast, too ugly for her tastes, and intruding its utter realness, like a scabrous dog, into the middle ground of her holiday landscape.

I came home charged, reeking of cigarettes and sweat (the sour nervous sort) and bad coffee breath. My nails were bitten, my complexion as pale as a peeled potato. A glaucous-green cast had set in about my eyes, which were invariably bloodshot, and the green and red combination brought to mind a lurid parody of Christmas colors. In my foul language, originally affected with innocent resolve to harmonize with the fall from blue chip to blue collar, a hard note of authenticity now sounded, and I had made several rough additions to it, too, that were difficult even for me to work my mouth around. I took to wearing black, twisted my hair into a tight, nihilistic knot, held my cigarette between thumb and index, let my bike fall in a rusting tangle of materialism behind the yellow Cadillac, and occasionally, just to alarm her, I rattled off a defiant fart without so much as a twitch of recognition. As far as Dixie was concerned, I came home raving.

One night bicycling to work I noticed that my rear tire was losing air, and so at some point during my shift I telephoned Dixie to arrange for a ride home. She arrived about half an hour too early, sailing in like a sloop on opening day, her white cotton shift luffing in the balmy, jasmine-scented night breeze that seemed to push her gently through the open door; sailed into our workingman's harbor, looking preposterously clean and bright and frivolous among the old rusty tugs and trawlers neatly arranged in their cubicle slips. Dixie's wake rippled out, the tugs and trawlers shifted uneasily, but kept their bows snugged in tight, their eyes averted as if they were unbearably beyond—beyond appreciation, beyond wonder, beyond life, and slightly offended, too, to be reminded it was thus. The harbor master, Grif, observed. And noticing, Dixie flicked him a smile and trilled her fingers in greeting. His gaze tarried, he unwrapped his last Hershey's bar (though it was not time), half rose (upsetting fat Boy) as if to come out to meet her, then nudged his door shut. Not disposed after all.

I waved at her, gestured toward the coffee machine, and continued with my pitch which, from the quality of the silence on the other end of the line, seemed likely to succeed. Dixie reached for a cup from the top of the Styrofoam tower, then inspecting the condition of various accoutrements on the table as well as the jar with its taped injunction—*.25 a cup, no exceptions*—apparently changed her mind and wandered over to my cubicle in the corner.

"Yes, Mrs. Stevens, it's for the kids," I was saying. "No, it isn't very much, but, well, I guess if you consider how *popular The Herald* is, that's what I try to think about, all the folks like you subscribing, well, it all adds up, that's what we're counting on, that's what can *really* make a difference, is everybody helping, everybody just trying. I guess that's all we can do."

I could hear Dixie snickering behind me; tried motioning her away but she wouldn't budge.

"Yes, Mrs. Stevens. Just two months. And you can stop it any time, you know, if you take a holiday or something, all you have to do is call."

Directly behind me Dixie stood, so close I could smell her behind her own perfume. Then she put her hands over my eyes and I had to jerk my head free.

"Beg your pardon, Mrs. Stevens? Why? I guess they're just trying to do their part." Suddenly too many questions and I could tell I might lose her. "I don't know anyone personally at *The Herald*, but I heard there's a guy there pretty high up, his daughter, well, I guess she can't walk. So, I don't know, maybe it was his idea to help out the kids at HOPE because he knows what it's like."

231

An exhalation behind me, followed by the tiniest *faux* sob.

"But it's a good idea, whose ever it was, don't you think, it's the kind of idea this country needs."

Now she was humming the national anthem.

"Volunteer? No . . . not exactly. A nominal fee, that's what they call it," I said, giving a little laugh, as little, I hoped, as she imagined the fee was. "Well, I guess it is more than HOPE gets *per subscription*, but the thing to think about, Mrs. Stevens, is *all* the subscriptions adding up, everyone helping. And what's kinda nice about it, the side benefit is that it's a good newspaper. I mean, people seem to really like it. Me? I'm just trying to put myself through college because my dad, you see, my dad . . ." *When all else fails,* I thought, *tell your own sad story.*

At this point Dixie had fallen utterly silent.

"*I'm* not disabled, no, thank the Lord. I'm just trying to help, that's what we're all here to do, that's what it's about, and the newspaper is doing its share, too, for HOPE, but it can't do it without you. The newspaper, like I said before, Mrs. Stevens, has offered to donate . . . *huh? Oh.*"

I hung up. Did not turn around. Would not turn around.

Finally Dixie asked, "What'd she say?"

"She said the newspaper's full of shitty news. She said she's paralyzed and there *is* no hope." Twisting, I glared at Dixie as if it was her fault. "I called a crip with a bad fucking attitude."

I made her wait by the front door while I took my orders back to Grif, then deliberately paused to chat with Paul whose cubicle was the first by the door. Paul was not easy to understand except in an abstracted, oblique way, and even then I was never quite sure that there had been anything *to* understand, though it was my natural wont to assume there was. His words crept out at a pace that allowed for long parenthetical gazes-off in which I felt obliged to participate, and frequently I was unaware when our exchange had come to an end until he picked up the receiver and dialed the next number. It was just the sort of ethereal driftyness that drove Dixie to distraction. But I was still mad about the last pitch, figured I might have *had* Mrs. Stevens, paralysis, negative attitude and all, if not for Dixie in her white shift hovering behind me, like some dizzy angel of earthly delights whose purpose it seemed was to screw up my noble mission.

"It was better when you were Catholic," Dixie observed on the way home in the car.

"Why?" I replied, with my new perverse, reverse spiritual pride.

"I don't know . . . at least it was nice, the songs were pretty and everyone was supposed to try and be nice, and maybe I didn't think all that praying was an ice cream sundae of fun, I mean, it is stupido, heaven and sin and the guy hanging there 'cause he had all this love no one could figure out what to do with, and he was so good, too, like, that can really burn you, someone whose real good . . . but the whole thing wasn't so . . ."

"So what?"

"Dirty. That place is dirty, Sue."

"Life is dirty."

"Yeah," she said, disgusted, "but there are gobs of places where it's not, where it's beautiful, you know, like you. Like your hair, the way you used to wear it, and the brain you got, and your killer looks . . . what're you doing with all those stumble bums? I mean, it's a toilet job, Sue."

"It's real."

"It's for losers."

"We're all losers," I said.

"And what's with the guy in the back with the peeled eyes and the totally gross dog?"

"Boy," I said calmly.

"Boy, is that its name? Perf. Well you can tell that that's what he's got, that fat beggar crowding his feet, like, that's all he's got. A dog. Anyone can see that, anyone."

"I'd say he was lucky," I said, with less confidence, since it so happened she was right: Grif, I knew, had no family, had probably long driven them away with his drinking, and lived in an apartment on the east side of town near a fruit cannery.

"Lucky." She rolled her eyes. "Lucky is you, in case you got your eyes glued shut. You got friends, like me," she said, her voice slipping, "and a nice job at Sambo's, and you're going off to some fancy college with fancy scholarships, and suddenly you're all grooved on slumming, like you got to, you know, like it's your last shot before you get outta Dodge."

With dramatic abruptness, she stopped at a red light and simultaneously punched the cigarette lighter, waited, then tapped out one of her long slender numbers and said, "Real," inhaling the word as she lit up and accelerated with the green. "It's not really real for you. It's Disneyland, it's a ride, and you know you're getting off, so, like, it's a kick. But those guys, they're stuck, they're butt deep in cement and it's gone hard, that's what makes it real, the stuckness. Which you aren't."

I had to think about that.

"Look Sue, you know and I know that you used to think you were better than anyone, and now you're acting like you're worse than worse, except that, like, somehow, you're *still better.*"

"I don't know what you're talking about."

"Yeah, you do. You know what I'm talking about. It's like my grandma, she used to think she was something just 'cause she'd shove her bare hand in the toilet to clean it, and grandpa and my dad wouldn't do it, they'd wear a glove maybe or use a brush, but they wouldn't put their hand in there and splash around in the poopy water, and they sure didn't think if they did put their hand in there that it'd come out smelling like a rose. Like grandma did. Just 'cause she could do it, get down there on her knees and touch poop stains, she thought she was better. Like it was some big deal. That place is a toilet and you're lovin' it."

"No," I said, a little piqued. "But I am willing to be there, to live it and look at it, the unvarnished truth, survival and desperation and hardcore need, and you just can't stand it. Everything's got to be gussied up for you, everything's got to be pretty and fun and look like what it isn't. But it isn't pretty *all the time*, Dixie. That's impossible. Even your mother . . ."

She threw me a look as black as obsidian, and as shiny too, for it seemed she might cry or spit or collapse, and then I had to back off, way off. "Ah, cut me some fucking slack, Dixie. It's mostly the money."

"Take mine," she said quickly. "I've got it, you know I've got it."

"Yeah, I know." I stared at my cigarette—cheap, unfiltered, harsh—and stubbed it out, feeling exhausted and pathetic. "I want to earn it myself. Even if the job is crummy, there's some dignity in making it yourself. Even the hard cases, they have dignity, they're not asking anyone else to pay for their addictions, they're down there trying to make it any way they can."

"Like anyone would pay for it if they did ask?"

I smiled. "There's that. So. So they have no choice."

"But you do."

"No, I don't, Dixie. I'm eighteen, I have no skills and no money. My father, who is his own sort of human wreck and who is as much an alcoholic as any lush down there, is selling life insurance policies now . . . I love the irony of that. My mother, when she isn't pawning our baby spoons, is telling kids at the neighborhood library to shut up. I've got as much choice as, as that holy man, that cripple in the cave Paul was talking about."

"He the one you *parlayed* with?"

I nodded. "Did you hear what he said?"

"With the oatmeal skin and the slippers?

"Yeah."

"The ratty, pink, girl slippers?"

"Yes. *Yes.*"

"Like, what's that about, Sue? Slippers."

"It's about frostbite," I said, stiffening my voice. "He was a heroin addict. He's not now, but when he was, when he was up in the Sierra and he got high with some friends, he went out barefoot, I guess, and he ended up losing some toes, and the rest of his feet are in pretty bad shape, too, I guess. I mean, it just happened this last winter. So he's wearing slippers for awhile. That's all."

Silence.

Finally I said, "Do you want to hear what he told me?"

Slowly she moved her eyelids.

So. She didn't want to hear. And she knew I was going to tell her anyway.

"There's this holy man who lives in a cave in the Himalayas. He's crippled and he can't leave the cave, he just sits there all day looking out at the snowy mountains. Some trekkers come by and they're full of pity for him because he's stuck in the cave just staring at the same mountains day in and day out, but the thing is, the old man seems happy and they can't figure out why. So one of them says, 'What's it like, being here?' And the holy man replies, 'Oh, it's *wonderful*. And I have no choice.'"

Dixie coughed, an antiphon of petite, girlish gusts.

"They could've hauled the old geezer out," she said. "If it really bugged them, they could've stuck him in some posh place with a color TV and a remote."

"Right," I said. "Seventy-six channels, room service, and a Friday hooker. After enlightenment, what more could he ask for?"

We both needed to laugh, and when we had finished, the camaraderie lingered on the air, as though some lovely, self-possessed woman had wafted through, trailing fragrance. I remember noticing Dixie's exuberant blond hair, her white dress, how she seemed to be giving off light. I remember touching my hair, all tucked into a smooth black roll, all inward; then glancing down at my black tunic and black pants, the light disappearing in the fabric, and thinking that Dixie was here in the turquoise VW moving through the night, and that I could hardly be seen sitting next to her.

The moon wasn't up yet, but from the small flat city around us peachified lights diffused upward, blended with the black, and created a gray flannel canopy. Beneath it, the air was as soft and warm as flannel too, just out of the dryer, and we had both our windows open, Dixie driving with one hand on the wheel and the other, like a turn signal, supported by the wind of our passing. She glanced over at me with shaded eyes, but I could feel them, pupils like twin studs, keen and cool and piercing swiftly in. "Let me guess, you're going to date him," she said.

"Maybe I'm thinking about it. So?"

"So why?"

For some reason, possibly in the spirit of my new blunt reality, I felt honesty stumbling forward. "I suppose because he sits."

"We all sit."

"You know what I mean."

"Okeydokey, so he dropped smack and took up Zen."

237

"I'm into Zen. Currently. As you know."

"Ah, Sue, it's not Zen, and it's not selling newspapers for gimps, it's what you do to it, *you*, I mean. What you do to it in your head. It puts you in this creepy trance, and then you're not where you are, you don't have to be anymore, and I betcha that's why you do it, why everything goes to your head. Then you don't have to make it fun, you don't have to, like, live."

"Living is for the birds."

She sighed. "So you're gonna go out with this guy who deep-fried his brain and freeze-dried his feet so basically all he can do is sit anywhose . . . like, he's the one with no choice, Sue. He says Zen so he doesn't look like such a loser, which he is, and you dig it because he's perf, a holy dope and totally not the Pope, who you dumped. What I don't get is how scrambling your brains means you're holy someways. I mean, it's like Halloween and the dumber you are the freakier your costume, and you get to babble things like *keep good company* and everyone goes off all wow-ed to meditate about that. Hell's bells, your mom probably told you *that* when you were six years old, not to bum around with punks. And all this sitting till your butt goes to sleep, and breathing like you're some kind of machine, all this dead silence, what a downer."

"It's too hot to do much else," I muttered absently, and feeling just as she had inferred—down.

"Well, I say crank up the tunes and shake 'n' bake." She put out her cigarette and popped a lifesaver in her mouth. "Yeah, it was eons better when you thought God was cool."

"I really don't know why you say that? I really don't."

"At least He was a *he* and you thought He might could be out there somewheres, checking up on things. Now it's like there's *nothing*. In this totally weirdo vice-a reversa, you don't believe in anything."

"Oh, but I do, Dixie, I do believe," I said with arch mystery.

"What? That toilet you call a job?" She shook her head. "Why don't you just quit, Sue. Al, he'll give you some night shifts, you know he will. He can't say no."

"No shit," I said, remembering my shame.

"Naw, naw, that's not why. 'Cause he likes you, he, like, thinks you're going to be someone, you know. And he's not, he's got kids, a wife, he's *there*." Pausing as though momentarily confused, she cast a troubled look at the dark road ahead, then shook it off and said gayly, "We could pull some graveyards together, that'd be fun. A lot of cops come in then, ready eddie to par-tee."

"Everyone smiles at Sambo's Pancake Paradise. I'd have to smile."

"Yeah," she smiled. "So?"

"I don't feel like smiling," I said, which made me suddenly and desperately miserable, so I added, "Smiling is *déclassé*." Maybe I was trying to annoy her, or maybe I was just trying to stop her: too much of what she had said wobbled in toward a kind of truth. "*Déclassé*," I repeated.

"I give up."

"Good."

Swinging into the Penthouse parking lot, she cut the lights, got out, went front and popped the hood to release my bike, then came back to the driver's side and leaned in. "Take a shower," she said. "You stink." And off she sailed in her white shift, lovely and spectral, not a figment of my imagination, I decided, watching her disappear. But if Life itself could imagine, if it could dream up a creature in its own likeness, a living monument to living, its name would be Dixie Darling.

Which left me sifting through the ashes.

I did take a shower, a long one. And I persisted, too, in

my work at the bungalow, though with less enthusiasm and less confidence in the glories of grubby survival which, as she had implied, was not something I could pack in my suitcase, like some medal for honorable shame proving I had been there and could now leave, could now simply carry the episode with me up the gilded ladder, a small neat metallic object slipped between the folds of expensive future fabric. I had less confidence in confidence too, after that.

About the time the weather cooled—really, it was ever so little, a few degrees—and activity became at least imaginably more agreeable, I abandoned Zen. I told myself it wasn't simply a function of the heat. I told myself that I had not found enlightenment through the suffering and desire in the *The Herald's* bungalow, had not transcended experience, but that I had been snubbing experience, as Dixie had suggested that night in her peerless, curlicued logic of the moment.

But it was weeks before the weather really cooled, before we got some relief; and by then it was too late. While I became richer, more relaxed, excited about college and moving on, Dixie's life seemed to heat up inexorably.

# 13

One week Dixie came home pregnant; that is, while she was assembling a liverwurst and sauerkraut sandwich, sweet pickles, dabs of mustard, sliced Havarti, she mentioned by way of explanation that she had been for awhile—pregnant.

"Pregnant?" I said, marveling at the small yet significant weight of the word as it toddled into my brain.

"I'm getting an appointment," she replied with delicate nonchalance, and taking a large and obviously much anticipated bite of her creation. Desire slaked.

Naturally I never asked her who, not because not knowing the answer would have embarrassed her, but because it wouldn't have. And because I'd have been searching her eyes for some familiar flicker of sentiment, for something I could understand, but they would have been—I was certain—bright and strangely blameless, like the eyes of a wild animal whose gaze one could never hold for long, and never without recognition, perhaps nostalgia.

Just days before the scheduled termination, at about 2:30 a.m.—it was Dixie's night off and she was uncharacteristically home and early to bed—she began to miscarry. The blood was everywhere, black-red, pudding consistency. I stuffed a towel between her legs, threw a

241

raincoat on over her negligee, and got her down to the car and off to the hospital. It took them less than forty-five minutes to scrape her out, an hour or two for the worst of the anesthesia to wear off, then the doctor came by and told me—because there was no one else to tell—that her electrolytes were a little low but that she could still leave. No baths, no swimming for a week, infection was the concern; as a precaution, he wrote out a prescription for antibiotics, another for "discomfort." And I bundled her back in the car where she reclined in groggy pain against the window, saying nothing except "what time is it?" and again, several minutes later, "what time is it?" as though there was something about her presence at that particular moment she couldn't quite reconcile, or maybe she thought she ought to have been somewhere else and was late.

Her gaze was blank, her body crumpled against the door, and she looked like an abandoned marionette, though now and then her body jerked and her lashes fluttered, and then her eyes were wild blue flames, the microscopic holes of her pupils plunging into the maw that was opening up behind her gaze; I couldn't decide if it was just another bad cramp, or if some startling thought had bolted forward only to vanish as abruptly. She looked like someone who had seen God, or an equally awesome vision.

The VW's engine turned with its customary squeal, settled at once into the continuous, high-pitched chatter I had learned to appreciate for its reliability, and I motored cautiously away from the hospital, half afraid someone might notice an undiagnosed being escaping the wonders of modern medicine.

Just to get it out of the way, I observed that it was already warm. Dixie seemed not to hear.

I had acquired a new habit: no longer cursing the heat,

I now calmly acknowledged it before it became especially uncomfortable, as if recognition might somehow lessen its severity, even disarm it. The heat might pull its punch if I conceded it champ. Whereas Dixie had simply and instantly fallen in with *heat* in its essential reality, in step with it, and didn't appear to mind it or not to mind it, didn't yearn for change if indeed she thought it possible.

In any case, it was already warm, hopelessly warm. The sun had hardly set out on its slow path across the sky, and my stomach, in anticipation of another searing dusty day, felt about as sound as a sinkhole into which I would have gladly crawled just to escape the surface temperatures.

There was a dewless inertia lingering above the sunrise streets. The uneven and angular distribution of light together with its peculiar cast—mustard-gray and lacking any of the rosy hues of promise or of absolution generally accompanying the birth of a day—brought to mind a leaking corrosive. In the downtown area, office buildings stood acid etched into a sky of blinding sheet metal, while below them the ragged shadows of ornamental trees began their creeping, fearful retreat from across the pavement, which had never really cooled and which was already warping the air just above it in preparation for the full-scale thermal hallucinations of the midday sun. Everywhere the surfaces of things were so manifest, so *de facto*, that sight and touch merged and I experienced a kind of textural vision. Abrasive masonry walls, the gravel of vacant lots, the weathered, peeling boards of a park bench, the lacerating glint of a broken bottle—all were so completely revealed that I winced at the sight of them, their details keenly defined, and unhappily not one of them omitted. Sheer perception, alas. The world was getting to me through its bits and pieces, but nothing was in any order, any ranking, there were no comforting inequalities. Perhaps it was the prematurity of the hour and the light seeming to contradict it with a tarnish of age and infirmity; or perhaps it had more to do with Dixie, the night hollowed out by her little loss, and the day afraid to make meaning of it, everything slow-moving and slow-coming and nothing censored, everything suffering the indignity of overexposure. The evidence was overwhelming, but of what? Was the world grinding to a halt and was that why I could see it so excruciatingly well? Had it slowed to a perceivable pace? Was what seemed to me too real, simply the real fully received? Driving along, I thought about it, and while thinking seemed to have little if any effect on this state of affairs—the hard light, the details on all sides, the sad, foul smell of poor Dixie, my charge—there was nevertheless something redemptive, something *transcendent*, about the twenty/twenty sight of it all. It seemed, strangely and momentarily, that we had nothing left to lose. I was exhausted, Dixie was in pain, and we had alone/together another day of tortuous heat: stated, the matter seemed reduced to that . . . yet reduced was not how I felt.

Leaving downtown, we passed through the encircling margin of older elegant homes toward the outlying areas where the neighborhoods were homogenized and the restaurants franchised and the hills looked on with just alarm. The car window was open, but I detected none of night's elusive scents drying like perfume with the dawn; there was, apparently, not enough moisture to arouse them in the first place.

Really, there was no sense at all of a new day starting up, fresh, innocent, untried, no early players at the coffee spots or gas stations or news stands. It was as if we were being asked to witness—and participate in, too— the reenactment of a scene long gone stale until, I supposed, we got it right. But there was no *right*; we seemed to know that too, obliquely—that we would never get it right and that we had to behave *as if* we could get it right. As if the impossible were possible. What fools. What lovely, destitute fools, we.

In the curtained windows, in the newspapers yet to be retrieved from driveways, across the gray parchment of lots, and especially at intersections where we met no one and waited obediently for no one to pass by, we continued to behave *as if*. In the foolishness of waiting, I wished we would in fact meet no one who might privately mock our docile and thoroughly fatuous compliance with the law of man; I began to sense a pervasive reluctance in the unseen and unencountered inhabitants, in the town, perhaps in life itself, to issue forth and try again and fail again—to get it right. I sensed an exhilarating loss of hope.

The red light peered down at us like a desperate, monocled eye, worried we might disobey, yet we kept on heeding its caveat. It meant nothing. Alone, there was no need of this red light, this directive to stop and let others pass; if there was no Other, there was no need of the law as mediator, or as guide, or as a dam against the jungle instincts. The heat had simply gone on too long: it was not a reminder any longer, it was a contagion. What we had constructed—our relationships springing up and dying off like weeds, and the delicate, rare ones too, pruned and cultivated, our shops and streets, our town, our magnificent law—all seemed to quake beneath the huge indifference of the weather. Not the intensity but the monotony, that was what drove it—and us—beyond. We seemed to be wandering half blind across a hot, vast plateau, and one day, perhaps this day, we would simply step off the edge. One could only hope (if hope was the word) that one was in full stride as one took that last step.

Heat. Now the heat had transcended its own physical

properties, had become an abstraction whose symptoms ranged from sweat to vague anxiety to genuine grief to existential panic. Also, it began to reproduce itself: in the eyes of my fellow victims I noticed a cooked, bleak indifference. And seeing it, I felt the absurdity of our predicament.

Glancing over at Dixie, I wondered if in fact it was the long strain of the heat that had perpetrated the fetus' expulsion. Of course, what did it matter? I thought, she'd've killed it herself three days hence, though that reality seemed to be of little comfort. It is one thing to act, it is another thing to be acted upon; or worse, to be simply caught up in a scheme of chaotic, dispassionate acts—which is not a scheme at all, which is nothing. Death was the only real scheme. Whether or not one eventually lost the baby or the battle or the whole match struck me as considerably less important than how. Though even *how*—losing with dignity or cowardice, with reason or complete absence of thought—even *belief in how* was beginning to be undermined by itself. How could one attend to belief when the outcome was always the same? *She'd've killed it anyway.* We were all going to die anyway. We were all going to die of ourselves, in effect. Nature of the beast, etc. It was living, it was striding, or crawling, or being dragged by Time itself, across the plateau, that would kill us—nothing less. The only truly serious question was whether or not to open one's eyes wide.

And if living begat death, could it not be said that death begat life? And what if the two had sex? How incestuous! But think of the collision, the point of contact and the terrible beautiful union, and think of *being* in that keen and (of course) simultaneous orgasm within the relentless present tense. And what, I wondered, would be the progeny of that union? A work of art, I supposed; and never finished, either. No, it could never really be finished. But I was getting away from things . . .

In silence, we tooled the bleached and desolate roads of the town, heading home, which for the first time and probably only by virtue of the anticipated dusky light of the apartment, seemed indeed a home, however temporary. Every time I had to brake, I threw out my right arm to keep Dixie from slumping forward, and the funny thing was that I think it was my protective arm and not the miserable episode itself that occasioned two large teardrops which my roommate, so exposed and reduced, did not bother to conceal.

The other funny thing was that on that day alone among all the days of the long spell, Dixie noticed the heat. She drew her fingers over her face and murmured, "I can't stand it anymore."

I said, "I wish we had air conditioning."

She gazed at me, almost fearfully it seemed, and, as if across a soundless abyss, did not try to respond.

Then I felt even more sorry for her, for myself. We had helped each other over the years whether or not we had wanted to because there wasn't anything else to do. I wondered if it made any difference. Probably not . . . but maybe some. Maybe the whole of the difference lay tucked, like a bittersweet secret, in the pocket of that paradox.

Once out of the car, she needed to lean on me as we hitched across the parking lot and up the elevator, then before starting down the long hall, we paused to rest. Opening her raincoat, she stared vacantly at the carpet, and seemed to attend only to her breathing which on the intake was long and quiet, on the outtake forcefully abrupt, imparting a sense of closure, as if she wasn't going to bother inhaling again, she had quite finished with that. And yet she did take a breath, and another, concentrating, it seemed, on the cost and dearness of each one.

Presently, a young man—blue suit, red tie, slender attache, hair still wet from his morning ablutions, cologne in the plenitude of power—hurried by, pushed the elevator button, then with time to spare and taking curious note of us, he strayed over to where we stood three yards away, enlisting the aid of the wall.

"Is that you, Dixie?" he inquired, canting his glossy head.

The insipid eyes I faintly recalled. Maybe from the party. Maybe at the door, picking up Dixie. Maybe he was the one responsible. Insipid eyes casing her bare feet, her raincoat, bloodstained negligee tattering out; observing too, through the semi-sheer bodice, her breasts, so sadly full and perky for what Life had briefly intended.

Now I could not hear Dixie breathe.

"It can't be you." His lips were swollen and bruised-looking, as though someone had punched him there, and when they wriggled around a toothy grin, I had to look away. "Can it?" he said.

From Dixie—head bowed and isolated behind a cage of undone curls—there came no answer.

I tried glaring at him. He was so clean and pressed and orderly, so self-complacently ready for his little day, it was really unbearable, and somehow it was indecent, too.

"Hey, what's the deal here?" he said with a hard voice now, as if our silence was vulgar.

So, with icy composure—because it was true—I said, "Fuck off."

The elevator *dinged*, and into it he fled, though just as the doors were closing, his safety assured, I heard a savage guffaw and the words, "town pump."

Which led me to assume that he had concluded Dixie had run into some trouble with a lover, had been roughed up. Had deserved it. And if one took the view that Life was Dixie's lover, then his conclusion was not unreasonable.

In the apartment Dixie clung to the breakfast bar while I fetched sheets and pillows for the couch where I had predetermined it would be more pleasant for her, with the TV and balcony view and the sun projecting a saffron haze against the west hills as the leading edge of dawn slid down from the ridgeline and across the valley toward us, like the approaching menace it was. Another day abandoned to heat, another bout with lassitude and hope.

She smelled of musty, dried blood and antiseptic and sour sweat, but I never let on, made a point of getting close to her as I settled her on the couch, made a point of being casually competent as though I had done this every day. I turned on the TV. Called Lemucchi whom we had made, oddly enough, privy to virtually all our activities, to tell him I could not come in, to tell him what had happened.

"You poor girls," he said. "I'll come by later with . . ." he couldn't think what, "with something," he said, frustrated. "Candy, or something. You girls just take it easy." The quintessential nice guy, A. L. Lemucchi, and I felt at that moment not only a warm rush of gratitude for his concern, for the presumption of fellowship he embodied, but for the first time since it had happened, profoundly glad I had fucked him. It seemed the least I could have done. And fortunately for both of us, the event had not given rise to the obligatory fumble and grasp at meaning of which we instinctively knew there was a shortage. A moment of need, or narcissistic affirmation, perhaps even a dream of oneness, but meaning? No. Calling him, that had meaning perhaps; and his answer, even the helplessness in his voice and the voice sounding in spite of that helplessness, (ridiculous!)—that had meaning too. He would come later, as soon as he could, bringing something that would be of no use but nice all the same, to be here with us for a few minutes until he had to leave. It was strangely moving.

I went to the grocery store and gathered up pads, popsicles, sherbet, juice and booze for piña coladas, and for later when her appetite would return, T-bone steak (she liked steaks, especially T-bones because they occupied an extravagant lot of her plate), and baked potatoes with butter, sour cream, and Baco-bits which she distributed on an unlikely spectrum of food items, and broccoli to show her someone really cared, broccoli because in those days it seemed the future might hold something, and flowers *comme il faut*, and cigarettes because one was always stuck in the contradiction, because life was a precarious proposition anyway. A wire walk. Next door at the pharmacy, I had the prescriptions filled. I then found an appliance store and purchased a tiny, oscillating, "personal" fan which I set on the coffee table next to her, along with the latest *Vogue* and *Cosmopolitan*, and a third periodical devoted entirely to hair styles with dramatic before-and-after shots of satisfied victims, their smiles fabulous and specious, like converts to a new religion.

"They look like EST graduates," I said, trying to cheer her up—we both had it in for EST graduates—and Dixie did try to smile, but it was really more of a short and pathetic spasm of the small muscles bordering her lips, and did not pretend to engage any facial territory beyond.

Several times in an unfamiliar voice—small but intensely vivified—she murmured, "Thanks."

"Sure," I said, or "Of course," and once I only smiled and reached to move an errant curl from her pale, damp brow. Then she gazed at me wonderingly, as if she were trying to recall who I was; and when she slept through the morning news, I found myself gazing similarly at her, for I had never seen her so cut down, her vitality withered, her face unoccupied, her presence not flowing out but ebbing back and inward, as if retreating from the idea, *the very idea*, of Dixie Darling. Only in her voice did there remain a tremor of life.

It was just before noon when I noticed the smoke, a slender, white question mark in the distance.

The west hills, as the lowest and most eastward rank of the Coastal Mountains, ran in north-south ripples which broadened as they dropped down to the valley floor so that the visual effect was of a vast, green corrugation tilting up whose bottom half had been hammered and splayed. On one of these corrugations, about halfway down where the land was stretched and fully exposed to the sun, in a mix of brittle grass and desperate scrub, the fire began; the smoke, so sinuous and pretty, a pantomime of disaster. For awhile it was the question mark, then a white cobra, then the line resolved into graceful spirals, like a dancing wraith; for awhile there was something in it to be desired, to journey toward, the eyes gazing, the gaze shearing off only to return hypnotically again (but briefly, *oh briefly*) to the wavering line. Soon enough the line lost its integrity, began to blur and mass, and then the delicate twisting became muscular and the smoke rose in billows, swelling up from the earth, gray now and angry seeming, the dancing wraith overwhelmed. At a certain height the billows flattened, as if they had bumped into a ceiling, an air current perhaps, or heaven's very foundation, and the smoke spread east toward us, its acrid scent arriving first, an eerie, invisible messenger. I waited and watched as the billows lapsed into a shapeless thing, out there, cutting with languid confidence— nothing could hurry or stop it—an ever-widening swath through the blue field to which we had grown accustomed that summer, perhaps even taken for granted in spite of the irredeemable heat. I wondered how it moved, there was no breeze; and the longer I watched the more it seemed that it was not moving, that we were moving toward it, Dixie and I and everything in its path, but then it was our path and the path of the baby that could never have been and the paths of friends we had lost and friends we would find too, and we were all moving to meet the shapeless thing which itself had begun in the distant distance as a mere question . . . as a tenuous and provocative, dancing white wraith . . . as a silly contradiction far off on the ultimate landscape.

Obliquely I sensed a shift in the atmosphere, subtle yet unmistakable, a kind of vacuum, as if whatever and all that lay beyond our door had suddenly inhaled, and was trying now to inhale us, to pull us, like cartoon people, out under the absurdly unqualified door.

I glanced at Dixie, wondered about her low electrolytes, wondered what they were and why I hadn't asked the doctor, what had been so daunting?—the size of the word or the responsibility it implied or simply the distance when he told me, the distance between me in the empty, ill-lit waiting room adjacent to the exit, and Dixie lying somewhere in the fluorescent innermost of the hospital. It seemed she was always in the middle of something, and that I was always next to the exit.

*Electrolytes.* I made a search for the dictionary, but it was nowhere to be found. I thought of calling the hospital. I reasoned that it was just as likely to be *un*important as important. I told myself that if I had needed to know, the doctor would have explained. If I had wanted to know, if it was something that affected all of humanity, for instance, I supposed I would have asked. I might have felt inspired and if so, I would have rallied all of my resources, I would have committed myself with the fortitude that only the most glacial passion imparts, steady and slow-moving and unrelenting, uncompromising. But it was just Dixie. Just one, eighteen-year-old woman with a small problem of her own making, decidedly correctable. I had got it wrong, I had switched them: Dixie was not an example of humanity, humanity was my case study. Which struck me as a most dangerous reverse exercise of synecdoche.

Probably just asking the doctor, the wanting to know would have come; if I had faked it, if I had behaved *as if*, I might have tricked myself, I might have lured a brilliant, fingerling of love to the surface and offered it up to Dixie. He said "electrolytes" and it was I who felt weakened by the word, maybe even annoyed; it was possible that I was afraid to know what it meant, afraid to know what I could do, what I would have to do, to help a single human being for one day of our circumstantial alliance. Afraid because I was unqualified. We were all unqualified. We were all we had, too.

Still, in spite of not knowing, I found myself blindly trying, perhaps only for the sake of those two teardrops in the car, one (it could be said) for each of us.

Outside the light seemed to falter as though a great hand were making ambient mood adjustments, settling a curtain here, dimming a lamp there, in preparation for some long-awaited event, and when the light faltered for the last time and finally went murky, I stood up to close the balcony door to keep out the smoke, though by then it was really too late. The air was visible, swirling as I passed through, and in the kitchen where it was especially trapped, it seemed to sag in the corner like the obligatory unwanted guest at a party. As matters stood, I regarded the "personal" fan swinging busily back and forth, debated its utility, then flipped it off and returned to my post in the chair beside the couch. Dixie was still asleep, her breathing soft and trustful, and meeting incongruously the sound of distant sirens. Listening, I felt. For one moment loosed from time I felt complete solidarity, and sewn into the lining of that unbound moment, the blessedness and utter futility of it.

Maybe I dozed. The long night and the thick, plum-pudding blood, the doctor telling me things because there was no one else to tell the things to, the smoke in our midst, and Dixie's innocent breathing—the whole of it, the immediacy of it, seemed to drain me of purpose. It was all I could do to sit. To sleep. Later when I opened my eyes, I was again aware of the light outside, not opaque as I had expected, but a translucent gray, and the air some-how mobile, as if a dark veil had been thrown over the world and was quivering, quivering tenebrously.

She was still asleep.

It struck me that something ought to be done, that perhaps I—in view of Dixie's nonpresence—that *I* really ought to do something, but I couldn't think what, and for the longest while yet I maintained a deathly stasis. It seemed easier not to move. Maybe the phone would ring, maybe Lemucchi would knock at the door and I would be compelled to stir. The room was a pool of silence, and if I lifted a hand, even flicked a finger, not orderly ripples but a disturbing chaos would surround us, overcome us. I meditated, attended to my own breathing—*in, out, pause, in, out, pause lengthening, reluctance, reluctantly in, then out with relief*—but Dixie's breathing was an in-terference, and anyway, the meditation was all pretense to begin with.

Finally, not at the strong urging of my mind, and not out of boredom or hunger, but for no defensible reason— really, there was nothing to do and nothing I had to do, no action that would make a difference, put out the fire or stop her suffering, nothing that would lead to know-ing *why* anything had happened, why this decrement, this small erosion of humanity that would have with time been a willful act, no thinking, no formulations that could explain once and for all the source of the fire or the source of Dixie's troubles, and no deed at the moment that could alter the night before or change the course of the day with its stifling heat, no prayer that would find a god, no god in attendance, just me—finally *for no reason at all*, not even for the smug awareness of the lack of a reason, maybe only because I was free to or not to, damned free, I stood and walked into the kitchen and sliced some peaches. They were cool and slick and sweet, and seemed to mock—I practically laughed with exaltation as I slid each one in—the burnt smell and heat of the day, the bloody night, the bloody nights that would come. Then I sliced another and plopped some of Dixie's whipped cream on top, and ate it all fast, without thought. Afterward, I found some of Dixie's anchovy paste, slathered it on half a dozen wheat crackers, and washed them down with a tumbler of chilled white wine. The wine seemed to mitigate the aftereffects of the sleepless night, so I made a spritzer of more, with cranberry and soda and lime slices squeezed over the brilliant, hissing liquid. I thought maybe to move even more, so I tidied up the bedroom, changing and soaking the bloodied sheets, and ran a couple of loads of wash down to the laundry room, scrubbed the bathroom, emptied ashtrays, popping into the kitchen between completed tasks to eat, which had proved such a success, such a tiny and magnificent force. The fact that I wasn't hungry, that the apartment was relatively clean and even if it wasn't, it would get dirty again, that nothing I was doing mattered or would be noticed by anyone seemed to unlock a kind of gleeful and profane defiance. I was satisfying no dire need. I was furthering no plan: there was no plan. If the question had been, if nothing mattered, why bother? now with a sleight of hand it was, if nothing mattered, why not? Still, I couldn't quite escape the feeling, the *necessary* feeling that *something* mattered.

Maybe *she* mattered. My friend, Dixie. Or maybe it was only that *mattering* mattered.

That day in her spiritual absence I became Dixie Darling. Maybe to invoke her, or to revive her. Maybe because I realized for the first time that whoever I was needed whoever she was. And without colliding, without a point of contact, nothing true had a chance.

The vacuum awakened her, and through several rounds of backgammon (my suggestion) I willingly struggled. Dixie, with a drooping of fingers or a faint nod, indicated her advice on which pieces I should move, but she never uttered a word, never registered a feeling.

At intervals I helped her to the bathroom to change her pad. She did not turn on the light, keeping her head down as her shape moved with the shade in the mirror, as if to avoid even the dimmest reflection of the present. I thought to make her a nice warm shower though I never suggested it for fear of intimating that I was offended by her malodor, but a shower seemed not to occur to her. I fluffed her pillows whenever she was away from the couch, luffed the sheets when she returned; checked my watch, administered on schedule her medications, took her temperature now and then, worried about the cryptic electrolytes. Was too embarrassed to call the hospital. Never found the dictionary.

When in the afternoon the soap operas began she wandered from one to the next with broken interest, her eyes unlit, her gaze flat and drifting from the parodical angst on the TV screen to the glass balcony door and beyond through the quivering veil of smoke to the west hills, now a cinereal green, still silent and distant and ever-present, then back to the thirty minute tragedies, again to the irreconcilable west, until at last a heavy sleep released Dixie from the cross-purposes displayed before her.

Between the lunch shift and the dinner shift Lemucchi,

in his touching, brown-study attire, arrived with a box of cherry-filled chocolates. Dixie rolled over, faced the back of the couch, wouldn't see him. Wasn't even polite.

"Gosh," he said, then again "gosh," peering into his hands as if to discover exactly what it was they had done.

I walked him to the elevator.

"She's taking it awfully hard," he said. "Was she thinking of going through with it? That never occurred to me, that she was going to."

"No."

"Then I don't understand."

"Maybe it's just the whole idea . . ."

Confused, he shook his head. "You girls . . ." he said softly. Even when he didn't understand, maybe especially then, Lemucchi's habit (*oh*, it was a lovely habit) was to assume that there was something admirable, a fine and dewy sprout of virtue, trembling at the heart of any mysterious matter.

That night she picked at the T-bone, drank too much, and never once mentioned the smoke, as if it was simply part and parcel of the whole episode. Which, indeed, it came to seem to me.

Throughout that entire day we never actually saw the flames. Just smoke.

There was only one phone call, from the caretaker at the stables where Dixie boarded her horse, saying that the forest service had advised them to move all the animals, that the fire had jumped the line and was headed their direction.

"She got to come get him," he said. "All owners, they got to come now."

"It's impossible," I said. "She's ill."

"Well, what I'm sposed to do? You ask her."

"She doesn't even own a trailer," I said. "Make arrangements. She'll pay whatever."

"Yeah, *arrangements*, I heard that before. Five times, five calls. Don't nobody wanna get up here and mess with a fire-blind horse." He gave himself over to explosive coughing which at last thinned to a desperate and wheezy subjoinder, "You tell her nobody but somebody, they gonna pay, and not Ephraim Armstead. You tell her."

Of course I didn't that day. And I didn't tell her the next day either, she was so cheerful, so normal, I couldn't bear to upset what, by virtue of sheer contrast, I concluded was an unreliable mood. I couldn't bear for her to vanish again. Though I confess to one thing: there was something about that day, about Dixie that day, that I missed with a deep and wrenching tenderness—her smell, unmasked, unprotected, her usual camouflage plunging to its absolute naked nadir. Old sweat and old blood and hard time, and her unwillingness, the *dignity* of her unwillingness to do anything about it. The dignity of her foul, foulest smell.

The cheerful mood stuck. And the horses, as it turned out, were not evacuated, though they were all pretty keyed up from the smoke and smell of the scorched land, especially the stallion. And in a way, as Ephraim Armstead had warned, Dixie paid.

It took them several days to get the fire under control, another several to stamp out hot spots. Everyone seemed to make two wild assumptions. First, that the threat of fire was now gone, when in fact *nothing had changed*; the degree of threat was uniform, the threat itself perpetual. Second and wilder still, that with the fire, the fever had broken, as it were, and the weather would now cool off, when in fact the heat persisted with oblivious vengeance. "It has to stop," we said, though there was nothing it *had* to do and nothing it could be *made* to do, and nothing *we* could do except make the best of it, though there were many times when that resolve was undermined by the relative successlessness of the task at hand.

A week later Dixie discovered she had crabs, which inspired a far more frontal reaction than the pregnancy. I heard through the bathroom door the moment of discovery.

"Stupid, selfish jerk." A blast of water. Cupboards slamming. "H. E. double hockey sticks!" Then more garbled execrations.

"What is it?" I called. "What's happened?"

Out she burst, hair flying, face flushed, and a gun metal glint in her eyes. "Crabs. He gave me crabs. Like, he could've said so, he could have *informed* me, the jerko."

She was standing there in her robe, doing a kind of stifled Saint Vitus' dance, twitching about, and trying to keep her hands from herself. "Itchy little guys, like, *wow*," and she gave a bob and jiggle, "they are totally kicking *alive*. I'll tell you one thing for sure," she said, flouncing about, "I'm not dating that stud-muffin again."

It seemed such an unnecessary thing to say. I realized though that it held a quaint reality for Dixie, represented the extremity of action she might take against a man. Probably she had never said no to any of them, and I was both impressed and beguiled by the retribution.

"What would you have done if he *had* told you . . . before?"

"I don't know . . . nothing, I guess."

"Nothing?" I was flabbergasted.

"Well, all I want is to know. I gotta right to know," she said, looking straight at me.

"But you'd've still contracted crabs!"

"Yeah," she said, in airy dismissal. "Maybe."

# 14

Mid-August, two weeks before my planned defection, Dixie asked me out to dinner in order to meet her proposed new roommate—not the Jewish art historian (who knows what happened to her?) but a nurse-in-training she'd met at the hospital during her brief and unhappy procedure. It was always a little unnerving, the speed with which Dixie established contact, in this case enough apparently to advocate living together. I was told only that her name was Katherine—no leave to shorten—and that she was "another Catholic," to which I responded (again) that I was not, as Dixie very well knew.

"Sure you are," she said, pinching my butt. "Still a pew buff 'cause it was. Some parts of you, like your sitter, just can't forget."

Which, in terms of summation psychology, made some sense. Also, it implied (and partially revealed) Dixie's philosophy of life as a rudderless ship in unexplored waters. Grueling acts of will, the calisthenics of the overconsidered choice, the reason of reasoning, brought about nothing more than lost time and eventually chronic aches and pains. One could not *choose* not to be it; one simply encountered it (whatever *it* was), and in encountering it, acquired it to some extent, and while one may sooner or later toss the thing itself overboard, one could not shake the encountering experience, the taste and stench of it, the phantom feel of it lingering in hands that had once so confidently ejected it. We are what we were up to the pinpoint of the present—"the peak of my personal and exclusive heap of me myself and I" as Dixie was fond of saying—and what we were, for Dixie, was wholly a matter of chance and seemed not to oblige conscious memory or to inspire any regrets. What we would be (including dead) did not interest her. Hope did not interest her. Faith was a foreign language.

So, as far as Dixie was concerned, it didn't matter what I said, Catholicism was down there in my personal heap of history, still taking up space and giving off odors while it moldered, as Zen was doing, and coconut macaroons, and Henry James and everything else I had encountered with (or without) zeal. And perhaps for the late-model roomie, Katherine, it would be likewise relegated to compost some day, but that evening of our first and last meeting, in the sunken garden of her soul, Catholicism was in full bloom.

Actually, I was looking forward to meeting her. I found myself trying to imagine her, came up with several implausible combinations of strawberry-blond giddiness (to bring her temperamentally closer to Dixie), and the scrubbed composure of nurse Katherine taking Mr. Peabody's anal temp (to factor in some realism), and lastly Catholic Katherine leaving anonymous knee dentlettes in the *prie-dieu* as she confessed . . . what? Sex? It was always sex with Catholic girls. So, what, *what* would Katherine say, how would, how *could* she negotiate Dixie Darling's live sexcapade?

In the end, I couldn't imagine Dixie with anyone but me. Which came as the kind of shock that, to the silent members of one's being crouching in obscure corners, is not a shock at all.

Though Dixie was by no description fat, she was in all her physical particulars generous, but perhaps because of the heat and the various stresses and strains of the summer, Dixie had steadily lost weight, and was now frequently attired in her mother's more subtle and tasteful raiment. Coincidentally, her ablutions became (if it can be envisioned) even more elaborate and at the same time more fixed: she seemed to cling to them as to the last surviving ritual of an abolished and, now, half dismantled faith, providing the comforts of rote, where before there had been something heartfelt and exciting, something inspired about the standards to which she paid religious attention.

So it all took longer, her *toilette*, and in terms of the essence of Dixie, was less successful, and because of her mother's clothes, even less authentic. But as long as I can remember, she was, during those last two desperate weeks of the summer of our dying youth, as beautiful as she had ever been, and would ever be, as it turned out.

We met Katherine at the restaurant, formerly a "family eatery," soon to be an "elegant dinner house," currently in the unseemly throes of evolution "under new management": the table linens were white and the glassware thin, but the waiter brought cocktail napkins (imprinted bar jokes) with the Burgundy—a lesser Clos Frantin—and knowingly did not question our age, no doubt because of the presumptive *quid pro quo* rise in his tip. Whenever the kitchen door swung it was with the preternatural slam-bang of a saloon followed by a sudden, momentary tumult, like a detonation, that brought to mind a crowd at a sporting event in which the home team (in the kitchen) was not doing so well.

Dixie ordered Steak Diane (?). I chose the wine and a fettuccine. And Katherine—rather pretty in a pre-molded way, contours smooth and undramatic, yet well proportioned, hair looped up, teeth small and even, like rows of pale baby corn—dear Katherine suffered through the bony corpse of a farmed trout.

She was too nice and too earnest and very nearly infuriatingly flawless, bucking for martyrdom, I decided, a fatal pursuit to all concerned; and Dixie was, throughout the conversation, too quiet. She was either waiting for my approval, or trying to insult me with this perfectly nice, squeaky-clean, socially anemic, Pollyanna proxy. Finally, out of boredom, I made a couple of cracks about religion that seemed to imply that I had developed beyond it, and that it was all really quite a clever ruse, wasn't it? Christianity, just to try to dupe mankind into moral conduct while enduring the inborn despair of life itself, and *Eternity*? wasn't *that* a fat little carrot cure for the incurable?—an argument which I thought would amuse Dixie since she regarded organized belief with about as much solemnity as a kid at a traveling circus. But it didn't somehow amuse her.

Katherine was having a real time of it with the trout. At some point (just after the carrot-of-Eternity bit) she abandoned her careful dissection and began hacking randomly at the corpse, using her fingers, spitting bones, and at the end her plate seemed to bear not the remains of a savory meal but of a small grisly explosion—fleshy shrapnel scattered about, caught in the micro branches of broccoli, floating in the vacant trench of a baked potato, even pasted to the stem of her wine glass. Between me and the fish bomb, she was looking about as puncture-proof as a tight balloon, though when the coffee arrived (in the thick, aboriginal mugs of the "family eatery") I could tell she was still trying to be perfect—*Would you care for sugar, Susan?* said she, turning her fourth or fifth cheek. I took this as the challenge it was, and before the sugar had dissolved in the black depths of my cup (and of my heart, I later mourned) I made some gay reference to Jesus as the first hippie. At which point she did lose it. Shoving away from the table, her eyes tiny and pinked (like fish eggs, I remember thinking with satisfaction), she said I hadn't got any right insulting other people's religions. Whereupon I said that it *was* my religion which not only gave me *every* right to insult it, I rather considered it my duty. Which, once again, I thought would please Dixie, since she had just that afternoon asserted that I would, in effect, always be Catholic. But it didn't somehow please Dixie.

Then Dixie paid the tab, and the rest of the two of us mimed our thank you's, and on the way home in the car I acted stunned and amazed, said something vaguely charitable about Katherine's "sensitivity," but Dixie held her peace, kept her eyes on the road.

The next morning I told her I was sorry. She shrugged, said it didn't matter. I felt worse. I said that Katherine was perfectly nice, really a very nice person, I didn't know what had gotten into me. "Oh well," she said, handing me a cup of coffee (*sans* whipped cream, I noted). I said I guessed I was just stressed out by the move and all.

Stepping out onto the balcony, she lit a cigarette. For awhile I watched the back of her and the west hills in the distance, the great black amoebic scar the fire had left, Dixie smoking, an eerie tranquility about her, and no breeze, not a tick of movement anywhere, it seemed, except the smoke from her cigarette rising in a nearly straight line before attenuating and vanishing of its own account. Finally I said that I guessed I'd run down to the grocery store and get some boxes to pack up before it got too hot and I lost all incentive and gave myself over to bonbons and TV—just to lighten up the mood.

"I have to turn the horse out this afternoon," she said

in a flat voice, and keeping her back to me. "You wanna come?"

It was Saturday, we were both off. Now and then I had enjoyed accompanying her to watch her ride, or to read a book beneath a spreading oak, or simply to get away from my two jobs and the urban broil of summer. And, aside from wanting to make amends, I was beginning to feel that I would miss Dixie Darling even while I couldn't wait to get away with my own kind in a college of my choice. Everything about my current predicament—my relationship with Dixie, my job, my address and, more often than not, the company I kept and the places I went—was accidental. I yearned to take up my original plans and proceed apace. But it was true, I would miss her, I would miss her bubbly, embarrassing, unruly ways, so pathetically alive, I would miss how she cared which was never meant to *show me*, but was always and plainly the helpless brimming over of how she felt, a kind of failure of containment. Whereas I, unhappily, had too often succeeded in containing my feelings, they were so inveterately small and easy to stifle. So I said, yes, and to convince her, added, "I would really like to," in a deliberate, emphatic manner, smiling though she couldn't see me.

Then Dixie had to cough; probably she'd inhaled too deeply—that was what I thought. It was early morning, after all, and one's lungs, having enjoyed an eight-hour respite, naturally balked at the resumption of torture. But later I had to wonder.

I had to assume that she knew her father was coming that morning (though she hadn't mentioned it) because he'd only visited her at the apartment twice, each time following overly elaborate discussions which left them with very little to say once the visit became fact. I had to figure that because it was not mentioned to me, the usual overly elaborate discussion must not have taken place,

and the purpose of his visit was therefore ostensibly unknown. Which meant that it *was* known, especially and
utterly known. Which meant that whatever Dixie knew
was intolerable . . . that she was there on the balcony
anticipating it . . . that the night before, and the boxes of
my departure, and Slade's news, and maybe even the mis-
carriage and the crabs and the dragging heat, and the
black swath of death in the middle, *right in the middle* of
our once hilly green view, had all combined to under-
mine her. So when I returned with the boxes and saw Bill
Slade in our living room I had to wonder if she had
coughed or if she was choking back the first intimations
of her own undoing. And of mine, it could be said.

He turned when he heard the door, an expression of
futility raggedly edged with anger persisting through my
interruption. In our matchbox living room he was hulky
and awkward, an overgrown child. His hair, sparse but
erect, had been recently butched and formed a dusty boxy
corona about the light bulb of his head. Except for a pair
of very clean, very large white tennis shoes with red darts
along their sides, his clothes were undistinguished. The
off-duty inspector.

I thought he might try to involve me somehow, or escape through the door just behind me, because he seemed
reluctant to turn back to Dixie, but since she hadn't even
acknowledged my arrival, I only nodded, fled with wild
relief to the bedroom, and closed our exceedingly feck-
less, hollow-core door which no doubt had provided substantial savings (multiplied out) to the owners of the
Penthouse, but no aural privacy to its less prosperous inhabitants. I heard everything.

"Why didn't you ever sleep with her?"

"I won't have this conversation with you."

"Why didn't you screw her?" Incredibly, it was Dixie's
voice, *not* Dixie. No. Not ever Dixie.

Long silence. Then Slade, quiet, exasperated. "Dixie, Chickadee, I have a right to remarry."

"*Hermia?*"

"She's been good to me. To all of us, your mother especially."

"Everyone was good to her. We were all good to her, we were all *so* good to her, we were all just *as nice as could be*, her agent, Sharp, and all the kiss-the-camera guys, and the slobs selling cars and cigarettes and life-o-matics, they were nice too, and you, you kept her nice and like, safe, and yeah, Hermia was good to her too, Hermia cleaned and polished the furniture and mom and more furniture, and you know what? I was nice to her too, I was really really good to her and what difference did it make? What difference?"

"I don't know why she . . . look, we'll never know why, there's no use in this."

"We niced her to death."

"You're too upset."

"She never had a chance," Dixie cried.

"No," from Slade, voice strangled.

"If you screwed her, if you yelled at her, if I had . . . if she had something, *anything* to, to, to, like, bump into, but there was *nothing* there ever, just niceness, empty niceness all around her." Pause, then in rapid fire: "She was vacuum-packed."

"Your mother was a very delicate woman . . . from the beginning. Even when I married her . . ."

"Marry? You engraved her."

"Dixie, you can't, you can *not* talk . . ."

"And then you kept playing. You were a big-time player, I know, I know about the others, the Hermia hicks. Meat 'n' potato women."

No sound. A heavy, suffocating presence just there on the other side of my hollow-core door.

Finally him. In policeman monotone. Control pushing rupture. "She couldn't handle it and I had needs. Normal needs. The normal, everyday needs of any man."

"Yeah, what about her? What did she need every day? Does anybody have *any* idea?"

"I, we all, tried not to disturb her."

"Disturb?" Dixie said, her voice shattering. "Disturb her?"

"Look, Dixie, she never knew, she was completely protected."

There was a shuffling about sound, as though they had moved to different places, sat down maybe, far apart. "You just don't get it," she said.

"That's right, I don't, I never did understand your mother, no one did. But I have more information than you. People said delicate, or sensitive, I said that, I told myself things from the very beginning, that I'd have to take care of her, and I wanted to, believe me, she was beautiful and simple, like a bird. But it was worse, Dixie, you have to know that, you really should know. She was unstable. Who knows why? We went to see a man in New York just after you were born. She couldn't even handle her own baggage, let alone a baby. He said, he said she was the most passive human being he'd ever met. He said other things, too, *abulia* maybe, maybe some kind of that, but he couldn't say for sure, and I didn't ask. The thing is, he didn't want to see her."

"Why?" Dixie asked with obvious confusion. Then I heard sounds from the kitchen, the clink of glassware, rattling ice. It had to be Dixie, it had to be she was pouring herself a drink. In those late summer days she drank at odd times, denying the propriety of The Hour, refusing to participate in the moral sport of delayed gratification; ignoring, too, by a kind of total eclipse of the mind, the standard signs and symptoms, the terrible promise that she was cultivating a drinking problem, like some seed of a weed that happened to have landed in her garden and which, through sheer unparticularness, she was raising up like a prize rose. As the ultimate hostess Dixie embraced everything, even alcoholism, even me. The totality of her being—body, spirit, heart—was a veritable welcome mat, and life thundered across it. One could not help but wonder, though, what would be left of her once the dust had cleared.

"Why didn't he want to see her?" she asked again, the words thrumming the eardrum of my hollow-core door as she passed on her way back to the living room.

"I don't know, I don't know. I guess she'd hardly said anything during the sessions, or what she'd said didn't say much, even behind the saying. 'Resistance,' he said, 'that would be interesting, that would tell me something.' But she wasn't resistant. He seemed disgusted, and I couldn't see that, how you could be, how anyone could be *disgusted* with Cheryl, so I got angry, said to hell with this, and in the end he just gave her prescriptions and another name to call. Never even cashed my check. Then it's hopeless, I thought."

From Dixie, a muted echo: "Hopeless."

"That's why we needed help, why Hermia and the ones before, and why you were sent to boarding schools, and why there were always private rooms for your mother. For the peace and quiet, so that she wouldn't be disturbed."

"Her rooms . . . what did she do in her rooms?" A conciliatory note had entered Dixie's voice. "I don't even know, I couldn't see, what she did up there . . . with time."

(At that point I remembered Dixie's steno notebooks containing a detailed accounting of how *she* spent her time; and the photographs, *yes*, I realized, the hundreds of photographs of every stupid insignificant act, the most trivial encounters, the most passing acquaintances, and none—save those ones we took of each other being the other—none of them posed, all of them wretchedly blunt and tedious and thoroughly flawed, thoroughly artless, the uncensored facts of her unbridled life.)

"Oh, she got a lot of magazines," Slade was saying, sounding relieved, eager to mollify, to play the witness instead of the villain, "and she listened to musicals if it was a good day, Broadway hits, *Hello, Dolly*, you know, and others. She liked Dean Martin, too, that whole crowd. And Brahms, it didn't seem to matter. Most of the time, though, she was tired from the trips. Cameras took it out of her, she said, she said she had to respond, it was what made her good, you know, she responded to the camera. That's the trick, I guess. Remember the one with the hi-fi? Like she was hearing music from heaven, and the camera caught it all."

"Yeah, it did."

"Sold a lot of hi-fi's, I bet."

There was a long silence then. He cleared his throat. He cleared it again. In between I could hear Dixie's glass clicking thrice on the coffee table.

"But the work was . . ." Slade began, "the word she used was *draining*. When she came home she needed to rest. And headaches . . . you know. Sometimes even sunlight . . ." Unable to finish his sentence, he moved on in a solemn key. "So then came more pills, pills for headaches, pills for anxiety attacks, pills to put her to sleep and pills to keep her awake if she could stand it. A lot of time she couldn't stand it. The smallest things would . . . they could really bust her up."

Then Dixie, her voice rising on a wave of desperation: "What do you mean? What are you talking about? I don't know what you're talking about. What things? What things?" She was back in the kitchen. I heard ice cubes falling to the linoleum, the cupboard door (with its tell-tale squeak) where we kept the liquor.

"Come on, Chickadee, you don't need anymore of that."

"Who says need? Need? *Want* is happening here," she replied, jingling the cubes in her glass. "Want. And I want to know what you're talking about. What things? She was fine when I saw her, holidays and summer, like, she was just fine. So what things could *bust her up*? What are you *talking about*?"

Apparently taking offense, he said "I don't know," with mulish defiance.

"What *things*? I want to know." She was on the brink of crying, it seemed, the words struggling against backed-up feeling.

"Little things, all right? Always little things. We were always on egg shells. And when you get around to admitting it, you were too, Dixie. I remember once I was cleaning the garage, and she came out, oh, just to see, I guess, and she was standing there in the big opening, no shoes and wearing a silk shift, pale and blue like a piece of sky, and her yellow hair at the top and the light kind of like a flash behind her, like an explosion. This was in Florida, summertime, it was muggy hot and I was a mess from the work, but she was like a cool blue angel there in the opening and it flustered me, she flustered me, so I kept moving things, boxes and stuff, thinking she would just kind of float away back to the house or wherever, or maybe waiting for her say something and maybe hoping that she wouldn't because then I'd've had to stop and think about it and figure out how to answer right. I could never figure out how to answer some of the things she said." He paused. "Dixie, I really don't think there's any use in . . ."

What kind of look Dixie gave him then I don't know, but he did go on.

"Okay, but it's nothing, a little thing, no big deal to me or you or anyone, that's the point. So . . . so I shoved this trunk, an old family steamer trunk of hers, and I could feel her behind me moving only it was like she was being blown into the garage, like the exploding light behind her was pushing her in, into where it was dark, to see something. And what it was—because then I looked too—it was a rat, pretty far gone, I mean, there was just a patch of foamy gray fur and then the point of nose and a long naked tail and four scratch marks that were feet, and right next to it, *eating*, was the prettiest green frog, shiny and bright and as tiny as a brooch too, the kind women wore then, of insects and animals with jewel eyes. Your mother had one, I think."

"Yeah, she does," Dixie said. (I noticed the present tense. And the brooch . . . actually, the brooch Dixie had given me to wear for the party.)

"Well, your mother stood there in her blue silk and bare feet and saw it, the rat and the baby frog eating all alone, I mean, that was what *I* was thinking, why is this frog all alone, how did it get in here? Then right before it happened, I looked at Cheryl, at your mother, and I swear she was, well, it was small and maybe she wasn't, maybe she was trying not to, but it might've been a smile, and I remember feeling relieved and funny too that it hadn't upset her. But by then the frog had figured out that the jig was up, so he hopped, only it was a silly giant hop with a slapping sound when he landed on the cement, like wet skin makes, and then another loopy hop, it was really ridiculous, how high it was, and out of the corner of my eye I saw your mother twitch each time that crazy little thing hopped, and it was hopping right for her. She gave a shaky look at her feet, which were bare, like I said, and instead of running out of the garage she ran *into* it, as far back behind the steamer trunk as she could squeeze herself, back there with the rat. I had to coax her out, pulling the whole time. All I could think of to say was, 'I didn't know frogs were carnivorous.'"

"What, what did she say?"

"Oh, I don't know, something about not wanting it to touch her and the thing is, she was standing right on it, her eyes were closed and she was standing right on that dead rat. She called me Billy, too, 'Billy, don't let it touch me,' I remember that. Billy . . . I was just a rookie then."

A pause. A tinkle of ice, a click of a glass.

"That's one thing she never wanted to know anything about, my being a cop, what I did, any of the day-to-day details. But I know, well, I think she liked the idea of it. Maybe it didn't matter, who knows? She didn't have to stay with me, she was a first-class ticket all the way, and when she really moved into the world of glamor and high fashion, well, I figured that was it, she'd be gone, she'd meet some big shot with big bucks. But she came back. After every job she came home. I don't think it ever crossed her mind, leaving. In a funny way that about broke my heart." He tried to clear his throat then, said something about a glass of water, went into the kitchen. "Anyway," he said, returning, "the frog put her out of commission for two days."

"I don't miss her," Dixie said with a kind of numb bitterness, as though she might have been angry, she might have *spent* her anger if she'd had anything or anyone to spend it on.

"Sure you do, we both do. It's just hard, not knowing why. People blame themselves, that's how it goes. I've seen it a dozen times, the family blames themselves, think they've failed some way, but we didn't. I've thought about it, you can bet on it, and we really didn't fail her, Dixie. We adored her, and when she was working too, it was the same, everyone adored her. Something inside just broke, that's all."

"No," said Dixie, apparently not listening. "I don't miss her. What's there to miss except glossies? And clothes, the way she wore them, and the way she wore her face too. I used to make up what she was saying, you know, like it was for me. Only it wasn't. It was for everyone or, or it was for nobody, yeah, it was for nobody, it was like for the camera and its eye, its one little empty eye sucking her all up into a little black box, like she was smoke, like she wasn't there really. No, it wasn't for me."

"Ah, she loved you, Chickadee."

"Yeah, d'ja catch it on camera?" she said, as if jerked awake.

"She just didn't know the first thing about raising kids, and even if she'd wanted to try, she wasn't psychologically . . . she just didn't have the equipment. She was sort of like a kid herself. She loved you in her way. *I* love you, Chickadee."

"And Hermia."

"For god's sake, I have a right to remarry."

So. They were back where they started.

"At least *she's* not too good for you," Dixie said.

"Good? I don't know what that is," he said coldly. It was Slade the cop talking, Slade the trained realist. "Your mother was harmless. Beautiful and harmless until, well, until she wasn't."

"I'll tell you what," Dixie said, "I'll tell you something, mom didn't off herself. We did, all of everyone of us who looked at her pictures, who looked in their own piddly wobbly mirror and saw her looking at them and had wet dreams about a fancy white lady, anyone who bought the package deal, the make-up or the clothes, the Gidgets, the handy-dandy-do-it-for-me-babes, every single dirty ugly one of us who lined up to 'adore' her, like you said, to look and not touch, not ever touch until she couldn't probably remember, couldn't probably figure it out, couldn't *stand* touch, it was like too scary, too much . . . we did it. We may as well've each one of us've dropped one of those pills in her mouth, and all she had to do was swallow it. And she did. Finally she did, she said, yeah okay I get the message. And the thing is nothing's changed because it can't change now because she's still nailed to the wall, like a abject D of art, D for dead, which we made her and she let us, and, and we better remember."

Then I thought. I thought, *do this in remembrance of me. Do.* I thought, if Dixie was remembering—and it seemed there could be no doubting that—she was remembering with outright defiance, *in* outright defiance of the memory. She was *doing* when her mother hadn't, she was *being* as her mother couldn't, she was *taking note* of every passing increment of time, every sign, every encounter, every man, creating her own reality or illusion—who could say?—and entirely present for it; she was throwing herself with glittering abandon under the juggernaut, hoping only that it would touch every inch of her body before it crushed the awareness out of her. With her own life, in deed, *with acts*, she was rejecting her mother's life. A kind of tribute, I supposed. And the tribute lay not in the repudiation so much as its extremity, in the sheer amplitude of her voice raised in glorious and loving contempt against it. Yet oddly it seemed to drown out the repudiation, the words indistinguishable. In the end, what would she conclude? Would she worry about "holding onto the real," as Cheryl had? Would she feel that it had gotten lost in the incredible shuffle? Really, I had to wonder. Because there was something dark, something *inside* the *out*, there was something strangely imitative about Dixie's counter-tribute.

I could hear movement, Slade walking heavily toward the door, the door opening. "Just tell me," he said from the vestibule, his voice tired, disheartened, painfully gentle, "tell me *why* my remarrying is so hard for you."

"Because, *because*," she sputtered, "you're not, just not *remembering*."

"I remember," he said bitterly, "and I'm moving on."

"Daddy, please don't not . . ."

"Don't what," he said, the words so bleak and final that for the longest moment I hated him and everything he seemed to represent—ordinary life plodding dangerously forward, head bent, gaze narrowly fixed on the careful placement of feet in a world dispossessed of spirit. Plus, I couldn't for the life of me remember when Dixie had ever made an appeal to anyone, and it seemed heinous not to grant her some kind of stay. To say if only for the sake of the saying that he would always remember, that Hermia was merely a sorry distraction from the memory of *HER*, the memory of beauty and innocence leaning too far out over its own frontier and falling irrevocably away. It could even be said that Cheryl Darling was more human, more truthful than any of us; at the very least she had taken up pen and written in the blackest of ink, definitively, the answer—life was not worth living. It was too full of harm, or not to be understood, or it required of her such that she was unwilling or incapable of doing. As for some of the rest of us, we seemed to be trying desperately to recuse ourselves from the vote.

"You never believed in her," Dixie was saying, "you're just a scumbag hypocrite."

"Dixie . . ."

"Traitor."

Quietly the door closed.

Then without delay I heard the shower, the commencement of Dixie's morning rituals, and I had to wonder what other purposes, beyond basic hygiene and the requirements of acceptable self-esteem, they served.

Still shaken, I crept from my lair. The bathroom door was shut, steam sliding out from beneath it. From habit, I gazed upward imploringly but it was to the mirrored ceiling of our vestibule, and not the face of God I found but my own, sick-eyed and pale and blurring to mere presence behind Dixie's rising steam.

One hour. I had approximately one hour to figure out what to say to her. But I didn't have to. She never mentioned it. And I took my cues. Truly, I *wanted* to say something, though almost anything would have been a kind of lie. Maybe if I'd simply said her name, "Dixie . . ." or "Gee, Dixie . . ." in a sorry, commiserative sort of unfinishable way, but that might have been insulting, and anyway, at that moment—like several others in the past and one more moment that would inevitably come—I was struck by the absurdity of her name, and in all honesty could not have said it right. So nothing was said.

We drove up into the west hills in her turquoise VW with the radio on, and she was as composed as a good Christian after Easter Sunday services, Christ risen from the dead, the slate of humanity wiped clean.

# 15

It had been over two weeks since the fire, longer since Dixie had ridden the horse. She'd gone up, of course, to throw him some alfalfa and grain, to turn him out into the paddock, because Ephraim Armstead, the caretaker, didn't have permission to do that. He could feed the horse when she didn't come, but not turn him out—probably wouldn't have wanted to. The stallion was a Thoroughbred with an obscure background, high-strung and rank, a purpose of his own. The original owners had sent him to a local breeding farm to stand at stud, but when the breeders realized he was rank, they didn't want him in with any of their mares. So the owners decided to cut their losses, put an ad in the newspaper; not any trade journals, I suspected, probably just the local rag where someone who didn't understand (in any prohibitive way) how totally useless a horse of this nature was, or someone who fancied the *idea* of a pure Thoroughbred, or someone (like Dixie) who thought it might be "fun" to have an "amped-up stud."

Naturally they didn't want anything coming back to bite them—the horse or a lawsuit—so in their way they told Dixie everything, using long, soft words as moldable as warm clay, eminently and variously construable, and when they were finished it almost seemed they were sorry to let the rogue go, he'd provided them with such sport.

Dixie just said *oh*, and I kept my mouth shut, knowing a lot less about horses than Dixie, and having certain respect for her riding skills, and being, like her, intrigued by this purebred delinquent.

We went out to the pasture to watch him, came back an hour later and she gave them the full $2000 in cash, and then they had her sign a bunch of forms she didn't care to read. They even trailered him up to the stables Dixie had arranged for, holding their breaths all the way, I bet. Threw in some tack, too, just as they were leaving, looking sheepishly lucky and in a big hurry to dig out.

"You don't want to use an easy snaffle on him," the former owner said, handing her the bridle.

"Yeah?" Raising her eyebrows, she held the bridle out as if she'd never seen one before, turned it about once or twice, poked a curious finger through the snaffle rings.

"No," he said nervously. "You got to use the heavy one. He likes to be in control." There was a wisp of fatherly concern in his eyes as he gazed at Dixie, but his partner waiting in the cab of the truck honked impatiently, and all he had time to say was, "Heck, no, Miss Darling, he'll clamp down on the easy ones, lock his neck. And his neck's clear out-to-out muscle."

Shrugging, Dixie said, "Okay," all singsong, dimples, and blue button eyes.

Then he turned and fled, never looked back, unable, it would seem, to bear the sight of what he thought he had done.

Armstead wasn't around when we arrived; no one was. And I could see why. Once we'd reached a certain elevation, the road up into the hills encountered the burnscape in all its dreadful black reduction. We skirted its edge for a mile or so, then, girding round a hill, came upon dusty yellow fields still intact, and scattered live oaks with their billowing tops like green cumuli, and dipping down into a canyon, other trees, lean and straight and reaching sunward, and delicately tangled undergrowth, and the scent of mud in phantom snatches from the creek wending invisibly along the crease at the bottom; and then it seemed for a space that everything was okay, there was light and shadow and colors, there was hope, but up over another hill, we met yet another of the advancing edges of the burn—shapeless, consuming all color into a void of one, cinder smell and windblown indifference, the naked fact of black conveying at once like a blow the unforeseeable certainty that it would happen again.

The thirty-acre swath to the north of the stables through which the road passed was burned; the west meadow directly above, spared; the open fields and forest below where many of the riding trails led off, utterly blackened—a hopscotch of ruin which suggested a disquieting component of volition, as if the fire had paused and *chosen* which to take and which to pass over. Though I knew it was all random, fires were known to jump, a function of wind or of something equally natural—and entirely out of one's reckoning.

We parked and headed for the barn, our shoes sinking into the soft mix of ash and dirt along the edge of the road, sending up fine clouds that stung the eyes. The sunlight, for all its midday volume, disappeared into the charred expanse below us, and seemed only to render the black more black, in the same way that death was somehow vivified when life was, if not in contact, at least in the vicinity. I wondered where we would sit while the horse had his time in the paddock, for the oak under which I had read Chekhov and Camus, Dickens and Dostoyevsky, the great oak was a fright wig of twisted black, half gone on one side where the fire had first struck, and on the other, a stark frazzle of scorched and brittled twigs reaching up into the listless blue silence, as if to grasp what was irretrievably lost.

"It's just awful," I said. "Incredible. I had no idea."

Dixie glanced back, preoccupied, and gave a little twitching frown as though my voice had reminded her I was there following behind her; said nothing. Of course she'd been up to the stables, seen it already. Plus, she was especially intent on getting to the horse.

The barn was T-shaped, stalls lining all sides. We didn't enter through the main opening. The stallion was kept in an extra large stall at the bottom of the T, purposely isolated by a vacant stall on the inward side, another vacancy across, and the end wall of the barn. So we swung around the outside toward the bottom door, and from no less than twenty yards away I could hear him.

"How long has it been since . . . ?"

"Four days," she said.

*In this heat*, I thought.

He was a big horse, over 16 hands, about five years old, a dark bay with a black mane and tail and black stockings. There was a gashing scar across his chest where he'd run into a fence, and various smaller cuts on his legs from barbed wire; otherwise, no other markings. Most Thoroughbreds are lean and long, and indeed his shadow conformed to the hereditary precedents, his legs like inverted reeds, tapering with proper grace; but the muscles of his thighs and shoulders as well as his chest, formidably broad, were more developed and hinted of the "obscure background" of which we'd been cursorily informed. He had an unusually pronounced poll, too, that reminded me of a war horse. His face was strong and fine, like a pen and ink drawing, lines angling down to the sculpted coves of his nostrils and a youthfully taut

Lynn Stegner

nose. His ears, in-pointing like an Arabian's and thinly outlined in black, were never quiet, turning, flicking, ever aware. Above his cheeks and running down from his eyes were two veins, one on each side, always full, it seemed, and pulsing no matter his level of activity, as though he was perpetually *on*. But it was his eyes, not peacefully large and knowing like Bucky's, her childhood horse; no, these were smaller, and while they too seemed to know something, whatever it was made him by turns wild and enchanting—it was his eyes that made him an altogether disconcerting creature.

After the noon sun the barn was pitchy, and we paused in the entry to let our eyes adjust, listening to him kick his stall door with his knees, and then the back of the stall with his hooves, whinny and snort and swish his tail. He knew, he could see.

Dixie went in and observed him through the upper bars of the stall. I followed.

"I know, boy, I know," she said, her voice matter-of-fact.

He swung his head about, alternately pinned back his ears, then stood them at attention, tossed his nose up and down.

"Yeah, okay," she said. "I know." She moved to the side of the stall door, fingered through some tack hanging from a peg, twisted up her mouth, peered through the bars into the stall at other pegs—halter, cross ties, etc.—then returned to the outer peg and grabbed a bridle.

"I thought you weren't going to ride him," I said.

"Changed my mind."

"But you haven't ridden him for, well, forever."

"Might could be it's time."

The horse let out a couple of solid kicks to the back wall, made a complete turn, and did it again.

"He seems pretty keyed up," I said. "Shouldn't he run

282

off some of that excess in the paddock, then ride him?"

"It's too hot," she said, "to do both." She was inspecting the bridle dangling from her hand, working the bit as if she was trying to decide something.

I nodded at the bridle. "Is that his? That's not even his, is it?" I asked, feeling vaguely nervous.

"Nope," she said. "This here's a hollow-mouth snaffle, kinda beat-up, too. Ephraim must have his. Ephraim's, like, a real neatnik. He's probably cleaning it."

So he didn't think she was going to ride either. And why would he? The horse hadn't been turned out for four days, it was over 100 degrees and no breeze, most of the trails, the fields and woods surrounding the barn, were a charred wasteland unexperienced by the stallion, and the smell, the unmitigated blackness, the crunching sound of it under hoof might . . . and then there were the permanent incalculables—temperament, testosterone, *Dixie*. And how much *did* she drink that morning? The sheer accumulation of factors argued against it, *I* argued against it, but she was already in the stall, snapping the cross ties to his halter, then with the curry comb, the hard brush followed by the soft brush and a rag. And throughout, he pawed, he jerked on the cross ties, he threw his head up and down, he swished his long sooty tail, straining to watch her every move, his skin quivering under the brush, his eyes terribly alive. Then out came the hoof pick and he simply stopped and stood strangely quiescent, as though he knew that any movement during this more delicate procedure might hurt him, or her; or as if he knew—and of this I was reasonably certain—that the ritual of grooming was nearing completion, that it was almost time to run.

The whole thing was painful to watch, and I wandered off through the barn. There was something so calculated about her impetuosity, the insanity of it, and yet it excited me, too, the prospect of witnessing them, each in extremity, come together. As I passed along the stalls some of the horses let out low, grumbling whinnies, others simply snorted incuriously, too hot and too lethargic to care, one mare shied away as if I might require something of her. When I returned Dixie had him tacked up and was opening the stall door.

"Horse," she uttered in an unfamiliar voice, not as if she was intoning with childlike indiscriminateness a generic example of *Equus caballus*, but as if she was summoning the founding myth itself to accompany her out from the dark womb of the barn and into the oppressive, dazzling light of our eighteenth August on the planet. "Horse," she said again.

Of course he did have a name, one of those regally hyphenated strings that track announcers love to drawl out with straining decibels as the pack heads into the homestretch, but which trainer and groomer and rider alike never use, preferring some friendly nickname that describes a special characteristic or quirk of the animal, and which is given not only to personalize but to establish and reaffirm relationship. His official name was typed throughout the forms Dixie hadn't cared to read. Apparently as far as she was concerned, the animal had no past, no associations. What she thought about the future I don't know, except maybe that it couldn't be counted on. The present she kept as uncluttered, as free as possible, free of names, free of interference, free of the inhibitions of time and its forever contentious siblings, past and future, free of regrets, free of hope. With the present (which seemed to be all there was to time for her) she cast her fate, and everything was left undecided, everything was a surprise, everything was a sudden ride on a hot sudden day.

There were, however, some telling drawbacks. For one thing, it seemed rather abstract, rather cold, not to give one's own horse a nice name. It seemed reductive. And as I watched her lead him out to the mounting block, I found myself thinking of all her men and that it hardly mattered to her *who* they were, their names and such, only *that* they were. And that they were *with* her, consummately with her. She didn't seem to want to *have* a life in the way that I did, a good, purposeful, meaningful life; she wanted to *fuse* with it in a kind of sublime meltdown of self.

The mounting block was around the barn, near the paddock, and while I watched the horse drag her forward and jerk her back, trot, walk, abruptly jounce up in a mini-levitation and land lightly only to commence stomping with bullish impatience, as I watched the aggravation, the complete passion of the animal wanting only to diffuse it, get rid of it, I suffered a futile blink of hope that she would change her mind and ride him into the paddock where a fence could provide some backup containment. He never even stood still at the mounting block, he was already moving away as she swung up, but her hands were quick with the reins, her heels pulled down and inward like pincers along his ribs, her backbone so gracefully erect it seemed a length of cord someone had merely tugged gently upward, and her eyes, her eyes were *electric* blue shocks of purpose known only to her and seemingly utterly devoid of any restraint, of anything that might extinguish the charge, so bright and so blue, so actual. Suddenly it was the horse I was worried about.

She stutter-stepped him past the paddock and then they were in the wasteland. Trotting, she posted rhythmically, then coming back across, she let him into a smooth canter, turned him midway, and worked the opposite side, in total control it seemed until at one point he appeared to stumble and instantly she eased off the reins and then he broke into a full gallop. A flash of teeth, Dixie hauling back, keenly focused, and she walked him—or he walked, it was hard to tell who was in charge—the length of the wasteland with spooky poise, as if he was feigning contrition for the stumble ruse, and as if she knew he was, it was all a game whose rules they had silently agreed upon. Now they looked comfortable, relaxed, working gradually through the sequence of gaits, like old trusted friends. I lost them in the half-denuded woods at the bottom edge of the field, but minutes later they re-emerged, threading through the spiked remains of two Douglas firs at a lovely, easy, rocking gallop coming toward me, but before we might have made eye contact, she turned him sharply south across and down the wasteland again. I remember feeling disappointed; I had wanted to wave, or smile, I had wanted to normalize the day with some thumbs-up gesture.

Back into the woods, longer this time but where the trees were less dense, fraying into field, and I could see weaving movement among the blackened columns, then out they burst and she gave him rein only to take it back for no reason, because they'd hardly started up the field. At which point he threw his head down and she snapped forward over his withers, and I swear I heard her laugh with weird delight. Pushing herself back on the saddle— she was using an English saddle those days—she picked up the reins with coy formality, and he took her down toward the woods, his long tail flaring up like a pretty black flame. Just before entering, I saw her—*oh, it was crazy*—I saw her heels fly out and she kicked him up so hard that his hindquarters instantly coalesced into a massive ball of muscle, then his back legs sprang down and back, catapulting them into the barren woods descending out of view.

It was a half hour before I saw them again. I climbed up on the paddock railing to wait, to see better. The sun made a hot polished dome of my head, and eventually I went over to the spigot attached to the barn and let the rusty water stream across my scalp, then I doused my face and neck, took a long drink, and returned to my post on the railing. I was worried about Dixie now. I was worried he might try to knock her off against a tree, or cut corners too tight, or that he might trip over a root. Maybe I would have to hike down, look for her, but where to enter the woods, where to begin, and then which direction to take? And first there was the blazing expanse of the wasteland to cross, and I was already feeling faint from the heat, from the possibilities. The longer I waited and the hotter it got, the more real the fantasy became until, gazing through the undulating heat across the wasteland to the edge of the woods, trees like spiring black grave markers, and no sound in there, I imagined, no color, no little live things twitting in a soft breeze, until I was convinced that they would never emerge.

Then here they came, not from the woods but from the west somehow, from nowhere it seemed, his black stockings disappearing so fast into the black desert that he seemed to have lost the bottom half of his legs, to be flying on invisible wings, his body gleaming, his tail a smoky back draft. And Dixie, Dixie crushed down like a lover against him, her face tucked in along the side of his straining neck, his mane whipping black striations, weaving through the yellow blaze of her hair, as if they had already begun to lose themselves, to twist into each other, hair for hair. Her arms, her clothes, her legs were black with dirt and ash, and a cloud following behind, chasing them it seemed, as though they were fleeing the very fires of Hell. The rumbling three-beat of his hooves, muffled in the distance, sharpened as they approached, and my heart took it up, and then I heard a scream and I realized it was mine. Leaping off the railing, I sprinted toward them, but Dixie jerked the reins hard right when she saw me and they headed for the woods, and then the strangely seductive game of dipping in and out from woods to field, from wasteland to wooded graveyard, began again in deadly earnest.

Several things I had seen in that moment of turning: that he did not see me, that he was running blank and blind, that he was in a full lather, sweat foaming between his hind legs, across his chest and in along his flanks, and that while Dixie still held the reins, he was clenched hard over the bit which at some point he must have worked in between his front and back teeth in that small, irreclaimable gap belonging solely to him. The other thing I had seen was not that Dixie was or was not trying to break his resistance, not that she did not care what was happening; the question was irrelevant. No, what I saw was that she was simply *not there*, or so *there*, so *present* that she had vanished in time and space, and had entered an immeasurable, impenetrable dimension of being. It was like a living death.

Twenty paces into the field I stood shaking as if chilled to the bone, and feeling so desperately helpless that it was several minutes before I noticed tears stinging down my sunburnt cheeks. They were not toying with each other anymore, trading control and cunning, power for servitude, pain and pleasure, back and forth. I understood that now. The game, the delicious foreplay, was over. No, now, simply and bluntly and without apology, they were using each other—and the aim was oblivion.

I walked back past the paddock and slumped down in the ash against the burned trunk of the oak. What difference did it make how well I could see? I could see well enough. Idly, bleakly, I thought of the phone lines, temporarily down on account of the fire; they were bringing in new poles—we had seen them lying along the sides of the road—changing the whole wiring configuration in the hills, rebuilding for a better future, an invincible future. I could not call anyone if calling would've helped. There was no one to call. There was no time to do anything if doing would've helped. I thought about trying . . . trying *anything*, but it all seemed so chancy—running out into the wasteland, waving my arms, or maybe white rags, or simply placing my body in their way which was harm's way, and forcing them to stop or to turn at the very least and slow long enough to come to their senses, I even thought of filling a pail of water and sloshing it across them as they flew by in the hope that the shock of cold water might bring them back—I did think about trying but thinking about it seemed to handily defeat it, the success of anything I might try was so clearly, terribly uncertain, failure practically a given, and so I didn't try anything. I didn't really have a choice—I told myself that. Several times.

I sat in the ashy dirt with hopeless intent and waited, feeling a shame that was not only past comprehension, but in its way groundless, in view of the Lady of Reason whose perfect skirts I clung to, hiding. Later I told myself that it was not from cowardice I hid, but from life: some consolation, a slight upgrading, but not much.

I thought of the heat, too, the midday heat, that kept Armstead from his appointed rounds until later in the day, that kept other owners of other horses from their charges until later, until the long summer twilight dimmed the black reality, and a ride among the western hills offered some of the old, sweet, incongruous pleasure. I sat in the torn shade of the oak, light beating through what was left of the branches with pitiless accuracy on my face, and I waited. *Oh*, I waited. When I heard the hooves again it was only my heart that leapt in response. And when I saw the animal slow and stagger, his front knees folding, and Dixie sailing off in slow motion, landing flat on her back, and I rose and began the inevitable trip into the inevitable wasteland, it was with a sickening and grim foreknowledge, a movie I had watched before and of which I seemed to be an unwilling part.

I saw him from a distance flopping about. The shape of stillness lying beside him was Dixie. When I reached them the flopping had stopped, his eyes had rolled backward, his whole body quivered once, and that was it. Dixie blinked up at me, not moving. Her legs were splayed, her hands placed carefully along her sides, pressing palms down into the black earth, as if to keep something from escaping. Nothing appeared wrong with her except that she wasn't breathing; she'd had her wind knocked out, that was all, her lungs had collapsed. But the funny thing was, she wasn't in any panic about it, she wasn't gulping for air, she wasn't struggling, she wasn't even moving. She was just looking at me with those blue eyes of hers, and then she was looking through me into the impossible blue.

Of course it was the right thing to do, the doctor said later, the lungs will expand naturally, and if she had gasped, if she had fought for it, it would have taken considerably longer for her to regain breathing. But I don't think Dixie knew that. I think she simply didn't care which way it went.

Armstead came and went away, and then he came back with a man who had a flatbed truck, and they winched the body of the horse up and took it away.

Dixie said, "I need a shower."

There was an autopsy. I don't know who ordered it, maybe Slade, maybe Armstead who didn't want any responsibility. The autopsy said heart attack; the autopsy said maybe weak spots in the artery which, with the exertion, blew out. The autopsy said predisposition. But Dixie never read it. Dixie knew.

# 16

All those men . . . those many, many men. Young men and the not so very young, smooth and rough ones, the mad and the quite mad, lean, stout, rank and rube, all those differently identical men proving and in their numbers negating the same point; name after name after name in the book, arriving, signing, giving sex and other evidence, departing, departing . . . all those men here and gone, the purpose served but never satisfied . . . all those many protestations, men, credible instruments of incredible proof, those many, many, many men for one woman in pain.

I came home Tuesday night.

I came home Tuesday night after my second date with Paul. We had left directly from work, the two of us, Grif watching with his sad, collusive eyes, smile vanishing even as it appeared as though editing itself. We had taken in a late movie, then pizza, and when we went out to the car he put his arm around my waist and his hip shifted with poignant awkwardness against me. The pink slippers were gone, his feet were improving, but he limped. The doctor had told him he might always limp. I liked the limp: it was grotesquely real and stirred in me a tenderness that was not pity but a form of camaraderie. It seemed to make him more predictable, too. Handicaps of any kind generally do that—make one more predictable.

In the parking lot of the Penthouse in his old gray Impala we exchanged the courtesies and, without serious intent, sampled a kiss or two, and then I got out, smiling and waving, and when the Impala turned the corner, I took the outside stairs instead of the elevator for the vivid night air and the extra time to relive the kisses, wakened lust darting up from the secret depths and fizzling somewhere between my stomach and diaphragm . . . tiny flares, so potent and fun, so momentarily immortal. I climbed the outside stairs, five flights, because it would take longer; because I had noticed Dixie's VW in the lot, and guessed she had called in sick. She was doing that now, even when she wasn't. Al was concerned. So was I, but didn't want to be. Was annoyed by it. Wanted to put off the having to care. It was painful, having to care.

I came home Tuesday night and found the lights in the apartment dimmed down low, hardly there, like something just dying. But I could see bulky shapes in the living room, two on the couch, one leaning with a detached air against the breakfast bar, cigarette in hand, another standing by the stereo, standing very near her. She was naked except that she wasn't. There were painted daisies surrounding both nipples, a kind of tiara arcing over her pubis, a stripe between her buttocks, a star exploding from the core of her navel, ten glowingly pink teardrops at the ends of her fingers; and there were words too, names. Names I refused to assimilate, my brain clenching and the names glancing off like stray bullets. The paint was fluorescent—pink, green, yellow. All the rage those days, fluorescents. All the rage.

The music, like the lights, was hardly there too, faint cries, a woman's voice, notes sparking desperately up now and then, falling back into the murky, murmuring silence.

Neighbors would not complain. An altogether quiet and respectful assembly, it was. Except that it wasn't.

Even Dixie's dancing was slow and languorous as if she was immersed in a thick liquid, and with the night glass of the balcony behind her, she was like a human specimen in a glass jar, a lovely, twisting, tortured animal, brilliantly colored.

The shape nearest her, hips thrust forward, was masturbating with lingering deliberation toward her undulating form. She drew a hand under his member, the hand continuing through the air along the same line his erection described, fingers feathering at the end toward her own flesh as if to summon, to extend, to connect, and went on dancing, oblivious when his fluid came spattering across her belly.

I moved in among the shapes and said firmly but not unkindly (because in a way it wasn't their fault, because I was afraid and didn't want to provoke them, because I had to, I had to say it) "Please leave now." I was glad for the dimness, for not seeing eyes, expressions. Their names would be in the book. Their names were on her body, they had signed her, like idle boys carving on a piece of deadwood. Names were meaningless. I wanted them not to mean. For Dixie's sake. I wanted them not to mean and I knew that they did not and I knew that that meant everything.

I took Dixie by the hand, the same hand that had drawn desire from these men, I took Dixie by that hand and led her swiftly into the bathroom, closed and locked the door, turned on the light, turned on the fan. Waited.

I could hear them moving about, angry words, a call and jeer, then knocking on the bathroom door, five-beat syncopation presuming the old, two-beat response, and again the mocking five beats and my rigid silence, my hand squeezing Dixie's wrist into quiescence when she

cooed in answer, the insensible waif; and then further
away I heard a reasoning voice, calm and older sounding, reasoning with the others, and presently, miraculously, the front door was opened and they were leaving,
and I knew in the reasoning voice there was some com-
passion; and with the sort of frantic, illogical logic of
extreme moments, as if I might run out and say his name
and beg his help, I searched quickly the names on the
body before me and saw that there were only three names
and I knew that that one voice had spared her this last,
most brutal indignity.

Then empty silence. Blessed emptiness. The white noise
of the fan. Desultory breathing. Dixie.

She was so drunk her eyes seemed to bob and dip, like
blue buoys in a white sea. I placed my fingertips under
her chin and gently raised her head, made her see me. In
recognition, she slurred out my name and loosed a smile
that went slack when the experience of an obscure un-
pleasantness—the overhead light—finally achieved cog-
nition. Besides her perfume, there was a faint marine scent
about her, and I realized it was semen, tracks of it running down from her vagina, dried patches at the corner
of her mouth, on her neck, clumped in her hair, flaking
off her breasts, and the still-wet deposits festooning her
stomach.

I made a point not to confuse by asking; I told her I
was going to put her in the shower, and I eased her down
onto the toilet lid to wait there while the water tempered.
Her mascara had run as if she'd been crying, and I thought
that maybe one of them had hurt her. The thought was
blunt and sudden and so complete, igniting such a mess
of feeling, that I held my breath against it, choked it off.
When I finally got her in the shower and adjusted the
spray, I stood back to allow her to wash. But she just
gazed with dreamy, floating eyes through the veil of wa-

ter, not helplessly, but as though she had no idea that there was something she was to do besides stand there gazing out at me. So I removed my own clothes and stepped in with her.

Twice I shampooed her hair, then, soaping up a wash-cloth, I began with her face, circling her eyes, her lips, over and around the small, perky nose, making soft spi-rals on her cheeks, then down, rubbing the pale column of her neck, moving still downward to breasts, each of which in turn I cupped with my left hand and gently dabbed at with my right until the nipples were pinked and tight, then belly and the fiddle-curving back, and buttocks, the ever generous thighs, and between them too, particularly—because there was no other way, because it held the most secret and malignant of crimes—with fin-gers cloaked discreetly in the washcloth, from the pubic bone down toward the vulva, in and around the labial folds and up inside her a modest distance . . .

"Don't . . ." she gasped, "stop."

I stopped but didn't move, looked at her face. Her eyes were no longer swimmy and soft but piercingly fixed on me, her hands clasped my shoulders, her legs quivered.

"Don't stop," she said with a voice so weak and yet so intense that even if I'd wanted to I could not have moved. I did not move.

But Dixie did, squatting down hard against my hand so that my finger rose abruptly inside her and my palm brushed up against her clitoris, then up and down once more she moved, and a kind of fearful cry tore lose from her, moaning and quivering and fingernails digging into my shoulders, and it went on forever, and I felt the most fantastic horror and it was in my hand and pulsing up my arm through the rest of my body, I was holding it in my hand, and still couldn't, wouldn't move, watching the fluorescent paint streaking psychedelic blood down her body, down the white walls, mixing to black in the porcelain tub and swirling round our feet like the disappointed tide, watching and waiting for Dixie to finish what I had unwittingly begun.


I don't think Dixie remembered much of that night. In most ways I hoped she wouldn't. She remembered the four men, the fluorescent paint (giddy, half-proud laughter), and sex with the first or second. After that she looked vague, lit a cigarette, asked about my date with Paul. I said, "This isn't a brothel," but with hardly any force, since I was moving out soon and she could make of her home what she liked, and then nurse Katherine could run interference if she felt so inclined. And since, too, I felt I was up against something much larger than run-of-the-mill promiscuity, and that it was simply not my job to reform Dixie Darling, or psychoanalyze her, or even anymore to try to attend her. Whatever else the shower told me, it confirmed the utter inappropriateness of my help. I was in way over my head.

But.

But I couldn't resist asking her *why*. *Why all those men?* I even added before she'd had a chance to answer, and with a certain callous note in my voice, something about multiple orgasms which, like fluorescent paint, was the rage those days. We were all supposed to have them in couplets and triplets, and theoretically *ad infinitum*, or at least until the wine and roses ran out—whichever came first. Redundant orgasms, a Madison Avenue fad, enthusiastically promoted mostly by men who sought to accrue virility with each multiple they triggered. Since, barring recuperative time-outs, they were stuck with a singleton. So I wondered if Dixie, by way of her customary gift-giving excess, was keen on more than the commensurate one.

With a chirpy, flippant sort of challenge, she said, "Never had one."

It seemed there was something wrong with my ears. "One what?" I had to ask.

"Or-ga-smmm," she drawled.

"What?"

"My comer's busted."

"What?"

"On the fritz-ola," she said, trying again and with some irritation. "Why are you looking at me like that? It's no big deal."

"You've never . . ."

"Never, ever. You got it."

"But . . . then . . ."

"Well coming isn't the whole taco, *Sue*. It's just The End, and who wants it to end?" she said, and a jaunty smile of self-assurance almost persuaded me.

In the kitchen behind the breakfast bar I stood, thankful for the partial barrier between us, because at that moment I swear my hidden right hand began to tingle, as if to contradict, to remind.

She was looking at me, waiting; she was *staring* at me, I realized, and the smile was beginning to wane, and the blues of her eyes had gone dusky, and the skin of her brow twitched ever so slightly the way a horse will twitch away a noisome fly he can only feel, cannot see. And I thought that maybe, *maybe*, the night before—the end of it—had poked through the surface of her reality, had momentarily cast its shadow, then plunged back down, and all so fast that she couldn't quite recognize what it was but sensed that it was tangled up with me.

Rising, she went over to the TV, turned it on. "So," she said, drifting back to the couch where she sat down, tucked her legs up to one side, and with equal, ladylike precision, smoothed her robe over an exposed length of calf. "So." Another pause. "So when'd they split?"

My heart was pounding. "When I got home," I said. "I told them to."

"Hey, Sue, maybe you should'a . . . who knows, take off your hose," she sang, but the tension showed.

At first I said nothing; then, watching her, I said, "I don't think so."

"No, huh?" Redoubling her effort, she said, "Seriously, Sue, it might've been a kick. I'd've shared. Two for each, *perf.*"

I dropped my eyes, couldn't bear to watch her struggle, the paper-thin cheerfulness, the stupid and eerie lie. Who was she kidding?

"You never take me seriously, do you?" Suddenly her tone had lowered and flattened, as though her insides had bottomed out. "No one ever takes me seriously."

"Why should they? You've . . . *you* never . . ." But I broke off. It seemed useless. Too late. There was another long pause.

As if to fill up the space, Dixie coughed elaborately, but soon launched herself again in pursuit of the lost narrative. "So you eighty-sixed them. And then I guess I . . ." she frowned and glanced down over her person, ran her fingers through her uncoiffed hair, clean and limp, the dark roots more apparent, "I guess I must've . . ."

"Taken a shower," I blurted out, heading for the bedroom. "What else? What else would you do?" There was anger in my voice. I didn't know why. I sat down on my bed and reached for a book from the bedside orange crate, tossed it in one of the packing boxes that were strewn about, picked up another book, skimmed through it and read a paragraph or two without the slightest attention. I heard her turn up the volume on the TV. Then I began throwing things in the boxes. *Eleven more days*, I thought, *then it's over, I'm gone.*

That was Wednesday morning.

Since I'd given notice at Sambo's Pancake Paradise, Lemucchi had cut back on my shifts, was working in the new girl, another college-bound pauper. So I was home now more often than not, getting ready to move out and away from this messy, unpurposed interruption in the sleek flow of my life. I kept the night job at the *Herald's* bungalow because that was where the bigger money could be had, tax-free, and with a lot less time and foot strain. I didn't bother mentioning my imminent departure to Grif: the way people fell in and out of that place, the bone-pit of reality, it would have been a laughable and faintly embarrassing formality, giving notice. He would have thought I was putting on airs.

So that was Wednesday morning and I was home. The Friday night before was dinner with the new roommate. Then came Saturday morning and Dixie's head-on with her father. Saturday afternoon the horse died. Tuesday night, Dixie danced for the four shadows. And Wednesday morning I was home. As I said. Then Thursday, Friday, Saturday trundled by. And on Sunday, a mere four days after the night of fluorescence, Dixie came home married.

"*Un*real."

"Isn't it *just?*" she replied, glaringly pleased with herself, the air tingling around her as she whirled into the apartment. Her smile was as bright as beach light, her eyes shattered, glinting panes of blue. Then, perforce, here came Himself with the bags. (Why all the bags?)

His name was Anthony J. Aiken. "T.J. to my buds," he told me, though I had to wonder if he had any, and I noticed Dixie always called him Tony. I said "Okay, T.J.," and shrugged, beyond caring. Way beyond. Past. Past tense. I thought, *seven more days.*

She'd met him at Sambo's on Wednesday night during the graveyard shift. I hadn't seen much of her since then, just the usual to-ing-and-fro-ing; nothing ever mentioned. She'd been gone all day Saturday and Saturday night. It had been a kind of relief, her being gone.

He was a cop. ("Natch," said Dixie, winking.) He was a cop, except that he was on three-month suspension for some "unfortunate mix-up over confiscated drugs." *Yeah, right*, I thought, because he laughed too loud.

So, Sunday morning, 10:00 a.m., here came Mrs. Dixie, all smiles, flouncing about the apartment with a hyped-up, showy air. They'd left Reno at 5:00 a.m., driven straight through, and were still in their casino/wedding clothes—halter-top dress of purple and red lamé, midcalf length, and purple patent leather slings, formal blacks for the Mister—reeking emphatically of booze and cigarettes, and T.J. (not Dixie) snuffling with theatrical intent about the "heavy-duty pollen this summer." And indeed, there was a rime of white about his nostrils of which he seemed to be carelessly aware, because clearly he was aware that I was aware that the world was aware he was lying with insolent glee.

Dixie kicked off the purple sling-backs, said she was "starved," intended to "pork out," and presently she was swishing about in the kitchen where I was doing dishes, rummaging for salami, crackers, mayo, pickles. He was not hungry (in view of the "pollen," no doubt) and proceeded to uncork a bottle of cheap pink champagne which he drew from a police-issue duffel bag full of wadded clothes. (The duffel bags began to nuzzle the back door of my brain; why was it here, why so many clothes?)

"Ready, fire, aim," he said, and the plastic cork rocketed up, leaving a distinct and somehow irreverent pockmark in our cottage-cheese-glitter ceiling.

"No bubbly, Sister Sue?" he said, offering it for the second time, his arm snaking not-very-persuasively around my waist.

"No bubbly, T.J.," I replied, ignoring the agile arm and persisting with the dishes.

He talked a lot and laughed a lot, mostly at Dixie who didn't seem to mind, and he strolled around our place—*our* place—picking up things, like someone not serious at a rummage sale. When he emerged from the bathroom (another bout with the ersatz pollen), rolling from one hand to the other a small, alabaster swan dish that had belonged to Dixie's mother, I took it from him. "It's breakable," I said.

"Good thing," he said, laughing his happy, contemptuous laugh.

That settled it for me: I hated him.

Most of what there is to say about Anthony J. Aiken probably isn't worth the saying, because it could have been any one of them, what happened. And it's too late now, it's all too late. For the saying or the not saying. For words and other emblems of approximation. But at that point, at that *moment* in Dixie's life, I figured who he was, the particulars and all, hadn't mattered one whit to her: like her horse, T.J./he/they had finally been denatured, transmuted to purely symbolic form. And not merely to *HE*, the male representative of the species—it reached far beyond that, far into the heart, and the heart was mired down deep in the swampy past. No. *HE* became *IT*, and *IT* became intolerable. From its mire the heart would out.

But she married this one, and she . . . well, now it seems the right thing, the right and proper thing, to grant him his particulars. So.

He was handsome (she'd had handsome ones before,

lots), dark hair, an attractively weathered face, features cut clean without any disturbing shortages or excesses, the eyes small and alert, like a night creature's. In heels Dixie was taller, but he was nicely proportioned. The two-day growth of beard he was sporting when I met him that Sunday morning he managed to sustain throughout the seven days of our proximity. His taste in clothes was simple, nothing too noticeable, nothing too tight—shirts of quiet stripes, jeans and khakis, coordinating socks, sleeveless, V-necked undershirts, aviator shades. There were a couple of rings: police academy insignia, and a bulky gold affair full of diamond chips, the latter removed whenever he was on duty, he told Dixie. Because of his service revolver, he told Dixie. In case he needed to use it. The fingers themselves were stubby, nails bitten to the quick, and seemed not to square with the rest of him— the agitation they implied together with the primitive, club-like effect of forearm and hand. He wore too much cologne, but who could complain? Dixie wore too much perfume. And he had a hip way of talking, but so did Dixie, except hers was corny and somehow more whole-some, his, cool and backhanded. In speech and gesture he was instantly familiar; of course so was Dixie, though her manner seemed to have more to do with anticipated love and his seemed to have more to do with anticipated use.

But the feature that in its way defined him—not in-trinsically but *ex*trinsically—the thing that was memo-rable, that seemed to invite too much and to excuse too much, was his smile: he had the sweetest, most disarming smile I have ever been exposed to. That was how I felt, too, *exposed to it*, as if it was giving off some dangerous, invisible radiation even while it seemed to warm beyond words. It was the smile of a protective, older brother, and if it did indeed have words it would have said, "You are dear and darling to me, I understand you, I will be here always for you." Perhaps it was that smile Dixie needed to hear, perhaps only that. I don't know.

Dixie marrying after just three days, I reasoned, could easily have been a function of a) wanton enthusiasm, b) sudden uncontainable affection, and c) her enigmatic, reckless attachment to the present which to me was seeming more and more like a form of self-imprisonment. For anyone else, for Anthony J. Aiken (smile notwithstanding) it struck me as suspicious, marrying like a shot. Still, if they looked into each other's mirrors, one image did indeed counter-reflect the other. Alas, they appeared to be desperately alike. Yet I couldn't help feeling—or hoping—that there was some fundamental discrepancy, some place inside, maybe the place where identity takes its first irrevocable steps, from which Dixie Darling and Anthony J. Aiken diverged at right angles.


"Teeny hitch," Dixie said, "'bout us getting hitched."

It was less than an hour after their arrival, and they were settling down some, worn out from the all-nighter and the drive, mellowing with the champagne. T.J. turned on a ball game. Dixie followed me into the bedroom where I had planned to peruse for the third or fourth time and with anticipation stoked to a blaze by the gust of Dixie's nuptial news, the catalogue of courses from U.C. Berkeley for the upcoming fall quarter.

"Hitch?" said I.

"Teeny."

"How teeny?"

"Well," she said, "I'm married now."

"Evidently."

"And we wanna be together."

"Naturally."

She surveyed the bedroom and giggled. At which point, remembering the bags, I took her meaning. "He lives some place, I assume, your husband. And I'm only here seven more days, Dixie. Can't you go there temporarily, shack up at his place?"

She winced. "That wasn't nice. We're married. It's, like, the real thing now."

"Sorry. This is all so sudden."

"Yeah, isn't it?" And she giggled again.

"You'll have to negotiate the Katherine question, too. Have you thought about that? Your new roommate?"

"No problemo. She'll understand. She's Catholic, remember? Marriage is, like, one of the seven sacrifices."

"Sacraments."

"Same difference," she said, smiling. "Anywhose, Sue, seriously, there is a eeny-weeny hitch. Tony's sorta not actually living, like, any place right now. His roommates said he did something . . ."

"What." There was not a ting of inflection in the word. Since their arrival not only had my voice lost tone and pitch, the cadences of feeling, but my manner in general seemed void of any and all susceptibilities. I was not stunned by the turn of events, I was *glaciated*. "What did he do," I repeated, glazing the ice.

"I don't know. It bums him out, talking about it. They were his buddies, that's the thing."

"Cocaine, *that's* the thing, I bet."

"Coke? No, why? It's no big deal. He had to drive, he was braindead by the time we left Reno. So he did some dust."

"He's not driving now."

"A lot of people party with it, Sue. That's all he pretty much does is party with it."

"Maybe he's marketing it, too. Have you thought of that?"

"That's redundant."

"Ridiculous."

"I said. Anyway, he's, like, a cop. It's totally redundant. He's a cop."

"Suspended."

"A mistake."

"Whose?"

"Not Tony's," she said.

"Somehow I'm not convinced."

She moved to her bed, sat down facing me, and though the baseball game was on so loud T.J. couldn't have heard us if we'd screamed, she lowered her voice. "Don't you like him?"

"I don't even know him. And for that matter, neither do you. What are you trying to prove?"

"Nothing," she cried—an alarming flash of anger.

"Well, I think . . ."

"Cut with the thinking, will ya. I'm sick of your thinking. And for your information, I need all I know, I mean I, I know Tony. Anyway, what difference does it make to you . . . what d'you care? You're history."

"Yes, I'm history," I said with feeling, a strange catch in my throat. "But, Dixie . . ."

"You're history and I'm here," she interrupted. "So you mind sleeping on the couch for your last week so Tony and I can, like, *live*? Is that okay with you?"

"Dandy."

So that was what happened. They hauled the twin beds back to the countless, empty guest rooms at her father's house (I wondered what *he* thought about Dixie's marriage, the dueling nuptials), and moved in T.J.'s waterbed, (left, along with his other impedimenta, on the lawn of his former residence by his former buds); then they spent a morning filling it and the afternoon frolicking in it; and I was relegated to the couch, and what remained of *my* impedimenta—not quite boxed and ready—to an untidy heap in a corner of the living room. My father offered to come down on my last weekend and drive it all up to the house of my family in San Francisco where most of it was to be stored. Whatever the dorm room at U.C. Berkeley could accommodate would then come with me. It never occurred to me—or maybe it did, fleetingly—to move home for the last week. Father would have welcomed me, father would have been exultant, overjoyed, over-everything. Mother would have liked me home, too, but she couldn't say so. I was to live with my decisions. It was a question of honor. I thought so too. Though it would have been nice to be home. Really nice. And it would have changed everything. *Oh*, it would have changed *all*.

The week dragged forward, the days still hot though not impossible, temperatures fawning about the ninety mark. Afternoons usually roused a breeze, but by then, by the end of August, the air was so congested with dust and pollen and dander from the withered gray grasses and other flora of the west hills desiccated by a summer of relentless heat that one was almost glad when the droughty air fell silent, and ceased to redden the eyes and crust up sinuses and betray the youthful skin with fine white tracings in the crackwork, intimations of decay.

I spent most of my time reading in the library which was air-conditioned and only two blocks away from the Penthouse. They were interminably home, it seemed, the apparent pair—sprawled out by the pool with icy drinks or sprawled out in the living room with icy drinks or sprawled out in the waterbed, followed by the prescriptive icy drinks and more nomadic sprawling.

I asked about a honeymoon (hoping, by some windfall

of the gods, that it might commence immediately some place far away).

"Hawaii," she said. "In December, when the weather's best," she said, adding, however, that she was taking this week off, had already alerted Al (he was terribly permissive with "us girls"), and that a junket to Hollywood was planned for the weekend following my departure. She wanted to see some "stars," she said. And T.J. had "doings," she said, in "la-la land," she said.

"Why wait?" I inquired feebly. But Dixie only stared back at me with those twinkling blue eyes of hers as if to say "What concern is it of yours?" and went on with the strange business of parading (flaunting?) her ridiculous marriage.

I felt disoriented and obscurely frightened, but the feelings were connected to nothing tangible, or at least to nothing conscious. Maybe it was moving, starting college, the prospect of having to make friends and the certainty that there would be enemies made too. Maybe it was because I had worked my last shift at Sambo's Pancake Paradise which left my days empty, only there wasn't much left for me to do before next Sunday, my date of departure. Or maybe it was just Dixie. Dixie marrying—on a whim and a quirk—one of those many, many men. Why would she get married to anyone? In itself, it was an act that ran counter to almost everything she stood for, it was an act with a future, with built-in checks and balances. Worst of all, it was mapped out, that future—babies, bills, picket fences—all of which was as likely as not to be fine with Dixie, just fine. But the map? No, not ever the map. Not Dixie. What she stood for—if it could be said she stood for anything—was mapless, and paid not one breath's notice to what was around the next bend. So *what* was she trying to prove? And to whom?

The *Herald's* bungalow served as a four-hour, night-time refuge, and on two of the nights of that last week Paul and I went out after work for coffee and dessert at a cafe popular with students, and on another of the nights I went and saw the same movie Paul and I had seen the week before though it did not bear re-viewing. But it seemed I couldn't stay out late enough to come home and find the happy couple safely localized in the bedroom. When they did finally retire, the notorious hollow-core doors of the Penthouse Apartments afforded me with yet another opportunity to hear them in their disport among the warm waves of T.J. Aiken's evicted and movable sea.

Plus, there was this *other thing*. T.J. and his oh-so-familiar gestures.

It was one thing for Dixie to slap my behind: I regarded it as the roommate equivalent to the congratulatory or commiserative or supportive or even regulation butt-patting of professional football players—nothing more. It was another thing altogether for her husband, just out of the gate, as it were, to pass his hand—and not just once, and not in any cursory fashion either, but clinging to slow contours—over my southern bumps. So far he hadn't headed up-map to the northern bumps, but I wasn't terribly sanguine, and worried about an impetuous migration.

Of course I never said peep. Not even to him. I simply moved, without comment, out of reach, out of the room when that sufficed, and later when it didn't, out of the apartment, taking care not to expose myself to the smile which I knew was yoked like a rank beast to the trailing, vainglorious chuckle that his gestures/my exits invariably occasioned. No, I never enjoyed, I never objected: I *blinked.*

To say anything would have been to recognize what he did, and to recognize what he did would have been to recognize *him*, and to recognize him would have been to recognize a whole loaded-down half-submerged raft of *stuff* having a lot to do with Dixie, and a little to do with me, and everything to do with everyone, all of us stuck here together with the same stopping place, how to live and how to *keep* living after, after this or that, the unshakable, the unforgivable, the exquisitely unbearable, and how to love past the meaning of love, and live before the meaning of life, to love what was as we could and through that somehow to be better than we really were, to make it better somehow, beautiful if we could, decent, somehow . . . a whole raft of *stuff* I didn't want to think about or care about, things that were no longer my concern. Since I was history. And I *wanted* to be history. Believe me.

*Four more days.*

*Three more days,* I told myself, leaving a tiny row of thumbnail notches in the wall above the couch.

Then Friday afternoon.

Early Friday afternoon of that last week of our time together the coastal fog made it all the way over the west hills and spilled down on us like the second coming, pouring through the streets, tangling in trees, drifting past windows in long gray banners. From my chair in the library I leapt up and hurried with others to the door, and then I could smell it, where it had come from and where it had been along the way, every blade of withered grass it had combed through, every bough, every cracked pan of dirt, every brittled shrub it had gently coolly swaddled up in passing, and the ocean back and behind, the ocean, I could smell it too, marine broth churning at the far edge, I could smell all the clinging life, long subdued, hardly there, come from the heat of the summer bearing down, come awake from deathlike hibernation, come alive, come gathering together in the soft, moist, cool breath of a dream of a Friday afternoon coming on.

I jogged home. I wanted to run, I really wanted to, but I thought people might wonder. Then even the jogging concerned me, so I tried to walk, but when I reached the Penthouse parking lot I broke into a sprint across it and up the outside stairs two at a time because the thought of waiting for the elevator was intolerable. The thought of waiting for anything any longer was intolerable. I had to find Dixie. To celebrate with her the coming fall, the coming cold—*oh*, it was getting splendidly cold suddenly—celebrate the end of summer, the end of our time, too, our crazy, painful, intense time together forever to be remembered, celebrate the beginning of college, and *okay*, the beginning of her marriage, I didn't care, it was fine, whatever she wanted was fine now, whatever. To celebrate with her *change*. That was all. Only change.

And bless her, praise her, she was out on the balcony in *it*, turning as she heard the door, and giving me *that smile*, that big, carried-away, wide-open, homecoming smile of hers.

"Fog!" I cried, throwing my arms around her. And then she kissed me right on the mouth.

"Fog!" I cried again.

She tossed up her hands like a pair of white doves, she gave a lovely laugh. "Drizzle."

And it was. It was *drizzling* the tiniest soft wet jewels of relief all over us, everywhere, around the whole world, it seemed. It was webbing up in our hair, it was darkening the cement, it was misting up windows, walls, railings, the mother of mist come comforting finally, finally. We opened our palms, and for a time, *for a time*, we held open our hearts. That was all that could be asked of any of us, to stay open for a time, to have known that.

"Sweaters," I said, grabbing her shoulders as if I had just discovered the meaning of the universe. "We need sweaters, lots of sweaters, don't we? shouldn't we put on beautiful sweaters?"

So we rushed in and pulled out all of hers and tossed them like giant confetti about the living room, and then we dug out mine from the heap in the corner and added them to hers, and then we just looked at them and poked each other and shook our heads, laughing, laughing, for there wasn't a chance in hell we were going to wear sweaters and forgo being deliciously cold.

Then, placing her finger along the side of her nose as if to keep me from speaking—*Santa Dixie*, I thought—she went to the stereo, slipped a record from its sheath in a way meant to conceal its title, and *lo*, it was Schubert, a Schubert piano sonata, fluid notes swirling up around us until we were floating away; Schubert, a favorite of mine.

Somehow I jammed two chairs out onto our miniature balcony, and there we sat for well over two hours, feet up on the railing, getting wetter and colder and more content by the second, drinking the Irish coffees of yore with Dixie's whipped cream, Dixie's wonderful, enduring whipped cream of the heart.

The music changed from mine to hers, back to mine, and after awhile it didn't matter, there wasn't any difference, it was music. The mood softened. We hardly spoke.

At one point I said, "You hated it too . . . the heat."

"Did I?" she said. "Maybe."

"You never said so."

"No, I never said."

"But it bothered you, right?"

"I don't know. I guess. It's hard to remember."

I laughed. "Why, because you're cold now?"

"Because now it's cold." An enigmatic look, then a minute or two later she said in afterthought, "Pretty soon you'll wish it was hot."

The gritty light of dusk and the now dank fog eventually sent us back inside where we made popcorn and watched an old black-and-white movie, reminiscing during the commercials about our own old movies, St. Agatha's, people we had both known, *and gently, gently and carefully,* about Cheryl, *just seven months gone,* I thought with wonder. When the movie ended I called Grif, told him I wouldn't be coming in that evening, then I suggested dinner and mentioned T.J.—to include him, *comme il faut,* in the celebratory meal.

"I don't know," she shrugged.

"You don't know about dinner or T.J.?"

"Tony."

"He didn't say when he'd be home?"

"Yeah, 'later,' that's what he said."

"Well, I'll make spaghetti for all of us," I offered.

But by 8:00 he still hadn't showed, and we'd already eaten and cleaned up.

Prompted by the ousted sweaters, I began neatening up my bags and boxes, sorting things for home storage, things for Berkeley, rearranging interiors. "Only two more days," I said, mostly to myself.

Dixie seemed at a loss. She went into the bedroom, came out, rattled through a drawer in the kitchen, drifted into the bathroom, brushed her hair, stood for the longest time (I couldn't help noticing) before the shower (maybe only debating, that's all, a nice warm shower before bed?), came back to the living room for a magazine, paused to watch me folding and fitting things into boxes, set the magazine down, pushed at the sliding glass door though it was already shut tight, picked the magazine up again, disappeared into the bedroom, returned and again stood watching me, the magazine clutched like a shield to her breast. And throughout all of this aimless movement, every so often, I distinctly heard her say, "No."

"No what?" I finally asked.

She gazed at me.

"You've been saying 'no' for the last half hour."

"I have?"

"Yes, haven't you heard yourself?"

"I don't know." There was something wrong with her voice, a flutter in it, small and breathless, like a trapped bird.

"Are you worried about T.J.?"

That seemed to revive her. "No." Silence. Then, "He's just like me, isn't he, Sue? Wherever he goes, there he is."

"Where *did* he go?"

"I don't know. Out."

"Well," I said, "he probably ran into some friends, that's all." But she wasn't listening, I knew she wasn't; she may not have even cared. She was fanning the upper right corner of the magazine which was still clutched against her, thumb working the page edges over and over, like a dealer anxious about the next concealed card. I was kneeling on the carpet, and beside me was a spot that seemed to have captured all of Dixie's attention, because she kept gazing there at the unseeable thing, her lips parted, her expression raveling and unraveling as though half of her was struggling with the thing and the other half kept fleeing.

"No," she said in a guttural whisper.

I snapped about. "There. Did you hear yourself? Did you hear it that time? 'No.' That's what you said, Dixie. You did say it."

"I heard," she said. *Her voice . . .* the trapped flutter again.

"What are you thinking?"

She frowned. "I dunno."

"You don't know what you're thinking about?"

"Nothing. I'm, I'm not thinking, it's . . . I feel . . ."

"What? Are you sick?"

"No, I dunno, it's nothing, forget it, let's forget it, I'm

just tired, I'm seriously tired. I should, like, hit the hay wagon . . . I guess . . . I guess that's what I should do." But she didn't do what she should have done. She just kept standing there, as if waiting for something to happen, thumbing the page edges, her smile shaky and everything else about her uncertain too, all in pieces. It was terrible to see, terribly unlike Dixie.

I didn't know what to do. I picked up some loose photos of Dixie and me—at a sidewalk cafe, at a concert, by the pool—tucked them inside a book, put the book in a box; then, holding up a swimsuit, I turned and with a happy-go-lucky replica of a grin, said, "I guess I won't be needing this."

Honestly, she looked scared to death. "No."

"Jeez, Dixie, you're giving me the freebles. Go to bed." *Freebles*, her word, one of her silly inventions, this one without any conceivable etymology, and I used it to try to pull her out of whatever pit she'd fallen into. But it didn't work, she didn't come out.

I began to feel clammy and chilled; lit a cigarette—my hands trembling—pulled the ashtray off the coffee table and set it next to me on the carpet on the staring spot to eclipse it, make it go away, make her go away, then I propped the cigarette, went on with my packing, kept my back to her.

"No." Said curtly, as if the matter was just about settled.

This time I ignored it.

Several minutes later, the mere tatter of a breath: "*No.*"

Then I heard her walk away, and called out, "Night," with a geniality so strained, so casual-to-a-fault that I nearly choked on it, and didn't dare turn to look until I thought she would be well along the dedicated path to another room, another world. But she did not make the turn—so small, so crucial—into the bedroom. She vectored straight into the bathroom and only to vacate it immediately, having done nothing except flip on the light and the fan.

Another chill crept like a detached hand up my spine, slid up under my hair and clove coldly to my scalp.

She resumed her post behind me.

Something had to be said, anything, anything normal and commonplace, maybe even something in bad taste; vulgar things had power, even while they offended.

"Shit," I said with over-loud enthusiasm, "this box is full as a tick."

No response.

Her mother's gown, the one I had worn at the party, was lying mixed up with my own dresses; trying a different tack, I held it out admiringly. "Are you sure you want me to take this? Probably aren't a whole lot of occasions that a lowly freshman and future famous lawyer . . ."

"No, no, no, no, no . . ."

"What's the matter, what the hell's the matter, Dixie? What *is* it?"

The sobbing started then. Ragged, whole-body sobbing, and she crumpled down like a shot animal, and I couldn't get her to stop, I couldn't get her to hear me. I wrapped myself over her back, lifted her up enough to rest her forehead in the crook of my arm, and there we were, the two of us entangled, blind, confused, scared, together and not-together, the asana of human misery, while at the glass door the night fog pressed eternally, eternally, eternally.

"No don't, don't go, please don't leave me again, please," she sobbed.

"Again?"

I don't remember the exact words, exactly what things I said after that. Tried to say. Intelligent, reasonable, explanatory things . . .

"Please don't go . . ."

. . . about college and babies and the law and marriage . . .

"I can't stand it, please, no, you can't leave . . ."

. . . about time and friendships, the vicissitudes of geography . . .

"No, no, I love you, no, I can't stand it, don't leave again . . ."

. . . about life-in-general (*oh*, it was not, was it? not general, not ever, it was details, little, pathetic, precious details escaping the maelstrom, a half memory, a lucid image, a name softly said, a green pond on a yellow day, a hot forehead in the crook of one's arm) . . .

"No, not again, no, no . . ."

. . . about remembering always and letters weekly and holidays each season . . .

"No, no, no . . ."

. . . about her context and my context and changing contexts . . .

"I love you, I love you . . ."

. . . stupid, repulsively kind, hideously reasonable things of so small value that I prayed to god she wouldn't actually hear, hating god and praying to god she might notice, that was all, might only feel the muted bump and fumble of my hobbled comfort. And still she wouldn't stop, she couldn't stop.

I said, "I'll miss you too, Dixie," and added, "I will," undoing all.

I would miss her, I would, but she was dying and couldn't be bothered, couldn't be saved by mere missing.

Finally, pulling her up, I said, "Let's get you into bed. I'll fix up a cold washcloth for your face, and a, a glass of white wine. You're just tired. It's been an eventful . . ." that was the word I used, eventful, *god help me*, ". . . week. Too much change at once," I said. "Maybe your period," I said. (For that I truly hated myself.)

Willing or unwilling, she shuffled into the bedroom,

my arm around her waist, half holding her up and guiding her.

"I'll be right back," I said, and the wild relief I felt in having two inconsequential tasks to perform—and so avoid, for the time they required, her despair—left me feeling ashamed of my life-in-general.

When I returned it was like returning to someone's deathbed after a transient escape to the hospital cafeteria with still nothing to say, nothing really that could be said, words grotesquely inadequate, clubbed hands for heart surgery that would fail regardless; the right words in fact not available, never invented, and nothing to offer except the embarrassing contradiction of one's presence, of life, my life, the brute fact of it, continuing on while hers was playing out.

She had undressed to bra and panties and was sinking back into the waterbed. Not sobbing now. Whimpering. The whimpering was infinitely worse. The whimpering said she knew. The whimpering tore me up. There was a rocky obstruction in my throat, a ringing in my ears, my stomach was a cold pit of regret.

I placed the washcloth on her forehead, the wine on the bedside orange crate. She watched me with eyes as listless as a dead sea. When I straightened I saw her wince. It was as though whatever it was inside her that had broken down and that lay as quashed and weakened as her physical form was pained anew by my very erectness. I stood, she lay. I could walk out, walk on; I was in a position to do so—at the ready. I was vertical, not vulnerable. I had always been in a position to walk away. Not Dixie. Dixie lay within the framed confines of her seabed, lay on her back, on the surface, unaware of its murky depths, her body and her life shifting in little back-and-forths with the unseen currents.

"Will you lie down with me, Susan?" Her voice was

urgent, pleading, different, so different, and yet, though I had never heard this voice—not with me, not that I could recall—I recognized it as utterly *authentic*. "Just a little bit. Just . . . just ten minutes?"

Ten minutes. The specificity of a child, charmingly uncomprehending, deeply meant, deeply touching—*I'm gonna eat cake for ten whole years, I love you as big as a big house, will you love me for ten lifetimes, for ten minutes?* Thereat, whensoever, as long as and during, throughout no matter when, once and anon, until and up to and including at that instant pending, whereupon for a time of ten eternities you lie with me. Susan. Ten minutes.

"Okay," I said softly. What else could I say, what reason give? There was no reason, no reason at all, no reason left. It was all gone, it was all here. The reason.

And so down I went, fully clothed, into the troubled sea, as though I had merely lost my footing and plunged in.

Between us the water moved in warm slow swells, Dixie floating up as I drifted down, then up I listed and down she settled until, the both of us lying perfectly still, the water smoothed within its plastic bag and we heard only the occasional gurgle, felt the subdued churn of the sea imprisoned beneath our bodies.

She was not whimpering anymore.

I couldn't think what to say. I had said everything and everything was nothing. There was nothing to say. And it was clear that these ten minutes, these increments of eternity, had nothing to do with saying. Only doing.

Dixie seemed to be waiting.

Both of us at a loss. A terrible loss.

Something was supposed to happen, something that had already happened, something that could never be.

*All those men,* I thought. With Dixie. *T.J.,* I thought. With Dixie. *Me,* I thought. With Dixie. *In bed,* I thought.

Always with Dixie. Always with. Desperately with.

It was out of the question, *I* was out of the question, and yet I *was* the question. At that moment for Dixie I was the only question.

Someone shifted a leg, rippling the water. *Rough water*, I thought. *Hazardous currents.*

The silence was enormous, more than silence, a vastly held breath, an atmospheric imbalance, pushing out, pressing in.

It was at that point I did the unspeakable thing: I glanced at my watch—though I had no idea how long it had been, ten seconds, ten eons, and no place to go—I glanced at my watch and I said, "I have to go now." And in that instant of glancing Dixie snatched up my hand and cried out with piercing anguish one name, the wrong name that had always been the right name, the one name, and gave herself up to her loss.

*"Mom!"*

At the door I added—and there was anger in my voice, as if surely she ought to understand there were things to do, places to go, other people to meet, others and other things that were more important than her ten lousy minutes, ten, impossible, petrifying minutes with her, surely she ought to understand that what was asked was not possible, surely she ought to see that, forgive that—at the door I twisted about and added, "I have to go to work, Dixie."

*Work.* Though I did not. *I have to*, as if anything—work, play, death, life—*anything*, could justify my failure, my . . . inhumanity.

*God, oh god*, it would have cost me almost nothing, that littlest of lies, and who could say, really, who could say it would have been a lie? I could not say, I would never again be able to say, that it would have been entirely a lie, to have lain with her, to have been with her, to be with another human being, to have reached in and given another human being in a parallel world of pain, help. Whatever help. Help for the time being, the human being. Not cure. Just a little help for some time of our little time being together. For ten minutes, say.

Sex?

It was always sex; it was obviously sex; it was never sex. Sometimes. Sometimes truth suffers the obvious, the way a quiet man suffers the crowd. And what is he do-ing, that quiet man in the midst of the crowd? He is wait-ing, listening for someone, perhaps a friend if he's lucky, someone to whisper his name.

In the religion of despair there are many prayers. Dixie had but one. That night she needed me to help her pray. That was all. Just someone to pray with. It was the only prayer she knew.


Years later, driving down a street in San Francisco, I ran over a yellow cat. Not actually over it with the tires—there would have been some mercy in that. No, it had darted out just as I was passing, and got caught under-neath the car, and for thirty yards or so it pinballed be-tween the chassis and the pavement, each soft thud a sound I could feel until finally, glancing in the rearview mirror, I saw it hurled up behind the car, its back stiffly arched, claws spread like small, exploding stars, its mouth thrown open to pain, and its teeth flashing in fury, a fury that was utterly and beautifully impotent against the sud-den effrontery of death.

I drove on to the nearest business, and from there called the S.P.C.A., and from there went on to work, shaken, appalled, my soul squirming.

Why didn't I stop when I saw it dart out?

I suppose it had seemed too late. And somehow not

my concern. Not my fault. I was afraid, too. There was that.

Why didn't I stop when I felt the first thud?

Then it seemed even more too late. And I wanted it out from underneath my car. I couldn't stand it under me, suffering.

Why didn't I slow at least, give it a chance to escape?

I was late, I was always late for . . . something. And I wanted it out from under my car, I wanted to get away from what was happening as fast as possible, from the pain my passing was causing, from its howling mouth, from its sinuous body rigidified with pain, I wanted to get away from the fear, I wanted to get away from its fate that was for a moment mine . . . ours.

And I didn't pull over either, to run back, to see if it could be helped, or to put it out of its misery. Because I was late, as usual. Because it was too late: the series of hesitations, creeping hesitations, one plus one plus another, increments of weakness—one could hardly halt such indubitable additions once they'd begun. They had a strength of their own.

It was an accident, I told myself. An accident. "That's so, that's so," I said aloud. But that's not all.

To this day and for the rest of my life, for the remainder of those ten everlasting minutes, when I think of Dixie I think of that yellow cat.

# 17

The name of the state prison—California Institution for Women—used to include the suffix *at Corona*, a town forty-five miles east of Los Angeles, but citizens objected to the inglorious stigma, and so location was replaced with euphemism, "Frontera," Spanish (feminine) for frontier, which cannot be found on any map in any gender or application.

Disregarding the conspicuous geographical absence, and the optimistic connotations of change and renewal, CIW-Frontera is, sadly, a literal place—one hundred and twenty double-fenced acres of hardpan on the eastern edge of the L.A. basin. To that place they send women whose abuse of society achieved clear extremities. To that place in the winter of 1973, six months after the actual crime, they sent Dixie Darling. She was still eighteen. No one, not even her father who loved her, of course, not even A. L. Lemucchi who wept on the phone when he called to tell me what had happened and who loved her simply and who was never one of the many who lay with her, and not even I who loved her as I could, and could not have loved her more without more courage . . . no one thought that she didn't deserve to be there. There were times, though, when I thought I ought to have been there with her. There were times when I was there, in a prison of my own design.

I feel certain that Dixie hadn't meant to offend or outrage humanity, that, in a true and (unfortunately) eclipsed way, it was a marvelous act of self-defense and self-affirmation, never mind the contradictions in plain sight. That was the trouble—it required something beyond *plain sight*. But they—the lawyers and jurors, the relatives, the newspapers, the judge—they saw only the specious, the stuff *en evidence*, a chronological arrangement of visible facts as inexorable as stone. Facts could be turned and touched, worried at length, but they could not be entered with ease. In a court of law there isn't time really, there often isn't even inclination, particularly in cases as seemingly lucid and unequivocal as Dixie's, for the kind of deep inquiry that leads away from the comfortable surroundings of facts, familiar furniture in a familiar room, sunny and dust-free, toward a nebulous and very often countering truth residing in the storm cellar of the soul.

Truth is a dark-skinned alien in a white world: she is too much trouble to get to know, speaks a different language, a niggling threat to the status quo, her eyes hungry, perhaps even accusing, and yet she is a sister more like ourselves than we can peaceably tolerate.

There was no question she was guilty: that was a done deal, to use one of Dixie's ever-descriptive expressions. So the attorneys spent a lot time arguing *how* she was guilty, debating prepositional clauses—of the first or second degree, with or without malice aforethought—and adjectives too, fistfuls of them—voluntary or involuntary, express or implied malice, disturbed or distorted state of mind, overwhelming/underwhelming emotion, conscious/ unconscious disregard, etc. etc. and etc. In the end the jurors were left with a multiple-choice litter of modifiers for one immutable act, and a decision, finally, that seemed as subjective as what each of those twelve chose to wear to court that day.

Dixie had no chance. Probably she knew it. Probably at some point she stopped caring: she had done what she needed to do, and with that, time and illusion were fin- ished, the territory was all new. Dixie Darling was not to be conjured up any longer; she was to be witnessed. She was real. Now everyone took her seriously. The defen- dant. No one called her Dixie. Dixie was done for.

They gave her the maximum sentence because of the facts, while the truth remained shrouded and tastefully out of sight. I was perhaps the only one who could know why what happened happened, but then, there were those facts gleaming like tiger teeth, and though not blinded by them, I was afraid to point, to reach beyond them into the heart of the beast. I was young, I was intimidated, I was suddenly shy of contradiction and clung to the coat- tails of the throng. And I was guilty—there was that. So I, too, fingered through the facts—her activities, her friends, her statements—leaving the insides of things un- touched, my voice throughout testimony flat, my man- ner accommodating, my eyes rigorously cast down to a single, scuffed square of parquet lying midway between defense and prosecution. But the act itself, so large, so adult, yet so guileless—Dixie's act—seemed to have mes- merized me. After the trial and over the years, I fled into books, into college, into my reclaimed, reharnessed future, and into the clean and implacable assurance of The Law. I told myself that whatever I might have said would have had little force, the facts were too present, taking up most of the foreground. But the truth was, they might have made some allowance, Dixie's twelve peers, they might have felt obliged to at least look past the imposing brute bulk of the facts and glimpse, perhaps only obliquely, a shadow bending softly down and inward, as if crumpling, the sad shadow of Dixie's life.

At Paso Robles I turned east onto Route 46 through a wedge in the Cholame Hills, tawny and threadbare, then southeast between ranges, not mountains, not like hills either, unimpassioned anticlines, broad and vaguely curved, like tanned welts that would subside with time; then straight east across Antelope Valley toward Blackwells Corner, descending so gradually that a stopped car would not have rolled in either direction, passing oil derricks, vineyards, tomato fields, walnut trees, almond trees, peach trees, segregated and set in mathematical rows. Occasionally there was a farm house with its enclosing, squared windbreak, looking from a distance like a toy house inside an opened box, the box left upon a table that went on and on.

At Blackwells Corner I realized I had already crossed the western edge of the southern extension of the Great Central Valley: the purity of the horizontal premise, the brutal candor and exposure of the topography, every direction flat, unanimously flat and radiating out, like an echo of a voice whose reality one can't quite believe, one doesn't quite want to believe, so much of one thing and seemingly without check. There were cotton fields as far as the eye could see—spindly, leafless bushes with their haphazard growth of white bolls—rendering a variegated ocean of brown and white, and the road on which I traveled a raised, endless dike. And then again there were orchards, a yellow spattering of mustard weeds spoiling the austerity of the rows. Then came the green stripes of vineyards, cordon wires training the new shoots to submit to the mechanical pickers of the fall. To the south I noticed a relatively small patch, maybe a dozen acres, of nothing; that is, nothing planted by man—hard scrabble and sand, the remains of a shallow wash, and sagebrush, tumbleweed, greasewood, their muted colors washing into the noonday haze.

Boarding Interstate 5 at Lost Hills, I shot south past Bakersfield. Everywhere off to the west stood the nodding oil derricks of Kern County with their blind, mole eyes, drilling down, not with hopeful but with a relentless, arithmetic intent—so many barrels per day, so many dollars per barrel—predators without regret or apology strewn across the skinned, anticlinal humps and draws and flats. Between the derricks, connecting them, lay an exposed veinwork of pipes, the steam from the generators rising like smoke from a deathscape.

But I was driving, driving fast, and could claim no clear title to indignation. Like the gasoline in my car, guilt drove me on.

If there was a kind of terrible beauty in the earlier expanses of premeditated, homogeneous growth, the unpeopled land, patches of giant sameness, now with the oil fields came the genuinely terrible. All-out taking. Nothing would be replaced, nothing returned to the earth. About a mile below abandoned oil fields, I knew, were enormous subterranean cavities where the crude had once been. Dry holes in the heart of the land.

Behind me, Bakersfield vaporized in the bright ubiquitous haze of the valley. It was just past noon, the temperature over ninety. The Temblor Range skulked low beneath the heat warps in the west, and played itself out against the southern hook of the Tehachapi Mountains which rose in a pale, celery green blur fifteen miles ahead, signaling the bottom end of the Great Valley. Next to the Interstate, in the drained lakebed of Buena Vista, white dust devils whirled up from the alkaline soil. Except these ghosts, and the hypnotic penetration of the derricks, nothing else moved. Nothing grew. The wind whipped swiftly through and away, as if worried it too might be claimed for some use.

At that point on my drive down to Frontera, to Dixie, nothing less than the naked union of premise and purpose, and the soulless space it seemed to create, nothing less than the silent busyness in the emptiness surrounding, could have tapped the spiritual desolation left within me, like one of those derricks breaking into a subterranean cavity; nothing less could have driven me back in my mind to Dixie, back to the last August of our time together, that last unbearable morning in the Penthouse Apartments . . .

There was a note on the coffee table when I awoke. I saw that the handwriting was Dixie's and didn't read it, sinking back, instead, into soft pillows and into the abject relief her absence occasioned. Closing my eyes, I thought about the night before, the week before, the muddled time after St. Agatha's, and then in a kind of panic of waste, I pinched off all of that and let my thoughts spill across the sunny plains of the future, beginning with father's arrival tomorrow morning to take me away from here, home and then to Berkeley where I was sure to thrive in unison with others of my kind, where I could take up pick and hoe and raise up something worthwhile. Enough of this random growth, this weed patch.

When the phone rang, I scrambled up and into the kitchen to grab it before it waked T.J., wondering if in fact he had even returned last night. I hadn't gotten back (after fleeing Dixie) until past midnight, having spent three hours in a coffee shop reading magazines, watching other late-night diners, and trying to elude the troubling thoughts of her.

"Good morning. Is this Sue?" a young, honeyed voice inquired.

"Yes."

"Hi, Sue. This is . . . *Felicia*, Sue." She seemed to fall with comfortable importance into her own name.

"Felicia?"

"From last night." There was a significant pause, then she said, "Oh, I'm so sorry, you can't talk, can you, Sue?"

"Sure I can talk. What do you mean, I can't talk? Who are you?"

"Is this . . . ?" And she recited our phone number.

"Yes."

There was another significant pause. I could hear pages turning.

"It is not uncommon, Sue," she began, as if reading, "to feel some embarrassment, even shame, after . . ."

"After *what?*"

"After calling us," she said. I could tell that she was trying to stay calm and solicitous, but exasperation was shoving the back door. "Denial is another common aspect of the post-suicidal state."

"*Suicide?* Denial? Will you please tell me who you are?"

As though indulging a child, she said, "This is Felicia Ashworth of the San Jose Suicide Prevention Center. You called last night at . . . 10:41," she evidently read, "and we talked for nine minutes," she read on, "and I *told you*, Sue, that I would make a follow-up call this morning, I told you that things would look better in the morning, Sue."

"You didn't tell me anything because you got the wrong Sue. Felicia."

"Obviously, you *are* better," she replied with some irritation.

"I'm not better, I'm not anything. You've got the wrong number or the wrong Sue . . . you, you got it *all* wrong."

Felicia Ashworth hung up then.

The abrupt silence was eerie. Somewhere out there was another Sue with an almost identical phone number, maybe only one digit different or transposed, who was waiting this morning for the follow-up call to her moment of private and profane desperation; somewhere out there was another Sue who might not be "better." Gazing out the balcony doors at the leaden, impenetrable fog, and feeling a stupid anger at Felicia's well-meant but nevertheless bungled civic service, I noticed, lying halfway along the path of my vision, Dixie's note. Deliberately, nervously, I walked to it, picked it up, and read:

> Hi Sue,
> Got a facial with "Armand"—yum!
> See ya later a.m.
> I.l.y.,
> Dixie
>
> P.S. Last nite was tray weird, huh? Oh well,
> take it with a grain of salt and add tequila.

There were eyelashes drawn over the e's in "see," and a happy face next to her name.

So I decided Dixie was not the mislaid Sue. I also decided to accept the advice implied by the tone of her note—the express meanings themselves made practically no sense at all—and disregard (as a kindness to her) the night before. Clearly, this was what she wanted. Plus, it handily excused me from the squeamish task of having to offer comment on the events (or non-events), and worse, on my participation (or non-participation), and worse yet, on my failure, about which there was no question.

*One more day*, I told myself on the way to the shower.

When I emerged, T.J. was up and in the kitchen, wearing only a pair of nylon briefs, a sweatshirt, and white crew socks. It was 10:00. The TV was on, Saturday morning cartoons, Wile E. Coyote and the elusive Roadrunner. T.J. let out explosive guffaws every time Wile E. bit the dust, his malevolent schemes undone by the bird's last minute insights.

"Where's the little missus?" he said.

"Having a facial."

"I guess you don't need to do that."

"Neither does Dixie."

"Her skin's not perfect," he said.

"No one's is," I said, as I folded the blankets and sheets from my surrogate bed in the living room.

He watched until I'd finished. "What? You get up on the wrong side of the couch?"

"It only has one side. Straight."

"Ow, hot stuff." Whether he was referring to my temper or to the coffee he had just sloshed across his hand, I didn't know, but in any case, I took my own coffee and a book, grabbed a sweater, and went out to the balcony to read in the fog.

I found the actual fact of T.J. Aiken oppressive; add to that his snappy manner, his strangely insulting compliments, his lax ways immune to punishment or at the very least to examination, his disarming smile and his lubricious hands, and he was to me as noxious as a dead skunk. I couldn't stand to be in the same room with him, and hoped Dixie would return soon and carry him off to some weekend blowout far away.

Shortly later, the balcony door slid open behind me. I might have heard another door, but the TV was loud—college football now, prattling color commentators, the roar of the crowd—and anyway, I was distracted by his proximity. I kept reading, wouldn't turn around to face, which was to feel, the delusory warmth of his smile. It seemed he meant only to intimidate me, because I detected no purpose, no movement. Minutes passed, yet still, the flip observation, the question that evinced no interest whatsoever in an answer, the unfunny quip, never sallied forth. Casually I reached for my cup of coffee on the box beside my chair. It was then his hand closed around my wrist and guided *my* hand, placing it squarely against his genitals which were thinly sheathed in nylon.

"Meet the family jewels," he said with dark pride.

I yanked my hand away. "Jewels?" I snapped. "You mean the family zircons. And the rest of you is just as cheap and phony, too."

He seemed to think this was hysterical. It seemed also to increase his appreciation of me. "You're a sharp little tack, aren't you? How'd you end up with Dixie?"

"Dixie happens to be my friend. And your wife, in case you forgot."

Easing over to the side of the balcony, he leaned against the railing, and for the first time I saw him frown with something approaching serious reflection. "Dixie's a joke," he said, flicking his hair. Then, more to himself, "A bigger joke than I figured." Despite his incomplete attire, despite everything I had suspected about him and everything I was beginning to confirm about him, at that moment I regarded T.J. Aiken with the grave shock of someone learning then and there of a terminal illness in the family.

"But you're married," I said.

"The whole thing's a bad joke."

"You're married," I repeated dumbly.

"We're nothing. She's a piece of taff. Defective, too, by the way. Did you know that? She can't even get off."

"I don't want to know anything."

"You know plenty," he said with sinister flatness, and giving me his cold, dark-eyed rays. Then, lightly, as if to cover or dismiss, he said, "I'm just hanging here."

"What do you mean you're hanging? You made promises, you married Dixie. Doesn't that mean anything to you?"

"Yeah. It means I got a place to hang."

"But marriage is permanent."

He laughed, how he laughed. "Nothing's permanent." It reminded me of something Dixie had said once about the future, about there being "no such beastie." They kept *seeming* to be alike, T.J. and Dixie, but they were not. Not at all. He was the dark side of the same coin.

I stared at him. "Why? Why'd you do it then?"

"She's a cute act, you gotta admit, cute and tasty. Plus I did a lot of blow that night. And hey, I had a housing problem. She said you were moving out, there was an opening; it was cute the way she said that . . . 'I got an opening.' I thought she had the right attitude about it."

"You mean you thought she didn't take it seriously either?"

"Naw. How could she? Mostly she was excited about coming back married, surprising you and her dad, and the next door neighbors for all I know. The big wow, and who'd've thunk it, that kinda thing. But . . ."

"But what?"

"But on the way back she went all moody and mushy, kept asking if I really loved her and was I serious and did I want rug rats. *Rug rats* . . . yeah, right." He rolled his eyes. "What was I supposed to say? I'd done a couple of grams, I was torqued, and it was gonna be one, long, ugly drive if I didn't pick Door Number Three. So I said, sure I love you, why not?"

"But you don't."

"Give me a break."

Furious, disgusted, sick to my stomach, I said, "So what is your plan, T.J.?"

"Well, I'm not gonna shine it, if that's what you mean. They got drive-through divorces too, you know. You could lob a brick from the chapel to the courthouse in Reno. I expect in the next month or two, just about the time the department buffs my badge and I'm on the roll again, I'll be taking a short vacation in Nevada." He paused. "But whoa hey, this is strictly confidential. I don't want her to thrash my bed or something while I'm gone."

"And in the meantime you still need a place to *hang*, there's that."

He smiled.

"Like a cheap suit," I said. And then I excused myself, gathering up book and cup, and went into the apartment where I discovered Dixie propped against the wall of the vestibule, gaze aimed at the floor, as if holding something carefully in place, something that might slip away. I uttered her name, full of pain and apology.

Then, coming in behind me, T.J. said, "Whoops."

Her eyes locked like blue laser beams on T.J. To me, very gently, very gravely, she whispered, "I guess you better get out now, Susan." Susan, not Sue, everything official, everything on the record.

I don't know why, but I thanked her. Then I carried all my belongings, which were anyway ready to go, down the hall to the elevator, down the elevator to the lobby, stacking them unobtrusively in the corner by the main door. To expunge all evidence of my presence required less than twenty minutes, a fact in which I took the saddest pleasure. Throughout my comings and goings, Dixie never moved except to light a cigarette, the ashes dropping listlessly into the carpet.

T.J. had sprawled on the couch, and was making an obvious effort to watch the football game, but I knew he, too, was waiting for me to get out. I figured he thought he'd land on his feet somehow. But the whole thing felt pretty unpredictable to me.

When I'd made my final tour of the apartment, passing T.J., who gave me a conspiratorial *oh boy, am I in deep shit* look, brow raised theatrically, eyes wide, mouth drawn down, a look I studiously ignored; when I gazed one last time through the balcony glass for the view to which I had developed a fond attachment, though the fog obscured all and I was thus denied my farewell; when I laid my key on the counter and had my purse in hand, I tried again to think of something to say to Dixie. "Well," I began, "look, it's been . . ."

"Better . . . go," she said. Her hand was hanging against the wall, and at that moment it made a sad little flutter, like the last movements of a dying bird. I thought of her hand the night before, reaching for me; and then I thought of T.J.'s hand grabbing mine and pressing it into his groin; and I thought, *yes, go now, go, go, go.*

I called my father from the pay phone outside the library. Though he wasn't scheduled to come for me until the next day, he said, "I'm on my way," bless his soul.

I realized I couldn't wait to see him, to feel his warmth and to forgive it too, the trouble it had caused, the vulnerable state in which it had thrust us all. It seemed I would be carried home more human than I had departed it, and glad enough for that. Perhaps even mother and I would overlook each other's perfections, and find an endearing flaw or two of value, something to love.

As for Dixie, I told myself I would give her a call in the next day or so, see how she was doing, if she'd booted T.J. out or not. But three days passed and I did not call. Then I told myself it was a good idea anyway to give it all a rest; I told myself I would call her the following weekend, I'd have more to say by then, about Berkeley, about my new life. But by Wednesday night she'd already done it, and by Thursday Lemucchi called to tell me, and by Saturday—Saturday when I might have chatted brightly with her about the dorm rooms, about how she

was lucky to be shut of Mr. Aiken—by the time Saturday
slouched forward like a volunteer for duty long since carried out by others, by destiny, by time, it was all too late.
I was too late. It seemed I had always been late. Late for
life.

I took the Grapevine over the Tehachapi Mountains in
a bound, past the fume and growl of the diesel trucks
hauling up in the right lane which was reserved for their
struggle alone, and past them again on the downside,
though they barreled headlong, jockeying by inches to
lead the convoy south into the L.A. basin lying etherized
beneath the smog, like a victim of its own vast calamity.
San Fernando, Burbank, Glendale, Hollywood, Whittier—
just signs and exits, veins twisting off the I-5 artery and
out into the tissue of the body politic. Then turning east
onto 91, I knew by the atmospheric smudges in the southern sky and the distant, amalgamated hum, that Anaheim
and Orange were somewhere off to the right, but I was
left to presume life by the steady throb of traffic, cars
flowing in and out, glints from far-off steel and glass.
Twenty miles, twenty minutes, to Dixie. Finally, the freeway straightened and edged along the northern reach of
the Santa Ana Mountains where the spread of humanity
was temporarily checked.

A sign for Corona, five miles. No mention of Frontera.
Then a smaller sign along the side of the freeway—California Correctional Facility—and another just after it, warning travelers not to pick up hitchhikers. It was 3:00. I
estimated that by the time I parked and got through security checks it would be 3:30. 3:30 and I would be face
to face with Dixie.

At the bottom of one of the exit signs for outlying
Corona, printed out in reduced letters, as if in shame or

afterthought, were the words *California Institution for Women-Frontera*, and I bore off the freeway, turned left onto the Chino-Corona Road, following directions given me by the public relations lieutenant with whom I had spoken before leaving Monterey.

I found I was having a hard time breathing, and opened the window, but the rush of hot dry air seemed to make it worse. My face and fingertips began to tingle, my eyes stung, my heart was banging as though something had come loose, a critical bolt or bearing. Drought invaded my mouth. And with a sudden, violent urgency, I needed a restroom. It seemed I was withering inside and out.

The earlier idea of bringing Dixie a selection of favorite food items—pineapple milk shake, chorizo, etc.—was abandoned; I decided it was best to reach my destiny, if only to have done with it.

But what would I say? What could I say? So much time, so much pain. And I was so very very late.

She killed him, of course. Mr. Anthony J. Aiken. On Wednesday afternoon, September 3rd, at around 5:15 (there was some question about the exact time).

She was sitting on the outside stairs of the Penthouse Apartments, between the first and second floors, facing the parking lot. She was wearing a dress which was a matter of some import during the trial because it had a full skirt, a sleeveless, cotton, summer dress, flowered print, blue and pink and "pretty," said one of the witnesses. Her legs were loosely parted, and between them the full skirt hung in a kind of shallow well which bottomed out on the step, and in the well of flowered fabric was the gun—the service revolver belonging to Officer Aiken, as he was referred to throughout the trial. Hence, the gun—a 6" Colt Python, .357 caliber, with a vented rib running along the barrel for ease in aiming, weight, two pounds—was not visible. She sat there for approximately three hours. She was drinking tequila from a bottle which stood, like a little soldier sentry, loyal and unflinching, on the step below, about an inch from her naked calf. A dozen people saw her on their way in and out of the building, several noticed the bottle, but either out of discretion or a not-my-business attitude, none addressed her, none questioned her activity. One even passed her on the stairs, but he saw neither the gun nor the bottle, was focused, he said, on easing by her and down to the lot. He was late for an appointment, he was in a hurry: it was why he had taken the stairs. The other witnesses used the elevator and so were never close enough. At 5:10, T.J. drove up in his black and gold, rag-top Camaro. Along the south perimeter of the parking lot was an area where Penthouse residents could wash their cars, and at the time there was a woman engaged in just that. Upon exiting his own car, T.J. strolled over to her, suggesting she wash his car when she had finished hers. The woman laughed, she said. Then, she said, they heard a sound, the clink of the tequila bottle on the cement step, and both looked over and up at Dixie. She was still seated on the step in the same relaxed, late summer afternoon pose—legs parted, elbows on knees, chin propped in her left hand, the right hand dangling down into the hidden recesses of the flowered, cotton well. She was looking at T.J. with a blank, fixed quality, "like she'd never seen him before," the woman later testified. T.J. began walking toward Dixie. The woman resumed washing her car. There was a loud *crack*. The woman glanced up. Nothing seemed to have changed: T.J. was still upright, though he seemed unsteady, "like he changed his mind or forgot something in his car, like he was going to turn around," the woman said. Dixie was still exactly as she had been a moment earlier. A half second later T.J. crumpled to the pavement. There was a pause. The woman looked at T.J., looked at Dixie, and apparently froze. She testified the pause lasted maybe five seconds. Then the gun rose again from the well of flowers, the woman collapsed in fear beside her car, there were three more explosions, the body (for at that point it was merely a body) giving a slight jolt with each bullet's penetration. Dixie dropped both hands with the gun back into the skirt. She then reached with her left hand for the bottle and sipped "like a lady" (the woman testified); then she stood and climbed the stairs to her apartment on the fifth floor.

When the police arrived, they found her in the bathroom, taking a shower. The fog had long cleared and the westering sunlight swarmed through the balcony glass and around the apartment, exposing all. The gun was on the counter next to the empty tequila bottle. The radio was playing soft popular music, golden oldies. A cigarette burned in the living room ashtray. The flowered dress was lying in a heap on the floor of the entry. The waterbed had been drained, its plastic mattress neatly folded and placed inside the empty frame along with the spread and linens and the rest of Anthony J. Aiken's belongings, including the empty holster, apparently awaiting removal. On the couch—where she had evidently slept the night before—lay pillow and blanket, disheveled. In the kitchen sink were the partially burned remains of the guest register. There was a sliced peach on a plate, untouched, as though she had changed her mind. The apartment door was wide open.

The officers knocked on the bathroom door—a touching detail, I thought, the politeness, the attendance to matters of civility in the wake of brutality. She emerged wearing another summer dress, one of her mother's. She had not had time to curl her hair or to apply make-up.

One of the officers verified her name, stated her rights, asked if she understood, and said her name again: Dixie Darling. She was reported to have looked at him peculiarly, and to have said, "But the cast has died."

He then repeated the question about her rights.

She shrugged, it was reported, and replied, "Yes."

The newspaper photo showed a young woman, rather plain—looking like any one of us—in a simple, solid-colored dress, no jewelry, standing in front of the Penthouse Apartments and flanked by two policemen. Her expression was calm, though there seemed a hint of curiosity, as if she was seeing not a new world, but the world newly.

The initial bullet had entered T.J. Aiken's heart, which meant that the following trio of shots was, in actual killing terms, gratuitous. (A great to-do was made of the three superfluous shots.) In its way, the murder act itself was gratuitous. Officer Aiken, it was reported during the trial, had already made the run up to Reno, had already filed the divorce, and was coming by merely to pick up some of his things. Officer Aiken was already history, as it were. So, though there were the obvious literal aspects of the murder, it was in essence symbolic. It would change nothing that was not already in the process of changing, or already changed. It would not change her relationship with Officer Aiken, which had ended. (I found it interesting that though T.J. had been ingloriously suspended from the police department, dead he resumed his post in spirit and became again one of their own, and both the prosecution and his former fellow officers insisted on resurrecting his title, if not his somewhat tarnished memory.)

But I knew that the murder did change Dixie's relationship with Dixie. She did not kill a man. In her pretty summer dress that September afternoon she killed the first lie and all the lies that followed from it, and then in that same single act she killed any chance the truth had for a room, for a life, of its own.

Because with the first shot she affirmed herself, and I for one could not help but see it as a triumph of sorts, a triumph of human dignity. But in the pause between the single shot and the trio, a pause no longer than five or six seconds, she must have seen completely the self she had just authenticated and affirmed, and perhaps it was too frank or too real, and for Dixie, whose standards had always been fabulous, perhaps too ugly, and so again she raised the gun and fired three quick shots not into a tangle of flesh and bones, or into Anthony J. Aiken, or a man, or the symbolic man, or even into all of humanity or all of humanity's pain and pleasure, its good and evil, and least of all into God whose salvation she never desired, but into her own alias self who was, at that moment of birth, unbearable. Unbearably shocked and burning bright and alive, and for all of that, a kind of hell.

The things that worked against her seemed to work equally in her favor. She got drunk (to get up her courage)/*she got drunk (in an effort to soften her rage)*. Her father had taught her to use a gun (meaning she knew exactly what she was doing)/*her father had taught her to use a gun (meaning she couldn't have missed if she'd wanted to)*. She was wearing a full skirt (in order to conceal the weapon)/*she was wearing a full skirt (because it happened to be a summer dress and it was summer)*. She was waiting on the steps (to kill him)/*she was waiting on the steps (to express her anger, to scare him)*. It was malice (express)/*it was malice (implicit)*. She was in a jealous rage (which is basically malice)/*she was in a jealous rage (which is heat of passion)*. T.J. Aiken was an officer (of the peace)/*T.J. Aiken was an officer (suspended)*. He was shabby (but that didn't warrant homicide)/*he was shabby (and she was young and desperate and alone and mourning the suicide of her mother, upset by the recent mar-*

*riage of her father, and her best friend had just moved out, and her husband was a hoax, and her job was a nowhere job, and she had nothing and no one left, and she wanted to be taken seriously for a change . . . ).* Why should they have? the prosecution asked. She hadn't given anyone *reason* to take her seriously—the string of men, wanton behavior, whimsical marriage, the drinking at odd hours, the disregard for her horse, for the safety of others, for society's mores, the haphazard work attendance, haphazard meals (as her roommate testified), the haphazard life, as the record shows.

And the closing summations: defense argued that she was intoxicated and angry, her judgement was impaired, she raised the gun to scare or threaten him, and the gun went off; and seeing what she had done, distraught by what she had done, seeing him fall to the pavement, all the blood, the crackling silence, she then effectively went out of her mind and fired three more shots, emptying the gun—which was not fully loaded to begin with.

The state argued that she was intoxicated and angry, but she knew exactly what she was doing, she intended to kill Officer Aiken, she had to use both hands, she had to have *aimed* the gun because the shot went through the dead center of his heart, and she fired three more shots to make sure that she had done what she had intended with malice aforethought to do. Which was to end his life.

She's just eighteen (she has to be stopped now)/*she's just eighteen (give her a break)*.

In the end it was the pause. The five-second pause between the first shot and the trio of shots, the pause that settled all. There was more premeditation in that pause than in all of her life up to that point, the state argued. As for me, I would have emended that to say that all of her life was *contained* in that pause. It had erupted into it and hung there suspended as it were, until, in a despair of vision—clear and acute, dangerously inclusive, *ravening*—she blew it all apart.

The trial lasted eight days. With my parents I attended the third day, during which I testified. With my father alone I attended the eighth day, when the verdict was read.

Dixie did not testify. The court told the jurors that they must not use this fact against her, that she had a right like every other defendant in a case, to rely on the state of the evidence. And since what happened—so far as I could tell—had little to do with the state of the evidence, I thought she'd made the right choice. She would have had to have gone up there and to have told a completely separate, parallel story that had played itself out across the dimly-lit topography of her inner landscape. She would have had to mention me—more than once. It would have been an incredible story, one that only the best of psychoanalysts could have swallowed without complaint. And anyway, there was that single unavoidable fact: a human being was dead.

Defense asked for involuntary manslaughter.

Prosecution asked for second-degree murder.

The jury found her guilty of voluntary manslaughter. She got seven years plus two "for enhancement" because of the use of a dangerous and deadly weapon. She was delivered forthwith to CIW-Frontera.

There was some minor trouble at the second security check which employed more sensitive metal detectors. A strip search was mentioned. I stared at the guards in disbelief, and with some panic too, shrugging my innocence, grinning nervously. They had already searched through the contents of my purse, confiscating car keys, possible weapons; I had removed my jewelry; my pockets were empty; my shoes were examined; my underwire bra was established; my heart was pure. Three guards gathered around me, two men, one woman. Finally, the woman noticed the copper barrette holding back my hair, the mystery was solved, and I was allowed into the CIW visiting room.

It was a large, cafeteria-like room, with scattered round tables, plastic chairs, windows on two sides, an area for guards on the third, and along the fourth wall a bank of vending machines—cigarettes, candy, soft drinks, coffee, sandwiches. "Bring change for the machines," Dixie's note had said. So that mystery, too, was now solved.

I found a seat at an empty table and waited. They had taken her name, and she would be notified that she had a visitor. There was a separate security check room and a separate door through which inmates entered, and for twenty minutes or so, I watched the door as inmates arrived and departed, sometimes in tears; and then, giving up my discomfort in the fact of my presence here at all, and the further discomfort of conspicuous solitude, I rose and bought a cup of coffee and a tuna sandwich which was inedible.

This was the "contact" visiting room. There was a non-contact area reserved for inmates who did not conform to the rules and regulations. I was glad that Dixie was on the list for contact visits. I wanted to embrace her, to touch her. I wanted contact.

Another fifteen minutes passed. The room was thick with smoke; I bought another pack of cigarettes, the second of the day though this time it was Dixie's old brand, and lit one in her honor. There were probably a hundred or so people in the room, most of them talking, talking fast and perhaps too brightly, forsaking no silence; the time of the room was bound by silence, deep and vast and especially real. In the corner there was a woman holding a girl of about five. The woman was not talking; she was crying. The girl's eyes were closed. Seated next to them was a man looking at the floor. A minute or two passed. He touched his fingers to the woman's hair, and then he stood. The visit was ending. In the woman's eyes was desperation. I looked away.

*Please, Dixie,* I thought, *please hurry and come, please forgive me.*

What is really knowable? And what do we want to know finally? How much can we tolerate knowing?

I wanted to know everything—there would be safety in that. Which left me protected from life.

Dixie didn't want to know; mostly she wanted to be. Which left her susceptible to life.

And I wanted to know, to be assured, that there was Meaning, that there existed deeds and things of worth upon which I could depend. Dependable meaning to compensate the undependable condition. I wanted—and not necessarily for myself—immortality, the possibility of it. That was to be The Comfort. Not the eternal life offered by God—which was hardly reasonable—but the eternal meaning implied by the very fact of life. It was here, therefore it had to have a meaning, it simply *had to.* One had only to locate it.

I wanted to know that there existed a solution. The Solution. Somewhere out there. I believed it could be known, and I wanted to try to know it, and I was willing to cast aside the present, the living moment, for something larger and greater floating out on the ebbing tides of the future.

Dixie wanted to know that there was no solution. Or rather, she seemed to believe that nothing was knowable. Her life in all depended upon that.

I wanted love, too, I suppose, love by slow inches, moderate and manageable and not too much of a detour off the long straight path of meaning.

Dixie wanted love, perhaps to die of love, but at the very least to know that she was loveable. She was. I don't think she ever knew that—which left the wanting skewed. She wanted an extravagance of love, a waste of love, love in all forms at any time, a world made raw by love's being and doing and longing in hot excess; she wanted to be inundated and swept away by a tidal wave of desire coming at her, over and over. But there was something weightless about Dixie—the not knowing or the not believing that there existed within her stuff of value and gravity.

Her father gave her some love. Lemucchi loved her in his simple, unimpeachable way, the same way, though differently expressed, in which he had loved me. Some of the men, perhaps, loved fleetingly, not deeply, could walk away. There were friends here and there, occasional rifts from which love ascended like a vapor.

Her mother? I don't know. What escapes a human cave-in? Not love, certainly. Smoke, dust, ashes . . . and a certain knowledge: the knowledge that down in the dark shafts beneath the rubble a life had hoped to get out, perhaps had meant to get out but didn't know the way or the how, couldn't hear or wouldn't hear the directions and pleas called down from the light above . . . or perhaps there were no directions, no pleas; the knowledge that that life hadn't the strength or the luck or the will or the autonomy, the *necessary* lonely autonomy, to keep pushing through the tunnel; and most of all the knowledge that that life was far too easily crushed. A shame? A fault? A sin? Perhaps for that Dixie hated her mother, and perhaps that hatred was her greatest sorrow. Not for not loving Dixie, but for not being *able* to love Dixie.

And the terrible innocence, too, of Cheryl's incapacity, the helplessness, the sin of it. How to interpret that as a child, as a daughter? In the black-and-white reasoning of youngness, blame magnetizes inward: there is nowhere else it can safely go. Her mother—Beauty-and-Innocence—*would* love, *of course*! if the object was *worth* loving. Ah Dixie, dear Dixie.

Perhaps there was something of her mother in me, minus the innocence. Perhaps that was why Dixie made of me a cause. Perhaps that was why Dixie loved me—because I was autonomous, and had only to learn to let myself out from my beloved tunnel.

I did give Dixie some love. Not enough. It would never have been enough, though. I know that now.

For those seven months, through Dixie, I lived. She provided me with a refuge from myself and from my fears. I was not afraid of feeling, but of feeling too much, the uncontrollable, the extreme flow and flux of the wide-open present; I was afraid of the voices calling from the blinding light outside, afraid they might disappoint me, more afraid, much more, that they would fill me with song. Because songs inevitably end.

What I didn't know, perhaps couldn't know, was that it was in love I would find the only meaning upon which I could ultimately depend. That I could, if I dared, bring all the weight of living and of dying, of time and immortality, to bear upon the ephemeral connection—*love*—and that that connection would not break, *for a time*, and that in that space life, death, time and immortality would so commingle that all would be transcended.

What Dixie didn't know was that her life, just the fact of it, had meaning. That the sun in *her* eyes had meaning. That *her* next breath was not an appeal against her fate or our fate or the fate, but a necessary and sometimes conscious affirmation of the right to continue to be for the simple reason that one already was being. That it was *her life*, hers, and that significance lay merely and solely in *having it*—the possession.

With sex, with men, one after another, Dixie defended against the truth, which was the need for love, which was the despair of never having known it, or never having believed it, or never having believed it was deserved—it was all the same. And for the elemental worth of living, for dignity in the ephemeral, for love and the meaning in and of it, and then for the sublime unimportance of our time here, the sublimity of being open and staying open *as long as one dared*, and being thus together open to each other and making a passage across the night that fell away at our feet.

With sex, with men, she tried, perhaps little knowing that it was for her the costliest form of suicide, even while it was the only prayer she knew.

With men, not many, I established and honed the emotional control I seemed to require for a kind of comfort. A kind only. Not the real thing. Comfort could not really be had. Impassiveness was the nearest thing to comfort.

Dixie found in connections a self that didn't last, couldn't last, would be lost again and again, because it was not really Dixie who made those connections. Dixie was her own illusion conjured up from the desert, a shimmering blue evanescence into which many dove and emerged still thirsty, still looking, perhaps wondering what had just happened. *Oh*, but from a distance she was beautiful.

And the murder? The murder was despicable. The murder was a triumph. The murder was.

The murder left her separate, too; and the completeness of her separation from humanity seemed to stand in barren contrast to her life before, a life of glitter and graspings and easy losses, and briefly, by turns, desperate fusion.

Perhaps Dixie had no sense of her own worth. Perhaps I had a false sense of my own worth. Both, it would seem, led to despair.

She acted; I observed. She bolted; I plodded. She was overinvolved; I was underinvolved. She was painfully unreal; I was painfully real. She was fabulous; I was frank. We needed each other, to know the place where extremes meet, if only to know that they did meet.

She relied upon relationships to tell her who she was, but her relationships (by design) proved unreliable, and seemed only to further highlight the lie. I relied upon autonomy because it was reliable. It was ugly, too. It was a form of death.

She wanted to be taken seriously, defense said. This was absurd, prosecution argued, since *she* did not take herself seriously. There was nothing for it but to agree. At times I have thought that she was trying to do just that—to take herself seriously—the night before I left; that it was I who refused to take her seriously when she'd finally gotten up the courage and the blind will and the leap of hope, or when she'd finally had no where else to turn and had to do it, and so Dixie inside clawed up and reached out beyond Dixie outside . . . and there was no one to take her hand. At times I have thought that it was with *my eyes* she saw herself during The Pause, and that it was I who helped her to fire those last three shots.

At times I have wondered if she was in love with me as her surrogate mother. At times I have even wondered if she was a lesbian in love with me—certainly all those men argued more than desire, more than men; they may have been utterly beside the point, in direct opposition to the point, so perhaps an alternative preference *was* the point. But the surrogate mother theory, the lesbian theory, the zero-self-esteem theory, the objectified woman theory, the social deviant theory, the sexual deviant theory, the lost soul theory, etc. etc.—they were all so small, so limiting, and individually, lies. Cheap and easy and whores to the truth.

Deception. Finally that was what mattered. Not the content of the deception, but the enormous and actual fact of it, the life *composed* of deception. Just that.

Who was Dixie? Who *was* she? *Who?*

I know she was a lover. I know she loved me. Period. I know now that that was all I ought to have needed to know. Just the love. Her too: that was all she needed to know.

I was enchanted by Dixie, repelled by Dixie. I loved her as I could. I was afraid of sex; of happiness; of Dixie; of living. I was afraid of myself, as she was of herself, of knowing, of making the inbound connection—we had that in common. I used her too. Lovers do. She meant too little, she meant too much; time passed.

Who was she . . . maybe she was me, and I her; maybe for a time we could not have really said where one ended and the other began.


I sat waiting in the visiting room at CIW-Frontera, wanting to believe that I could love more freely and would love more deeply the young woman she had tried to keep hidden from us all, the young woman I was about to see; and needing that young woman's forgiveness now, as she had once needed my acceptance. But by then an hour had passed, visitors were thinning out, the smoke, too, was clearing, and I was beginning to wonder if she had changed her mind.

"Something has happened," I said to a guard. He had a matronly bulk, and so far as I could tell, he hadn't budged once from his post next to the inmate entrance, monolithically fixed and for that, imposing.

"What's the problem?" he said.

"Well, Dixie . . . I'm here to visit Dixie Darling, I've already informed one of the correctional officers, over an hour . . ."

"Dixie Darling," he interrupted, tapping a clipboard against his leg. In the way he said Dixie's name I realized Dixie was already present, though glancing around I felt only the slightest change in the overall configuration of the room. Then the corner, the corner swung back across my vision. The corner table. A profile. Short brown hair. Hands loosely folded. I could not have said—perhaps something in the hands, the careless pile of fingers like pick-up-sticks, perhaps only her solitariness—what identified her, because nothing in my memory of her was currently serviceable.

I approached, said her name—"Dixie"—and heard the fear.

"Hey," she said. Toneless. One hand opened, closed back over the other. "Sue," she added.

I sat down opposite her. The table was a gray plain between us—flat, cold, forbidding in its emptiness. A man-made material. "I've been sitting over there," I explained, gesturing, "all this time, and so preoccupied I guess I didn't see you come in. Plus, your hair . . ."

She reached up and pulled a tuft of it, as if to check that it was still there.

"But it must be much easier to take care of, and with the kind of heat you get down here . . ." *But*, I thought. *You*, I thought, *not me, down here in the heat, stuck. Better shut up, Sue.*

"It's real," Dixie said, and gave a small smile. "Hot today," she said in afterthought, though somehow it did not seem the least bit connected to *real*. Maybe the hair was real, maybe what it meant was real . . . I don't know, maybe all she meant was *natural*. It occurred to me then for the first time that what was real was not necessarily what was natural.

There was a tick-ticking silence.

"Oh, I brought change," I said finally, and too loud, "the change you mentioned . . . in your card." And out of my purse, onto the hard gray plain of the table the rolls thudded like petrified penises. An offering. The head of John the Baptist. The ear of Van Gogh. The finger of the pianist. Penises from another time.

Without any apparent embarrassment, without, in fact, any expression, she removed a fair number of coins, and excused herself with a nod. Watching her at the vending machines, moving right to left in rote fashion like a slot machine addict, with the money I had brought—*all the money she gave me*, I thought, *all of everything she gave me*—I had to swallow hard against the misery, it was a fist in my gullet.

She started back toward the table. She was wearing prison-issue clothes—light blue work shirt, jeans, no belt, tennis shoes—everything clean, stains faded to amorphous shadows. She could have had personal clothing sent to her, I knew she could've, if she had wanted. Or cared. Many of the others did. She could have worn make-up and painted her nails and dyed her hair; she could have held on to herself. But evidently Dixie had accepted homogenizing—at least symbolically. Something in her indifference repelled pity, turned it back on me: I was sorry for myself, for having to see her thus. For having to see. (And I did have to.) For driving all the way down just to see her like this. Though that had been part of the point, it was not what I expected; I expected to see her like this— plain and reduced—but I suppose I did not expect to believe what I saw. Which is to say, I expected her *like* this, but not *this*. I suppose I was waiting to wake up from this dream of reality. Waiting for Dixie to tell me it wasn't so. Somewhere at some point without my having paid proper attention, the punch line had already been delivered. I had encountered emptiness, only it was still alive, a living, breathing emptiness.

Arranging the candy bars and cigarettes in a neat pile—there was something unpleasant about the neatness, like a mortician arranging a cuff or an errant lock on a corpse, excruciating attention to details without meaning—she said, "Thanks," and with unnervingly dull composure resumed her seat.

I pushed the coin rolls toward her. "Keep the rest, for another time."

She twitched her head leftward; the economy of the gesture—meaning *no*, and referring to the purchases occupying the left edge of the table, and meaning also, *end of subject, escape/exit*—the economy of the gesture was so utterly unlike the young woman I had known, the richly flourished extravagance of her being, and so bluntly expressive of who she had become or perhaps even who she had been all along, that it produced in me a kind of psychological double take: I couldn't believe my eyes . . . or my ears, my heart and soul, I couldn't believe my experience of this woman who was implying to me that *she* was Dixie. My Dixie. My beloved stranger.

"Three more months," I said.

Maybe she lifted her brow.

"I mean until your release."

"Yeah, they say."

"So . . . what will you do? What are your plans?"

"No plans," she said, looking at me as if along a steel rod—*the shortest distance between two points is a straight line*. Unblinkingly straight. The eyes were still blue; of course, of course they had to be blue, they were always at least blue—one could not change the color of one's eyes. But now there was nothing beyond that, beyond the color blue; nothing to imagine or project, no diving allowed—in, through, back out. No bottom, infinite depth, a blue abyss; or perhaps no depth at all—flat. Two blue dots, a gray table—blue moons, cold light, gray expanse, the lunarscape of a life. I felt the slithering onset of panic, the subtle kind that promises not to be relentless—which was at least manageable—but panic of a capricious nature. Surprise.

"Will you come north, back to the Bay Area?"

"I don't know." She reached across the table and slipped a cigarette from the pack I had purchased an hour earlier. "Mind?"

"No, no, help yourself. Actually, I bought them for you. I quit years ago. Actually." So the cigarettes *she* had just purchased were to be hoarded; mine were expendable, a part of the lavish and endless present tense. She lit it, took a couple of drags, flicked the budding ash onto the linoleum, hanging her hand with the cigarette at her side, as if the entire arm had gone dead.

"Well, do you have any thoughts about what you might like to do . . . when you get out? I mean, I realize it's difficult to have an actual detailed plan, from here, but something you want to do?"

"No."

"Hair styling," I said. "For awhile back then you were training."

Almost imperceptibly, she tipped her short, brown-haired head.

"Okay, well you've got a job here, right?"

"Sure."

I stared expectantly at her.

"Recycling," she said. "Here we recycle everything. In the end it pretty much all looks the same. Little pieces."

"Maybe some of the skills you've acquired . . ."

Blinking slowly, she said, "Hey," and flipped her left hand open for a second, shut it back down on the table, a muted slap, "I don't have a plan."

"But you have a future, Dixie. You're getting out, it's almost over, this, this interruption."

"Interruption." She smiled. Though it was no longer beguiling it was still a nice smile in the way that most human smiles were nice—signifying amusement, peace, or perhaps only signifying a kind of gift to its witness, or an offering to the hope that some day it would indeed be so—the amusement, the large peace. But it did not seem to be for me, her smile, as it had been in the past; for me or for others, seldom the symptom of an inwrought condition. This time it was ironic, her smile, and might easily, very easily, have occasioned tears—if there had been anything worth crying over.

I said, "By that I meant it wasn't permanent. It's not."

"Permanent interruption," she said vaguely.

"Now you can start thinking about the rest of your life, you know, getting on with things."

"The rest of life," she said, as if to actually think about it. "Things," she said, as if they actually mattered.

I felt encouraged. "Yes, your life, Dixie, you're about to get it back, and I really want you to make the best of it, to . . ."

"What *do* you want?"

"What?"

"Why are you here?"

"Well . . ."

"With your change."

"You said . . . I thought . . . *oh Dixie*, I'm so sorry about everything, what happened, this place. Maybe I could have helped." I peered into the shallow of my hands, at the lines like broken smiles cutting across the palms, so many lines . . . "I know I could have helped her . . .

you."

   "Her." Again the ironic smile. "Right the first time."

   "What are you saying, Dixie?"

   "Look," she said, "there is no Dixie Darling."


   I could not go back the way I had come. It seemed unthinkable. I called Henry from a pay phone, left a message on the recording machine saying that I would be staying an extra night, and headed east past Riverside, up through Desert Hot Springs and around the western edge of Joshua Tree National Monument, not pausing, not looking. In Twentynine Palms I checked into a motel. It was 8:00. Showered, changed my clothes, eluded the mirror with success until moments before going out, a macabre interest overcame me and I peered into the glass: the face was smooth, placid, not in a self-possessed way but as though the sleeper had just waked, but the eyes, *the eyes,* enormous, dark, and so deeply open that, gazing into them, I worried I would never find a bottom.

   I went out and ate something—maybe chicken—and walked back to my room along the main street, the lights from the town washing out the lower atmosphere and confining what was left of the stars to a disc at the top of the sky, cold and tenuous specks, less like light than incipient perforations in a dark veil. In my room I undressed, climbed into the bed, decided I ought to take some Rolaids—in view of the meal, the day, everything—and got up and rummaged through my purse. There I found Dixie's postcard. *Sue—Dixie here—Saturday is visitors day—Bring change for the machines,* and then the letters, and her signature. Only there was something wrong: Henry had said, "f.y.i."—that's what he had said the letters were. He had glanced at it and had said without hesitation, matter-of-factly, "for your information." That's what he said. And I stuffed it into my purse, and never looked at it again. But now I looked at the letters, really looked at them, the fat, swirly script, her name below, and again the script, then again and again until I couldn't see through the tears pooling in my eyes. *I.l.y.*

The next morning I cut north over the Sheep Hole Mountains and down into the heart of the Mojave Desert, wandering along dirt roads, taking one then another as they appeared, no direction in mind, no destination. The early sun was colorless, yet vastly and immediately present over the tawny flats; desert light which was in essence complete exposure; and the desert itself—taupe and dun mountains, some rising abruptly, others sloping up like long slow waves taking shape across an earthen sea, jagged at the ridgeline, fanning down into alluvial aprons of sand and gravel, and from them the earth flowing across the vision to the ends of vision. Dry land, widely open and unprotected, and so evenly tufted with creosote and cactus, so lovely the arrangements imposed by aridity, that it was like a Japanese garden where value reposed equally in objects and in the spaces between them.

I pulled over and stopped. In the north a great dust plume trailed behind another vehicle too distant to see. Wind. Space. Dry, peppery air. A cloudless sky, faded blue. The *tick* and *scratch* of a tumbleweed against the right rear panel of the car. And everywhere around me in everything was the candid, lonely insistence of the desert to be as it is—unadorned, unpretending, unashamed. Such rights needed defending. And defended, they took one's breath away.

I sat there for awhile, maybe an hour. Presently in the east a lake appeared; or I noticed it. A broad, pale blue lake and just beyond it, a short range of mountains. The mountains were reflected in the lake with astonishing precision, each peak reproduced in fine detail, even the subtly shaded colors of the basins and outwashes, the sweeping curves, the rocky flanks, were cast without distortion in the lake's image. At some point I realized that the lake was a mirage. The mountains, I knew, were real. Bending light rays; distance; layers of varying air temperatures and densities—there were explanations, reasonable, measurable causes. But who could really describe the effect, the sensation, the hope and belief and appreciation, who could express the loveliness?

I thought about it for many miles, many years since—reality reflected in illusion. I thought about Dixie, Fata Morgana, the most beautiful of all mirages. I wondered, and still wonder, whether or not it matters if a thing is real, whether or not it behooves one to make such seemingly fixed and final determinations, so long as it reflects with accuracy and beauty some range of our existence. As Dixie had for me.

I wanted to believe that I would have loved Dixie as she was . . . just as I loved the candid desert. But perhaps in those early years it was the lake that enchanted me. And while I was afraid to get close to it and have it disappear or move off, Dixie longed for just that. To be herself. To be loved.